THE
AUCTION

THE
AUCTION

TOM GALVIN

Published by Drexel Books, Annapolis, MD

Edited and designed by Girl Friday Productions

Cover design: Emily Weigel

Image credits: cover © Shutterstock/kkssr, Shutterstock/The7Dew, Shutterstock/Hibrida

ISBN (paperback): 978-1-7375150-0-5
ISBN (e-book): 978-1-7375150-1-2

Library of Congress Control Number: 2021917559

To Jane and Tom, who loved words.

PROLOGUE

"Suction."

The lead surgeon lifted her scalpel so a nurse could clear the cavity of blood and fluid. A monitor kept a steady beat, although the future of the patient was not in doubt. Other than the doctor barking orders, the only sound came from the monitors. The surgeon didn't abide by the mundane chitchat so typical in many operating rooms.

The Fort Stewart morgue was the only such facility in the country with a surgical unit. If Global's plans came to fruition, there would be more. While the surgeon prepped the removal of the man's heart, another team concentrated on extracting the kidneys, pancreas, and intestines. The army had flown in the surgical units to handle the procedure, although it was routine.

MPs stood watch at the door.

"Saw," the surgeon ordered, holding out her hand.

A nurse placed the power tool in the doctor's hands. The room filled with the rhythmic sound of the electric device and the cracking of ribs. The surgeon held the saw to her right, and the nurse replaced it with a rib spreader. Once the chest was extended, the surgeon used a scalpel to separate the aorta and the pulmonary artery. She next sliced the pulmonary vein and aorta, causing a mass of blood to pulse from the heart.

On cue, the nurse suctioned the pooling blood. With the heart emptied, the surgeon expertly snipped the superior and inferior venae cavae, being careful to leave enough length for the transplant team. Once finished, she scooped the heart out of the cavity and placed it in a pan. Seconds later, a technician whisked the organ away.

She exhaled. "OK, now let's take out the lungs."

A technician assisting with the kidney removal took the opportunity to say, "I wonder what put this guy in a coma. He can't be over twenty-five years old and there's no trauma."

"Cut the chatter," the lead surgeon commanded, and once again the monitors were the only sound in the cramped room.

The teams, supplemented by other surgeons, removed the lungs, liver, pancreas, intestines, kidneys, spleen, eyes, and blood vessels. They would be put to good use. While mechanical organs were available, nothing was as effective as the real thing.

Six patients in Georgia—all Series As, the elites—would benefit.

The procedures completed, a technician removed the tubes keeping the man alive. An orderly wheeled away the body to prepare for cremation. After the surgical teams washed up, they were hustled off the base to a waiting Gulfstream VIII for a return flight to Fort Bliss.

As far as the personnel at Fort Stewart was concerned, the procedure never happened.

ONE

Sasha Cross gave a furtive glance at the man standing outside the parking garage across the street as she bounded up the concrete steps that led to an entrance to the Brooklyn Dome. She didn't like the way he stared at her. A security guard blocked her path. "This is the wrong side. Go around," he said, pointing to the sign that read, Auction Entrance This Way.

The man across the street pulled out a drone from a backpack and placed it on the ground. Sasha didn't have much time. "Can't you just let me in here?"

"Even if I could, you'd never find your way." The guard paused. "Wait, aren't you . . . ?"

"Yes," she said hurriedly, "so if there is any way you could help me?"

"I'll radio to send someone over to pick you up."

Sasha glanced over at the man by the garage. "Never mind," she said, and walked in the opposite direction as the drone approached.

The guard yelled after her, "You don't want to go that way!"

She broke into a trot, hoping her twenty-two-year-old legs could navigate the foot traffic clogging the busy Brooklyn thoroughfare better than the drone could manage the wires crisscrossing the street. A glance back confirmed her pursuer had halted the intrusive aircraft.

Smiling at her rare victory, she made a left-hand turn—smack into a throng of demonstrators massing to protest the Auction. Sasha froze. A man standing on the top of an SUV shouted into a bullhorn, warning the mob not to hurl objects at the police. Sasha looked back at her pursuer. Recovered, he elevated the drone to a higher altitude. She exhaled, put on sunglasses, and snaked through the gathering of mostly twentysomethings.

"Excuse me," she said, gently pushing aside bodies. Sasha kept her head down as she pressed through the crowd. Her foot got tangled, and she stumbled into a heavyset woman wearing an army jacket and backpack.

The woman's eyes went wide. "What are you doing here?"

"Sorry, just trying to pass through."

A murmur rippled through the crowd. "That's Sasha Cross."

Sasha intensified her efforts to extract herself. Thirty yards ahead she saw daylight. A man grabbed at her arm. "You don't belong here," he snarled as Sasha pulled away.

A woman intervened, "Let her go." Twenty yards to daylight. A hand pulled at her sunglasses. Sasha stopped momentarily when they left her face, then pressed on. Ten yards.

Using the bullhorn, the organizer yelled, "We've got royalty among us!" The crowd responded with boos and hisses as Sasha's stomach dropped. "Sasha, tell all the beautiful people waiting for you inside their day of reckoning is coming!"

A mix of anger, disdain, and empathy flashed on the faces of the mob. As she searched for an opening in the metal barricade, a voice called out, "Hey, Sasha!" She turned. *Thwack.* A freckled woman with a ponytail flung the contents of a strawberry smoothie into Sasha's face, splattering her from the waist up.

Stunned, Sasha blinked her eyes, and felt a hand upon her. An officer pushed her through an opening. He escorted her toward the Brooklyn Dome's Flatbush Avenue entrance as photographers snapped pictures. Guards scanned her eyes then waved her through, and Sasha dashed inside to find a bathroom. She dropped her hands to the counter and held back tears. The speakers in the bathroom crackled, and a moderator called the event to order. Sasha wiped the strawberry highlights out of her hair and dabbed wet paper towels onto her tan cotton shirt. It removed the mess but left her with a wet stain across her chest.

She splashed water on her face, wiped her eyes, and took a deep breath. Sasha peeked her head out of the bathroom in search of the closest entrance to the stadium seats. Finding it, she made her way down the steps and gazed at the thousands of twenty-two-year-olds listening to a woman. Behind her, screens displayed the words *Auction Combine.*

Sasha's device beeped, signaling an incoming video call from her father. Those closest to her turned their heads at the noise, and the commotion caused the moderator to pause.

"Devices should be off," the moderator barked. Sasha fumbled to silence her device and slunk to the back row of chairs in search of an empty seat. She averted her eyes from the gawkers staring at her appearance, but turned when she heard her name. Jason Harris pointed to a chair next to him.

"What the hell happened to you?"

"Don't ask," she whispered.

The disruption over, the moderator continued. "You're here because your Auction will take place in November. You have a lot of work ahead. Over the next two days, you'll learn more about the Auction and how we'll help you succeed."

Fifteen thousand Auction candidates from all over the country sat on folding chairs on the same surface where the Virtual Reality Olympics took place just days ago. The scene resembled a college graduation. Those seated were the cream of the crop—the nation's top twenty-two-year-olds poised to become the most financially successful of their generation.

In the months to come, the Big 7 companies that dominated the economy would bid to gain the rights to these young stars. Sasha recognized a few of them. Billy Edwards had spent a brief time in her business class at Berkeley before dropping out to launch a start-up now worth $5 billion. Loretta Sanchez, a world-renowned concert pianist, sat two rows away.

And then there was Jason.

He had been Sasha's first boyfriend. It fizzled out, but was replaced by something sweeter: Jason became the brother she never had, and his house a hideout when the Cross family drama spun out of control. That was before the accident that killed his parents and shattered his leg. Jason left Los Angeles to live with his aunt Ayana in Philadelphia, and Sasha lost her refuge.

The moderator gazed at the candidates. "Many of you are comfortable in the spotlight. The rest better get used to it. You are about to be worth millions of dollars."

Sasha was accustomed to attention, even though she did everything she could to avoid it. She presented herself blandly—plain clothes, limited makeup, nothing flashy—which was surprising given her background. The Cross family epitomized glamour and celebrity, even by Hollywood standards. Fame came with a price. Four years ago, TMZ had breathlessly covered her arrival at UC Berkeley, and a paparazzi photographer named Freddy Tangier made Sasha his pet project. When others grew bored with Sasha's college life, Freddy remained, lurking everywhere, making a living on photos of Sasha.

"As a Series A, you're special," the moderator told them as she wrapped up the session. "Your college friends will probably be Series Bs. Those who work administrative jobs may be Series Cs. And if you have family or friends who are restaurant workers, store clerks, or are in the military, they'll be Series Ds. The next six months will define the trajectory of your life. Use it well."

Soon after, the candidates filed out to the concourse. Turning to Sasha, Jason said, "I'd hug you, but not with that shirt. What gives?"

She glanced down at her still-damp clothes. "I ran into an admirer."

Jason opened his arms. "On second thought, you look like you need it."

Sasha slipped into his embrace. "Been a minute, Jay. What did the doctor say?"

"Not much. My leg's improved as much as it will. Ayana says hello."

Sasha brightened. "She's my hero. When are you coming to visit?"

"It's your turn," he replied. "I came for New Year's."

Sasha frowned. "There's more to do in San Francisco."

"Fine." He removed his jacket. "Wear this."

She slipped it on, and they walked down the corridor mobbed with Type A overachievers. Sasha squeezed his hand when they saw the sign pointing them to their required medical examinations and implantations. "The nightmare begins."

Twenty minutes later Sasha sat on an exam table as a nurse directed her to slip her left arm into a long metal sleeve. She shivered when the cold metal brushed her skin. The nurse fastened a clamp to tighten the sleeve, then sterilized her biceps with an alcohol swab.

"The doctor will be in soon."

Sasha eyed the plastic gun on the metal table. A sign on the door instructed patients to avoid strenuous physical activity for forty-eight hours after the implant. The doctor entered, did a double take when she realized it was Sasha, and got down to business.

"Hold still," she ordered. The doctor inserted a tiny object into the canister and held the gun to Sasha's biceps. Sasha flinched when the doctor pulled the trigger. A chip the size of a grain of rice was embedded in her biceps; it would enable the Big 7 companies to track her location. The doctor listened as a series of beeps confirmed the tracking device was operational. Series As were too valuable a commodity to be out of sight for a single moment.

After the nurse returned and stuck a needle in Sasha's right arm for blood work—genetic testing to be catalogued and analyzed—he directed Sasha to a room down the corridor, where she underwent a full body scan to check for cancer and other diseases. From there, more blood work followed. It was the most thorough medical appointment she'd ever experienced; various parts of her body ached, and a slight headache developed behind her eyes.

Dazed and hungry, Sasha walked aimlessly down the hall until her device beeped with a message from Jason: *Taco bar at section 102.* She set out to find him, ignoring the stares that came with her family fame. Her mother, Lacy Cross, had been an Oscar-winning actress and America's sweetheart. At the height of her career, Lacy was the most recognized woman in the world. Mother and daughter were inseparable, so it seemed fitting that seven-year-old Sasha play Lacy's on-screen daughter in her biggest film, *The Road Home.*

They were the only mother-daughter duo to win Academy Awards in the same year. Sasha melted hearts when she sobbed over her mother's lifeless body in the final scene. Audiences didn't know the director had actually told Sasha her mother was dead. Her award-winning pain had been genuine.

As she grew into a carbon copy of her mother, the young star captivated America. She appeared on magazine covers and was a regular at trendy hot spots frequented by young celebrities. But by the time she left high school, something had changed and Sasha sightings were few and far between.

Despite—or because of—her efforts to stay out of the spotlight, she remained a source of fascination. Her grandmother nicknamed her "Princess Di," a reference Sasha had to look up to understand. When she made a rare public appearance for a Cross family event the summer after her high school graduation, the media paid as much attention to her as to her mother.

Her father pressed for Sasha to return to acting, but she'd insisted on attending Berkeley, just across the Bay Bridge from San Francisco. She hoped to be another face in the crowd there . . . but then Freddy Tangier appeared.

Life imitated art. In the middle of Sasha's sophomore year, a maid discovered her mother's lifeless body at the home of a well-known Hollywood agent. An autopsy confirmed Lacy died of a drug overdose. Television crews and paparazzi camped outside the Crosses' Hollywood Hills estate to report on the star's death and catch a glimpse of Sasha and her sister, Kelsie. Her classmates wondered if they would see her again. She returned the following fall but shut down questions about her family.

Now, with her Auction looming, she faced a return of the harsh spotlight she dreaded, and the reality of what was to come settled on her like a heavy blanket. Fellow candidates milled around, searching for tables. She discovered Jason sitting with an attractive, well-built man wearing a Michigan State sweatshirt.

"Thanks for saving me a seat," Sasha snarked as she stared at the stranger.

The blond-haired man smiled. "You don't remember me, do you?"

Sasha frowned. She didn't like being put on the spot. Then she saw it: around his eyes and the way he smiled. It wasn't a pleasant discovery. "Avery?"

"It's been a long time. Eighth grade."

Sasha's stomach seized as she was transported back to middle school. Eagerly waiting outside the school entrance for her celebrity crush to swing by to say hello. Unlike most thirteen-year-olds, she'd actually met her crush. Her father had introduced the YouTube singing sensation to her at a fundraiser.

Two days later, she had received a text from the fourteen-year-old object of her admiration. He wanted to see her again. Could they meet at her school? She waited, wearing her best dress and a bit too much makeup for the 3:00 p.m. date.

By 3:10, she was antsy. Ten minutes later, she repeatedly checked her device for a message. By 3:30, she couldn't help it. She typed, *Where are you?*

Her device beeped immediately with the answer, *Behind you.*

She turned to find Avery and a dozen others laughing. At *her.* Another girl, a supposed friend who Sasha had warned against dating Avery, smirked and put her arm around him. Avery held his device, recording Sasha's humiliation. Within days, the video had spread from her school to sites that mocked celebrities. Nearly a decade later, the video was still online.

A stinging sensation buzzed in Sasha's throat at the memory. The shame. Not long after the incident Avery's family relocated to Michigan, but he'd made his mark: From that point on, Sasha kept everyone at arm's length. They'd never humiliate her again.

"Don't you love this?" Avery interrupted her flashback. "The Combine is live on CNBC right now. I feel like a stud athlete about to be drafted."

"I'm so sure CNBC is here for you," Sasha responded.

Ignoring the insult, Avery focused his attention on Jason. "You must be a big deal to earn an Auction invite."

Sasha blurted out hotly, "He's a professional e-gamer."

"What game?"

"Basketball. I play on a team based in Philly."

Avery raised an eyebrow. "Guess the bum leg held you back from the real thing."

Jason placed his hand on Sasha's wrist. He knew her so well, he could sense she was about to jump out of her seat. "Car accident in high school messed me up. It's not all bad. The 76ers are talking to me about joining its NBA e-sports team."

Sasha's face was blank. "Where did you move to, Avery?"

"Outside Detroit. My mom and dad grew up there, so it was a homecoming. It took a long time to get used to the cold weather." He sighed. "I miss LA."

Good, Sasha thought. Avery's device beeped, signaling his next interview. As he stood, he offered, "Maybe the three of us can have dinner tonight."

"We'll get back to you on that," said Sasha.

Avery got the hint and departed without another word. They sat in silence until he was out of earshot and Sasha couldn't hold it in anymore. "What a dick."

Jason sipped his drink. "He's not the only one in New York this week."

"Who else?"

"Denton." He let the name linger. "He's here for a concert, wants to meet up."

"I haven't heard his name in a long time. Why is he in New York?"

"He's a ticket broker."

Sasha rolled her eyes. "Right. Not a drug dealer to concert organizers."

"I don't know."

"Be careful, Jason," said Sasha. "I never understood why you stay in touch with him."

"It's always complicated with Denton."

———

"And we're live in five, four, three . . ."

The floor director completed a silent count as CNBC staffers hustled into place. Britney Reynolds adjusted her ear mic, cleared her throat, pressed her lips together.

At the right time, she burst into a smooth, distant smile.

"A big day for the markets as the Series A Combine gets underway in Brooklyn in what will be a hectic week," Reynolds read from the prompter. "But first, proof the economy shows no sign of slowing down. The government today reported the lowest unemployment rate in half a century. More on that later."

Reynolds pivoted back to the Auction, introducing an analyst named Andrew Barby. He'd been on her show many times before—and indeed, had grown too comfortable, if his hand on her knee at the previous night's happy hour was any indication—and he beamed in the spotlight.

"Today's the day the Big 7 take a first peek at the biggest prospects for the annual Auction. A lot of money is riding on it. What are the companies seeking to learn?" she asked.

Barby styled himself as an expert on the most valuable twenty-two-year-olds up for bid. With dyed jet-black hair that covered his head like a helmet, a bulging forehead, and a Kelly green Notre Dame tie, Barby looked like a cartoon character. He explained, "While all twenty-two-year-olds will go through the Auction in November, only the elite are here in Brooklyn. This week is about everything from medical exams to psychological tests to learning who burns to succeed."

As Barby talked, the ticker at the bottom of the screen displayed the names of the top candidates. Reynolds interrupted with a nod. "For those viewers who might not know the basics, can you simplify what's happening this week?"

"The Auction may seem complicated, but let's not overthink it. Every twenty-two-year-old in the country goes through it. The companies bid on those they think will make the most money in their careers. It's a merit-based system: if you have a bright future, you'll receive a high bid."

"How hard is it to be selected as a Series A?"

Barby took off his glasses for effect. "It's as rare as Charlie finding the golden ticket to get into Willy Wonka's chocolate factory. This year five million Americans will turn twenty-two years old, but only one in five hundred will be a Series A."

"And how do companies acquire their rights?"

"Companies place bids on candidates. If they win, they receive 25 percent of that person's income. For example, if Global Holdings bids for an entrepreneur and that person makes $500 million over her lifetime, Global receives $125 million of it."

Reynolds smiled without showing her teeth. "What do you say to critics who claim the Auction is stealing from these young people and handing their earnings over to their parents and the Big 7 corporations?"

If Barby was surprised, he didn't show it. Instead, he shook his head. "They're misinformed. The Big 7 help these kids build successful careers." He pointed toward the stadium floor. "The people down there are everyone's bets to join the ranks of CEOs, YouTubers, and inventors of the future. Because the Big 7 have a lot invested in them, they do everything they can to help them realize their dreams. It's a win-win."

"Andrew, what happens to those who aren't here today?" she asked, getting ready to wrap up the segment. Her brain was already jumping ahead to her next guest.

"Every twenty-two-year-old goes through the Auction," he answered. "But their value dictates what they become. Doctors, lawyers, and business executives pegged to make a lot of money will end up as Series Bs; most middle-class workers end up as Series Cs."

"And the rest?"

"The 1 million who aren't selected become Series Ds. Most are low-wage workers. They are treated differently."

CNBC cameras panned the demonstrators congregated outside the Brooklyn Dome. Reynolds let the footage tell its own story before she continued. "Speaking of Series Ds, it wouldn't be an Auction without protesters."

Barby jumped in. "There will always be the naysayers. But the Auction helps so many. Parents rely on money from the Auction to pay for their retirement, so this is an important obligation for their children."

"Mmmm," Reynolds said, pivoting. "One of those parents is our next guest . . ."

The camera zoomed in on a man sitting to Reynolds's side. His tight smile hid the nerves that had overtaken his stomach a few minutes before air. His jitters were understandable: after twenty-two years of raising a child, he'd soon learn whether his hard work resulted in millions of dollars of retirement money. All parents were eager to find out what prices their children would fetch.

———

Global executives peered down from a luxury box, searching for clues about which of the candidates below would be the best bets. "There's Sasha Cross," an analyst said, pointing as the young woman returned from lunch.

"Talk about being born with a silver spoon in your mouth," said another.

Clad in a no-nonsense plain black suit, Jessica Garulli stepped forward. Her heels echoed on the tile floor. "Say what you want, but there isn't another here whose picture has been taken as many times or who has been on as many magazine covers as Sasha Cross. And yet she's still a riddle to us."

The analyst sneered. "She's easy to figure out. An entitled princess who's famous because she looks like her dead mother. Who cares?"

"It's your job to care," said Jessica, watching as Sasha ignored those who pulled out their devices to snap a photo or take a video as she glided through the crowd. The young celebrity lived behind a mask; it was Jessica's job to pierce it and reveal the real Sasha.

As Global's head of security, Jessica oversaw the collection of information on Series A candidates. If they had a weakness—a drug problem, family issues, or disease—she and her team had to find it. No matter what it took. Global installed video and listening devices in the lobbies, hallways, corridors, and hotel rooms Series A candidates stayed in during the Combine. Those surveillance cameras had already caught a twenty-two-year-old YouTuber from Omaha poking herself with a needle and a Harvard student planting cocaine in the suitcase of a supposed friend.

Jessica pulled up Sasha's file. No arrests. High citizenship score. Business major. Graduating in May. Worked for a member of a California state commission investigating the Auction's fairness. One of the Big 7 companies would bet big that whatever Sasha chose to do with her life, the company would make tens of millions of dollars. When you're a Sasha Cross, you can do whatever you want. Jessica studied the young woman, arms crossed, brow furrowed.

———

A half hour later, Global wasn't the only Big 7 company asking questions.

"Does suicide run in your family?" a Beech analyst grilled Sasha, barely looking up from her laptop.

She didn't answer. Throughout her ten-minute interview—though "Spanish Inquisition" was a more apt term for it—she could overhear the same conversation taking place in the cubicle next door. That meant whoever was in there had heard the interviewer ask if Sasha Cross planned on killing herself like her mother had.

"Does it?" the Beech analyst pressed. Of the Big 7 companies, only Global was bigger or more powerful.

Sasha leaned forward, eyes flashing. "No, does it in yours?"

The analyst paused, then moved on. "Tell me about this commission."

Sasha exhaled. "My professor asked if I wanted a research position, so I took it."

"And what have you learned?"

"That your job probably pays well."

"Do you want my job?"

Sasha shrugged. "No. I have to look myself in the mirror every morning."

"Then why not pursue a career in movies or television?"

"Are those my only choices?" Sasha's casual way of asking the rhetorical question hid her frustration. "Whore myself out to Hollywood or become a stooge for the Big 7?"

The analyst put down her clipboard and smiled smoothly. "Of course not. But I'm trying to understand you. You won an Academy Award. You have a famous name. Why not pursue an obvious path?"

"It's not my thing." Sasha leaned back and crossed her arms.

"Then what is your thing?"

"Here's what I'd like my thing to be," she snapped. "I'd like to stop being treated as a product, for the paparazzi to stop stalking me, for my friends to stop trying to profit off my fame. How's that for a start? Is that good enough for your notes?"

A hoot came from the booth next door. "You go, girl."

"That answer won't help you in the Auction," the analyst replied, "but if you're rich already, I guess it doesn't matter. We're done."

Sasha left. She endured the same question at each meeting: Why don't you go into the family business and reap the millions of dollars that await you? A handsome young Latino man nodded and greeted her by name, but she passed by without replying. Only later did she realize he was the pop singer who had played at her sister's birthday party.

Her device distracted her. She had two messages. The first, from her father, Judah, read: *Play nice. It's important.* The second, from Jason, asked where to meet for dinner.

She turned away when she noticed Avery sitting on a bench peering at his device. Outside, Jason's oversized jacket protected her from the harsh wind that whipped across Flatbush Avenue. So much for springtime. Her mind wandered to the four days they spent together over New Year's. She knew the death of Jason's parents still haunted him. Gaming was his escape, and now it appeared it could be a career.

At least one of them had it figured out.

Flatbush Avenue hopped. The smells from Patsy's Pizzeria made Sasha rethink their Thai dinner plans. For a moment she considered messaging her father for the address of the Brooklyn walk-up that had been her parents' first home years ago, but thought better of it.

She passed a shabby two-story building that housed a public health care facility. The bottom rung of the Auction, Series Ds, weren't provided private benefits. Instead, the government provided care and, based on the sign on the door, not often. It read, Open Monday and Wednesday, 10 a.m.–2 p.m.

As she approached Sixth Avenue, Sasha spotted Jason and Denton. At six feet two and 210 pounds, Denton might have played lacrosse at USC, but fate placed him in the back seat of the car the night of the accident that killed Jason's parents. His injuries ended his sports career.

When she walked up to him, Denton bellowed, "The famous Sasha Cross."

Passersby turned their heads, and Sasha's stomach tightened. She relaxed when no one approached her. "Hey, Denton, heard you were in town."

He sized her up. "Looking good, girl. I saw a pic of you at the Staples Center last month. Whenever you need tickets, I'll be your hookup."

"I'll keep that in mind," said Sasha. She took Jason by the hand and led him away, but not before Denton yelled, "Get back to me, Jason."

They walked in silence before Sasha piped up, "What did he want?"

"He says he has a business proposition."

"Are you going to do it?"

Jason stared ahead. "I don't know."

"He's still dealing, isn't he?" she hissed. "I thought you were past that."

"No clue, Sasha, and I am. Give me space."

Sasha raised her hands in surrender. "I'm just worried about you. If you're gonna be like that, I'm picking dinner."

"I thought we decided on Thai?"

She grabbed his hand again and did a U-turn. "Ever hear of Patsy's Pizza?"

"Lead on. By the way, want to know who you're dating?"

"I'd love to."

Jason fished his device out of his pocket and showed Sasha a gossip site with a picture of the two of them arm in arm walking up the stadium stairs. "Me."

It was clear one of their fellow Series As snapped a photo and then sold it to the celebrity site. "Wouldn't that be nice," she said as she wrapped her arm around his.

"You know you were the first and last girl I ever kissed?"

"That bad, huh?"

"Yeah, your kissing skills are why I like boys."

Sasha bundled his coat to protect against the wind. While she often messaged and video-chatted with Jason, she rarely spent actual time with him, and she enjoyed the feeling of holding him tight while they walked together. A vendor pushing a pretzel cart barreled toward them, jarring Sasha out of her thoughts. She moved to the side.

"Speaking of boys, any to talk about?"

He shrugged. "None worth mentioning. You?"

"You'd already know."

"Or I'd read about it in *StAuctor*," he laughed.

"Right. Hey, there's a job for me. I could spy on people."

"That photographer still harass you?" asked Jason as he opened the door to the pizzeria. A hostess picked up two menus and led them to a table. Sasha nodded and sat down.

"Freddy? He's still around. Next to Brianna, he's my most constant companion."

"What losers we are. You're desperate to be left alone. And I'm desperate for attention. If I can't convince the e-76ers to take a chance on me, I've got nothing."

Sasha held his hand. "That's what's so messed up. We're twenty-two years old. Our whole lives are ahead of us. This should be an exciting time! Instead it's the Life Olympics, and the outcome dictates our entire future. Then they wonder why so many of us have anxiety."

A woman furtively approached the table. Sasha recognized the look on her face—desperate to impress. "Ms. Cross, I just wanted to say how much I admired your mother. Can I have an autograph?"

Sasha bit her lip and took the pen the woman held in her hand. After asking her name, Sasha scribbled a note and her signature on a napkin. The woman smiled, then frowned after reading it and skulked back to her table.

Jason smirked as he read his menu. "What did you write?"

Sasha pulled a baseball cap out of her bag and tugged it over her head, shading her face. "I wrote, 'My mother taught me manners.'"

Jason shook his head. "That will sell for double on eBay."

———

Analysts rubbed their eyes and stared at monitors tracking Series A candidates. Their empty takeout containers littered the tables at the facility across the water in New Jersey. The silence broke when one of the roving supervisors was beckoned by an analyst.

"What's up?"

"You told me to track Sasha Cross," said the analyst, pointing to the blinking light on the screen.

"Anything to report?"

"Not about her, but her companion, Jason Harris. He had an interaction with a man named Denton Long. Facial recognition flagged him as a felon, and the system alerted me when he came in contact with Harris. Cross showed up minutes later, just as Long left."

"Have they entered Red Zones?" the supervisor asked, referring to parts of the city known for prostitution, gambling, and drug sales.

"No," the analyst reported. The chip implanted in the arm of Series As set off an alert if the candidates entered those danger areas. If so, an analyst filed a report. In cases of high-priority candidates, such as Sasha, the team dispatched an operative to investigate.

The supervisor stared at the screen. Sasha and Jason were inside Patsy's. "Send an alert about Denton Long."

Her supervisor departed; the analyst turned her attention to the screen. Dozens of others tracked priority Series A candidates. She pulled out a day-old egg-salad sandwich, a pickle, and a warm bottle of seltzer. It wasn't a coal-fired margherita pie, but it would have to do.

TWO

Jason cradled his morning coffee as he navigated his way through the stadium. He fished his buzzing device out of his pocket. A message from Denton read, *Tonight at 6 p.m.*

Candidates snaked their way through the concourse. At the top of the aisle, Sasha grasped his arm so hard his coffee splashed over his hand. He jolted. "Sorry," Sasha said. "But if it takes the Auction for us to have time together, then it's worth it." He squeezed back before they went their separate ways.

Jason's first interview of the day was with Global. In his assigned cube, a coffee stain dotted the beige rug. The interviewer sat in a plastic lawn chair. "Who is Denton Long?"

Jason froze. How . . . ? Oh, right. He remembered the pinch in his arm from the prior day. He, like everyone else, was being tracked. Constantly, apparently. "Guy I went to school with when I lived in Los Angeles."

The analyst scanned his device. "And he's a friend?"

"We were tight in high school. Don't see him often anymore."

"Was he involved in the accident?"

Jason nodded. "Is that important?"

"I'm getting to know you better. When did you last see him?"

Jason hesitated. "Not much since I moved to Philadelphia."

"You didn't see him last night?"

"He was outside the stadium, so we caught up. Is that a problem?"

The analyst raised an eyebrow. "You know he's a convicted drug dealer, right?"

"He used to do that stuff . . ."

"You used to deal with him."

"I never sold." Jason shook his head sharply.

"Did he give you drugs last night?"

His jaw tightened. "No."

The analyst glanced up from his device. "We'll need to redo your blood work. Anything illegal, we're required to pass it on to the authorities. He's not someone we would expect a potential Series A to associate with. Thank you for coming in. You can go."

Jason's head spun as he walked through the makeshift corridor. He stumbled through his remaining Big 7 interviews and skipped a session with a career counselor. Sasha discovered him sitting in an end-zone seat under a massive New York Jets banner.

"What's going on?" she asked as she sat down next to him.

"Um, not much."

Sasha touched his forehead. "You're clammy. Are you sick?"

"I'm fine. Hey, I gotta go to my next meeting."

"Cool—sure you're OK? Dinner?"

Jason stood. "I'll message you."

As he ran up the aisle, Sasha yelled, "Are you meeting with Denton?"

Jason didn't stop. He raced up the aisle, not slowing down until he opened the stadium doors and the cool air revived him. A few minutes later Jason found himself on the same street he and Sasha had strolled down last night. Jason stood outside the entrance of a crowded bar for five minutes. He started to go inside, stopped, turned around, and left.

He walked aimlessly until coming upon the Grand Army Plaza and the Soldiers and Sailors Arch, where he found an empty bench. *Pull it together,* he commanded himself. But still his mind reeled, his breathing labored. Jason dug into his pocket for his device and typed out a message to his aunt Ayana. *Got a minute? Need your help.*

She responded quickly. She always did. *Picking up Baker. Ten minutes?*

He waited, mulling over what to tell her. For most of his life, Jason had barely known his mother's older sister. When he came to after the accident, lying in a hospital bed, she was the first face he saw.

"How are Mom and Dad?" he had mumbled to her.

She clutched his hand. "Oh, baby, I'm so sorry. They didn't make it."

A police officer arrived to question him. "Who was driving the vehicle, Jason?"

Ayana answered for him. "Denton already told you my brother-in-law was driving. What else do you need to know?"

The officer glared at her. "Both Jason's and his father's chest wounds were consistent with being the driver. We need to nail this down. Were you driving?"

Jason glanced at Ayana. "No."

The officer flipped his notebook. "Were you under the influence of drugs?"

"No."

"Your blood work says something different."

"The boy's just learned he's lost his parents," said Ayana. "He told you he wasn't the driver. My brother is an LAPD captain, and if you need more information, go through our lawyer." She stared pointedly at the door, and the officer left.

Five years later, he couldn't imagine a world without Ayana. She had two grown daughters of her own. Neither lived nearby, nor wanted much to do with their overbearing mother. After the accident, Ayana moved Jason and his brother, Baker, to Philadelphia. She kept a photo on her night table. In it she stood between two teenage boys, chin out and ready for battle.

Jason's parents' estate was modest, and Ayana worked days at a dentist's office and nights at a diner. It took Jason two months to leave the rehab facility and longer to walk again, and that was with a limp. He'd holed up in his room and lost himself in video games and alcohol.

Baker struggled in his own way. Expelled from school for fighting, he seemed lost until Ayana found a private academy that valued his mixed martial arts skills. Over time, he steadied. Now he was one of the top-ranked amateur MMA fighters in the country.

Jason's device chirped, and his aunt's face appeared on the screen.

"What's wrong, baby?"

"How do you know something's wrong?"

"'Cause, I know you."

Jason hesitated. "Denton."

The energy on the call changed; Jason heard it in Ayana's voice. "Why was he there? To see you?"

"Business, he said."

Ayana leaned in close to the camera. "Listen, we worked too hard. Don't backslide now."

"It's not that. He wants to introduce me to an agent."

"Well, say no."

"I owe him for what happened. But a company I met with today asked why I saw him last night. They warned associating with Denton would hurt me in the Auction."

Ayana took a deep breath. "Listen, baby. There's a lot at stake here. Stick to the plan. You're the last of the family who goes through the Auction. First Keke and Rosalind, and now you. Baker doesn't count because he's number four."

"I know."

"We've come this far. Today's just a bad day. No backsliding. Denton doesn't need you and you don't need Denton. Cut him out of your life."

"OK, Ayana."

"I love you, baby. Team Harris, right?"

He nodded until their connection ended.

A swarm of commuters walked through the triumphal arch. The inscription read, To the Defenders of the Union, 1861–1865. The morning rain gave way to bursts of sun creeping through the clouds. He had an e-sports tournament on Saturday. Scouts would attend.

Ayana always had the answers. Six months. Ayana would make millions from his Auction, and he would receive a contract offer from the e-76ers. He searched his device, found Denton's message, and deleted it. Then he punched in a message to Sasha. *Thai tonight?*

———

"I can't talk, so tell your producer 'no thanks,'" said Sasha, quickening her pace through the stadium corridors.

The CNBC booker made a living by not taking no for an answer. Sasha topped the list of Series A candidates the news network hoped to bring in for a live interview. "It doesn't have to be today. We could do it tomorrow morning."

Sasha shook her head. "It's a hard no."

Outside the stadium she avoided the photographers and messaged her driver. Her late mother's closest friend lived on the other side of the East River, and she insisted on checking in when Sasha visited New York. An hour later she sat in a stylish living room in an apartment overlooking Central Park as Hannah Robbins carried over a tray of tea. Sasha followed the faint smell of hyacinth and found french doors that led to a small garden on Hannah's balcony.

On the morning of her mother's death, the only call she had made was to Hannah. Fate had placed Lacy's friend on an airplane, so she didn't receive it until it was too late. Hannah set a cup of tea on the table in front of her guest. "If it hadn't been for your mother, I would have been an actress."

Sasha took a small sip. She welcomed any stories about her mother, no matter how peripherally related. "How so?"

Hannah reached for a picture on the shelf behind them of her and Lacy taken many years ago. "I auditioned for a movie. They offered me the role. Honestly, not the greatest movie, but for a twenty-one-year-old, it was a big break. My father called me foolish when I moved to Los Angeles, so getting it meant a lot. I had the role for a week; then Lacy came by the studio to pick me up for lunch. Once the director met your mother, he dropped me and cast her."

Sasha paused. That sounded on brand for her mother—she'd been a showstopper. "You must have been angry."

"For a while, but a month later I met my Harold. So it worked out." Hannah stopped long enough to sip her tea. "What's this dog-and-pony show in Brooklyn about? Do they inspect your teeth and check your hind legs?"

Sasha snorted. "Basically. I dread it. And it's so pointless! It's not like my dad needs the money he'll receive from whoever bids on me."

"One thing I've learned, dear, is some people can never make enough money." Hannah stared at her visitor, then reached over and touched Sasha's hair. "You look just like her."

"Not really."

"You do, especially in the eyes. Your mother would be proud of you."

Sasha rubbed her temples. "I've done nothing to make her proud."

"You grew up well. Being the daughter of Lacy Cross may seem like a burden, but it's also an opportunity. You can do whatever you want."

"That's what my father always says, but what he really means is I can do whatever *he* wants me to do."

Hannah shrugged. "Some parents live through their children."

Sasha put her hands in her lap. "Can I ask a question?"

"Anything, dear."

It took a few beats for her to be confident she'd ask her question without her voice breaking. "What would my mom want for me?"

A sad smile curled Hannah's lips. "I know she'd not want you to fixate on that question. If she were here today, she'd ask what is it that *you* want."

"I want to be known as something other than Lacy Cross's daughter," Sasha blurted. "I need to find my own way without people telling me what to do. Why do I have to have all the answers now? Because the Big 7 say so?"

Hannah pursed her lips. She started to speak, then stopped. Finally, she spoke. "I knew Lacy before she was famous, while she was famous, and after she did something with her fame. She wouldn't have cared one bit as long as you make a difference in the world, and are happy."

Sasha pulled her sweater tight. "My dad says fame opens up the world to me. But I feel like it's put me in a cage."

Hannah took her hand. "You may look like your mother, but you don't have to *be* her."

———

In Lower Manhattan, longtime adversaries eyed each other in one of the world's most hallowed chambers. Global CEO Victor Armstrong and his fellow Big 7 chief executives sat in plush chairs on one side of the enormous horseshoe table used by the United Nations Security Council. Economic ministers from the world's largest economies sat across from them.

"Welcome to the UN," Secretary-General Joseph LeCartrion greeted his visitors.

Jessica sat in the row behind Armstrong, along with the other Big 7 staff. Armstrong and Beech CEO Ursula Johnson warily nodded at each other.

The historic meeting was years in the making and brought Armstrong a step closer to achieving his dream: expansion of the Auction to the rest of the world.

The Big 7 companies earned trillions of dollars in revenue and employed forty million Americans. They operated the country's largest banks, hospitals, news organizations, communications, and social media companies. But they wanted more.

Specifically, to bring the Auction overseas. The UN meeting signaled world leaders wanted to play ball. The reasons were obvious, if unmentioned. The leaders wanted to replicate America's economic success. In the decade since the Auction's introduction, the United States had boomed, the economy so hot companies struggled to find workers to fill jobs.

Americans paid a simple 10 percent tax rate that paid for the government services that hadn't been transferred to the Big 7. Under the new system, schools improved, every American had health care, and the nation's infrastructure was rebuilt.

Yes, there were malcontents who called the Auction immoral for putting a price tag on people and warned of the Big 7's growing power, but it had saved the US from collapse.

LeCartrion brought the meeting to order. A Belgian who lost his leg in Angola, the handsome ex–fighter pilot cut a heroic figure that belied his ineffectiveness. In comparison, Armstrong looked more like a high school math teacher than an elite CEO—he was of average height, paunchy, and appeared older than his sixty-odd years. But Armstrong had turned the company into a powerhouse with tentacles extending into every industry, every business, every home. Among the Big 7, Global had the most to gain if the Auction expanded worldwide.

After LeCartrion's smooth opening remarks, Armstrong cut to the chase.

"What the last decade has shown," he started, waiting for nods from his fellow CEOs before continuing, "is that you cannot succeed with an outdated economy or nostalgic view of how governments should operate."

He gazed around the table. "The Auction model works. Global is proof. We're prepared to offer you the same for your citizens. The only question is whether you want our help."

LeCartrion and his counterparts forced smiles at Armstrong's arrogance. The UN leader was a socialist and viewed the Big 7 as corporate devils. He resented that capitalist markets were once again winning the global battle for influence. Ever the statesman, LeCartrion smiled as he gazed at the CEOs. "We can learn from each other. Let's begin."

Later that day the *Wall Street Journal* reported that the meetings in New York put the Big 7 on the cusp of a breakthrough: a framework to expand the Auction, with Korea volunteering to be the first nation to adopt the US model.

Still, a storm cloud hung over the Big 7's plans. As they left the UN, the economic ministers gawked at a massive banner that Auction protesters hung off the roof of a nearby hotel. The message: A Reckoning Is Coming.

It took hours for police to access the roof, arrest the protesters, and remove the banner.

Armstrong and Jessica waited in the back of a town car in the bowels of the UN parking garage. The door opened, and Johnson slid into the leather seat across from them. The two CEOs shared a mutual dislike and distrust. Seventeen years younger than Armstrong, Johnson chafed at how the Global CEO dominated Big 7 discussions—and that it was Armstrong the White House relied on for advice. But today was not a day for that.

"Four trillion dollars' worth of opportunity is just sitting there in that room, and then the UN officials leave and see that bullshit?" Armstrong hissed.

"Not just here. An explosive device went off at our headquarters this morning. No one was injured, but Chicago police said it could have been much worse."

"We need to hit back," Armstrong said.

"We need to plan," replied Johnson as she stepped out of the vehicle.

Even with the bumps in the road, the Big 7 remained confident. Congress promised to allow the companies to operate Auctions overseas if the UN went along. Buoyed by the smiles of the Big 7 CEOs departing the UN, investors pumped tens of billions of dollars into their stocks.

———

As the Auction Combine came to a close, it was a weary-looking Britney Reynolds's job to wrap it up. "The best and the brightest twenty-two-year-olds came to Brooklyn this week, but we've got to wait six months to find out which of them will be selected as Series As," she reminded her viewers. Her fresh lipstick shone under the bright studio lights.

At the November Auction the companies would spend tens of billions of dollars on Series As, banking that the candidates would make the companies many times that amount.

The Big 7 called the Auction "the most democratic system in America." If you had value, regardless of what it was, you got selected as a Series A. It didn't matter your race, gender, who you liked, or where you were from. If you would make the Big 7 money, you got a high bid.

At least that's what they told the public.

"The next time the companies and candidates gather in Brooklyn, a feeding frenzy of bidding will determine this year's biggest prospects," Reynolds continued smoothly.

And for good reason. A typical Series A would earn half a billion dollars in his or her lifetime, meaning the company that owned their rights would recoup $125 million of that. That's why the Big 7 deployed war rooms to bid on Series A candidates as they flashed on a screen.

While the Series B Auction relied on computer programs to place bids for the contenders, they also paid off handsomely for the Big 7. The Series C process was a crapshoot. Clerks, nurses, and middle-class earners were randomly packaged in groups of one hundred and auctioned off. To the Big 7, they were grab bags they hoped would yield a prize. And they often did.

Those not selected during the first four days of the Auction became Series Ds. Their parents received a modest onetime payment, then both parent and child were forgotten. Unfair? Sure, but not every worker has value. But even among Series Ds, though, there were feel-good stories. Three years ago a waitress in Nashville named Rachel was hanging around open mic nights, hoping for her big break. When Paramount shot a film in the city, she tagged along to a call for extras and caught the eye of its famed director. Her voice had no range, but he sensed her ease and charm would make her a natural in front of the camera.

When Rachel won an Academy Award two years later, she brought the crowd to its feet with a rousing speech. "This is for all of those overlooked. You know your true value! Show the world what it is!"

The Big 7 companies spent lavishly on PR firms each year to promote the stories of the Rachels of the world. Someone had to sell the idea that America was still the land of opportunity.

———

"Take Jack Matra off the list," Jessica told the group of Global operatives late that night. They were ruling out hundreds of Series A candidates based on the results of their interviews and background checks; a dozen prospects would soon be notified that their body scans discovered cancer or other serious disease. Jessica didn't know whose job it was to deliver that kind of news to the Auction contenders, and frankly, she didn't much care.

"Why?"

She relished the silence in the room as she dropped the news. "He got busted with a prostitute."

The activity in the room came to a halt. Jack Matra was the son of the country's most powerful Christian televangelist. His father, Jeremiah, preached the Three Gs: God, Gospel, and Gold. Jack would someday take over the family's multibillion-dollar business. But six weeks ago a patrol car discovered Jack and his "date" in an SUV behind a marijuana dispensary in Shreveport, Louisiana. His father's power extended beyond the pulpit, and the police buried the incident report. Or so they thought.

Jessica had received a tip—she'd built enough of a reputation for herself that she often heard information that wasn't intended for her, but benefited her and her work greatly—and dispatched investigators to Louisiana. Getting answers had been easy; the wife of the arresting officer gave up the information in exchange for half a million dollars.

"Take him off the list," she repeated.

Her team got back to work. Jessica peered at the monitors listing hundreds of Series A candidates. Global's Auction list was a tightly guarded secret, known only to the analysts in the room and the company's senior leadership. The list would change as they collected more information. Matra would still be interviewed; no reason to alert other companies.

The analysts resumed bickering about candidates, and Jessica's ears perked up at the mention of Larry Mattison's name. "Mattison, what about him?" she asked, looking over at an analyst whose name she should know but could never remember.

"He died at the Combine. Who has a heart attack in their twenties?" the no-name muttered, thumbing through his file.

"Cyclist. The autopsy found a rare condition."

"What doctor examined him?"

"Hashmi, Dr. Ali Hashmi. Palo Alto."

Jessica took the file and scribbled a note on it. "Larry Mattison is of no use to us. We only care about the living. I want data from the Digital DNA Archive. Find out how many cardiac deaths have occurred in the last five years for Auction candidates."

The Digital DNA Archive facility was the world's most secure—and for good reason. From the time of their birth, every scrap of data available for every American—where they visited, medical records, jobs held, meals eaten, people met, thoughts uttered, any messages typed—was logged. The database offered a window into a person's soul: interests, fears, secrets, and, most of all, trustworthiness. The Big 7 and government used it to develop a citizenship score for each American. That score dictated what schools they or their children were accepted to, whether they'd qualify for a mortgage, or whether they could get a job deemed critical to the economy or national security. But Congress banned the Big 7 from using the information to target individuals.

Of course, there were ways around that. And Jessica knew them well.

"Three other cardiac deaths in the last five years," reported the analyst after he logged in to the database. "Do you want me to forward you the information?"

Jessica finished sending a text to her cousin—*Be there in two weeks, I'll find you*—before rolling her eyes and snapping, "Yes." Why couldn't her staff read her mind yet?

———

Vincente Arias smiled at his cousin's message, then peeked into room 306 to find his patient dozing while the dialysis machine cleansed his blood. Travis opened his eyes. "Any news?" Not a day passed that the patient didn't pepper Vincente with questions about when he'd get the transplant the doctors promised him.

Vincente moved closer to the bed. "Sorry, nothing to report. But hey, I have something for you. Let's check your blood pressure first."

Once completed, Vincente retrieved a package from the counter. He pulled out a chocolate cupcake. "Happy Birthday!"

"Thanks, man. I never thought I'd celebrate my thirtieth in a hospital. Drinking tequila surrounded by girls on Galveston Island was the plan."

"You'll do that next year," Vincente offered as a consolation. He held up the cupcake. "You want it now?"

Travis shifted in the hospital bed. "I have to pee."

Vincente pushed Travis to his side and placed a bedpan underneath him. He noticed Travis's ashen color. His kidneys were failing. He listened to Travis's stories of a trucker's life on the road. His army years. How he had passed out at a roadside

diner and woken up in a hospital bed with a doctor informing
him he needed a kidney transplant.

How did this happen? It turns out it's easy when you ignore
warning signs for years. As a Series D, he'd received only the
most basic health care. It caught up to him. Since the diagno-
sis, Travis had been in and out of veterans' hospitals while he
waited for a kidney. He'd come to the Fort Stewart medical
facility a month ago to take part in experimental treatments.

Travis lifted his body so Vincente could remove the pan.
Vincente emptied it in the toilet and washed his hands. He'd
joined the army to escape his hometown of Lukeville.

Fort Stewart used to serve as the home of the Third Infantry
Division before the Pentagon dissolved it during post-Auction
military cutbacks. Now the massive base had a small community of army personnel who worked in a medical unit and the
base morgue. The medical unit offered experimental drugs and
treatment.

When Vincente stepped out of the bathroom, Travis had
nodded off. Vincente counted his blessings. He didn't have
answers to the questions his patient asked. What Vincente
knew he didn't want to share: in his three months at the facility, no one had received a kidney transplant. He left the room.

After checking on another patient, his shift ended, and
Vincente made a beeline for the mess hall. It wasn't fair to call
it that. The Fort Stewart dining hall had to be the finest mess in
any medical facility in the country, and it was free to personnel.

Vincente eyed the choices of fresh salad and fruit lining
the wall. He did a brief dance when he learned the special of
the day was penne alla vodka.

He felt a poke in his side. "Nice jig, you dork."

"Lyra, are you coming or going?"

"Just starting my shift. You?"

"I'm out of here. Hey, what happened to Steven Jackson,
room 229?"

"Transferred."

As she answered, Vincente tried not to stare. Nurse specialist Lyra Angelos was the most beautiful woman he'd ever met. Greek, with long black hair, she could pass for a model. She was also engaged. If he'd ever had a shot, he blew it long ago.

They sat alone at a long table in the corner of the dining hall.

"How's Bryan?"

"Good." She pouted. "Just too far away."

"Fort Knox? What's that, a ten-hour drive?"

"Yep," she muttered. "Since he's not allowed on the base, it's not like it matters. I can't wait to leave here. What about you?"

Vincente picked at his penne. "I'm stuck. It was Fort Stewart or get kicked out."

"You never told me."

"My roomie during nurse specialist training stole painkillers. He hid them in my trunk and I got busted for them. I was up for a court-martial."

"Holy shit. What happened?"

"My cousin Jessica is a big shot at Global. Since the company is in charge of operating Fort Stewart, she arranged this assignment. I'm stuck here until my enlistment is up."

"You should message her we need booze."

"Great idea. You're living proof the army really does attract the dumb ones."

"Vincente, everyone who ever loved you was wrong." Lyra struggled to hold a straight face before breaking into a grin.

"That's harsh."

She giggled. "Remember, don't mess with me, boy, or I'll plant drugs in your bunk."

Vincente winced when he glanced at his device. He had promised his mother a video chat. He typed a message telling her he would contact her tomorrow.

"Booty call?"

"My mother, you freak."

"Sorry. How's she doing?"

"Not great. She works too hard. I need to visit."

Lyra leaned in to whisper. "I chatted with an MP. He said the higher-ups are planning to double the personnel here by the end of the year."

He stared a bit too long. "Maybe that's why Jessica is coming to visit."

She frowned. "I wouldn't want to be a patient here. They're guinea pigs."

She was halfway toward the door when Vincente called out. "Lyra!"

She turned.

"Don't kill any of your patients today."

The last thing he saw of her was her middle finger.

Later that night in a part of the base Vincente never visited and was not welcome, others took care of the business of disposal.

Specialist Malik Thurston stood behind a cardboard container on a gurney. "Ready?"

Clara picked up the paperwork. "No, this one's got a pacemaker. I need a minute." She made an incision above the left breast, secured the area with a clamp, and inserted her right hand, searching for the two-inch titanium device. She yanked it out and clipped the cords.

"All set."

"How many more today?" asked Malik as he pushed the container forward.

Clara counted. "Three."

Malik rolled the body from the stainless steel table into the container, then wheeled it a hundred yards to the crematorium. Gauze pads filled in the hollowed-out areas of the eyes, and a bandage covered the open incision that extended from the sternum to the abdomen. The corpses all had incisions where their organs had been removed.

He had never heard of a mortuary affairs specialist, let alone expected to become one. But as far as army jobs went, it was cushy, as long as you weren't squeamish.

Malik rolled the gurney to the incinerator preheated to 1,100 degrees Fahrenheit. The mechanized doors opened, and he pushed the cardboard box onto the rack of rolling metal pins that delivered the body into the chamber. The doors shut, and Malik pressed the button that ignited the fire. In two hours he would return to dispose of the ashes. After two months, it had become routine. The only thing he didn't understand was why so many had prison tattoos. Malik didn't have time to ponder it. He had more bodies to burn.

THREE

Berkeley bustled in the spring. Preparations had begun for Berkeley's upcoming graduation ceremonies, and Sasha marveled at the activity as she meandered down Sather Road. Incoming freshmen and their families scurried to keep up with a student guide explaining the significance of Sather Gate and the Campanile; across from Sproul Hall, she clapped in time as students danced under a Lindy on Sproul sign to French jazz and ragtime. A scruffy young man held out his hand, but she begged off. Sasha turned back to watch the dancers, feeling the lightest she had in weeks, before she headed toward the library. She almost made it uninterrupted.

"Don't you answer your messages anymore? Or just not mine?"

Sasha stopped in her tracks. "You don't think I've been busy?"

Brianna Coleman pouted. They had been friends since fourth grade, so Sasha knew her moods—and this one was manageable.

"I got back last night. Chill."

Brianna shrugged. "Whatever. How was it?"

"Exhausting. And creepy. And . . . overwhelming." She swallowed back the uneasy feeling thinking of the Auction always gave her. Then she brightened. "But I got to hang out with Jason."

"Our boy! I miss him. Did you tell him I said hi?"

"Yes."

Brianna saw through her. "You suck. How is he? How does he look? Does he have a boyfriend?"

"In reverse order, not that I know of, looks great, his leg is much better." Sasha hesitated. "But then Denton Long showed up."

"Ew. Never wanted to hear that name again." Brianna, Sasha, and Jason had, for a time, been as tight as the Three Musketeers. "Ready to pick up our dresses?"

"About that . . ."

Brianna glared at Sasha. "What now?"

Sasha's words rushed out in one fast exhale. "A rep from Rosie Assoulin reached out last week and offered me a dress if I tagged the design on my graduation pictures." Then, meekly: "Sorry I forgot to tell you."

"What?" Brianna's face fell. "But we picked out our dresses together."

"It just happened."

"Did you at least ask if they'd give one to me, too?"

"I didn't speak to the person. My dad's business manager handled it."

Brianna brooded for a minute, but Sasha flashed her one of her famous *please forgive me* smiles. It worked. "Well, at least come with me to pick up mine. I need your opinion on shoes."

Sasha pointed to Evans Hall. "I'll meet you there. Since I'm here, I'm gonna go say hi to my adviser."

"Screw your adviser," Brianna joked. She wiggled her eyebrows. "Unless you already have."

Sasha gasped. "Why would you say that? You know there's nothing between us."

Brianna flipped off her sunglasses. "All work and no play make Sasha a dull girl."

"Gross." She kissed Brianna's cheek. "See you there."

When she arrived at William Cosgrove's office, Sasha watched as he inspected a bottle of Swarovski Regent Vodka—a pricey gift from a graduating senior. He admired the crystal vase shape. The gift giver obviously didn't know his history. William noticed her staring. Embarrassed, she entered the office.

"So, have you decided?" he asked.

Sasha shrugged. "I'm not ready for graduate school."

"What will you do?"

"I'm not sure." She kept her voice light, but underneath was a roiling, bumpy sea. Couldn't everyone give her a minute to decide her future for herself? "Maybe I'll be a celebrity correspondent for a gossip site."

William frowned. "Really?"

She sighed. He was always so serious. "Hell no. But I actually got offered that this week."

"You did well in my business analytics course. Why not go work for a Big 7 company?"

"Double hell no."

"What about acting or directing?"

Sasha gave him a tight-lipped smile. "My dad would love that." Judah Cross developed reality TV shows, a far cry from his earlier years when he, too, seemed destined to win an Academy Award. His outlet for his disappointment was Sasha. Since Lacy's death, Judah pressed his daughter to embrace Hollywood. He was relentless.

Her adviser eyed her curiously. "What's stopping you?"

Sasha shifted in her seat. "For my sixth birthday, my mother was on location in Tunisia, so my dad organized a party. All I wanted was a pool party with my friends. But my dad made us go to this sushi place in Santa Monica. I didn't eat sushi; I still don't. He dressed me in this Chinese cheongsam dress. This director was there, supposedly by coincidence, and my dad took me into a private room and forced me to audition. For a role I didn't even care about."

William listened in silence.

"Halfway through, I started bawling. I hid in the bathroom and my friends left."

"But you acted after that. You won an Academy Award."

"Not my idea. I hated it."

Desperate to escape the waters he waded into, William said, "Did you know that this was once Ted Kaczynski's office?"

"The Unabomber? Really?"

William shrugged. "Eh, that's what they say."

One of Sasha's classmates appeared for a scheduled appointment. William beckoned him to come into the room. Sasha stood. "I'll leave you to it. I was in the neighborhood."

As she ducked out of the office, William called her name. She poked her head back in as he came around his desk with the bottle of vodka in his outstretched hand.

She grinned. "Are you allowed to give alcohol to students, Professor?"

"I'm sure they'd rather you drink it than me."

She tucked the bottle into her oversized purse and waved her fingers goodbye. She was riding that high again, that optimism that came so infrequently these days. It all came crashing down when she spotted Freddy Tangier outside. She hustled down the steps, ignoring his questions. "Sasha, did you see the Auction rankings? You're slipping. You need to raise your profile."

She turned right, toward the parking lot, but Freddy was persistent. "C'mon, Sasha, why can't we be friends?" He snapped away at his camera, and Sasha knew images of her would be sold to the highest bidder within the hour.

But out of nowhere, a campus police officer stepped in front of Freddy as he followed Sasha into the garage. "Knock it off," he ordered. Freddy raised his hands and took half a step back. Sasha wanted to smack the smirk off his face and spent the next twenty minutes imagining ways to do so before pulling up in front of the boutique where Brianna was outside, pacing.

"They close in ten minutes!" she hissed as Sasha parked her car.

"Sorry. I'm here now." Sasha squeezed her hand and held the front door open, mimicking a low bow. "After you!"

Inside, the boutique was hushed and pleasantly cool. An old song Sasha remembered from her teenage days sounded through the speakers, loud enough to dance to but quiet enough that she heard her name called almost immediately.

A well-dressed man approached them, his eyes shiny and wide at the sight of a famous guest in his shop. "Ms. Cross, hello, hello. My name is Silvio. Congratulations on your graduation. It's an honor to have you in our shop. Can I propose something?"

Her stomach fell a centimeter. She wished Brianna weren't here to witness this. "Is it about the dress?"

"Yes. It's magnificent. I made sure of it." He nodded expectantly. He was waiting for Sasha to fall all over herself in gratitude. *Well, he'll wait forever,* she decided. She crossed her arms and stared pointedly at him.

Eventually, he got the hint. "Um, well," Silvio stuttered.

Next to her, Brianna coughed into her hand in amusement.

Silvio continued. "We'd be honored if you'd wear our dress to this milestone occasion. And we're willing to give it to you gratis in exchange for promoting our store in public."

Brianna cleared her throat, loudly this time. "We're actually both getting dresses." She stuck out her hand as Silvio looked baffled. "Hi, I'm Sasha's best friend."

It only took a moment for Silvio to recover. "We're happy to extend the offer to both of you."

Sasha stiffened. "That's a nice offer, and I thank you for it. But we stopped by to tell you in person that I'm not going to be wearing one of your dresses to my graduation after all."

"Sasha!" Brianna huffed into her ear.

"Let's not make any decisions until you see the final product?" Silvio suggested smoothly. "I'll go get them from the back—please, have a seat. Champagne?" He nodded to a shopgirl who'd been gawking from behind the register. She held up two flutes and nearly fell over herself as she stumbled to the set of tufted purple chairs in front of the shop's windows.

When the champagne was poured and the shopgirl was back behind her register, Brianna tapped her flute against Sasha's. "You couldn't have kept your mouth shut so I got my dress for free?"

Sasha swallowed. "These things . . . they come with so many strings, Bri."

"Still," she sulked. "Free. Dress."

They drained their flutes. How could she explain to Brianna the way these transactions made her feel? Every time someone tried to milk her celebrity, another wall was erected around her, keeping the world from ever coming inside to the real her.

So she changed the subject. It was what she did best, she realized moodily. "How's this? After graduation, we could get away for a few days."

Brianna brightened. "Remember the Santa Cruz trip? You had so much fun."

Sasha rolled her eyes, but a smile curled her lips. "That was *your* idea of fun."

"C'mon! Music, those boys. We danced for, like, six straight hours."

"I seem to recall you doing more than dancing."

Brianna smacked her arm. "Enough with the slut-shaming, Sister Sasha of Beverly Hills. Why don't we go back?"

Sasha cringed. Brianna had given her that nickname in high school. "Um, no, not there. I'd be hounded."

"What, and I can go because no one cares about me?" Brianna mocked. Brianna's family was what her dad called "LA rich"—but, with a mother who worked behind the scenes as an accountant to the stars, they weren't "LA famous."

Sasha hated that those kinds of distinctions mattered. But they did.

They very much did.

"That's not what I was saying . . ." Sasha started to protest, but Brianna waved her off as she put their empty flutes on the table and stood up. Silvio was approaching them with two plastic-sheathed dresses slung over his shoulder.

"Girl, I was kidding. You've got to lighten up!"

Sasha thought about Brianna's directive for the rest of the afternoon, through trying on their dresses—even Sasha had to reluctantly admit Silvio had created the perfect thing for her, it was exactly her style, and Brianna looked sophisticated and smart in her dark-green sheath—and being slowly convinced by Silvio to accept his offer. She reluctantly accepted the dress, but didn't make any promises about promotion, or about lightening up.

On her drive home a buzzing message from her father interrupted her. *Need to talk.* She ignored it. Instead, she sent a message to Brianna. *Maybe Vegas?*

Instantly her device chirped with a reply. *Yessss.*

Sitting in traffic, Sasha wondered what would happen to their relationship after graduation—after the Auction determined their fate. Was twelve years of school the glue that held them together? Brianna planned to move back to Los Angeles in the summer to work for one of her mother's Hollywood clients. She had a plan, she had goals. Brianna would laugh to hear her say it, but Sasha was jealous. She had no idea where she wanted to be. *Who* she wanted to be.

Once home, Sasha locked the door and slumped in the overstuffed brown leather chair in her living room. A ray of sun pierced through the shades, blinding her, but she was too lazy to close them.

Her dad played with the settings on the camera. "Kelsie says hello."

"My sister could do that herself."

"You know how she is. Anyway, she's busy at Crossroads."

Sasha raised her eyebrow. She and her sister hadn't yet managed to sort out what their relationship was going to be. "How's work?"

"Funny you should ask. I think our problems are the same." Her father's back was to her, and with the sunlight, he was all shadows. *Fitting*, Sasha thought. Her father had always been the kind of guy with a million balls in the air, all of them spinning, most of them just out of reach.

She yawned, delaying her response to get under his skin. "Who said I have a problem?"

"You graduate in a week, you have no job, and the best I can tell, you don't have a clue about what you want to do." He turned around, his face hitting the light. He stared at Sasha with a no-nonsense expression, the kind he'd had to give her a lot when she was a kid. "I'd say you have a problem."

"I'd say I'm only twenty-two years old."

"It's because you're twenty-two that it's a problem. You don't want to be an Auction bust like that professor of yours."

Sasha would have thrown a shoe at him, but her father wasn't actually in the room with her. They communicated mostly by hologram these days. It looked so realistic in the shadows of the sunset, though, that Sasha had almost forgotten.

When she stayed silent, he continued, his voice softening. "Come home for the summer. I'm working on something and need an assistant."

"Too busy." She shook her head. "There's so much I need to do."

"Your generation, you think you have it so hard. When your mom and I were your age, we ate noodles every night in a ratty walk-up in Brooklyn."

Sasha cocked her head. "When you were eating your noodles, did you have to worry that if you messed up you'd cost your parents millions of dollars in retirement money?"

That got him. "Well, no . . ."

"Then maybe it's not a worthwhile conversation. I can't spend the summer in LA. And even if I could, I never see you when I'm home."

"If you worked for me this summer, we'd see each other all the time. When will you realize the world is open to you? You're Sasha Cross; you can do anything you want. And raising your profile will help you in the Auction."

"I'm so sick of talking about the Auction," Sasha fumed. "Besides, did you know Marita only got $50,000?"

Marita had been the Cross family housekeeper for years. Her son, Louis, had entered the Auction a year ago. Like most children of recent immigrants, he was a Series D, so his mother received the minimum payout. She'd have to work until her dying day to make ends meet. It wasn't fair.

As if reading her mind, her father said, "Life isn't fair, Sasha. You're too young to remember how bad it got. Banks were closed for a month. While you were in kindergarten, a third of the country got thrown out of work. Your mother almost had to sell her jewelry! The Auction saved this country, and it's irresponsible for you to bad-mouth it because things didn't work out for Marita."

Sasha waited for her dad to run out of steam. At any moment his ADHD would kick in, and he would get distracted by something else. It was the common thread in Hollywood. That, and heroin.

When his rant about the Auction was over—Sasha knew right when it happened, for Judah was like a broken record about it all—he waved goodbye and the hologram dissipated. The quiet in her apartment unsettled her. She meandered through it, checking to see if her plants were alive (they were . . . mostly) and her dishwasher had been emptied. She was bored, she realized. Unsettled. She suddenly regretted skipping all the job fairs that Berkeley had hosted that spring; maybe she'd have been inspired by something there, and she wouldn't be wasting time now.

She decided to take a bike ride and get out of her head a bit. Outside, it was magic hour—dusky skies and a warm breeze. She breathed in the air, letting it fill her lungs. It felt like the first deep breath she'd taken in days.

Grunk. Her front tire hit a pothole halfway through her ride, flinging her over her Surly Cross-Check handlebars. She lay flat on the asphalt for a few seconds, catching her breath. As she wheezed, she noticed the stars beginning to climb out of the darkening sky.

It hit her like a train, like a physical attack, how badly she wished she could just stay on that ground, staring up at the sky, where no one expected anything of her. Least of all herself.

But she climbed back onto her bike, her knee swollen and stiff. It was a long and bloody walk back to her house on Valle Vista Avenue. Abandoning her bike in her driveway, Sasha gripped the rail to steady herself as she limped up the red staircase.

Once inside, she washed down two Advil, stripped off her sweaty, stained clothes, and hobbled to the upstairs shower. When she saw her reflection in the mirror, she froze.

She looked just like her mom.

It had been nearly three years since her mother's death. A therapist would tell her that her lack of focus was her way of avoiding dealing with it. *Good thing I don't see a therapist.* She chuckled to herself, but the laughter seemed hollow even to her own ears. At the funeral home she had declined to view her mother's body. She'd never even read the news stories about her—the profiles, the glowing memorials. She rarely allowed herself time to think about her mother's death; if one of her old movies came on TV, she changed the channel.

She turned on the shower and waited for the steam to fill the room.

Why? Despite the scandalous circumstances of her death, Lacy Cross had been an amazing woman. She'd quit Hollywood at the top of her game to help others. She made a difference in the world. Her mother knew what she wanted and got it. Sasha turned to look at herself in the bathroom mirror again, but the steam had enveloped the room. Suddenly, she couldn't see herself at all.

———

Jessica watched Armstrong from a distance. The man was many things: cruel, ruthless, devious. But he was also a doting grandfather. She watched as his young granddaughter ran into his arms. "Cranpa!" she shouted his pet name. Armstrong scooped her up and tickled her belly.

When the little girl scooted down the hallway after her mother, Armstrong waved Jessica into his office.

She skipped the pleasantries and jumped right to the point of her visit. "I think I know why we've been unlucky with Series A candidates and heart attacks."

"Not just a coincidence?" Armstrong didn't sound surprised. More like resigned.

"I'll know tomorrow," she confirmed. "I'm taking a trip to Palo Alto."

"What for?"

A thin smile peeked out from her face. "Stress test."

Less than twenty-four hours later, Jessica sat in the neatly appointed waiting room of Dr. Ali Hashmi. The cardiologist enjoyed a robust practice split between San Francisco and Palo Alto. He counted among his patients Fortune 500 CEOs and professional hockey players; he was the best of the best in his field.

"Jessica Garulli?" From behind her desk, the receptionist surveyed the waiting room until she caught Jessica's eye. She beckoned her to approach. "Dr. Hashmi will see you."

The receptionist pointed to the doors leading to an exam room. Once inside, Jessica changed into one of the standard blue hospital gowns waiting for her on the chair and studied the radiology equipment. Video screens covered one of the walls above a small desk; next to them, a dispenser for hand sanitizer was mounted on the wall.

It took twenty minutes for Hashmi to enter the room—minutes Jessica would normally be livid about wasting, especially when there was so much work to be done. But she'd focused herself on the mission ahead. Her hand was steady, her pulse barely audible in her ears.

He smiled at Jessica before studying her chart on his device. "Tell me about the scars," he began, pointing at the skin grafts on her leg.

She hid a grimace. They were Jessica's constant reminder. On a fall morning just north of Al Wakrah, Jessica's Humvee had been leading a four-vehicle convoy of the US Army Corps of Engineers to a new Iraqi hospital when a blue bongo truck passing by detonated. The explosion propelled her thirty yards into a ditch. She suffered gruesome injuries to her legs, back, and torso. She'd been airlifted to a German hospital, where doctors called her "Humpty Dumpty" when they'd thought she couldn't hear them.

It was a long recovery, and once the army gave her a medical discharge, she'd moved to San Francisco to work for a security contractor. Its biggest client was Global Holdings. It didn't take long for Armstrong to notice how efficiently Jessica handled sensitive projects—and how flexible her moral code was. When he needed a new head of security, he poached her.

Jessica cleared the memory from her head and told the doctor the bare minimum about her legs. After the stress test, just as the nurse slipped out the door with the doctor on her heels, she caught his attention. "One more thing, Dr. Hashmi?"

He must have sensed the steel in her voice, because he paused, lingering for just a beat too long before reentering the exam room and closing the door behind him. Jessica felt the satisfaction of her ploy spread over her lungs, up her neck. Getting here had been the hard part; what remained was easy.

"Yes?" Dr. Hashmi prompted her, his demeanor different enough from the affable, competent one he'd had moments before. Jessica had always had that kind of effect on people, had always wielded it like a weapon.

She flashed a brilliant smile at him before fishing out large color prints of Mrs. Hashmi and their three children from her bag. She fanned them out and carefully laid them on the exam table where her bare, scarred legs had just been.

Dr. Hashmi glanced at them and blanched. His eyes darted back to Jessica's. They were, she noted without emotion, full of fear and confusion.

What she said next was second nature to her by that point; she'd performed the same routine so many times. Patiently, she explained that a man was outside his home at that very moment, awaiting her orders. She briefed the doctor on her knowledge of his family's daily routines—school drop-offs and pickups, grocery stores frequented, favorite coffee shops. All the things that make up the daily grind of a family's life.

Her voice was low, confident. Not a hitch of spare breath escaped her lips. The more she spoke, the grayer Dr. Hashmi's skin grew. His jaw fell slack.

She wasn't finished yet. It was time for specifics. She transitioned away from his wife's play-by-play and into his eldest daughter's. Nine-year-old Sandhi was, according to her records, probably waiting for her mother to pick her up at Nottingham Elementary School right now—"Wasn't she, Dr. Hashmi?"

He blinked while Jessica paused. Her question wasn't rhetorical, even though it sounded like it. She really was asking him to confirm her whereabouts. While he sputtered and choked back tears, Jessica wondered what his driving force had been. Could it really have been something as simple as greed?

Dr. Hashmi had been hired by the Auction Combine to check Series As for heart issues; no one wanted to invest millions of dollars in a risky bet. But promises of even more money had lured him into a lucrative side deal with Beech, where an old college buddy of his had risen in the ranks and kept in touch. The size of his medical-school bills made it a no-brainer, he'd convinced himself. His mission? To give the company inside health information on candidates while withholding it from the other companies. In other words, to cleanly and clearly break the rules that all medical providers of Auction services had sworn to uphold. Not to mention, to violate all sorts of medical resolutions passed by Congress generations ago, and to utterly betray his patients.

He'd justified his betrayals, of course, especially late at night when his family was asleep and he was alone in the dark, catching up on paperwork—the time of night when all your chickens come home to roost. Most of the time a candidate's heart issues would not surface for several years, so Dr. Hashmi had done the calculations and figured he was likely to never get caught.

He was wrong. *Men usually are,* Jessica reminded herself.

She cut off his pathetic attempts to explain himself. Instead, she patiently laid out her plans for him and his family. Unless, of course, he supplied the information she was after. "You have all the power here, sir," she said sweetly, crossing her arms. "The choice is yours."

The thing about Armstrong was, he rarely smiled. But when Jessica returned to the office with the names of two other Auction contractors who were feeding information to Beech, he broke into a grin that threatened to engulf his entire face.

A makeup artist applied foundation as Global staffers prepared the studio for Armstrong's interview to discuss the company's record financial results.

"One minute . . . ," the floor manager prompted Armstrong, who turned away from Jessica and nodded at the camera. He heard CNBC's Britney Reynolds's voice in his earpiece.

"Congratulations, Victor. What made this a record quarter?"

"We had strong growth in our US market. We continue to show how private companies do a better job running things like prisons and border operations."

Reynolds jumped in with a question. "An analyst noted a spike in 'Asset Protection.' What is that and why is it going up?"

Armstrong smiled the cool smile of someone who didn't want to answer. "It's a minor part of our operations focused on the well-being of our Auction investments and our commitment to the social welfare of Series Ds. It should go up."

Investors cheered his statements. Global's stock soared in after-hours trading. Already the most valuable company in the world, by morning it would be worth billions more.

It was hard to argue with the Auction's success. After years of costly wars and fending off deadly viruses that overloaded the health care system and crushed the economy, the country had been in disarray. Jobs disappeared, crime rates spiraled, and one in four Americans relied on public assistance to survive. Poor communities cut school to three days a week. The postal service operated on Mondays and Thursdays. The rich did well, blissfully out of touch and living in their gated communities. The shrinking middle class blamed immigrants. And the poor did what they always did—stayed poor. Unemployment reached 36 percent.

Then it got worse. The federal government warned Social Security would go bankrupt in eight years. It happened in four. Protesters burned government buildings, and millions of homeless people built tent cities across the country. The violence reached a peak when a mob stormed Congress and killed three senators. Collapse seemed imminent.

One day, someone had an idea. In back rooms and over martini lunches, a solution emerged: create a new stock market, but this time for human beings.

Already, college students were able to sell their future earnings in exchange for tuition; the new system just took it a step further, everyone said. A natural evolution. Within it, companies could bid on the most promising new minds. And when the new employees accepted an offer, the company that bid on them would receive 25 percent of their lifetime earnings.

Parents in particular loved it, seeing for the first time in generations the promise that their children would have security, and that they would have enough funds to retire. The Auction let them realize the value of their most precious asset: their children. Since Social Security was one of the many government programs abolished, the Auction could fill the void.

Soon, it was hard to tell where the Big 7's role ended, and the government's began.

Getting the Auction established in both practice and in people's hearts and minds had not been easy. The poor and those who distrusted government staged mass protests; on and on they raged until the reality of the economy—which had surged—proved the Auction's success, protests be damned. Government costs plummeted, and taxes were at a hundred-year low. America had the strongest, most vibrant economy in the world.

Finally, now, ten years later, Asia and Europe were coming around to the idea; and where they went, the rest of the world followed. The expansion would mean trillions of dollars for the Big 7 running the Auction. There was a lot to lose. Everyone knew the company that came out on top would be the one with the cleanest data that could be best leveraged. And Armstrong intended it to be Global.

After the interview with Reynolds ended, Jessica pulled her boss aside for some updates. "The mayor said he won't use force to break up the demonstrations."

Armstrong's face contorted with fury. "That son of a bitch."

He ranked among the most influential people in the world, but Armstrong had little juice in his hometown. San Francisco had elected a socialist who ran on the promise of curbing Global's power. What started as a smattering of protesters a few weeks ago had now swelled to an encampment at Justin Herman Plaza, blighting Armstrong's view of the San Francisco Bay.

"How many were out there today?" he asked.

"There's two hundred in front of the building. The rest are at the park."

He eyed Jessica. She was his fixer, and she knew that look on his face. "You better get on this," he hissed.

———

Behind the closed doors at Beech, one of Armstrong's biggest competitors, CEO Ursula Johnson was thinking. Planning. Her eyes were closed, and her fingers rested on her chin as she took deep breaths. Strategy was her strong suit, but she took her time with it. You couldn't rush these things, she'd patiently explained to the board of directors.

That morning's hologram call from Dr. Hashmi would have thrown any other CEO, no doubt. He'd been in tears when he'd appeared before her, shaking and inconsolable as he tendered his resignation and begged her to leave him and his family alone. She'd offered him more money, but he'd been resolute in his decision.

Whoever had gotten to him had done a good job, she noted. "We have other doctors," she'd told her staff. "But wait before we use them."

They would rebuild for the next Auction, she decided. It would take time and attention to the small details. She'd felt a thrill of satisfaction at that decision. After all, she'd taken over Beech by paying attention to those details.

She had her cousin Sophie to thank for that. Sophie's father, her uncle, had founded the company decades ago; growing up, Ursula and Sophie thought of each other as sisters. Ursula considered Uncle Julius a second father. He taught her to play chess, and they'd often have a running game. "Remember," he told her, "chess isn't limited to this board. It's your life, your career, everything you do." By her midteens, Ursula was nationally ranked.

Her uncle had built a powerhouse company, aided by his daughter and niece. The two moved up the ranks together,

Sophie expanding Beech's communications and media out-reach as Ursula fine-tuned its processes, turning it into a well-oiled machine. When her uncle suffered a stroke, he informed the board he was turning over day-to-day operations to his daughter.

The board, however, rejected his decision.

Instead, it installed Ursula as the CEO. Over the previous year, she had privately lobbied key board members, wielding her influence to best position herself. She laid out Sophie's pro-fessional and personal weaknesses, some of which she knew simply by having gained Sophie's confidences throughout their lives. Sophie had been blindsided by Ursula's deception, and fought for control. But six weeks later, her father died, and the board unanimously sided with Ursula in the battle of the cousins.

In the three years since she'd taken over, Ursula had taken a reluctant back seat to Armstrong's aggressive ways. But she had a plan to make Beech the world's most dominant company. Global had had its time.

It would just take attention to the small details.

"Tell the facial recognition team I want the results from the Combine," Johnson told her staff. "And why do we care about Sheryl Mangum?"

"She's pregnant."

The striking brunette, a Series A candidate, had set high jump records in college, and *Maxim* magazine wanted to include her in a profile of the hottest college athletes. She'd declined. Her parents were Christian conservatives from Orange County. They would be devastated by her pregnancy.

"Why do we care?"

"We're the only ones who know. She went to one of our doctors. She graduated early and works for Jessica Garulli at Global."

Johnson considered it. *Details.* "Pay her a visit. And bring everything you have on Garulli."

FOUR

Sasha had a vague memory of walking into her room as a young girl after soccer practice to find a strange man. He was tall, taller than her daddy, and his clothes were old and worn. He held one of her dresses.

Upon her arrival, he had smiled. "My little girl."

Sasha had shrieked and run for her mother; she found her in the living room. By the time Sasha dragged her back upstairs to show her the scary man, he was standing on the balcony outside Lacy's bedroom, a manic grin on his face. Lacy had screamed.

Alerted by the commotion, Lacy's security detail had arrived and coaxed the man they would later learn was named Larry Lodge out of their house. He loved Lacy, he kept saying, again and again, screaming about destiny. He confessed to writing the countless letters Lacy had been finding in their mailbox for the past few weeks.

Security had pinned him to the ground and waited for the police. When the handcuffs came out, the flashing lights making Sasha squint and cry, Larry turned violent. He screamed, "I came to see my little girl!"

Sasha remembered her mother's tear-streaked face. Lacy was always cool and collected, but not that day. She explained to Sasha that sometimes celebrities attract these kinds of people. Lacy's breath smelled like it did when she came back from a party.

"What people, Mommy?"

Lacy caressed her head. "People who aren't well. Some are sad and want what we have."

Sasha pondered what her mother told her. "He said I was his daughter."

"He's just confused, dear. You don't have to worry about him anymore."

Young Sasha didn't understand it at all, but that night she slept in her mother's bed.

Larry's obsession never dimmed. He tried to reenter the Cross house a year later. Charged with trespassing, he received a three-month sentence. Once out, he violated the restraining order mandating he stay at least two hundred yards away. Larry spent his remaining years in an institution, writing letters to Lacy and Sasha.

Years later, when teenage Sasha got her own stalker, it brought back memories of Larry. It started with letters to her publicist with offers to meet. Unlike Larry, Sasha's admirer didn't take no well. The letters became angry, then threatening, then downright scary.

Sasha gave him the name "Benjamin." She hadn't heard from him in quite a while, though, and she hoped that he'd found someone else to fixate on.

That day as she passed through Sather Gate and onto the long boulevard that connected the main campus buildings, he was the furthest thing from her mind. She laughed as incoming freshmen streamed out of Dwinelle Hall after orientation, eager to experience their first college parties. The bells that rang in the Campanile signaled it was 2:00 p.m. An idea came to her.

She took a shortcut to the corner of Bancroft Way and College Avenue. Sam's Burger Barn food truck, William's favorite guilty pleasure, was right where she hoped it would be. She ignored the snide comments as she passed a gaggle of Gamma Phi Beta girls, pretending not to notice the stares that came with her celebrity while she waited her turn. William often spoke of his friend Sam and his burgers. Sam barked orders to his cook while he dealt with customers. Without looking up, he asked Sasha, "What can I get you?"

"Your name is Sam, right? You're a friend of Professor Cosgrove?"

"Rummy? Everything he knows he learned from me. What'll you have?"

"Give me two of whatever he gets."

Sam called out: "Two Burl Ives!" He turned to Sasha. "So why are you ordering his burger? Something I should know?"

"Why does it have to mean anything?"

"If they're for my man William, it's on the house."

Five minutes later Sam handed her the bag. "That's two Burl Ives. Cheddar burgers with a hot dog sliced on top, BBQ sauce, and sweet pickles. With fries. Tell him I said hi."

Sasha dodged the skateboarders who sloped down the incline and barked at undergraduates hustling to summer classes in Stanley Hall. She bounded up the steps of Evans Hall. On the stairs between the sixth and seventh floors, Sasha passed a man she had seen on campus but couldn't place. He stared as she passed.

She knocked on William's office. When he didn't answer, she entered.

"Professor?"

Disappointed at not finding him, she turned to leave. And jumped. The odd man from the stairway stood an inch from her face. He pushed her into William's office.

"Is it him? You want him?"

"What? No, I . . . who are you?" Sasha sputtered.

"I wrote you. You think you're better? Better than me?"

Gaping at him, Sasha felt genuine, hot fear slash against her chest. The man had to be in his twenties, but his matted hair and ragged clothes were out of place even for a college. His bloodshot eyes gave him the appearance of someone who hadn't slept in days.

He moved; something glinted. Panic seized her when she realized it was a box cutter.

He's going to kill me, Sasha thought. "Please, I don't even know who you are! What do you want?"

He moved toward her. "I wrote you, but you Hollywood bitches are all the same!"

Her jaw dropped.

Benjamin.

Sasha retreated, using the desk as a shield. That made Benjamin furious, and he climbed up on it, glowering over her. "I wrote! You think you're better than me!"

She held up her hands in protection, tears blocking her vision.

A flash of someone familiar caught her attention. William, in the doorway. He held a finger to his lips—shhh—and Sasha inhaled sharply.

Too sharply. Benjamin whirled around and, when he saw William in the door, pounced. He caught him on the left arm with the box cutter. William shrieked; blood soaked his shirt.

Sasha began to see everything in slow motion. Benjamin stumbled as he lunged again. William steadied himself and connected a right punch that glanced off Benjamin's neck. The attacker swung the box cutter again but missed. William hit

Benjamin flush in the temple. The attacker's eyes rolled to the back of his head. Sasha watched as William moved in closer and connected an uppercut to the jaw. Benjamin made one last effort to wield the box cutter.

William grabbed his hand and pushed it against the desk. The box cutter fell.

By now, the ruckus had brought other faculty to William's office; chaos ensued. William thrust Benjamin back. He stumbled over a chair and fell to the ground as two colleagues gripped his shoulders, holding him down. William leaned on top of him, breathing heavily.

Benjamin screamed. "No! You bitch!"

Sasha almost laughed—part relief, part adrenaline, part lack of originality from Benjamin. Did he think being called a bitch was some kind of new, harmful insult? Had he ever met a child star before? She'd been called a bitch in the press more times by her thirteenth birthday than most women would in their lives.

Eventually, Sasha's breath evened out. Within seconds, building security swarmed them; Benjamin was hauled off. His actual name, Sasha learned, was Tyler Kroop. Security used a towel to apply pressure to William's bleeding forearm. Next to arrive were the campus police, who asked what triggered the attack. Sasha glanced at William, then turned to them.

"No idea at all."

William declined the police's offer to escort him to the hospital. And even though Sasha knew she was safe now, her arms hadn't received the message; they trembled; her teeth chattered. Eyeing her carefully, William thanked the other professors who'd shown up to help and shut the office door. He kept the towel pressed to his arm. They were alone except for the security detail who were taking photos of the wreck—bloodstains, broken chairs.

Sasha remembered something. She unearthed the brown bag—still warm—and held it up weakly. She smiled through tears. "I brought us burgers."

———

It took six hours for the media to discover the attack on Sasha, and six minutes from the publication of the first headline for her father to call her, screaming. "How is it I hear that a stalker attacked you from the goddamn media?"

Sasha was home, rolled tight under heavy blankets in her bed, the curtains drawn. She'd told William she was fine, they'd even eaten their burgers, but by the time she'd arrived at her house, her shaking had started again. "I'm fine," she lied, her voice feeling foreign, like someone else was speaking from inside her throat.

"This isn't a joke, Sasha! I'm out of my mind that you didn't call me!"

She could tell her father was serious—and seriously mad. But so what? She was fine. Right? "What difference would it make?"

He seethed through the call. "That's all you have to say? Don't you remember Larry Lodge?"

Did he really think she could ever forget? "Of course. What's your point? He got sent to prison."

"Do you know why?"

Sasha groaned. "Of course. He contacted Mom."

"No, because he *attacked* her. She walked out of the studio lot one day, and he jumped her. She broke a rib!" Her father huffed in frustration. "We kept it from you so you wouldn't be frightened."

"Oh," Sasha whispered. From outside her windows, an ambulance drove by, sirens roaring.

When she had convinced her father that everything was fine, that she didn't even have a mark on her, he reluctantly let her go. Some semblance of bravery had returned to her, so she scanned the headlines. "Sasha Attack Drama!" blared the *New York Post* headline.

No wonder her father had panicked.

It didn't take long for more paparazzi to decide Sasha was a good bet for a story. Three photographers joined Freddy Tangier in his pursuit, hoping to take the million-dollar shot of Sasha Cross, victim of a deranged stalker. For the next few days, everywhere she went, she had an unwelcome entourage. Secretly, though, she felt relieved. At least Freddy's stalking was predictable.

Her relief was short-lived, though. A copycat attacker attempted to break into her house weeks later. The tabloids loved it; Sasha began sleeping with her lights on.

At night—after a third-straight dinner of toast and eggs, the comfort food she so desperately needed—Sasha peered out the blinds at the gaggle of vultures perched on the sidewalk. It struck her: this was her life, forever.

———

Jason pulled his car up to his aunt's house in the Mount Airy neighborhood of Philadelphia. That feeling of hope, of home, filled his lungs, the way it always did at the sight of their house, even if the brick-and-stone dwelling had seen better days. As he approached the house, busy making a mental note to clear out the leaves that filled the bushes, from the corner of his eye he noticed a shadow looming.

"When did you get out of the hospital?"

Jason exhaled in relief at the sight of Denton. The man knew how to surprise people. "What are you talking about?"

Denton took the steps two at a time as he barked, "'Cause the only goddamned reason I can come up with for you blowing me off is that you were in the hospital!"

They met halfway up the walkway. "Sorry, Dent. Couldn't make it."

"You made me look like a chump," growled Denton, circling him. "So speak up, boy."

Jason exhaled, taking another step up the staircase. "Dude, twelve hours after you approached me on the street, I got asked what I was doing with you."

Denton put out his hands. "That's it? Listen, man, you're either a player or not a player. If you're a player, those companies will want you. It's all on you. You a player?"

"I'm trying to be, Denton, but I can't do anything to mess this up," Jason hissed. He glanced at the front door. "For Ayana. She took in Baker and me. I'm her last shot. The Auction doesn't pay out any money for a fourth kid, just the first three. I owe her that after what she did for me."

Denton lowered his voice. "And what about what I did for you?"

"Hey!" Ayana stormed out of her front door, waving an angry hand. "Get off my property!"

Denton smirked. "She fights your battles?"

Ayana stopped a half inch from Denton's face. "I'll fight 'em, I'll finish 'em."

Denton took a half step back, hands up in surrender. "You think you know what's up here."

"More than you," replied Ayana, pointing at the street. "Now out!"

Denton smirked, gave Jason a knowing nod, and disappeared down the street.

Rubbing his chin, Jason sighed and hugged his aunt. He held the door open for her and escorted her back inside. "Sorry."

"Baby," she started, and Jason held his breath for a lecture, but she surprised him. Maybe surprised herself, too, if her expression was any indication. "Let it go. You can't blame yourself. Look forward."

"Yeah, but . . . he's not going away." Jason knew this now, for a fact. Denton would always be in the shadows, no matter how much time passed.

Ayana touched his arm. "Remember when you first got here? Those boys who teased you because of your limp?"

"They didn't tease me, Ayana, they bullied me."

"And you told them not to mess with you because you had been a gang member in LA. Do you remember what happened?"

Jason rubbed his leg. "Yeah, they kicked my ass."

She burst out laughing. "They sure did! That should have taught you not to play their game. And you can't play Denton's game, either. You just have to be Jason Harris." She wrapped her arms around him. "Go practice. You have a big game tomorrow."

Jason's device chirped on his way up the stairs. He glanced at it; an old photo of him, Sasha, and Brianna at a Westlake freshman dance shone up at him. They looked so impossibly young. *Remember these three?* Sasha's message said.

Head down, he didn't see his brother in the hallway.

"That better not be gay porn you're looking at."

Jason burst into a smile as Baker came over for a hug. He stepped back to look at his younger brother. "Man, you are getting uglier by the day. How long are you home?"

Baker rubbed his belly, a habit since he was a toddler. "Just two weeks. I have a tournament in Atlanta."

"Any word?"

"Ranked number three. The guys ahead of me are both going pro this summer, so I might be the number one US MMA amateur fighter by fall."

Jason bear-hugged him. "When do you go pro?"

"It depends how well I do. How was New York?"

A muscle twitched in Jason's jaw. "Not worth talking about."

But memories of New York, of Denton, of Sasha, and most of all, of the Auction, occupied him all night and all through the next morning as he drove to the Sclavos Center, the massive sports complex where the e-league doubleheader was taking place. He watched the last seconds of the first game tick down, struggling to control his pregame jitters. Fans left their seats in search of food, rushing to make it back in time to watch a hip-hop star's between-game performance. He was sweating; his stomach was churning. Finally, the sound of loud and rhythmic music cascaded off the walls of the arena, signaling to Jason that it was time to retreat to the locker room and clear his head.

"Have you fixed your jump shot?" Jason turned to see the e-76ers scout who was a regular at his games.

Jason nodded, feigning confidence. "Getting better all the time."

"It's the only thing holding you back. Good luck."

Jason fled to the locker room. Interactions with scouts unnerved him, and today was an important game. If his team won, they would move into a tie for first place. E-league salaries were dictated by both an individual's ranking in the league and his or her team's performance.

His device beeped. A message from Ayana: *You got this!* He could hear the distant echoes of the music. He took deep breaths.

The players in Jason's minor league team all scrambled to reach the gaming big time: a spot in the e-NBA. Each original NBA team had a gaming counterpart. The gaming teams had eight players: five starters and three substitutes. The difference with the real thing was that starters rarely subbed out. Games lasted eighty minutes, so arenas scheduled doubleheaders and mixed in musical and comedy acts.

All sports leagues had one thing in common: unhappy fans.

Once the game started, Jason struggled to ignore the boos coming in as he stared at the huge monitor in the center of the court. He missed his first six shots, and his team was already down twelve. A buzzer signaled the end of the first quarter. Jason sat back in his recliner and cracked his knuckles, his hands stiff from gripping the controller.

He sipped water as the coach detailed everything that had gone wrong. "Jason, you're rushing! Slow down!" Jason nodded.

He glanced over at the scouts sitting in the first-row seats that surrounded the court. Jason took his last sip and sat forward in his chair. He finally made a shot but never got his rhythm. He scored six points and his team lost.

"Don't sweat it, J," his teammate Elijah consoled him. "We all played like crap."

Jason managed a weak smile, but his stomach turned as he slunk to the locker room. A lot was riding on these games. The better he played, the better his chances of making the e-76ers.

That meant money for him. And if his Auction stock rose, the more money a Big 7 company would bid on him. That meant financial security for Aunt Ayana. That was his priority, he reminded himself—his driving force. After all she'd done for him . . .

He couldn't help it. Sometimes, his mind wandered back to the night of the accident, replaying the events again and again. As he changed his clothes, it started again: vivid flashes, a flood of panic.

Jason would take it all back if he could.

No one had walked away from that accident whole.

———

"You were supposed to be here two days ago. Where have you been?"

Avery shrugged. He'd been hoping for a warm reception and maybe even an offer to show him around San Francisco, but Avery's brother was nothing if not blunt. He strode over to the windows of Garrett's office and studied the sweeping views. "I stuck around New York."

"Avery, that's not how this works. New York wasn't a vacation, and neither is San Francisco. This is work," he scolded. Garrett was young, but moving up the ranks at Global, and to Avery he looked like a little boy playing dress-up. But he was sneaky; he'd approached his boss with a clever idea: send Avery to Brooklyn posing as a Series A candidate so he could collect information. His bosses agreed.

Avery had learned at an early age that he couldn't compete with his big brother. At sixteen years old, Garrett had become a local celebrity when he won first prize at the Michigan state science fair. That same year Avery got expelled from a prep school for cheating. Things had gone on like that ever since—Garrett earning some kind of award, Avery barely escaping trouble. Avery was relieved when Garrett finally went off to college—first in his class in high school, he then graduated with honors from the University of Michigan—and after only three years on the job, Global executives pegged him as a rising star. Now he had his own office on the eighteenth floor of Global.

In contrast, Avery skated through high school and got into Michigan State only because of family connections. Thanks to poor grades, he needed to spend an additional semester there before he could graduate and end his mediocre academic career.

That record ruled him out of getting a Series A selection based on his merits. But Garrett promised that if Avery delivered information on candidates, Global would pick him. And,

despite his jealousy of his brother, he still hoped to follow in
Garrett's footsteps. Global was the biggest company in the
world; surely there was room for him. If not, he had an ace in
the hole: his girlfriend, Stephanie. She liked that they shared a
common interest—her. Stephanie could be shallow, selfish, and
downright cruel. But Avery had never dated a woman this hot,
and he enjoyed the looks on his friends' faces when they met
her. Better yet, her family owned the Texas Rangers. Perhaps
he could wrangle a job in Major League Baseball.

Amused, Avery picked up his brother's pride and joy: a
glass case holding the ball used to make the final out when the
Detroit Tigers won the World Series three years ago. Garrett
had bought it with the signing bonus Global paid him to join
the company. Garrett took it out of his brother's hand and put
it back on his desk. "What do you have for me?"

"About what?"

"About. The. Candidates. You. Met. In. Brooklyn."

"OK, you don't have to treat me like an idiot." Avery tapped
on his device to retrieve his notes. "At lunch I ran into Sasha
Cross, I knew her when she was in middle school."

"Really? My boss's boss showed a lot of interest in her.
What did you find out?"

"Well, she's still stuck-up as hell . . ."

"That doesn't matter!" Garrett was growing flustered. "Did
she say anything about her career plans?"

"She doesn't know. But if anyone knows, it's another guy
from LA, Jason Harris."

Garrett groaned. "And who is Jason Harris?"

"A professional e-gamer. He moved to Philly when his parents died."

Garrett accessed Jason's Auction rating on his device.
Global gave each candidate a score based on his or her job prospects, education, wealth, criminal record, quality of friends
and associates, health, and online activity. In Jason's case, his

scores had declined in the few days since the Auction talks had begun, jeopardizing his status as a Series A candidate. "Forget him. He's a weak candidate. He's got sketchy friends, lied at the Combine, and his disability is a strike against him. Go back to Sasha Cross. Did she say anything? Like about going back into entertainment?"

Avery went through his notes. "I already told you. She hates attention. Always has."

Garrett took a breath. "We didn't send you there to guess. We sent you there to bring us back real information. You aren't taking this seriously. You want to be a Series A, right?"

"Yeah, that's the deal we made," Avery said, his voice growing hot at the implication.

"The deal we made is you bring us valuable intel and Global selects you," his brother said through gritted teeth. "Make good on your part of the deal. Follow the plan. Let's start again."

They went through every interaction Avery had had with Sasha; an hour later, Garrett knew he'd gotten all he would from his brother. He wearily rubbed his eyes. "OK, that's it."

"Do we meet with your boss now?"

Garrett snorted. "I said we'd do that if you had something worthwhile. You need to work harder."

Avery rolled his eyes. "You sound like Mom and Dad."

"You should listen to them. Did Stephanie dump you yet?"

"You're just jealous."

Garrett laughed out loud. "Dude, I'm pulling in four mill, working for the most powerful company in the world. What makes you think I couldn't have anything of yours I want?"

He knew that would sting, and by the look in Avery's eyes, it did. Garrett had slept with Avery's girlfriend a few years back as revenge for the dent Avery had put in his new BMW.

Avery's face turned red. "Fuck off."

He walked down the long hallway. In each office a well-dressed man or woman with an air of importance spoke rapidly on video conference calls or pored over candidate lists. They made at least what Garrett earned, and likely more. Avery wanted what they had. He *had* to be a Series A, with all the advantages it offered.

If not Global, he would have the chance to impress Stephanie's family when she took him to Texas next month. Avery smiled as he got on the elevator. When he was twelve, his teacher asked him what he wanted to be when he grew up. Avery answered, "Rich."

He was so close to becoming what he always wanted to be. He could taste it.

———

"Say, are you Sheryl Mangum?"

The former track star placed her soy latte with no foam on the table in the corner of the Starbucks in downtown Palo Alto and turned around. As a well-known local athlete, she got a lot of attention. "Can I help you?" asked Sheryl.

A woman smiled back at her. "Maybe I can help you. I'm sure it's such a busy time in your life. Working at Global, the Auction . . . planning for the baby."

Sheryl stopped stirring her coffee. "What did you say?"

The woman slid into the seat next to her, smiling and calm.

"You know, the baby. Congratulations. I'm sure your parents are proud."

"Who, who are you . . . and how is this any of your business?" Sheryl stammered. Two pools of pink bloomed on her cheeks.

"It's all of our business now. The Big 7, we need to know who we are investing in."

"What company do you work for?"

"That doesn't matter. I just want to make sure your personal life stays private. Perhaps we can keep this hushed up. If others learned about it, it would cut your Auction value by over $2 million. That's a lot of money for your parents."

"What do you want?"

"Barely anything at all. Just Jessica Garulli's daily schedule."

FIVE

Sasha pinched the waist of her graduation dress as she gazed at herself in the mirror. She grimaced at how it hung, a result of her lack of appetite since the incident. She hadn't left her house in a week, which had led most of the media to end their stakeout. A search for her graduation cap led to its discovery under a pile of clothes in the corner of her room. She placed the cap on her head.

Her device buzzed. Where are you? asked Brianna. Sasha started to message back that she wasn't going, but an image of her mother popped into her head.

Be there soon, she replied. Twenty minutes later sweat beaded down her back as she half-jogged to Zellerbach Hall. A security guard her father had hired trailed behind her.

The bells rang just as she joined her excited classmates in the hall, the air thick with excitement. The soon-to-be graduates had a lot to smile about. Since the fall, recruiters for hundreds of companies had enticed them with offers of six-figure signing bonuses. The economy was growing at breakneck speed, and companies bid aggressively to get the best talent.

Sasha felt a poke and jumped.

"Are you ready?" Brianna asked.

"Let's get this over with."

Once seated, Sasha craned her neck looking for her father and sister but only saw a sea of excited families drenched in sweat. Zellerbach's AC couldn't keep up with the unseasonal temperature. William sat onstage. She caught his eye and waved.

It hit her then: this was it. Once she left the ceremony, she would be qualified to do . . . what? She had a summer reprieve working as William's research assistant. The governor had appointed him to a state commission looking into whether the Auction was fair to Series Ds. Graduate school remained an option. There was always a place for her at the Lacy Cross Foundation.

And then there was Hollywood. Her Academy Award gave her opportunities both in front of and behind the camera. Applause shook Sasha out of her thoughts. Sure, she had options. So why did it feel like she was caged?

After the ceremony, while she joined her father at a celebratory dinner, Sasha learned why she hadn't found her sister in the crowd.

"Don't be mad, she had a last-minute audition," her father said, popping a piece of bluefin tuna toro nigiri into his mouth.

"You always defend her."

"You know how she is." He raised his glass. "To my college graduate!"

She raised hers in return. At least the wine was tasty.

"How's the job search?"

She swallowed carefully. "I'm busy with my research position. And I'm lining up interviews."

An awkward silence permeated their dinner and then their drive home. Finally, her father cleared his throat. "I've got news."

Sasha braced for a hard sell.

"PicaFlix is producing a retrospective on your mother's life and career. And they want you, me, and Kelsie to participate."

Sasha hesitated, trying to think of a way out. She realized she couldn't object without looking like she didn't want to honor her mother. "When?"

"Next month. I'll send you details. It'll take a few days. Do you think you can do that?"

"Yes, just tell me when. I'll be there." She stepped out of her father's rental car. Sasha's device buzzed. Jason.

Congrats, girly! Survive your father?

She typed into her device, *He just left. He's pushing me to move back home.*

His response was quick, and perfectly Jason. *Tell him you're coming to Philly. Wawa is hiring.*

Lol. How's it going?

It took a while for Jason to respond. *No bueno. Can't hit a shot. The way it's going I'll be one register over from you at Wawa.*

Wouldn't that be nice, in a way? she wondered. But she knew he needed encouragement. *You'll get there, J. Look how far you've come already.*

When his reply came through, Sasha started to worry.

Not far enough.

Back in her home, Sasha felt a sense of unease as she put down her device. But she set it aside. She needed to pack. Determined to overcome her fear, Sasha refused to cancel her Vegas trip.

The next day, Sasha and Brianna buckled up as the plane's engines came to life.

"Is he going to be with us the whole time?" asked Brianna, pointing at the security guard seated in the adjoining row.

Sasha nodded. "He's my shadow."

Brianna glanced across the aisle at their protector. "He's cute. So, did you do it?"

"Do what?" Sasha shot back.

"The Bellagio."

Sasha bristled, hating that her friend had figured it out. Yes, Sasha had traded on her family connections to get a suite at the Bellagio. Among the oldest casinos on the Las Vegas Strip, it held significance for her. Her mother had filmed her last movie there.

"If you give me any shit about it, you can find your own room."

Brianna waved her hands. "Nah, I'm good. Did they comp it?"

"No comment."

"Sister Sasha of Beverly Hills!"

"Don't call me that. And shut up."

Brianna seized the opportunity. "Do you know Rogue Deluxe? The designer bags?" As a flight attendant dropped mini bags of pretzels on their trays, Brianna continued. "A representative approached me about the two of us doing a promo."

Sasha groaned. "Can I think about it?"

Brianna's enthusiasm dimmed. "Sure. Just thought it might be fun for us to do it together."

"Did they give you details? Like how many posts?"

"They sent me a proposal. Should I send it to your dad's manager or something?"

"No, I'll take a look. You know I'm careful about endorsements."

The flight attendant returned, offering drinks. Brianna sipped her wine and sulked until the flight arrived. She rallied once they reached the suite.

Later that night, in a rooftop private room that overlooked the twinkling lights of the Strip, waiters circled with sugary delights. "Oh my God, that one," Sasha gushed as she held out her plate. The waiter placed a fresh strawberry donut made with homemade brioche dough on it.

"Glutton much?" Brianna teased as she cut off a small piece of a chocolate layer cake.

"My Veg-as per-ogative," Sasha intoned in a singsong voice. Her eyes rolled as she bit into the decadent donut. Someone had set up a private tasting for them, and she'd allowed it. When in Vegas . . .

Brianna sipped prosecco. "Remember that time when we snuck into the wine cellar and drank that champagne and you hurled all over your dad's humidor?"

"Thanks for reminding me," she chuckled. Then she brightened. "I still remember the name. Armand de Brignac Midas, personally given to him by a French ambassador. My dad still brings that up."

Brianna raised a glass. "Here's to French ambassadors!"

"No, here's to sugar comas!"

———

Sasha's headaches, and not just from the sugar and champagne hangover, were waiting for her when she returned home.

"Vegas, huh?" Freddy tried to block her path as he peppered her with questions, but her security detail firmly pushed him aside.

"What's with the muscle, Sasha? Didn't seem your style."

She ignored him as she walked down Bancroft Way toward campus.

"C'mon, Sasha, give me something . . ."

The lunch crowd dining outside at various restaurants gawked as Freddy harassed her, clicking his camera and calling her name.

"So, Sasha, what's the deal? How come I never see you with a boyfriend? Maybe you're into girls? Was Vegas a romantic getaway for you and Brianna?"

In response, the guard put his hand over Freddy's camera.

"You can't do that!"

As Freddy ranted at her protector, Sasha spotted William's Acura. Her security detail opened the door. "Sure you want to go alone?"

"I'll be with him the whole time," she replied, and the door closed. The guard held up traffic so William could turn around and exit campus.

Five minutes later they eased onto the 80 East ramp toward Sacramento. In a little over an hour, they would be attending a session of the commission investigating the Auction. They passed the hills of San Pablo, and a wildfire billowed smoke across the highway, slowing traffic and obscuring the mountains. May had been dry, and the high June temperatures sparked fires from the mountains to the edge of the Pacific. Northern California had it backward. The trees and bushes turned a lush green in the winter and barren and brown in the summer.

"Why did you come out West?" she asked, making conversation.

William checked his speed after noticing a police drone hovering over the highway. "My investors insisted I base my start-up in San Francisco."

Sasha peered out the car window at the fires. "My dad can't imagine living anywhere but LA. I think because in a town of ruthless douchebags, he fits right in."

"That's harsh."

She turned toward him. "When he first moved out to LA, my uncle Jerry let him stay at his house. In exchange, my father helped him finish his screenplay. Nice, right? Then one day my uncle learned my dad had shopped it around as his own. He sold it and his career took off."

William was silent for a moment. "And your uncle?"

"He teaches at a community college." She thought for a moment before quietly adding, "I guess everyone hates their father a little."

William took a breath. "I don't. There's nothing to hate. I never met the man."

She was contrite. "Sorry."

After five minutes of silence, Sasha searched for something to say. "How did you end up on the commission?"

"Alcoholism."

"What?"

William lowered the music. For Sasha, that was reason enough to talk. Why white men loved seventy-five-year-old music played by dead white men was beyond her comprehension.

"I attend AA meetings at Good Shepherd Church. So does the chairwoman of the commission. We had a connection."

If Sasha had pressed, William probably would have given her all the details: Prior to his Auction, the Big 7 hadn't dug into the details of William's chaotic home life in a small Pennsylvania town. Or discovered his older brother, Henry, was at Pikesville Correctional Facility in Glenshaw, ten miles north of Pittsburgh. William's binge drinking seemed a youthful phase that would pass. It didn't. And within a few years of his Auction, it came crashing down in spectacular fashion.

When they made it to Sacramento and found their session, Sasha sat in the back and tried to make herself invisible so she could listen without gawkers staring at her. State commissions were dull affairs. Economists squabbled over whether Series Ds were treated fairly given their value. Only a smattering of onlookers showed up, and even then they spent most of their time checking their devices. But still, she was glad she went; she felt increasingly like she was on a fact-finding mission about herself. What interested her? What did she like? She'd take any insights, from anywhere, including boring commission meetings.

On their way back to Berkeley, a three-car accident snarled traffic just outside of Vacaville, so they pulled into a diner to wait it out. A rail-thin man with a massive belt buckle led them to a table in the corner near the window. William ordered a bacon cheeseburger, Sasha a Cobb salad.

When their food arrived, they dove in. In between bites, William said, "I have a confession."

"You have heart disease from eating bacon cheeseburgers?"

He chuckled. "I never saw your movie."

Sasha put her hands flat on the table and raised her eyebrows in amusement. "That's your confession?"

William reached for the salt. "I thought you should know."

"You need to work on your sins," she teased.

After a few minutes of warm silence, making their way through their meals, Sasha put down her fork and trained her eyes on him. "Do you think the Auction is fair?"

If he was surprised, he didn't show it. But he did take a long time swallowing. "I don't know. I suppose that's why I'm excited about the commission. That's what we're there to figure out."

"Sure," Sasha said agreeably. "But I'm asking for your opinion."

He threw down the remains of his burger. "You know my history. I flamed out. Tons of potential, a start-up on the road to success . . . and then I became a drunk when I couldn't handle the pressure. What does my opinion matter?"

"I'm about to turn twenty-two, yet I have no say in what happens to me." There. She said it. Out loud. She, Sasha Cross, was out of control—literally, the control over her life belonged to other people.

"You have a lot of say! You're the daughter of . . . I mean, you're . . . Sasha . . ."

She waved a hand and rolled her eyes. "Yeah, yeah, I'm Sasha Cross, and I can do whatever I want. Sure."

———

She thought of that meal with William a week later as she sailed into hour number two of a job interview. She was tired; a dull ache throbbed behind her eyes. They'd never really finished the conversation, but the fact that even William—who knew Sasha pretty well, who was a smart guy—seemed to think she had some semblance of control over her future kept her up at night. If he couldn't see how damaging this all was, who could? Who *would*?

"Tell us why you want to work here?"

Sasha flipped a lock of hair over her shoulder and tried to perk up. It was the most basic question that a prospective employer can ask, but as she opened her mouth to give a rote answer, she froze.

Why *did* she want to work here? Where even *was* "here"? She looked helplessly at the interviewer, some guy in his early thirties with a bad polo shirt and glasses, but he was a statue. She was on her own.

She fumbled some syllables before finding something appropriate to say. "I like the way you're making education accessible, especially in rural areas, and I'd like to go into communities and help them adopt your program."

As he processed her answer and jotted down notes, she was aware of a steady stream of people walking past the conference room, trying to catch a glimpse of her through the glass walls.

"Don't worry about them," the interviewer said assuredly. "We're not used to having celebrities in our office. I reviewed your transcript, and you did very well, but I don't see a focus on education. Why the interest now?"

Sasha wished she could tell the truth: because a friend told her about the opening, and she worried if she didn't find a job soon, she would be lured back to Los Angeles. But she could do better than that, right? She tried to dredge up some semblance of truth. Why had she agreed to come? What was she looking for?

What, above all else, did Sasha Cross want?

"It's true, I don't have a background in education," she admitted. "But I work for a commission that investigates social issues related to the Auction. One thing I noticed is the education gap among the poor."

"Excellent point. We have programs dedicated to that very issue. This job involves a lot of travel, and our staff stays in cheap hotels. Is that a problem?"

"Not at all."

He studied his notes. "Can I be honest with you?"

Sasha nodded. Her stomach twisted as he pulled off his glasses and stared intently at her.

"I don't see how this would work. Our reps go into small, rural towns to give presentations to town councils and school boards. If we sent in Sasha Cross . . . we would attract large crowds, but they'd only be there to see you, not hear about our proposals." He swallowed. "You'd be a distraction to the cause."

Sasha stood abruptly. "Thanks for taking the time."

The man stood, too. "I'm sorry. I wish you the best of luck."

Outside, she pulled on her darkest, biggest pair of sunglasses and treated herself to an iced coffee, trying to ignore the emotions creeping up her throat. She didn't know what bothered her more: that she didn't want the job or that they didn't want her.

———

"Ms. Garulli, we're here."

Jessica looked up from her briefing documents as the SUV reached the main gate of Fort Stewart. After clearing the gate, the driver navigated through the base to a medical facility under construction in the far reaches of the mammoth former army base. Her driver opened her door, then wiped the sweat off his brow. "Goddamn sauna out here."

"Do some time in Qatar and then get back to me on that." Jessica nodded at the newly installed Fort Stewart base commander and Global's chief medical officer, who awaited her. "Let's do this." Noise from the construction crews in what was once the Winn Army Community Hospital made it hard for Jessica to hear the medical officer.

"What was that?"

"In ten weeks, the expansion of the surgical facility will be complete," he said. "At that point, we'll be able to segregate personnel responsible for patients from those focused on disposal. Until then, they operate out of the same buildings but are kept separate."

"How many beds will we have?"

"About 350, but by the end of the year we can triple that number."

Jessica shaded her eyes from the Georgia sun. "How long are the patients here?"

"It depends on their condition and how much we need to do to get them ready. On average, eight weeks, give or take a week based on testing and compatibility."

"What's next?"

The base commander pointed toward the surgical wing. "We thought you'd like to see a demonstration of the type of work we're doing."

Twenty minutes later, Jessica and the commander looked down from a glass-enclosed booth at a surgical room. In it, two fifty-something-year-old men were strapped to tables. Each had a small portion of his skull exposed. Jessica watched as one of the patients flinched when a surgeon delicately inserted a small wireless Brain-Computer Interface chip into his brain.

"Is he awake?" she asked.

"Yes, they have to be for the experiment," said the commander.

When the surgeon inserted the chip in the second patient, he seized, but his scream was muted by his jaw being wired shut. With the implantation complete, the surgeon glanced at the booth across from Jessica, where a team of technicians peered at monitors that analyzed the brain function of each man. After studying the data, they gave the surgeon a thumbs-up.

He walked over to patient number two. "What do you want to communicate to him? Don't do it by speaking, think it."

Seconds later, each man jerked forward as if jolted with an electrical current.

The surgeon sought guidance. The technicians inched closer to the screen. Finally, the lead technician gave a thumbs-down. The surgeon responded by tinkering with the chip in patient number two. He put his hand on the man's shoulder. "Think something to your friend."

Once again, the men flailed. Patient number one whimpered. The surgeon asked him, "Did you get a communication?"

Whimpering, he responded, "He said he doesn't want to do this."

The surgeon put his hand on patient number two's shoulder. "Is that what you said?"

Unable to speak, he nodded, his eyes pleading with the doctor to stop.

The surgeon looked up at the booth, nodded, and said, "Let's try one more time. Tell your friend something happier this time."

The experiment was interrupted by banging from the technician booth. On the intercom, the lead technician announced, "Patient two is stroking. He's developed a clot."

Jessica focused on her breathing. She'd experienced and even participated in horrible acts as a soldier and nearly lost her life in the explosion that disfigured her. And they didn't haunt her. But she didn't know if she'd ever get the look of the man—his mouth sewn shut, wordlessly begging for them to stop manipulating his brain—out of her thoughts.

She eagerly followed when the commander stood up to leave. "As you can see, we've got a long way to go," he said.

Jessica took a last look back at the facility, then concentrated on her task at hand. "Any issue so far with the base restrictions?"

"No surprise, they don't like that they are prohibited from leaving the base during their tour of duty. But we offer incentive pay."

"Did they tell you one of them is my cousin, Vincente Arias? Where is he now?"

The commander nodded. "He's waiting for you in the mess hall."

An MP escorted Jessica past the security checkpoints. From the mess hall entrance, she spotted Vincente. A brief memory flashed before her eyes, and she almost smiled, surprising herself. Their families lived in adjoining houses in the Arizona border town of Lukeville, and due to the ten-year gap in their ages, she'd been more like a second mother to Vincente than a cousin.

When Vincente's mother became pregnant, the father wanted no part of it, so Jessica babysat while both of their mothers took whatever jobs they could find. Vincente was ten years old when Jessica left Lukeville. He took advantage of his newfound freedom to run around, skip school, and get into trouble. By the time he was sixteen, his record included a conviction for petty theft. It wasn't until age twenty that he realized his mistakes.

He got his GED, but the best jobs he could find were in fast food or as a janitor. He was a Series D all the way. Jessica offered financial support, but faced with few prospects, Vincente followed her path by joining the army. Then he got caught with his bunkmate's drugs, and only Jessica's intervention saved him from a dishonorable discharge.

She came up fast behind him and whispered in his ear, "Do people here know you wet the bed until you were nine years old?"

Vincente shot up and hugged her.

She took a step back. "Vinny, you look good. It's official, you're a man."

"An army man."

"The best kind. How's the base?"

"You know. Not much to do."

"That's the deal. You're paid extra for the hardship."

"Yep, my mom appreciates it, so thank you."

"How is she doing?" Jessica saw her aunt, his mom, in the crinkles around his eyes, the lines in his forehead. They'd been through some tough times, the two of them.

"She's still working two jobs."

"We were raised by stubborn women."

Vincente took a breath. "I'm sorry I couldn't be there for the funeral."

Jessica stiffened. "That's the rules. Your mom paid her respects, and my mom's Lukeville friends stopped by. No one came from Mexico, the borders are tight."

Just then Lyra approached the table. Jessica watched her cousin's eyes light up; she knew that look, and she knew it was a waste of time. "Jessica, this is my friend."

"Nice to meet you," Jessica responded coolly. "Vinny, I need to go. Walk me to the door."

On their way out, Vincente expertly guiding her as she pretended not to notice the attention she was attracting—it wasn't every day a tall, elegant businesswoman strolled through the mess hall—Jessica tapped his shoulder. "She's pretty. You're punching above your weight."

"I'm not punching anything, unfortunately."

"You know what they say." She smirked. "If you don't use it, it will fall off."

He guffawed. "Thanks for that visual."

She leaned in for a hug. "Stay out of trouble. Fort Stewart is not the place to take risks."

"Thanks for all you've done."

A senior-level official escorted her to the front entrance. Outside, the sun beat ceaselessly. As she escaped into the cool darkness of the waiting SUV, she pointed across the square at a large black wall under construction.

"What's going there?" she asked the chief medical officer as he stood by to see her off.

He cleared his throat. "That's where the new crematorium will be."

She nodded, and the driver shut the door. In the silence, she closed her eyes and settled back; a nap during the thirty-minute trip to the airfield was just what she needed.

She got about three minutes in before her device rang.

"Where are you?" Armstrong's voice thundered.

"Fort Stewart. What's wrong?"

He roared. "Someone stole my daughter!"

———

Expecting the worst—a kidnapping, a ransom, anonymous phone calls, the works—Jessica ran through all her resources on the private plane, only to learn it wasn't quite a kidnapping. Instead, the Auction rights to Armstrong's daughter, Candace, had been mistakenly put back on the market. Or was it a mistake? Jessica wondered, toying with the idea.

The Big 7 honored an informal agreement: they didn't bid on each other's children in the Auction. It was a point of pride that a CEO's children weren't bought and sold. And once a Big 7 company acquired the earnings rights for someone in the Auction, they could sell those rights on the secondary market. Like stock, the companies dumped people who didn't pan out.

But because of a glitch, the rights to Candace had been reentered into the database, effectively placing her back up for sale. A small company snapped her up in the minutes between the transaction going live and one of Armstrong's assistants noticing it, and they were refusing to honor the unspoken agreement.

"Jessica, you better fix this!" barked Armstrong after her quick flight and even quicker drive to the office. She'd told the driver to eschew the speed limits and get her to her destination . . . or else.

"Dracon Analytics took her. Their CEO, Carl Esko, is traveling and currently unreachable—supposedly—and his staff is claiming a $5 million price tag for her." She pointed to one of the staffers hovering over Armstrong. "You. Find out where Carl Esko is and why he's pretending to be unavailable."

Ninety minutes later the staffer finally got confirmation, and Jessica had her plan: Esko was holed up in Tahoe at a "spiritual retreat," his traveling companion a twenty-six-year-old analyst who worked for Dracon.

Jessica sighed. "Refuel the plane."

———

Carl Esko was drying his hair when a series of knocks reverberated through the room. *Perfect,* he thought. *Lunch.*

Linda, an analyst from the company's Entertainment Division, was still at her Pilates class, but he knew she'd be back any second. Unfortunately—if he was being honest. The fling had been fun, but it was time to break it off. He didn't expect a scene. She'd gotten a nice little vacation out of it, and a round trip on his private plane.

But when a well-dressed woman greeted him with a smile and handshake after he opened the door, he peered past her, looking for the tray. His stomach growled. "Mr. Esko, my name is Jessica Garulli. I'm here on behalf of Global Holdings to clear up the issue with Candace Armstrong."

Esko stiffened. "This is highly inappropriate. If you have an issue, call my office." He began to push the door closed, but Jessica persisted.

"Since this was a misunderstanding, we brought the paperwork to reverse the transaction."

"Now why would I do that?" he barked. His face reddened; the audacity of this woman! "Take it up with my office. I have a lunch meeting."

"Oh yes, I imagine that would be with Ms. Pescarelli?" Jessica tipped her head meaningfully toward the two sets of luggage—one dark and masculine, the other patterned in yellow-and-pink paisley. "She's finishing up in the gym. My associate is with her."

He sputtered. "So you've been spying on me. Is that what this is?"

"Not at all, Mr. Esko, just a fortunate coincidence. We were at the spa, realized you were here, and thought we could clear up this matter."

"I'll tell you what. Leave now and I won't call security. If you want Candace Armstrong back, I'll entertain an offer."

Jessica never lost her smile. "OK, Mr. Esko. I understand your position. I don't want to inconvenience you. Enjoy your stay. If you change your mind, here's my card."

Esko only took her card because she practically forced it on him. He slammed the door and then locked it—both locks—and rested his head against it, thinking. His heart raced. Joyce, his wife, already had suspicions. She remained on the board of Dracon Analytics, which her grandfather had founded thirty-five years ago, so remaining in her good graces was crucial. When he was sure Jessica was gone, he dashed to the gym and accosted the first trainer he saw. "Excuse me, my colleague was down here. A tall blonde. Do you know if she's in the ladies' locker room?"

"Linda?" The trainer brightened. "Great flexibility, perfect form. She left an hour ago with her brother."

Esko's jaw fell open. "Her brother?"

"Yes, he came to find her. It sounded like a family issue. She seemed upset."

The trainer started to tell him about the afternoon class, but he was already out the door. He locked himself up tight in his room and gripped the card Jessica had given him. Seething, he dialed her number. "Where is Linda?"

"Oh, hello, Mr. Esko. Linda? You mean your colleague? I wouldn't know. Why do you ask?"

"Don't yank my chain. Where is she?"

"I don't understand what you're talking about. But since I have you, do you want to reconsider our earlier conversation?"

Esko chewed his inside cheek. "I'm not playing these bullshit games. Get back to my room and we can talk."

The conversation didn't take long. And when Jessica left the resort, her spirit, much like their brochures advertised, felt lighter. She carried with her a document that made Candace Armstrong once again Global property. Meanwhile, Carl Esko and Linda Pescarelli sat in a town car heading toward the airport. The flight aboard Dracon's corporate jet would be a short thirty minutes. Neither uttered a word.

Armstrong was relieved about his daughter, and showed the typical level of gratitude toward Jessica for handling it—which is to say, not enough—so it wasn't without a sliver of glee that she delivered the bad news she'd been sitting on since she got on the plane.

It was what she'd initially suspected, and she told him as much. "Sir, there wasn't a glitch. Our data has pinpointed that a low-level engineer released your daughter into the system to protest what he calls the Auction's corruption. He even leaked it to the media, but we killed the story."

Armstrong sneered. "Now we're being attacked from the inside."

———

"Avery?"

He turned to see who called him. Bad move. The ceramic lamp slid off the box he carried and smashed into pieces when it hit the sidewalk.

"Damn it!"

He raised his head to see the culprit. Suni Yosar. He had met her in Fundamentals of Public Speaking last fall. They went on one date, and the night ended early. She was cute enough, but not a party girl. So he'd made up an excuse and ditched her to find his friends.

"I'm so sorry!" She bent down to pick up the shattered pieces.

"Forget it."

"Congratulations on graduating."

Avery stood. "I didn't."

"You told me you were a senior."

"I'm six credits short."

"You were at the Combine in Brooklyn. I assumed that meant you graduated."

Avery put the box in the tailgate of his roommate's pickup truck. "Nope, I have to take remote courses this summer. Lucky me." A few weeks ago, Avery would have meant it. But most of his friends left after graduation, and the landlord kicked him and his roommates out of their house after a forgotten pot on the stove caused a kitchen fire.

"What about you?"

The wind blew Suni's long black hair in her face, so she tucked it behind her ears. "I have a tryout this summer with the Michigan Philharmonic."

A gust blew open the box on the tailgate; Avery chased down papers. "Good to see you. Congrats on the job."

Suni nodded. "You too. Have a nice summer."

A half hour later Suni was a distant memory. Avery wrenched a desk chair into the packed cargo bed and signaled his roommate Liam. They had no permanent place to live, so they were moving their belongings to the basement of his family's house in Plymouth. His summer was off to a rocky start. At least he would fly to Dallas next week to meet Stephanie's parents.

SIX

An early-morning car alarm jolted Sasha out of a pleasant dream and afterward, despite her best efforts, sleep eluded her. She stared at the ceiling, then, as a black bug in the corner inched its way toward her. She wished she hadn't seen it. So, as the rays of a June morning snuck into her bedroom, she kicked the fluffy teal comforter off her legs and plodded downstairs for coffee.

A chime signaled a message from her virtual assistant: *Sasha, you asked me to remind you to renew your driver's license.* A screen appeared with a list of documents she needed. A half hour later, frustrated and hungry, she hit "submit" and put down her device.

She weighed her options. Good Sasha would put on sweats and go for a three-mile run. She decided there had already been too much Good Sasha for one morning and plopped down on the couch to lose herself in mindless television.

During a commercial, she messaged Brianna. *OK.*
OK, what?
I'll do Rogue Deluxe.

She could practically hear Brianna's squeal through her device. *OMG! This will be fun. I'll reach out after I find out the details. Love you!*

Her device alerted her to a story about her mother, and she transferred it to the monitor on her wall. CNBC was reporting that her father had filed papers to close the Lacy Cross Foundation, saying it had accomplished its mission. Sasha gritted her teeth. Why couldn't he have told her in advance? She inhaled the whole story, holding her breath through it. It appeared the shutdown was likely connected to an outside investigation of the foundation's finances.

Great. Her mother's reputation was pristine, and Sasha was not about to let her father mess it up. She went to call her father, a lecture already forming on her tongue, then thought better of it. He was a master at spinning stories, and she wanted to look him in the eye when she asked him. She'd be in Los Angeles in a couple weeks; she could wait.

She spent too many more minutes clicking through related stories about her mother, which led her to stories about herself. Apparently she was in a new relationship, according to some gossip sites, as photos showed her in what appeared to be a romantic embrace with an unknown man. Sasha guffawed out loud. It was just a picture of her hugging Jason during one of their Auction events.

The reminder of the Auction made her decide to get to work. William had requested specific Auction-related research. What she found unnerved her. The oldest class of Auction candidates were now in their early thirties, and Series Ds were dying at twice the rate of Series As. Soaring suicide rates were the primary cause. The Big 7 trumpeted that anybody could be a Series A—all it took was talent—but the overwhelming majority came from affluent white families. Money followed money.

Suddenly, Sasha realized how dry her mouth was. She looked up from her screen and widened her eyes. It was dark out; a ray of moonlight crawled through her apartment.

She'd spent all afternoon buried in horrible stories about the Auction. Reluctantly, she put down her device and did some stretches, her body creaking from being in the same hunched-over position for so long. Then she inhaled whatever was edible in her fridge—some old cheese, a bunch of browning grapes, the remains of her Thai food from earlier in the week—and chugged two bottles of water.

When she turned in to bed, the stories of all the Auction deaths she'd compiled—suicides, unexpected illnesses, poverty-based diseases—flashed behind her eyes. She dreamed of those haunted faces, those doomed stories, all night.

———

At his keyboard, eyes red and blurry, Jason practiced the drills his coach had assigned him after that disastrous game. The drills were easy, but he knew he deserved the boredom, the punishment. A rope of desperation had been pulling him forward ever since the game, after his coach subbed him out in the second quarter.

He took a shot of an energy drink and wiped his eyes. *Focus, dude,* he told himself. Eye on the prize.

Last week, his coach had cut two players. He couldn't let it be him next.

Through the repetition of the drills, Ayana's voice echoed in his ears: *You're it.*

Yeah, it was a lot of pressure. Ridiculous, really, when you thought about it. Jason wondered why most people *didn't* think about it, about the fact that parents, or guardians in Ayana's case, only received Auction payments for the first three of their children. Supposedly, the rule was intended to discourage parents from breeding large families and pinning their hopes on the possibility that one of their kids would earn them a windfall; practically, it punished lots of families who chose to have more than three children—for religious, cultural, or whatever reasons.

Also practically speaking, it meant Jason was the family's last hope.

He practiced the same move over and over. *Click, click, whiz. Click, click, whiz.* His fingers ached.

When his device buzzed, Jason ignored it and took a swig of water. But the buzzing continued, breaking his concentration as he tried to turn his attention back to the monitor. Frustrated, he grabbed it.

Denton messaged, *Got an idea.*

Jason grimaced, paused. His fingers hovered over the keys. Then: ?

Let's talk.

Jason needed time. He put down his device. He'd deal with Denton later.

His brother stepped into the room. "I'm leaving for Atlanta in the morning."

"Message me after the fight. Break a leg."

Baker glared. "Never say that to an MMA fighter!"

———

Vincente opened his refrigerator. Nothing. Despite his gripes about feeling cooped up, Fort Stewart's accommodations were plush. His apartment featured a separate bedroom, a spacious living room, a kitchen, and a sizable bathroom. And he didn't pay a cent for it. Between the comped room and extra pay he received for the Fort Stewart assignment, he sent plenty of money to his mother and socked away the rest. Not bad for a Series D.

He felt a pang of guilt. With her sister's death, his mother needed him now more than ever. He yearned to return to Lukeville and take care of her. First, he had to endure his time at Fort Stewart. The truth was, despite the space and the pay, he chafed under its restrictions. He could only stare at the bone-white walls for so long. He'd made few friends besides Lyra. The army monitored his communications. And if it wasn't enough that there was little chance for socializing, the medical experiments he was working on didn't seem particularly groundbreaking either. It all added up to *boring*. And he still had thirteen months left.

For two weeks, his mother had been complaining of headaches, so he grabbed his device to resume his search for a neurologist who could take her. Just as he did, a message came through. His eyes lit up.

I'm bored. Want to watch a movie?

I'm climbing the walls! he messaged back.

Let me take a shower. Then I'll come to your place?

Cool! I'll go to the mess and pick up snacks.

Maybe Fort Stewart wasn't so bad.

Vincente hustled to the commissary for pizza, soda, and chips. By the time he got back, a wet-haired Lyra was leaning on his front door. Breathtaking. Afraid his puppy-dog look would give him away, he lowered his eyes, mumbled a hello, and opened the door.

An hour later only a few pieces of crust remained. The movie was dull.

Lyra lay across his couch, her feet propped on his lap. She pointed her leg at the screen and a scene from the Alamo. "The one and only time I got arrested was in San Antonio. After basic training, I visited my boyfriend. Driving home, drunk as a skunk, I got pulled over."

"Shit, you were arrested?"

"Let me finish. When we came to a stop, my boyfriend handed me a bottle of vodka and told me to step out of the car and chug it so the camera on the cruiser would see it. It scared the shit out of me, but he screamed, and I was drunk, so I did."

"Why the hell did he tell you to do that?" Vincente was befuddled, in awe that someone like her would listen to some creep like that.

"He said that way they couldn't bust me for a DUI because me drinking *after* getting out of the car would invalidate the breathalyzer."

He paused, considering. "Did it work?"

She scowled. "I got charged with a DUI *and* public intoxication. I broke up with him the next day. Two months later I met Bryan."

"Ah." Vincente stretched out his feet on the cheap coffee table in front of him, his toe dangerously close to landing in the pizza box. "At least you have him now."

"He's so far away." Lyra took a swig of Vincente's beer. "At least I have an excuse why I'm not hooking up with anyone. Why aren't you?"

He tried to play it cool, to pretend his pulse hadn't started racing. "Not that many ladies on the base worth a look."

She rolled her eyes "There must be someone here you're interested in."

Vincente tensed. The choices! Lie and sound like he wasn't interested in her. Tell the truth and be barraged by a flurry of questions about the lucky lady.

He took option number three: the easy way out. "I need a glass of water. Be right back."

When Vincente returned, Lyra's eyes were closed. Once again, sleep saved him. He cleaned up the mess, then draped a blanket across her. Vincente stared at the beautiful woman on his couch, then turned off the light and walked to his bedroom.

A handwritten message next to his pillow greeted him when he awoke.

Sorry I passed out. At least you got a girl to sleep over. xoxo.

———

"Ladies and gentlemen, let me be the first to welcome you to Dallas Fort Worth International Airport."

Avery unbuckled his seat belt while Stephanie collected her handbag. They waited while a heavyset man in the aisle seat struggled to stand. The trip was off to a bumpy start, and not just the landing. Avery didn't like that she had taken the window seat without comment, leaving him to rub elbows with the heavyset man.

But he resolved to make it a great weekend. "Ready, babe?"

Ignoring him, Stephanie stood, cutting in front of someone to make it to the exit first.

When they reached the rental car kiosk, she turned to him. "Listen, this is a big weekend. My family makes me crazy, and you need to understand that this isn't State and my family aren't your friends, OK? Be cool."

"Sure thing," he assured her, touching her arm.

During the thirty-five-minute trek from the airport, Stephanie prepared him for what to expect.

"I don't think you'll meet my dad until the game tomorrow. Don't ask him questions about the Rangers. Don't talk to him unless he asks you a question." She ticked off her fingers. "My mom will be home. If she offers you a drink, say no."

Avery expected Stephanie's house to be nice, but nothing could have prepared him for when she pulled the rental car up to the sixteen-acre estate in Highland Park. They passed through sloping arches and maneuvered through the winding driveway to arrive at a mammoth stone mansion that had the appearance of a museum more than a family home. Avery grabbed the luggage while his girlfriend opened a custom wrought iron balustrade gate that framed the front entry and veranda.

As they entered the foyer, he gawked at an authentic Jackson Pollock on a wall overlooking a massive banquet hall. Stephanie's mother, Lorene, a smile fixed on a face stretched too tight from plastic surgery, greeted them.

"Is that a Jackson Pollock, Mrs. Simpson?" He had taken a boring art history class sophomore year, but now it paid off.

"Yes, it is, Avery. Does your family have an art collection?"

"No, I just recognized the work."

Leaving the bags, they followed Stephanie's mother to a sitting area.

"When do you graduate, Avery?" she asked.

"This summer."

"What are you studying?"

"Business analytics."

Stephanie touched his back. "Avery attended the Auction Combine in New York. That means he's likely to be a Series A."

"Impressive."

After a minute of silence, Lorene stood. "I'm sure you two want to get settled. Nice to meet you, Avery."

For the first time that day, Stephanie flashed a smile.

The family dinner was uneventful, and Avery offered smart commentary about the economy that he picked up from a professor. Stephanie's brothers, Taylor and Robert, invited him for an early round of golf the next morning and even loaned him clubs and shoes. On the tenth hole, the brothers cracked a beer and Avery took one. Taylor and Robert knocked back a beer a hole from that point on, and Avery drove them home. The conversation flowed, and her brothers took a liking to him.

When Stephanie ventured to his room to say good night, he made a point of keeping the door open. She left with praise. "I've seen a new side of you this weekend."

The drive to the stadium was the first time Avery witnessed the family flash its power. Avery sat with Stephanie and her brothers in the back of an SUV while a police escort cut through the traffic. A stadium employee met them at the gate and ushered them through the stadium, offering them drinks and food and leading them to the field so they could watch batting practice. And for the first time all weekend, Stephanie held his hand.

He was so busy enjoying himself that he almost didn't notice one of the players approach their group. He jogged over to Stephanie and wrapped her in a hug. Stung, Avery's jaw dropped. They whispered to each other, and Stephanie threw her head back, laughing.

When he left, grunting in Avery's direction, he felt uneasy. "Who's that?"

"He plays centerfield. We dated a while back."

Avery turned to watch the player step into the batting cage. He felt the need to put his arm around Stephanie's shoulder. Soon, Security escorted them to the owner's suite, which overlooked home plate. A spread of crab cakes, shrimp, and lobster rolls awaited them.

When Stephanie left to find her parents at the bar, Taylor approached him. "We have a tradition. For each run the Rangers score, we drink a rum and Coke."

Avery smirked. "Nice. Why that drink?"

"Our dad doesn't like us to drink, so it looks like soda."

"Aw, man." He ran his fingers through his hair. "I don't think Stephanie would like that . . ."

Taylor handed him a cup. "She'll never find out. Pretend it's Coke."

By the time Stephanie made it back, the Rangers jumped to a 4–0 lead and Avery relaxed. She settled in next to him, then swatted his hand when he caressed her back.

The drinks kept coming—secretly. Avery excused himself to use the bathroom. When he opened the door, Taylor waited with a cup. "Two-run double!"

The scoring came to a halt, and Avery had a fighting chance to sober up. Then the opposing pitcher walked a run in, and another runner came in on an error.

By the sixth inning Avery sat glassy-eyed with his head in his hands.

"What's up with you?" asked Stephanie. Her brow furrowed, and she tasted his drink. Disgusted, she pushed it away. "How many?"

Avery stared hard at the scoreboard. "Eight?"

"You asshole!"

Avery pointed to her brothers. "It's their tradition."

Taylor, overhearing the whole exchange, chuckled and shrugged. "Dude, I've been drinking Cokes all day."

Stephanie sprang into action. "We're leaving. Grab your stuff." Avery stumbled toward the door, right into the chest of Rutherford Simpson, who had meandered over to meet the bright young man who so impressed his wife. The smirking drunk in front of him didn't qualify. Avery slurred a few words before Stephanie grabbed him.

"Sorry," she said, averting her father's glare.

"Get him out of here."

If hell exists, it's the two flights it takes to travel from Dallas to Lansing. Stephanie tried unsuccessfully to switch her flight. When the plane touched down in Michigan, she bolted out of her seat. Avery lingered behind her while she rolled her suitcase down the jetway at Capital Region International Airport. He took the hint and ordered his own car.

———

The chip implanted in the upper arm of a Series A candidate enabled Global to track that person's location, but that was all. For Suni Yosar, a cellist on tryout for the Michigan Philharmonic, it needed more. Seventy-four million dollars was at stake.

In a nondescript building near Plymouth, Michigan, hackers sat in an alcove on the third floor of Benson Computer Analysts.

Ted Colston glanced at his partner. "Anything?"

"Only if you like jazz," answered Aaron Randle.

Ted and Aaron fixed devices, installed digital assistants, and personalized artificial intelligence. For a fee, they would illegally hack into computers. That usually meant investigating employees suspected of stealing company secrets or embezzling. They'd never had a target like Suni Yosar. They'd hesitated when they'd been offered the job, but the six-figure offer swayed them. Now, the two hovered over the screen, checking the sound levels in case audio was available.

All they learned today was Suni's love for Thelonious Monk and that her mother complained . . . a lot. The audio picked up the sounds of a distant shower, but that didn't do them any good. Unlike with other targets, such as actors or pop stars, the aim wasn't skin. The client—whoever that was; they weren't clear on this assignment—didn't have an interest in nude shots. Just information.

Hacking the Yosar home hadn't been difficult. They accessed Anika's device by sending a message that appeared to come from a distant relative. Once she opened the message, it installed a virus that gave access to her files and took over the cameras on the computer, the doorbell, and the nanny cam the Yosars installed in the living room to keep an eye on their cat.

Honestly, the cat turned out to be the most interesting of the three. Suni hid in her room a lot, and her mother spent most of her time cleaning the house, watching reruns of old

TV series, and gossiping with relatives in Bangladesh in a language that Ted and Aaron didn't speak.

As assigned, the two hackers regularly reported their findings, mundane as they were. Their orders were to continue the surveillance, but they could sense that their client's patience was running out.

SEVEN

The world froze around Jason.

He had stopped breathing. He was conscious of the pulse in his ears, the pressure on his fingertips, but nothing else.

The moment seemed to stretch out, lasting an eternity.

And then: boom! Cheers and screams and flashes of light and the unmistakable feeling of relief, of gut-wrecking joy, flooding his entire body.

Delirium.

Before he could breathe again, his teammates mobbed him, slapping his back, grabbing his shoulders, punching the air around him. Jason had just made the biggest shot in the biggest tournament of his life. And in doing so, he earned his league team an invitation to the Junior National Championships, an assembly of the best semipro e-basketball teams in the country.

He did it. He actually did it. He sat, dazed, his limbs thawing out, trying to take in the moment.

A huge underdog, his squad had hung in and trailed by only two points with eight seconds left in the game. What followed next was chaos: a loose ball, both teams scrambling, a tangled mess of players, the ball in Jason's hands, and a buzzer-beating three-pointer that bounced on the rim, bounced again, and fell in.

"Jayyyy-sonnnn!!!!" was all he heard at the bottom of a scrum halfway under the table, where the players' monitors shook from the mayhem. Extricating himself from the pile, Jason peered up into the stands. He wanted to remember what seven thousand fans screaming for him looked like.

Incredible.

His coach buried him in a bear hug as they made their way to the locker room. Jason tugged at his drenched shirt. Temperatures in the arena were high, and his concentration had made his whole body tense up and sweat. At his locker, he found dozens of messages lighting up his device.

He opened two. The first from Ayana: *So proud. Team Harris!*

The second from Sasha. *I get to say I know you!*

Still on for tonight? he messaged. She shot back with, *Brianna and I are leaving now!* and a million kissy emojis.

Jason chuckled. Brianna would grill him about his love life, which was nonexistent. He wished he had gossip for them, but the truth was, he had struggled through an abusive relationship a few years back that ended with a restraining order. There was lots of unexamined trauma there, he knew, but he didn't have the time or energy to examine it. There was enough pressure on him already.

A teammate brought him a bottle of prosecco. "Celebrate tonight, dude!"

Jason thanked him, but once his friend left, he nodded to his coach, who took the bottle from him. As he walked into the corridor, everyone from stadium attendants to scouts to fans wanted to high-five or shake his hand. He glowed with pride.

The moment ended too soon, though. Outside, near his car, he found Denton waiting.

Jason swallowed, racking his brain. He knew Denton wasn't afraid of making a scene in public, and he really, really didn't want a scene today—not after his big win. He nodded at Denton and pinged him the name of a nearby coffee shop.

Over steaming mugs, Jason tried to convey a sense of casual normalcy. "So, what's your idea?"

Denton sipped his coffee. "I just found out there's betting, not just on e-NBA games but even your league."

Cold dread coursed through Jason's veins. "I heard something about it."

"Well, this is an opportunity for us both. All we gotta do is find games where your team is the favorite and make sure you don't cover the spread. Win-win."

Jason stirred another sugar into his mug and dropped his voice even lower. "Dude, I'd like to help, but that's called point-shaving. Guys go to jail for it."

"Happens all the time and no one gets caught." Denton stretched his arms up over his head.

"This is a dangerous conversation," Jason hissed. His fear had turned to anger. "If it came out, I'd be banned from playing in the e-NBA."

"Well, then let's not talk about it," Denton said, emphasizing the *talk*. "I'll send a signal, and now you'll understand what I want you to do." Denton rolled up his shirtsleeve to expose the skin grafts on his arm. "Check this out. The doctor says I need another surgery. How you think I'm gonna pay for that?"

Jason stared at the grafts as Denton stared at him. He felt like he had during that last moment of the game—like time had frozen, like this was an undeniably important moment in his life.

Without a word, Denton drained his coffee, plopped the mug on the table, and stood. "I got a long ride back. Good to see you, my man. Just think, when you go on road trips for the 76ers, we'll hang out all the time."

Jason watched Denton leave, the bell on the top of the door to the café jingling.

Denton hadn't just ruined his whole day; he'd threatened to ruin his life. And there was no one, not even Sasha, he could talk to about it.

An hour later he faked a smile as Sasha and Brianna rushed to hug him. His miracle shot circulated all over social media and sports news programs.

Brianna kissed his cheek. "This must be the greatest night of your life!"

Sasha showed him a clip of his shot and his teammates mobbing him.

"Amazing!" She hugged him again.

Jason pointed at the buff man standing in the corner. "Who's he?"

"My dad insisted. Now I have a chaperone."

"It's not the worst idea," he countered, studying his friend's face. "That had to be scary."

Sasha rolled her eyes. "I don't want to talk about it."

They settled into a Tex-Mex restaurant. Brianna quizzed him about the e-NBA, when he might receive an offer, whether he was dating, whom he was dating, why he wasn't dating. When she got nothing out of him, she popped up to call an ex-boyfriend.

Sasha squeezed his hand. "Jason, what's up? You're acting weird. I thought you'd be on cloud nine all day."

His mouth went dry. Maybe he could tell her some of it, he thought. Maybe it would help him gain a new perspective—a way out. "Um . . . Denton came to see me."

"Ugh!" Sasha groaned. She slapped his hand. "Why are you letting that asshole worm his way back into your life?"

"It's complicated," he said earnestly.

"Jason, look at me," she said, placing her hands on his face and peering into his eyes. "You didn't cause that accident. I

know it's hard. But it wasn't you! You can't hold on to something that wasn't your fault. Fuck Denton and his manipulative
bullshit!"

"Whose bullshit?" Brianna asked as she plopped back
down into her seat.

Sasha sighed. "Denton showed up tonight. Killed Jason's
buzz."

Brianna made a face. "Yuck. Jason, why were you ever
friends with him?"

"You didn't know him like I did," Jason argued. He owed
it to Denton to be real about where they had come from, what
they had been through. Didn't he? "He was the first person
I met at school. He helped me earn a spot on the basketball
team. You weren't in the car that night. The accident ended
anything good for him."

Sasha rubbed his shoulder. "Jason, he's always been trouble. He even robbed my house."

"When?" Jason scoffed.

"Remember that tenth-grade pool party?" She jabbed a finger at him. "I had a deejay and everything?"

Jason thought back. "What did he do? How can you be
sure?"

"I saw the video." She slapped her hand on the table. "You
think the Cross house wasn't loaded with spy cams? He snuck
upstairs while we were all outside and took some stuff from my
mom's old jewelry box."

"Why didn't you say anything about it?" He was aghast.
"We tell each other everything, Sash." *Almost everything*, he
reminded himself.

"My dad didn't want the publicity," she explained, exasperated. "And . . . well . . . because of you, Jason. I didn't turn
Denton in because of you."

EIGHT

"Do you know Suni Yosar?"

Avery peered at the holographic image of his brother, Garrett.

"I ran into her just the other day. She's a cellist in an orchestra."

"Michigan Philharmonic. Do you know her well?"

Avery lifted a box off the pullout couch. His parents had turned his old room into an office, so now he settled for a musty alcove that smelled of workout equipment and dirty socks. "I took her out once. Boring as hell. I think she's still into me."

From his San Francisco office, Garrett reread Suni's biography. Born in Bangladesh. Moved to Michigan with her parents when she was five years old. Lived with her mother after the divorce. Full scholarship. Summer tryout with the Michigan Philharmonic.

Nothing in the file suggested Suni would be a Series A until the last pages: her father had founded a medical device company that hit it big and was purchased by one of the Big 7 companies. His net worth stood at $370 million.

He never remarried, and Suni was his only known child. If she inherited his money, Beech would stand to gain $74 million if it won her bidding rights. But if her father left her out of the will, Suni became just a poorly paid cellist and unworthy of Series A consideration.

"Avery, this is important. Reconnect with her. Do what you have to do but find out what type of relationship she has with her father. OK?"

"What's the deal with him?"

"Don't worry about it. Just find out. If this goes well, you'll be an A."

"I thought that was already the deal."

"It is." Garrett peered out the window at the growing throng of protesters outside Global's headquarters. "Listen, dude, I gotta go. Do it soon and keep me in the loop."

Was it fate that, two days later, Avery spotted Suni lugging her cello case down the stairs of the orchestra hall? He didn't know, or particularly care, but he seized the opportunity, plastering a wide smile on his face. "Suni?"

She turned and frowned. "What are you doing here?"

"Let me take a side." The two carried the cello down to the street. "I'm living in Plymouth, and I noticed the Philharmonic just down the street from my house. I've never been to a symphony, so here I am."

"I never thought of you as a symphony-type guy."

"I'm not, but it's time to expand my horizons."

"We just had a rehearsal. We don't play until Friday, and it's not here. It's in Detroit."

"That's fine. How do I get a ticket?"

She eyed him. "If you want to go, I'll put your name on a guest list."

"Cool! Why don't I drive you there? It's the least I can do for a free ticket."

"If I say yes, you're not going to bail on me, are you?"

Avery put his hand on his heart. "Scout's honor."

"You were never a Boy Scout," she laughed, "but I'll trust you."

"You are right, I wasn't. But give me your address and I'll be there."

Two days later, five minutes before the agreed pickup time, Avery knocked on Suni's door. He carried her cello, opened the passenger door for her, and had already inputted the concert hall address into his car's self-driving system.

"I have a confession to make."

"What's that?"

"I had a backup ride just in case you didn't show."

"That's harsh."

She gave him a look. "Well, it's happened once before."

"What are you talking about?"

"That night we went out. We had a pizza at that gross bar. You ordered shots. I didn't want one. A half hour later you disappeared."

"I did not! I dropped you off at home," Avery insisted.

"You were drunk; I was sober. I remember the night better."

"Holy shit, did I do that?" Avery experienced a weird sensation: shame.

"It's OK," she told him. "I met Derrick that night. We stayed up all night talking. We dated for two years. You did me a favor. We planned to marry."

"Then why did you break up?"

Suni glared at him. "We didn't break up. He died. In that bus crash last year coming back from the Michigan game."

"I didn't know that." Another weird sensation: empathy. He reached out and held her hand. "How did you deal with that?"

"I didn't. Not sure I have. So be nice to me, Avery."

———

"Let's get these beautiful young women into makeup." Sasha's father beamed as he led his two daughters through the hallways of the PicaFlix studios.

Kelsie couldn't contain her excitement. "Sasha, did you hear I'm playing Elphaba?"

"That's great, Kels. When do rehearsals start?" The trio navigated the props and signs that cluttered the soundstage. Workers set up a fake living room with four chairs where the family interview would take place.

"Next week. Will you come opening night?" she asked.

Kelsie's sole objective was fame. But she didn't have Sasha's *je ne sais quoi*. In the fall she would start her senior year at Crossroads School for Arts & Sciences in Santa Monica. Getting a lead role in the school rendition of *Wicked* convinced her she had what it took to make it in Hollywood. Now, millions of people would see her in a PicaFlix special. She'd spent the last two weeks practicing; Sasha suspected she wanted to be able to tear up at just the right times.

When Sasha didn't answer right away, Kelsie repeated, "You'll come, right?"

"I'll do my best." An assistant ushered Sasha into makeup.

The last time Judah had his daughters together for more than a lunch or dinner was their mother's memorial. Now, Lacy Cross brought them together again. In the fall PicaFlix would air *The Lady in the Red Dress: A Tribute to Lacy Cross*.

The three years since Lacy's death had not been easy for any of them. The well-wishers at Lacy's memorial had drifted off, and Judah'd struggled to get his calls returned from Hollywood's elite. It turned out the "power couple" was actually a power actress and activist who had a boorish husband that others tolerated because of his wife. In the halls of PicaFlix's Sunset Boulevard campus, Judah struggled to attract interest in the reality shows he developed.

He paced in the makeup room as stylists played with Kelsie's hair. "Beautiful, Kelsie. I love that look," he assured her.

"How long are we here for, again?" Sasha asked.

"I need you here all day," he reminded her.

Twenty minutes later the Cross family sat in comfy chairs. The glare of the lights made Sasha uncomfortable. Judah sat between the sisters, his hands interlocked with theirs.

Andre Walker, the host of the special, leaned in. "Let's talk about Lacy Cross . . ."

"An amazing woman and a loving mother." Judah turned to gaze at his daughters. "We had a rule: one of us would always be home to tuck our sweet girls into bed. Lacy insisted on that."

Sasha and Kelsie shared a look. Marita spent so many nights at the house that she got her own room. When Sasha broke her arm at a lacrosse game her freshman year, she called her housekeeper out of habit. Marita stopped cleaning and drove her to the emergency room—all while Judah sat at his desk in his home office.

As the interview wore on, Judah and Kelsie dominated the conversation. Sasha didn't mind. The less she said, the better, in her opinion. Only at the end when Andre asked her to name her mother's favorite movie did Sasha smile. "The ones we made in the basement," she said, and the camera caught her reliving the moment. "We recreated old movies. Mom loved to play the villain."

Kelsie laughed out loud. "I remember those! I wonder if we still have them?"

Sasha's smile disappeared. "If we do, they stay with us."

Andre turned to a monitor that showed Lacy Cross in her early twenties, next to a current photo of Sasha. "You and your mother could've been twins. Is that a tough legacy to follow?"

Sasha felt the air thicken with resentment. She shot a glance at her sister. Sasha and Lacy had always looked so similar; Kelsie, though, had inherited the strong features from their father's side. She'd never gotten over her genetic bad luck. That, combined with the fact that Sasha had been given a costarring role with her mother—while Kelsie had never been given the same chance—meant that this was a supremely sensitive topic in the Cross family.

And the interviewer had just blasted it wide open. On camera.

"Is it?" Andre asked again, snapping Sasha back into reality.

"I think what Mom accomplished is a burden for both her daughters."

Kelsie leaned in to answer, but Andre changed the subject before she could.

After the taping, Sasha was checking her messages when her father approached.

"Where's Kelsie?" she asked.

"I asked a talent scout to meet with her."

Judah led his oldest daughter to a bench overlooking Sunset Boulevard. He asked about school, her friends. He told Sasha to block off the date on her calendar so she could attend her sister's play. And then, when the small talk was done, he got down to business.

"I have an idea that would benefit all of us," her father started. Sasha coughed. Did her father know how transparent he was? she wondered. "There is a lot of interest in the Auction, especially now with the protests. None of the networks have done what I would call good work diving into it."

Years ago CNN aired an ill-thought-out documentary about potential Series As. Since then, the Auction got covered as either gossip or business news.

"The CNN show failed because it was boring and had a bunch of no-names. If it had tracked someone well known, it would have worked."

An uncomfortable feeling started tingling in Sasha's stomach. "What does this have to do with us?"

He grinned widely. "I want to develop a show starring you."
Sasha's head whipped toward him. "You can't be serious."
But she knew already, without a doubt, he was. This was her
father, after all—a man who seemed to only see dollar signs
when he looked at his daughter.

Like the rest of the world.

"Hold on, hold on," he said, waving his hands around. "The
difference is that I would be producing. I could control the
story. I can sell the idea to PicaFlix. And if you do this, you are
a sure Series A no matter what. All the attention . . . you are
smart, talented, attractive . . ."

"Dad!" Sasha took a second to control the rage building
inside of her. "How can you pimp me out like this? You know
I'm not interested in doing what Mom did. Or what you do!"

"It's just a six-week project, a limited series. Then it goes
away," he tried to soothe her. "Just the lead-up to the Auction
and a few after-Auction interviews, and promotion."

"No." Sasha shook her head resolutely. *Fuck no,* she wanted
to say, but thought better of it.

Judah rose with her. "Don't make snap decisions. This
could benefit us."

Us? Sasha froze.

"There is good that could come from this," her father continued. "First off, it would sell. And this attention will increase
your Auction value."

She closed her eyes and struggled to calm her temper.
Money, money, money. That's what it always came down to,
didn't it? No matter how much he and her mother had earned,
her father had always wanted more. Her eyes flew open. It was
time to ask him. "Money? Is that what this is all about? Why,
Dad? You don't need money."

"It's a great idea, and you know your sister wants to be an
actress," he explained. Sasha could hear it in his voice: he was

losing patience. Well, so was she. And she demanded answers. "If the project goes well, Kelsie could star in a sequel."

"Oh, so this is about Kelsie? Then wait until she can do it. She wants to and you do, too. Win-win."

He shook his head. "It won't work that way. Someone else will do it before then, and we'll lose the franchise. We have to do it now."

She set her jaw. "Tell me, Dad. Why now?"

"Because, Sasha!" He exploded, throwing his hands up in the air. "Because it's a big payday, and we could use it!"

Sasha opened her mouth to respond, but she found she didn't know what to say.

Lacy's fortune . . .

She thought of all the hundreds of millions of dollars her mother had earned—and, she'd thought, wisely invested. Their massive mansion in the best section of Los Angeles. Their private planes, their fashions, their cars. Her father's diamond-studded watch glinted in the sunlight as he stared at the ground, ashamed, and absentmindedly rubbed at his beard.

"How bad is it?"

Her father was quiet. Eventually he mumbled, "I don't want you to worry about it."

"No, you just want to pimp me out," she countered. "I said, how bad is it?"

"Let's just say this would help." He straightened up and shot his dazzling smile at her, the one she'd seen him flash at every entertainment executive in town.

She steeled herself. God, her mother would be *so* disappointed in him. "I will walk away right now unless you tell me. How bad is it?"

Judah sighed. He gritted his teeth. "We're tight. Projects I counted on didn't come through; investments didn't pan out. I owe important people money, more than we'll get for your Auction. I can't sell the house because it's mortgaged. I tried to work through it, and when I pitched PicaFlix, they proposed this."

"You already pitched to PicaFlix?" She didn't think she could get any angrier, but wow, had she been mistaken. "And we're broke? Does Kelsie have to leave her school?" Crossroads was pricey.

"If we don't do the show, yes, Kelsie would have to leave Crossroads."

Sasha couldn't breathe. It occurred to her then: this was blackmail. Do it, and she would become everything she detested—a Hollywood brat with her own reality show. Say no, and she would be the bitch who crushed her sister's future and destroyed her family.

Sasha had no choice but to do what she always did when she needed to think: leave.

"I'm going back to Berkeley."

Her father couldn't even meet her eyes. "I understand. Just . . . think about it. For us."

She stood to leave. "Dad . . ."

Hopefully, he smiled at her. "Yes, honey?"

She exhaled a long, loud sigh. "You really, really suck."

NINE

From her bedroom window, Sasha watched the kids at the elementary school across the street chase each other in the playground, shrieking with joy, with life, with childish abandon. She couldn't imagine how simple their lives seemed, how picture-perfect. At that age, she had already won an Academy Award. Envy tugged at her insides.

Three pictures hung on the wall by her bed. One was of her at eight years old, lying in a hammock with her mom. Another was of her with Jason and Brianna on a class trip to the Griffith Observatory. The third was a black-and-white shot of her fighting off a defender in the last lacrosse game of her senior year of high school. Turning away from the view outside her window, she studied the pictures, dredging up old memories. Old dreams.

When she got in these moods, she liked to check in with someone who could ground her. She messaged Jason: *Why aren't you here?*

Jason messaged back: *When did you become a morning person?*

Can't sleep.

Her device beeped, signaling a video call.

Jason's image appeared. "What's up?"

Sasha fixed him with a stare. "My dad made a deal. I need to star in a reality show."

Jason uttered a one-word reaction: "Fuck."

She shook her head, feeling a frustrating bout of tears well up. "Two days ago I dreaded the Auction. Now I need it to save my family from bankruptcy. What the hell!"

"When does your dad need an answer?"

She glanced at the school. The lot was empty; the kids had gone inside, and it was almost like they'd never even been there at all. A light rain splattered on the asphalt of the playground. "He calls me three times a day. I think it's safe to say I'm out of time."

Jason whistled. "What will you do?"

She stared out the window a few moments longer. When she turned back to her best friend's hologram, she was resigned, resolute. "I guess . . . be a reality star."

A week later she returned to Los Angeles to sign the deal to star in *Auction Diaries*. The terms called for a three-month run, longer than her father promised, with shows twice a week—more than he said it would be. It would end a week after the November Auction. She had to allow cameras in her house and conduct media interviews.

When she signed her name, she considered writing something else: *Screw you*, maybe, or *Ha ha ha, this is a joke, right?*

But somehow, "Sasha Cross" shone up at her, her regular handwriting perfectly visible.

It was done.

She and her father walked down a long green hallway covered with images of the award-winning movies and TV series PicaFlix produced. Not one was a reality show.

"Don't be surprised if by the end of this you're begging me to introduce you to directors," her father teased her. Ever since she'd told him her answer, he'd been acting like this had all been her idea, like she'd been jumping at the chance to star in a reality show.

Sasha shook her head. She felt empty inside, like all her emotions had been hollowed out. "Don't be surprised if by the end of this you wish you'd never asked me."

At the end of the hallway, Judah opened a door to a roomful of producers, editors, camera operators, technicians, and production assistants who made up the team he would supervise as executive producer. They sat; Sasha kept her gaze lowered to avoid showing everyone exactly how little she wanted to be there. Next to her, her father nonchalantly discussed how they'd invade her life. There would be a stylist to help with her wardrobe, makeup, and hairstyle; any dates she went on, the crew would be present. A smarmy woman sitting next to her father encouraged her to invite friends to her house for "heartfelt chats about their hopes and dreams."

Each week the show would document her life and what she had to do to prepare for the Auction. And during each week's live show, Sasha would take questions on social media and from a studio audience.

The details kept coming. Finally, an hour later, numb and ready to escape, she stumbled as she got out of her chair to leave. A man grabbed her arm. "Sorry," she mumbled.

Her father took her hand. "Sasha, this is Raymond Mix, he's a PA."

"Mix?" A memory danced across her mind and brought her back to the present moment. "Oh, I played lacrosse against a girl with that name."

"Was it Deanna Mix?" he asked.

"Yes!" She grinned, her first genuine facial expression in what felt like days.

"She's my sister," he replied. He had a nice smile.

Judah stepped between them. "Small world," he said, taking Sasha by the arm.

On the way down the hall, he boomed, "We need to call Kelsie! This is amazing!"

Sasha messaged Jason: *I'm in hell.*

———

Jason didn't see the message, at least not right away. He spotted his brother behind a shed next to a warehouse. The flames from a burning truck cast a shadow across the building. Jason inched up behind Baker, pulled out his Glock, and pointed it. *Bam!*

"Crap!" Baker yelled, putting down the controller. On-screen, his virtual self slumped to the ground. "How did you find me?"

Jason rose and stretched. "You always go through the warehouse."

"Which other way is there to go? I hate that you're better at this than me."

Jason searched for a hint that Baker realized the day's anniversary. Apparently not. Baker crouched into a fighter's stance, but Jason knew better. The last time he tangled with Baker was on his little brother's eighteenth birthday, and Jason got his butt kicked.

Jason picked up his keys. "You owe me a pizza. Let's go."

He navigated his Jeep down Germantown Avenue. "When's the fight?"

"Three weeks."

"Cool. Can you score a ticket for your big bro?"

Baker rubbed his belly. "You're coming to Miami?"

"If I can," Jason said, then hesitated. "Is there betting on your fights?"

"Are you planning to make a wager?"

"Just curious."

"We hear rumors from time to time. It's all underground."

"Are guys approached by gamblers?"

"Where's this coming from?"

Jason made a left onto Mt. Airy Avenue. "There's legal betting on my games."

"And do gamblers approach you?"

Jason glanced over. "To throw a game? Never."

"I had a fight in Atlanta two months ago," said Baker. "A middleweight got jumped outside the arena. They broke his jaw and messed up his eye. Word got around he took money to throw a fight, then reneged. He's blind in that eye."

Jason eased his car into the parking lot. "That sucks."

"Yep, once they get their hooks in you, there's no getting out."

The implied warning lingered. An hour later Jason sat at his terminal practicing his three-point shot. He felt a presence at his door and turned to find Ayana staring at him.

"What's up?"

"I brought you something." She held a bowl of cookies-n-cream ice cream.

Jason's eyes brightened, and he hit "pause" on the training program. "Not sure what I did to deserve this, but I'll take it."

She rubbed his back. "Did your mom and dad ever tell you how they met?"

Jason answered as he dipped his spoon into the bowl. "A blind date, I think."

"Back when your mom and I lived in Hollywood Hills. What your parents didn't tell you was your father had a blind date with me that night. When he showed up, Sheila answered the door and pretended to be me."

"Really?"

"I thought David stood me up. I left him a nasty message. But he didn't receive it because Sheila made him turn off his device. By the time he realized it didn't matter."

"When did *you* figure it out?"

"Later that night. A car pulled up and I saw Sheila and your father making out."

Jason roared. "My mom was a snake!"

Ayana laughed. "She could be. My brother, Bobby, wanted to kill your father. But your mom had a way about her."

"I don't think Baker realizes today's the anniversary of the crash."

"He's wired differently than you."

Jason nodded. "Dad would've turned fifty next month."

"What a party that would have been. And Sheila would have made him clean the whole damn thing up."

Jason gazed at a framed picture on the wall. His parents sat on a bench holding hands and laughing, while the smiling brothers crowded in behind them. Jason wished he could remember what his mother and father were laughing about.

"I don't say this enough, but I'm proud of you, baby." She reached out to touch his hand. "Get some rest. You have a big game this week."

———

"I'm the world's best-paid babysitter," Jessica grumbled as her driver dropped her off in front of the Contra Costa Superior Court. The courthouse had seen better days. Gloom seeped off the raised dark-wood bench that Judge Lucius Mertle had presided over for more than two decades.

Jessica watched the prosecutor fight a losing battle to press down the veneer peeling on the table. The decrepit jury box was to the left of the bench, which was fortunate for the judge, given an injury that limited his ability to turn his neck.

Jessica nodded at a well-dressed man sitting in the gallery. Five minutes later a deputy escorted a shell-shocked young man wearing designer sneakers, skinny jeans, and a T-shirt into the courtroom.

"All rise," the bailiff ordered. Judge Mertle entered moments later.

The bailiff called out, "State of California versus Parker."

Silas Parker and his Global-appointed lawyer stood. Jessica took a seat behind the defendant's table. Judge Mertle examined the paperwork. "How does the defendant plead?"

Parker's lawyer stepped forward. "Not guilty, Your Honor, and I would like to approach." The judge waved him up. The prosecutor scurried to join.

"Your Honor, Mr. Parker is a victim of mistaken identity," Parker's lawyer said, handing the judge a document. "I have an affidavit from the alleged victim acknowledging that Mr. Parker is not the man who attacked her."

The state's attorney held up his own document. "Hold on. The victim, a college student, provided a statement that Mr. Parker met her at a Danville bar, drugged her, and then sexually assaulted her in his Bugatti at Hap Magee Ranch Park."

While the lawyers made their points, Jessica opened Parker's file. An advertising executive, he had been in trouble before. In a night of selfish and destructive decisions, the only smart thing Parker had done was fish out the card in his wallet that Global issued to all its Series As with contact information should they ever be in legal trouble.

She messaged an underling: *Are you with her?*

The answer came quickly. *Yes, at the airport.*

Parker's lawyer pointed at the affidavit. "She was in shock and later realized her mistake. Given this, I hope the state's attorney will drop the charges."

The prosecutor turned back to his deputy, who shrugged. "I want to talk to her."

Parker's lawyer expected that. "My understanding is she had a long-planned trip to Europe. She is on her way to Oakland to catch her flight."

Appealing to the judge, the lawyer added, "Given her affidavit, I don't see why you'd want to add to her trauma by delaying her trip. I do, however, have her contact information, and we can do a video conference right now if you'd like to hear it from her."

The judge stalled a moment, then shook his head. "No, no, we have other cases here and can't fuss with a conference call. Enter your plea."

The lawyer turned and nodded at Parker, who said, "Not guilty, Your Honor."

The judge pointed at the confused state's attorney. "Ronald, figure this out."

Once the courtroom cleared, Jessica sent another message. *Have her board the plane.*

Once she sent it, one immediately came back to her. It wasn't the one she expected.

Mom had a stroke, Vincente informed her.

"Oh shit," she muttered. *What do you need?*

———

Vincente heard his flight called and gathered his bags. It would take two more connections and a bus before he reached Lukeville; his early-morning flight wouldn't deliver him home until nearly the end of the day. He hoped he would make it in time.

His mother, Gabriela, had collapsed in a men's bathroom in the office building she cleaned at night. It wasn't until morning that an employee discovered her. He had already lost valuable time. The army had only approved his emergency leave after Jessica intervened, and then it took an additional sixteen hours for Fort Stewart to process his paperwork.

He settled into his middle seat and checked for messages. His mother's brain had swelled so much that doctors had drilled a hole into her skull to ease the pressure. None of his mom's friends had the time or money to devote the months it would take for her to recover. He reminded himself to check on rehab facilities and government support programs. Maybe he could get her placed in a facility close to Fort Stewart, and the higher-ups would grant him permission to visit.

Maybe.

The doctors were noncommittal about her prospects. He hustled to Concourse A and Gate 35 just as they announced final boarding. Hours later, starving and exhausted and, most of all, anxious, when Vincente finally reached the hospital, he choked back tears at his mom's condition. He collapsed into a chair by her side.

Gabriela had not regained consciousness since her stroke. The ventilator masked her face. A bandage covered her shaved head. An IV drip snaked to the nook between her left biceps and forearm, which was purple from multiple failed attempts. Restraints prevented her from flailing her arms should she wake. The heart monitor lulled Vincente to sleep, but he shook it off to keep a lookout for a doctor or nurse.

Beep! Beep! Beep!

He awoke with a start. The machine alerted nurses that the IV bag needed changing. He left to find someone, but the nurses' station was unoccupied. The two other patients in the cramped room groaned at the disruption.

Vincente waited until he couldn't take the incessant noise. "Hello! Nurse?" he called. He walked the corridor in search of someone. He spotted a man in the stairwell.

"My mom's IV bag is empty. Can you help?"

Twenty minutes of incessant, nerve-racking beeping later, the nurse swapped out the bag, barely glancing at them.

After four days Gabriela's condition stabilized enough to arrange a transfer to a facility Jessica found that specialized in brain injuries. Vincente slumped into the chair. He reached over to adjust the bandage covering his mother's head. He slept uncomfortably in the wooden chair until he was startled awake at 4:15 a.m., when a janitor barged in to collect the garbage.

He checked his mother, then fell back to sleep. Eventually, the sun shining through the room's drab blinds prodded Vincente to open his eyes. His eyes landed right on his mother, who looked calm. Peaceful.

He peered closer. His heart thudded. She looked *too* peaceful.

Inching closer, his insides screaming at him what his brain didn't want to acknowledge, he touched her skin.

She was cold.

A doctor would explain it later: sometime in the night her body had surrendered to the stroke; her heart had stopped. Because of a faulty connection on the monitor, neither Vincente nor the nurses' station had received an alert.

It was a hospital for people without much money. As a Series D, he knew the signs by heart. What had he expected?

Vincente held her hand. Now he didn't want the doctors or nurses, just time with his mother before they would take her away. He caressed her fingers. He apologized for the pain he'd caused and thanked her for the sacrifices she had made.

Eventually, an orderly came to remove the body. He straightened her bandage, put his hand on her cheek, and leaned down for a last kiss.

"Goodbye, Mom," he whispered. He could swear he felt a small piece of his heart chip off and float away just then.

Two days later, Jessica and Vincente laid Gabriela to rest next to her sister. They held hands as they walked out of the cemetery.

Jessica was uncharacteristically quiet. Finally she whispered, "I'm sorry I couldn't do more, Vinny."

"You did a lot," he assured her. "And the doctors say she would have had brain damage. Mom wouldn't have wanted to live that way. To be a burden."

Jessica wrapped her arm around him. "I'll come to Fort Stewart for Thanksgiving."

"Let's just make sure to check that the oven works. I'll never forget my mom's face when she opened it up after three hours and found a stone-cold turkey."

"Don't bring that up! It wasn't broken. I got mad at her and unplugged it."

Vincente's eyes went wide. "Holy crap."

"Not my proudest moment."

"Why were you angry?" He wondered, enjoying the memory.

"Your mom wanted my mom to force me to stay."

"That's right, you left a month later."

"I did. And your mom worried what would happen to you once I left." Jessica took his hand. She seemed more earnest than usual, and more subdued. "I'm sorry, Vinny, maybe things would have been different if I'd stayed."

"No. Anything that happened was all my doing. Anyway, it wasn't you. I learned my dad wanted me to make a visit to Mexico but Mom refused. I actually hitched a ride to the border when I was thirteen."

"What happened?"

"That's where I learned what a passport was."

The SUV pulled up to take Jessica away. "I guess we're orphans," she said, embracing him. Vincente watched as the only family he had left stepped into the vehicle and drove away.

On the flight back to Georgia, Vincente took stock of his life. He had no family besides his cousin, few friends, and a dead-end job. He resolved to live to the fullest. Once he left the army, he would enroll in community college. But first, Lyra.

————

Suni eyed Avery. "Are you sure you want to do this?"

"Absolutely," he said, without meaning it. Together they walked into the Detroit Center for Performing Arts for an evening of modern poetry. "Do you do this kind of thing a lot?"

"Go out on dates or poetry?"

"Um, both?"

"Dates? No, not since Derrick. And he hated poetry. I love it. It's the only thing that makes me feel the way I do when I play the cello. It speaks in rhythms if you listen."

"How did you become interested? Your parents?"

She hesitated a second. "My mom."

"What about your dad?"

"He wasn't in the picture much. What about your parents?"

"Mine? They were too busy with my brother. Garrett is the golden child."

"It can't be all that bad."

"When I was ten years old, my mother left for a week to visit her mother in Tennessee. Once she left, my dad took me to a doctor to give a blood sample. He didn't believe I was his."

"Wow."

"I've never told anyone that before. You're lucky you're an only child."

"How do you know I'm an only child?"

Dumb mistake, but Avery recovered. "I just assumed. You didn't mention having brothers or sisters."

It worked. "You're right. It's just me."

"Have you ever been back to Bangladesh?"

"Just when I was six years old, my mom wouldn't let me go with my dad after the divorce. She was afraid he wouldn't bring me back."

An elderly man hobbled onto the stage to a standing ovation. With a halting voice, the man recited one of his poems. Try as he might, Avery could not hear the rhythms that Suni spoke about. He glanced over at her. She had a funny way of scrunching up her nose.

When she sniffled, he reached over to grasp her hand. She tensed, glanced at Avery, then intertwined their fingers. A funny thing happened. During the second poem, Suni squeezed his hand in rhythm with the man's recital. Between the words and Suni's form of Morse code, the poem's feelings and emotions flooded his senses. He pushed back tears.

Later, Suni sipped hot tea at a late-night diner a few blocks from the theater. "Tell me the truth, did you hate it?"

"No."

"Ah, you're just being nice. I know you'd rather be partying with your friends."

Her words stung Avery, but he had given her reason to say them. He changed the subject. "When's your next concert?"

"Next Saturday in Plymouth."

"Can I come?"

She took a bite of a cinnamon cookie. "Sure, but tell me, what's going on? We passed each other on campus dozens of times. What's the sudden interest?"

Because my brother is making me do it, he thought in his head. But that wasn't true now. "I don't know. I like being around you."

She put down her tea. "I'm not having sex with you."

"Wow. That's right out there. OK, I won't have sex with you, either."

Suni laughed. "I'll get you a ticket."

Later that night Avery sat in the cramped basement of his parents' home relaying to his brother what he'd learned about Suni's family.

"It doesn't sound like much of a relationship. Don't push too hard, too fast. You know how this works. Once you get close, they always open up, especially about how they hate their fathers." Garrett signed off, and Avery felt a mixture of exhilaration and disgust.

TEN

Sasha was in the middle of a strange dream when she shifted in bed just enough to rouse herself from sleep. Immediately, in the quiet shadows of her room, what felt like an electrical current shocked her fully awake. She was going to star in a reality show.

Struggling to even out her breathing, her mind raced. The clock read 4:48 a.m. Groaning, she willed herself back to sleep, but she couldn't escape her thoughts.

Reality star.

She rubbed her temples, and her mind turned to William. It had been a week since she'd committed to PicaFlix, but Sasha had yet to tell him the news. It reminded her of her childhood panic prior to informing her mother she didn't want to appear in any more movies. Her parents knew something was up—at age eight, Sasha suddenly regressed back to sleeping in their bed every night—but they couldn't figure it out. So one day, after an audition, in the passenger seat of her mother's Mercedes, trembling, she confessed. At the slightest touch from her mother, Sasha burst into tears. Lacy held her close and promised she never had to appear on film again. A year later, Lacy herself retired from acting and devoted herself to philanthropic causes.

With William, there would be no tears, Sasha reasoned with herself—just embarrassment. She wasn't sure, but she suspected he thought better of her than this. He would wonder why the change of heart, and she didn't want to reveal her family's financial plight.

Sasha rolled over onto her side, staring out the window. Streetlights cast a yellow sheen over the navy sky. William wasn't the only person on her mind. Kelsie had sent a furious message accusing her of doing the show for attention.

By morning—actual morning, not this 5:00 a.m. bullshit—Sasha had long given up on sleep and instead spent her time productively—exercising, cleaning her apartment, cooking breakfast. Really, it was all a distraction.

On campus, she took a sip of her third cup of coffee and peeked out her alcove at William's office door. Shut. It didn't take much for her to convince herself today wasn't the right day to let him know about her change in circumstances.

She instructed her digital assistant to save her documents, packed her bag, and headed toward the elevator. It opened. William. "Do you have a few minutes?" he asked.

"Is it OK if we wait? I'm late for a meeting."

"Sure, no problem."

As she hustled to her car, Jason messaged her. *You tell William?*

She messaged back. *Did you cut off Denton?*

Her small victory of the day: Freddy Tangier sprinted to catch her just as she pulled her Fiat Spider out of the parking lot and turned onto Barrow Lane. She glanced in her rearview mirror as Freddy threw his hands up in frustration.

Forty-five minutes later she pulled into an underground parking lot in San Francisco. She took the elevator to a twenty-third-floor office that had recently been a sperm bank. A year ago young men sat in that office awkwardly waiting their turn. Now it was twenty-two-year-old men and women who sat awkwardly waiting their turn.

After thirty minutes, a receptionist called out, "Sasha Cross?" She stood up, ignored the stares, and walked to the desk marked Auction Registration. A heavyset middle-aged woman named Trudy led her to a cubicle.

"Put your thumb on the screen," said Trudy, pointing to a monitor.

Within seconds Sasha's personal information and family history appeared.

"Oh." Trudy looked up. "You're *that* Sasha Cross. Such a shame about your mother."

"Thank you."

"You look like her." Trudy handed Sasha her passport. "You can go inside."

Sasha went through the monthly ritual of getting blood drawn so the Big 7 could double-check her health. The companies used the tests to pare down the list of candidates.

The next day Sasha summoned her courage and stopped by William's office. *Variety* would break the story of the reality show, and Sasha wanted him to hear it from her.

He smiled and welcomed her into his office. "Hey there, stranger, where have you been?"

"It's been a little busy and I have news."

"Me too. The commission asked me to go to New York in November to observe the Auction. What ya got?"

For a moment Sasha brightened. She needed someone to help her through it, even more so now. If it hadn't been for him, it would all be too much.

Then she remembered why she was there. "I know this will come as a surprise, but . . . there will be a show, a PicaFlix series, that chronicles my Auction process."

William stared at her for a moment, his face surprisingly neutral. "That *is* a surprise. You caught the bug?"

She scoffed. "That's one way to look at it."

"You must have your reasons."

Sasha glanced at the floor. "I do."

"Congratulations, I guess. I'll have to find a new research assistant."

Her head spun. "I could still do it. I can juggle."

William cut her off. "It wouldn't work. You can't promote the Auction on your show and then investigate it with me. And, anyway, you'll be busy."

They weathered an awkward pause.

"Good luck with the show." William turned to his papers.

Sasha hurried out the door. Brianna was waiting outside Evans Hall. "How did it go?"

Furious, Sasha stomped over to her best friend, eager for some sympathy. She hadn't expected to lose her job on top of everything else—the one thing she actually thought mattered. "I'm so screwed. Why do awful things always happen to me?"

Brianna's face contorted. "Oh, that's right. Poor little rich girl wants to work on a dumb commission and gets handed the job. Hates Hollywood but gets offered her own PicaFlix show." She rolled her eyes.

Sasha blinked, stunned. "What?"

"You live in a candy factory but hate sweets," Brianna continued, her lips pinched in a funny way Sasha had never before noticed. "I get it, Sasha, but give it a rest."

"Why are you being like this?" Sasha cried.

Brianna stared at her, anger etched on her face. Then she sighed, eyes drooping into something like sadness. "My dad lost his job. I have to help pay back my student loans."

"That sucks." Sasha reached over and squeezed her friend's hand. "What can I do?"

"Do you have $450,000?"

Sasha's eyes widened. She definitely did not, but she had an idea. "If it helps, come stay with me."

"No, thanks. I'm not another Cross family charity case." Brianna grimaced. "Sorry, Sash."

"It's OK," Sasha said quietly. "You're upset and I'm your favorite punching bag."

Her friend left and Sasha sat on a bench across from Evans Hall as the sun faded behind the building and the shadows bathed her in self-pity. She lingered a while longer.

She had nowhere to go and no one to see.

———

To counter the protests, the Big 7 kicked their PR efforts into high gear, starting with a series of CNBC specials looking back at the crisis America faced a decade ago. Britney Reynolds didn't mind hosting them; she just hated that Victor Armstrong ordered her to do it. But since Global Holdings owned her network, there was little she could say.

She recorded the introduction for the first special in a cramped studio. A monitor showed images of a tent city of homeless people on the outskirts of Chicago as Britney read from the script: "The economic situation was so dire, for the first time since the Civil War, the prospect of the country splintering into regions became a real possibility."

She paused when her producer came into the voice-over studio. "We're good. We can clean up any issues in editing. Is it true that Armstrong prepped you on what to say?"

The CEO's meddling was an embarrassment to Britney. "It's worse than that. Armstrong 'suggested' we give less play to the protests."

"What did you say?"

"I asked him if he had any summer vacation plans."

The producer bit into a granola bar that would pass as lunch. "What should we do?"

Britney shrugged. "Just do our job and hope Armstrong doesn't watch."

Britney was old enough to have missed the first Auction by a couple years, which meant her parents missed out on a windfall. Instead, they were among the last to receive Social Security payments, which paled compared to the amount received from so-called Auction babies. Her device beeped, and she returned to the control room. *Parental Payback*, CNBC's most popular evening show, was starting. It mixed investment advice for parents about how to manage the money from the Auction with tips on how to prepare their children to be a success, and it played on the surge in interest from parents over their children's financial futures. Nobody wanted to become what the show called "empty nest-eggers."

Britney shuffled her papers, almost chuckling at the changes she'd seen in just her relatively short lifetime. "Helicopter parents" were a thing of the past. "Asset managers" was the new moniker for overinvolved parents. An industry of tutors, preteen career counselors, and leadership coaches emerged to help parents shape their sons and daughters into financial successes that would pay off with a big Auction bid. Parents quickly demanded schools focus on careers that offered the most lucrative future—their children's own interests and passions tossed aside like empty coffee cups. Their children were like a reverse mortgage—parents wanted to make sure they earned them mansions, not garden apartments.

As the show started, the host, a comedian turned financial adviser, introduced the first guest, an Oberlin College professor with a novel idea. He formed a group of educators who pooled their expertise and resources to prepare their children for lucrative careers.

"How does this work?" the host asked.

"I realized on a professor's salary I couldn't pay for tutors and career counselors, but I had access to expertise at my school. So we organized."

A graphic on the screen displayed his daughter Kira's weekly schedule: piano lessons three days a week; courses in accounting, financial strategy, and engineering; and a regular session on leadership skills. Kira also played soccer on a club team.

"This is on top of her schoolwork?"

The professor nodded. "I can't count on the public school to prepare her."

"Oberlin has a well-earned reputation as being liberal. How does this square with that?"

"There's no contradiction. I want my daughter to be a justice warrior, but being socially woke doesn't mean she has to be financially broke."

"When do you find out if all this hard work has paid off? Is she in this year's Auction?"

The professor shook his head. "Oh, no. My daughter is nine years old."

"She's nine? And she does all this? Is she the youngest in your group?"

"Not at all. The children range from seven years old to twelve," he replied.

"You don't think that's a bit much?"

"I chose a profession that doesn't pay well, and then America changed the rules. I'm doing what's best for me and my daughter."

The host wrapped up the session, then teased next week's guest: a husband and wife who had five children in six years before learning that parents only financially benefited from the first three that went through the Auction. Now they were suing the Big 7.

—

Armstrong's ego obliterated any goodwill the Big 7 PR campaign created. Asked on CNBC whether the swelling number of demonstrators had legitimate gripes, Armstrong scoffed, "Their support comes from those who whine because they don't apply themselves and can't make a living. A movement of Series Ds will not make a difference."

Within days, the protesters launched the D Movement.

Rallies were now routine outside the headquarters of the Big 7. Chestfin, located in Philadelphia, shut down for two days over fears of violence.

But Global bore the worst of it. The San Francisco mayor refused to enforce the laws that made large demonstrations illegal without a permit. The mob had the upper hand and weren't letting up. When the mayor wouldn't help, Armstrong ordered a ring of barricades around the complex and brought in a private army of security. Police kept a careful distance.

The first day, it worked. Barriers kept protesters from getting close to the complex. But as if in reaction, the size of the crowds swelled. The understaffed security force struggled to contain the larger crowd. On day three, it came to a head.

The sun beat in Deval Fumley's eyes as he stood watch with fellow police officers at the stairs leading to the commuter transit station across the street. He hated the sun, and he was hungry, and those facts combined with the increasingly defiant D Movement protesters made him start counting down until his security shift ended. Today's shift had been different than yesterday's; there was something in the air. Deval had enough experience in security to know whatever was coming wouldn't be good.

Suddenly, the energy shifted. He blinked, jolted—his upper arm stung. "What the fuck!" Deval mumbled, holding his hand to his burning skin.

He watched them fly through the air, projectiles coming at him and his fellow officers lining the street, landing at their feet and glistening in the sun: a steady supply of D batteries.

"Those fuckers," Deval shouted.

He couldn't see who was throwing the batteries at them; the culprits hid behind a parked city bus. He and the rest of the guards lifted their riot gear. A yelp caught his attention. It was an officer half a block away—she had taken a direct hit to the left eye socket. The paramedics who'd been quietly eating lunch at the other end of the corner dropped their sandwiches and rushed into action.

"Hell no," Fumley mumbled. His shift was almost over, and he wasn't interested in overtime. He stormed over to tell the protesters to cut the bullshit.

He made the mistake of going alone.

Batteries rained down on him, followed by shouts. "Go back to your pen, mercenary!"

Fumley screamed obscenities at them. When he whirled his head around to block an onslaught, one of his friends must've thought he was giving him some kind of secret signal. With a yell, he grabbed three other nearby guards—they made a run for it across the street, toward the protesters. The rest of the guards followed suit, and Fumley saw a sea of dark-blue uniforms swarm the street.

He felt it, then: that unmistakable moment where something happens that can't be undone.

He opened his mouth, the word *Stop* on the tip of his tongue.

But it was too late.

With a ringing, lingering clash, protesters broke through the barricades.

In seconds, a rush of police responded with batons, pepper spray, and tasers. Distant shots rang out. Nobody could say who fired. But what happened next was not in dispute. Fumley panicked and unsheathed a Glock he kept on his belt.

Later, footage would show a half-dozen protesters crouching at the sight of the gun. Those that didn't weren't as lucky. A car's exhaust backfired. Spooked, Fumley unloaded his clip.

The gunshots set off a stampede that injured dozens of people—protesters and officers alike.

But Fumley didn't care about the injuries. He stared at the ground in front of him. He felt hollowed out, empty. Like a walking shadow.

There were two bodies there, on the ground, darkness leaking from them where his bullets had entered.

Dead.

The footage was clear. It didn't matter that investigators found hundreds of D batteries strewn on the ground, that the protesters had clearly started the attack. Because it turned out, the protester who'd called Fumley a mercenary was one of the ones Fumley had shot. And he was the nephew of a city councilman.

The next day, Fumley understood what would happen. He'd take the fall on the ground, but the mayor would pin the blame on Armstrong.

The backlash reverberated nationwide.

Armstrong wasn't the only target. Protesters pelted the CEO of Beech, Ursula Johnson, with rocks a few days later as she attended her young daughter's soccer game. Boston police arrested six members of the D Movement for setting fire to a fleet of Big 7 trucks.

Bunkered in his office at Global's headquarters, Armstrong bit his tongue as fellow Big 7 CEOs took turns scolding him, blaming him for putting them and their families in danger. Only Johnson remained silent.

After twenty minutes of a verbal flogging, Armstrong had enough. "Got it all out of your systems?" he barked at the CEO images on the large screen on the wall. "Because this bitch session isn't doing anything to rid us of the protesters outside our doors."

Once the meeting ended, Armstrong poured a glass of whiskey and turned to Jessica. "If the police aren't going to protect us, we need our own army."

ELEVEN

"No comment."

Sasha hustled up the steps to Evans Hall. She muttered a thank-you that the young man with the camera didn't follow her into the building. In the days since the news broke about the show, the paparazzi had really stepped up their game.

The *Variety* headline blared: "Sasha Cross Steps Back into the Spotlight." But the rest of the coverage was cruel. Talk show hosts mocked her as a spoiled product of Hollywood exploiting her family's celebrity. "Her mom gave up Hollywood to help the poor. Sasha Cross's great cause is shilling for Hollywood. What reality does she represent?" asked one reporter with long blond hair that she kept flipping over her shoulders. Sasha remembered her and her fake concern when her mother had died.

Bitch, Sasha thought.

Reporters followed her on campus; interviews with Sasha's "friends"—really, those whom she'd once had a class with or who'd been at the same random party—peppered the magazines and newspapers.

The attention triggered flashbacks to the days after her mother's death. A steady thrum of panic lit up her insides; she stopped sleeping. She avoided even her tight circle of friends. A frost chilled her relationship with William; they barely spoke when they were working together. If he was searching for her replacement, he wasn't talking about it.

Sasha reminded herself that wasn't her problem anymore. She had a new, bigger problem in its place: being a reality star.

How the hell did this happen?!

On cue, her father messaged her. *Come over to the office. We need to pick your wardrobe.* Sighing, Sasha ventured out of Evans Hall, looking around carefully. A heavy storm had scattered the usual photographers. Except for Freddy. Sasha moved down the steps, ignoring his questions.

"I'm hurt. You could have told me about the show," Freddy baited her as he snapped away. "That would have made my month."

Sasha ignored him as she crossed over the Hearst Mining Circle.

"Your Auction price doubled," Freddy pressed on. "I bet if I keep taking pictures, it will go up even higher." He walked backward as she made her way to the parking lot. As they reached her car, he stumbled and fell.

She hesitated. "Get up," she said, offering her hand.

Freddy stared in surprise, then reached out. She pulled him to his feet.

"Thanks."

At her father's home office, she stabbed at her chicken salad. Without fail, whenever Judah ordered lunch, he got her a chicken salad, despite her telling him multiple times that she hated chicken salad. It was Kelsie who liked it.

Judah was now a regular in Berkeley. It was ironic, in a way; Sasha had always thought about spending more quality time with her father, but his schedule had always been so booked. Apparently, all she had to do to get quality time with him was reveal her life story to America. He kept an apartment in the El

Granada building across the street from the PicaFlix satellite production office.

He got down to business. "Let's talk about what you'll wear."

"What's wrong with the way I dress?" she asked, looking down at her gold Berkeley T-shirt and faded jeans.

Her dad eyed her outfit. "You look like a grungy college student, not the multimillion-dollar Auction star you're about to be. Didn't you ever hear the phrase 'Dress for Success'?"

"Didn't you ever hear the phrase 'Stop Pimping Me Out'?" she countered.

Judah sipped his tea and let the moment pass. "We have eight weeks. And if we fight over every detail, we will exhaust each other."

Sasha brooded. Her father moved on. "Berkeley couldn't be more cooperative. They've agreed to make that professor of yours available, so we can shoot scenes with him advising you about the Auction. Given his history, it's perfect."

Her mouth dropped open. "You coerced William into this?"

"I wouldn't say 'coerced.' He'll get exposure. It will lead to other opportunities. I'm sure he didn't expect to spend his life teaching."

When Sasha didn't respond, Judah put his hand on her shoulder. "These are just jitters. Your mom had them, too. And after this, you, and Kelsie, will be very rich."

Sasha pushed her half-eaten salad away. "Anything else?"

"I can't wait to spend this time with you. Kelsie is so jealous."

As she left, Sasha reminded herself to bring her own lunch next time.

———

The clock ticked down as the crowd chanted "Jason! Jason! Jason!" Their hero acknowledged them with a wave. Ever since his miracle shot, Jason had been on a roll. Tonight's game made it four in a row where he scored at least twenty points.

The buzzer sounded, and he leaned back in his chair. His coach nodded and fist-bumped him. He stood and glanced at the crowd. So much for the adulation; they were already heading for the exits and the long Fourth of July weekend.

Where are u? he messaged Baker.

I'm at the gym. How'd it go?

Jason couldn't hide the smile as he thumbed his response. *Great. Twenty-two points.*

Killer!

Plans? Want to celebrate.

Sorry, bro, early night. I leave for Richmond at the ass crack of dawn.

Jason made a half-hearted effort to get his teammates together, but they declined. That didn't deter him. He had carried his team to another win, and he hadn't heard from Denton in weeks. Jason deserved to have fun. He'd earned it.

As Jason neared his home, he noticed a liquor store on Stenton Avenue. He drove past, then made a quick U-turn and turned into the strip mall. He waited in his car for a couple of minutes, then got out and walked toward the store. The signs on the window offered deals on a twenty-four-can pack of Sleeman's and a bottle of Seagram's whiskey. Jason zeroed in on a bottle of Bombora grape vodka.

A woman stared at him as she exited. The last time Jason had tasted alcohol was outside the Tranquility Recovery Center nearly two years ago. Actually, he corrected himself, it was exactly twenty-one months and fifteen days ago, but who was counting?

A river of shame rushed over his body. *He* was counting. He'd been sober for so long now. Was he really going to throw it all away?

He leaned against his car door, jingling his keys. Remembering. His reliance on alcohol had come as a surprise to him, even though the people around him had noticed it months and months before he had. And then one night, he passed out, completely sloshed—like, physically slumped over and fell. No big deal . . . except he happened to be sitting around a campfire at that moment.

When he'd come to, bandages covered his shoulder and neck; his skin had been scorched. He hadn't been able to look Ayana in the eyes when she'd found him in the hospital room.

He told anyone who would listen that his drinking had been a means to numb the pain from his mangled leg. He was lying to them, though, of course; the actual pain stemmed from something else.

After his discharge, Ayana had driven in the opposite direction of their home. Jason had suspected what was coming, and sure enough, when she turned onto a pine-lined street, he saw the inconspicuous sign: Tranquility Recovery Center.

Ayana had packed for him, organized his stay, paid the bill upfront. In a no-nonsense tone, she said, "Here's the deal." Then she pulled out a bottle and waved it around.

He had stared, salivating. Vodka, crystal clear and deeply inviting.

She held it in front of his face. "Take your last drink. Because if I ever see you with a bottle again, you're dead to me."

Jason had licked his lips, his mouth suddenly dry. He shook his head.

Ayana thrust it into his hands. "Take it! I want to see."

He put the bottle of vodka to his lips and sipped. She snatched it back. Her eyes were fiery.

"I don't have a lot in my life," she said, her voice loud and strong, but Jason could have sworn he heard a tremor underneath. "I can't lose you. I've got all my hopes wrapped up in you boys." She pointed at the rehab entrance. "Now go in there and figure it out."

And so, Jason had figured it out. As much as he could, anyway. Standing in front of the liquor store, Jason remembered his counselor's warning on the day of his release: the urge to drink would be most acute when things were really bad or really good.

It was weird how this felt like a little bit of both.

A man exiting the store shook Jason from his thoughts.

"Are you going in?" the man asked, holding the door open.

Jason turned toward him, then back to the Bombora grape vodka in the window. "No."

He held it together until he slumped into the driver's seat of his car. He lowered his head to the steering wheel so passersby couldn't see him bawling. "Just a few more months," he repeated over and over again. Security for Ayana. A future for him. Just a few more months.

Jason wiped his eyes and stepped back out of the car. This time he didn't stop at the liquor store door. He entered, headed straight to the vodka section, and found the Bombora grape. Jason didn't hesitate at the counter. The clerk scanned the chip embedded in his palm and handed him a receipt. Jason gripped the bottle by the neck. He slammed the door as he left.

Alarmed, the clerk watched as Jason stormed away, reached his car, raised the bottle to the sky, and smashed it to pieces on the ground.

———

Avery handed shots of tequila to Garrett and his friend Jeff. "Cheers!" Avery smiled at his older brother. His visit was a welcome surprise.

Garrett had asked him to arrange a weekend away. His buddy Jeff's marriage was on the rocks, and a trip to Michigan could combine business with pleasure. Tasked with organizing the pleasure part, Avery obliged with a day of barhopping that ended at a plush hotel on Lake Lansing.

As the sun set, partiers jumped up to a beat as a local rapper dropped lines on a makeshift stage that overlooked the lake. Jeff wandered off, and the brothers fell into wicker chairs. "Love this, bro," Avery slurred.

"Me too." Garrett sipped water and turned his head toward the bar.

Jeff returned with more shots. He raised his glass.

"To Garrett, the first guy I met at work and the smartest man I know."

Avery downed the shot. "Jeff, you work at Global?"

"Yeah, why?"

"It's just . . . you seem so mellow compared to everyone I've met there."

Garrett spoke. "Maybe that's why he's getting promoted."

Jeff put down the empty shot glass. "Not a done deal, dude. And even if I'm promoted, it won't matter if Lois insists we move to Scottsdale."

"What's in Scottsdale?" Avery asked.

"Not a damn thing but her family," said Jeff.

"Enough," Garrett ordered. "This is a party. Let's go to the hotel bar."

Twenty-five minutes later the trio sat on stools at Mac's Bar while a hip-hop crew serenaded the crowd. Garrett headed toward the dance floor. Avery surveyed the scene. For four years he had lived for this, but tonight it felt empty. His device beeped.

It was Suni. *Not sure if you're around. Just wondering.*

He pondered sending a message, but put his device away.

An attractive brunette walked up to the table, straight past Avery, and set her eyes on Jeff. "You look familiar."

Jeff ran his fingers through his receding hairline. "I would have remembered you."

She squeezed into the booth. "Buy me a drink?"

"Sure." Jeff got up to get it, but she put her hand on his. "I'm sure your friend wouldn't mind getting us a round."

Avery recognized the hustle, but he let it slide. "I got this."

On the way to the bar, he took out his device and messaged Suni. *At a party but I'd rather be with you.* He scanned the dance floor, searching for his brother, then glanced back at the table. Jeff looked like a deer in the headlights as the woman draped her arm around him and giggled in his ear.

By the time he returned with the drinks, a different woman was standing over Jeff—and she was screaming. "You're away one day, and this is what you do?"

Jeff's extraordinary effort to extract himself from behind the booth would have been comical if he hadn't tripped and smashed his head on the table. He stood, blood pouring from his forehead. Avery gaped.

"I need a Band-Aid," he mumbled, swaying.

A small crowd gathered to watch the bleeding man beg his wife for forgiveness. Neither the brunette nor Garrett was in sight.

Avery handed Jeff paper towels as Lois led her husband out the door. Avery made a last sweep for his brother then messaged him. *Jeff's wife showed up. Big scene. I'm heading back to the room.*

As the hotel elevator beeped with each floor, he dreaded telling his brother that the weekend away ended in disaster. The elevator opened. The brunette stood before him.

"Have a good night," she cooed as she passed.

Garrett watched from the open door of his room.

Avery waited until the elevator shut. "What's she doing here?"

"Don't worry about it."

"You hired her, didn't you? And sent for Jeff's wife. Why? He's your friend."

Garrett smirked. "First off, he's not that good a friend."

"But why ruin his life?"

Garrett shook his head. "I didn't ruin his life. He'll be happier in Scottsdale. I did him a favor."

"He doesn't want to move there."

"I know Lois. He's moving to Scottsdale, and this will be the last boys' weekend for Jeff."

"And let me guess, you'll get the promotion."

Garrett slapped his brother's shoulder. "Thanks to you."

Avery woke with a headache and a half-dozen messages from his brother. He staggered to the bathroom, washed the cotton out of his dry mouth, and sat down on the edge of the bed. His device beeped, signaling an incoming video call from Garrett.

His brother appeared agitated. "I need your help."

Avery tried to clear his head. "Where are you?"

"I had to meet Jeff. I left my device in the hotel room. Please tell me you're still there."

"Yeah, I'm here."

"Thank God. Check the nightstand."

Avery glanced over. "Yep, I see it."

"I need you to do something, and you can't mess it up. I need you to access the Global database and send Jeff files. First, scan your fingerprints, and when that doesn't work, there's a bypass using a series of codes. Write them down . . ."

Ten minutes later Avery sent the files.

Garrett did something he had never done before: he thanked Avery. "Dude, you don't know how much you just saved me. Don't tell anyone you did this and forget those codes."

"How's Jeff today?" asked Avery.

Garrett offered a bright smile. "Great. He's moving to Scottsdale."

———

"What an ordeal."

Lyra opened his travel bag and removed his clothes. "I don't know what I'd do if that was my mom. At least mine has my dad to take care of her."

Vincente unpacked the rest of his things. "It doesn't feel real."

Lyra touched his arm. "My mom's my world, too. I message her every night. I told her last night about what happened, and she's sending you a card."

The weight of the trip hit Vincente. He changed the subject. "So, what's going on around here? Feels like it's been forever."

Lyra turned to face him, her eyes searching his. "Well . . . I broke up with Bryan."

"What?" It came out a little too excited. Vincente toned it down. "What happened?"

She was quiet for a moment. When she spoke, it rushed out. "We got into a fight over the timing of the wedding. I thought we should wait. He accused me of cheating. I told him I hate not being trusted. He hung up, and I got drunk."

"Is it fixable?"

She smiled sadly. "I don't think so. I realized I'll never love him like he loves me, and that's not fair to either of us."

"Wow." Vincente rubbed his chin. He paced. His legs twitched. "And you're doing OK?"

She chuckled. "Yeah. I mean, it sucks. It was, like, two years. But once that doubt enters . . . what can you do?"

"I'm sorry I wasn't here to help you through it."

"C'mon, you were going through worse shit. And the others here have been great." She hugged him. "Anyway, I'm glad you're back. No one makes me laugh like you do. You're such a good friend."

Over the next few days, Vincente mustered up the courage to reveal his feelings, and spent all his spare time wondering if she was ready to hear them. But time with Lyra turned out to be hard to get. She declined dinner invitations. During a lunch break, he nearly confessed how he felt about her but coworkers joined them.

Then fate intervened. Fort Stewart scheduled a day trip for personnel to an amusement park near Savannah. Given the base restrictions, everyone jumped at the chance to ride go-karts, play a round of miniature golf, and waste money on arcade games.

Fort Stewart scheduled two shifts to the park. The first shift left at 6:00 a.m. for Savannah and returned at 3:00 p.m. Vincente and Lyra chose the afternoon bus. He hoped the excursion would open the door to a new relationship. On the big day he searched for Lyra at the gathering point for the charter bus. Seventy-five men and women in casual attire stood with Vincente by the Troupe Gate.

Vincente nodded to the others awaiting a break from the base. He messaged Lyra: *Hurry, we're leaving soon.*

At that moment, a silver charter bus rolled down East Fourth Street and stopped at the gate. The gate opened, and the bus came to a stop in front of the gathering. When Lyra stepped out of it, his heart fell.

"I thought we were going together," he confronted her, wounded.

"Sorry. I got asked to cover a shift."

He swallowed his disappointment. "I wish you'd have told me. I would have switched, too."

A man he had seen around stepped out of the bus. "That was great, Lyra." She waved.

"Who's that?"

"Malik. He works in the morgue."

"Cool. How do you know him?"

"He dated one of the nurse specialists."

The event organizer made a last call. Vincente hesitated. If he didn't get on the bus, he'd look pathetic and be miserable. If he did, he'd just be miserable.

He signaled the organizer and turned toward Lyra. "See ya later."

She waved at him. "Have fun!"

TWELVE

Avery watched a Jack Russell face-plant after stumbling over the bar. Undeterred, the terrier bounced to her feet and completed the course. The crowd at the Calhoun County Fairgrounds awarded the exuberance with loud applause.

Avery pointed at the hapless terrier. "That's a Series D right there."

Suni shook her head. "Don't be a jerk."

The annual dog show was a popular event, and each of the four thousand arena seats was filled, while hundreds of other people walked the fairgrounds in search of corn dogs, T-shirts, and games.

An attractive blond girl walked by, making sure Avery noticed her staring at him.

But Suni noticed, too. "Do you think she's good-looking?"

Avery weighed his options. Then he grinned. "That's a trick question."

She smiled. "You're too smart for me."

"Tell me about the orchestra."

"It's a start. It's got a solid reputation, and if I do well, in a few years I'll be noticed. My dream job is to play with the New York Philharmonic."

Avery eyed a beer vendor. He felt a nudge.

"You can have a drink."

"I'm OK. You come here every year?"

Suni waited until the announcer introduced Ollie, a seventy-pound boxer who bounded onto the obstacle course trailed by a slight man who seemed on the verge of losing control of him.

"If I can. My parents took me for the first time when I was seven years old."

Ollie navigated the course. The boxer had appeared the last three years and was a crowd favorite. After the run was completed, his owner led the dog into a shaded area to escape the heat.

"I didn't figure you to be a dog person," Avery said, sipping on water.

Suni shrugged. "You know I'm an only child. Our neighbors had a min pin. When they moved, they couldn't take her, and I convinced my parents to let me have her. I think the only reason they agreed was that they were splitting up and wanted me to have a companion."

"You said your parents took you to the fair together?"

"They did. That was why I looked forward to it. They wouldn't do much together after the divorce, but they did this. At least until I stopped seeing my dad."

Avery tensed. "You don't see him?"

Suni kept her eyes on the field as the competition shifted to show dogs. An Irish setter, a golden retriever, an English pointer, and a standard poodle entered the arena alongside their handlers. Three judges eyed them closely.

"The last time I saw my dad was the day I entered Michigan State."

"Does he at least call?"

"I got a birthday card a year ago."

"Well, that sucks. I'm sorry."

"I'm used to it. He's rich and selfish and self-centered. Kinda like you."

Avery turned to her. "What?"

She gripped his arm. "Oh my God, did I say that out loud?"

"Is that what you think of me?"

"No, no, I'm sorry. That's what I *thought* of you. Now I'm not sure."

The golden retriever pranced around the infield. It didn't take an expert to know that dog was a shoo-in to win the category. Ten minutes later the judges made it official.

Avery turned to Suni. "I appreciate you inviting me, but I have class in the morning. Do you mind if we make it an early night?"

The drive back to Plymouth was quiet. Suni played with the entertainment system. Avery kept his eyes fixed on the road, in particular on an SUV that rode up on his tail. He felt road rage rise inside him but thought better of it and switched lanes. The SUV sped past Avery and shot into the middle lane, narrowly missing a silver Acura, which swerved to avoid a collision. The driver of the Acura lost control, sliding across two lanes into a guardrail.

The SUV didn't stop. "Crap!" Avery yelled, shifting lanes and coming to a stop on the shoulder. He jumped out of the car and ran to the Acura. When Suni reached the wrecked car, Avery shouted, "Call 911." He wrenched open the dented driver's side door, where a dazed woman held her head.

"You OK?"

"I think so. That SUV . . . ," the driver mumbled.

"I know. What an asshole," he said, looking around to see if this patch of highway had surveillance cameras, but in the darkness, he didn't find any. "Do you want to get out?"

The driver put her hand on top of the door to pull herself up. Avery and Suni held her elbows, and she lifted herself out of the battered car. They leaned against the guardrail to wait for emergency vehicles. Avery gave his contact information to the police officer before they left the scene.

A little while later, they pulled up to Suni's apartment. "Well, thanks again," he said.

She leaned in and kissed him. "Avery, it doesn't matter what I think. You get to be whoever you want to be. I'll call you tomorrow."

Back home, Avery reported what he had learned. Garrett mulled over the information. "Not since her first day of college?" Avery thumbed through the notes on his device. "That's what she told me."

"That's interesting. So she didn't give any hint whether she was his heir?"

"I didn't push it. But based on how she said it, I doubt she expects a dime from him. I think she would have said something if so." As he spoke, Garrett's attitude shifted toward him. He ridiculed less, listened more.

"Who gets all the money? The mom?"

Avery paused. "She didn't talk much about her mom, just that her dad's rich, selfish, and self-centered."

"Jeez. That's gotta suck to hear. He must be a real tool."

"Yeah."

"Keep on it," Garrett instructed. "You're close to giving us something that we can use."

Avery hesitated. "Are you sure we don't have enough? She's a sweet girl, and it's getting harder to push her for information the more I get to know her."

"Don't be a wuss." The Garrett of old had returned. "You knew going into the deal. I can't ask Global to make a $75 million decision based on feelings. We need more."

"How am I supposed to get it?"

Garrett stuck his face right into the camera. "You and I are a lot alike. We do what we need to. You showed that with the Jeff situation. Every bit of intel I deliver gives me more power to bring you along. Avery, you're close."

Avery surrendered. "I'll do what I can."

That weekend Avery sat in the plush living room of Suni's home. The four-bedroom ranch was a mix of cultures. On the outside, the brick and aluminum siding screamed of America. Inside, Bangladeshi clay pottery and handicrafts adorned the room. Matching sofas made of white wood and blue upholstery faced each other. Avery and Suni sat on one side, Anika Yosar on the other.

Avery was on uncertain ground. Suni had insulted him, then they shared a first kiss. And now he sat in her living room meeting her mother. Avery hadn't expected this.

Neither had Suni, who whispered, "I'm sorry."

Anika stared at him without comment. A regal woman, she gave off the appearance of money, but from what Avery had learned, she had only what her ex-husband shared to support his daughter. Anika pieced together a comfortable life as a paralegal. She had high hopes for her daughter. They didn't appear to include Avery.

He couldn't agree more. Each day he spent with Suni left him guilt-ridden.

Anika focused her gaze on him. "Tell me about your parents."

He cleared his throat. "My mom's the CEO of a pharmaceutical company. My father is a corporate lawyer in Ann Arbor."

"And what do you do?"

"I'll graduate from Michigan State this winter."

"What are you studying?"

"Marketing." Was that a frown? Avery was sure Anika had just frowned.

"Maybe that's why Suni has never mentioned you."

Suni crossed her arms. "I never mentioned him because we've only been hanging out for a few weeks. Do I need to run all my friends by you?"

"You do as you wish. You always have." Anika sipped her tea.

Desperate, Avery stood. "I think I left my car running."

Suni sprang to her feet. "I'll go with you. I left my bag in your car."

In the hallway she grabbed his arm. "She wasn't supposed to be home. Do you want to leave?"

"I don't want to be rude. I'll stay a bit and then head out, OK?"

"My mom hasn't seen me with a guy since Derrick. The third-degree tonight will be brutal." She headed back to her mother.

As Avery passed through the foyer, a letter on the mantel caught his eye. When he moved close, he saw it was from Suni's father. He heard voices in the living room. Avery reached for the envelope. It had been opened. He tugged at the letter inside.

"Can I help you?" It was Suni's mother. Avery jumped.

He put the envelope down and returned to Suni, who spoke on her device. When she hung up, she announced the orchestra director needed to meet with her the next day. She used it as an excuse to call it a night.

Avery fled.

For a moment he considered messaging Garrett but couldn't stomach his brother's disapproval. He saw a sign for I-96 and lurched his car to the right. He remembered a party at Michigan State. In an hour he would be drunk and forget about what just happened.

———

As Jessica's vehicle pulled into Global's headquarters, her eyes caught a flash of light followed by a loud noise and shock wave.

"Stop!" she yelled. Jumping out, she sprinted to the plume of smoke rising over the northwest corner of the main Global building.

She fought through the crowd of onlookers to get to the corner of Drumm and Clay Streets. Shattered glass, pieces of concrete, and metal surrounded bodies, some lifeless, others writhing in pain. There was a gaping hole in the building.

Jessica pushed past the crowd. Blood splattered across the G on the Global sign affixed to the building. She heard the sirens of the oncoming emergency vehicles. She counted at least nine lifeless bodies strewn across the pavement. She didn't immediately recognize any of the dead or wounded as Global employees, but some were mangled beyond recognition.

"Establish a perimeter," she barked to her security team. For a moment, she felt woozy; she couldn't remember if she was back in Iraq, or if this was present day. In a blink, her security team had created a pathway for the paramedics, who were running toward them, shouting into radios and signaling to each other. Jessica fought to control her anger as she backed away from the crowd.

She alerted Armstrong: *Explosion at Drumm and Clay. A dozen or more victims. Extensive damage.*

"Come with me," she told a Global security guard. They reentered the building and made a right to the control room to review security footage. The FBI would soon arrive, and she wanted to know what they would find. On the tapes, a solitary man carrying a cardboard box loitered on the corner. When the street's stoplight turned green, he placed the box against the building and hustled across the street. Three minutes later a member of Global's security team arrived and kneeled to peer inside it. Just as he did, a massive flash of light blinded the cameras.

When the flash dissipated, Jessica could only see smoke. As it cleared, the footage showed the carnage of bodies, glass, and twisted metal she had just left.

The day flew by in a blur: more tape reviews, meetings with Armstrong's PR team and legal counsel, interviews with investigators. Employees had been sent home; a statement for the media was being prepped. Jessica popped some aspirin and chugged water. It was going to be a long day.

Midday, Armstrong's assistant rushed into the conference room Jessica and her team had turned into a war room. "Turn on CNBC!"

Anchor Britney Reynolds struggled to read a note put in front of her. "We will come back to the Global bombing in a moment. This is preliminary news, so we need to double-check it, but we have a report from our markets reporter that the Auction's proprietary software system has suffered a complete shutdown."

On-screen, Reynolds adjusted her glasses. "To repeat, and we don't yet have corroboration, we have a report that the computers the Auction uses to place bids are malfunctioning."

Jessica jabbed a finger at an underling. "Get a report from IT. Immediately."

She refocused her attention back to Reynolds's segment and ticked off what she knew about the Auction's data system. There were seven systems, each operated by one of the Big 7. If a system had an outage, it triggered an immediate handoff. Shutting down all seven networks at the same time was next to impossible. Supposedly.

With a start, Jessica realized: the Auction had been hacked.

Within minutes, Reynolds interrupted her software analyst with more breaking news. At the same time, Jessica's junior agent reappeared and handed her a compilation of headlines and rumors about what had happened.

"I'm Britney Reynolds, and I have additional breaking news to report," Reynolds said when the camera cut back to her. "Sources are confirming the Auction has been hacked by the D Movement. Again, the group of protesters who have been staging riots in cities across America have hacked into the system used by all of the Big 7 to complete the Auction process."

She fiddled with her glasses again. Jessica could hear her own heartbeat in her ears.

For a moment, she genuinely worried Armstrong was going to have a heart attack, right here in his offices.

"We're back with the breaking news," Reynolds said again. "And now we have a statement from the D Movement, taking credit for the breach. Let me read this to you now: 'The D Movement has inside, confirmed knowledge of the Big 7. We are monitoring their efforts and disabling these systems. We know your next moves. Without your systems, there is no Auction.'"

Before Jessica could even process the statement, Reynolds interrupted herself again; a new chyron appeared on-screen.

"The news keeps coming," Reynolds said. Her skin was pale. She touched the earpiece in her left ear and nodded briefly before refocusing her attention to the camera. "If you're just joining us, there was a fatal explosion at Global headquarters. The Auction's systems are down, and the D Movement has taken credit for the hack. Now, we're getting reports that protesters have rushed the police barricades at the intersection of Wall and Nassau Streets in New York City. There are unconfirmed reports of a resulting stampede."

On air, Reynolds swallowed. In the conference room at Global, Jessica held her breath.

"Folks, this is ugly," Reynolds remarked quietly.

———

"What happened to Peter Richards?" asked Vincente.

The woman staffing the nurses' station typed in the name. "He died last night."

Vincente sighed. "That's a shame. He was doing so well."

He flipped through the charts just as Lyra passed by. She had been extra nice since the amusement park miscommunication, and he yearned to confess his feelings. His heart leaped just seeing her.

"Do you have the new guy?" she asked.

"Yeah, why?"

"He's a piece of work. Prison lifer."

"Ugh." Vincente rolled his eyes. The last thing he wanted on a Friday.

As he entered room 226, Mickey Callahan shuffled back to his bed.

"Mr. Callahan, my name is Vincente, I'm here . . ."

"Boy, I haven't been Mr. Callahan since I got put away nineteen years ago."

Vincente ignored the comment and examined the patient's chart. The middle-aged man groaned as he lowered himself onto the bed. "Why am I here?"

Vincente faced him. "Fort Stewart offers new drugs to treat liver cancer."

Mickey waved him away. "Boy, I'm hollowed out. No doctor can fix me. Stop wasting my time and leave me alone."

Vincente put down the chart. "Did you serve in the military?"

"Can't say I did."

"Then can you stop calling me, an enlisted army man, 'boy'?"

Mickey eyed him. "What should I call you?"

He smiled grimly. "Vincente works fine."

"Vincente, let's not bullshit each other. Why am I here? I have four months to live, tops. Why should the army care about me?"

Vincente hesitated. "Honestly? I'm not sure. So many patients come through here. I'm not a doctor, but while you're here, I'll make sure you're comfortable, and maybe we can make you better. Deal?"

The prisoner-turned-patient nodded. "Call me Mickey. You Mexican?"

"Yes, why?"

"Mexicans ran Elkton. Can't say I ever met a Mexican who didn't try to slit my throat."

"How long were you there?"

"Eight years. Why, do you have a relative in there I should know about?"

"No. Just trying to figure out how long it takes to make someone a racist."

Mickey chuckled. "Everyone's a racist in prison. That's how you stay alive."

Vincente closed out the chart. "Here, you stay alive by listening to the doctors. And me."

"We'll see about that."

Vincente asked, "We've had other inmates here. What prisons have you been in?"

"Before Elkton, Terre Haute. And a brief stretch in Pierre."

"Better weather here."

The inmate scoffed. "When do I get to enjoy it?"

Vincente left without comment. Lyra wheeled a patient down the hallway. "So?"

He shrugged. "Just as advertised."

THIRTEEN

Jason's device beeped as he walked into the Sclavos arena. *Six.*

He deleted the message. The opponent tonight was the weakest team in the league and a ten-point underdog. Denton, however, didn't want to take any chances. Jason's team had to win by less than six points. That way a last-minute three-pointer wouldn't ruin the fix.

His coach waved him into his office. "I've seen this before."

Jason's stomach clenched. His coach continued. "A player makes an amazing shot, and it unlocks something. Gives him confidence. Your last three games are the best I've seen you play. Keep doing what you're doing."

The rhythms of the between-game entertainment shook the walls. Jason leaned back in his chair and closed his eyes. He had a plan: Instead of shooting, he would pass more. That way when they missed the shots, he wouldn't take the blame. If that didn't work, he would muff a few passes in the second half to keep the game close.

Now that he had a plan, he sprinted to the bathroom to vomit.

A teammate stood outside the stall. "Are you OK?"

He coughed. His stomach reeled. "Don't know if I can play. I'm sick."

"I'll go get Coach."

Jason slid down onto the bathroom floor. He could run away; that always solved things, right? But then he thought of Ayana. The e-76ers scout was in the crowd. If he bailed today, Denton would just make him try the next game. He vomited into the toilet again. Then he lifted himself off the floor, cleaned himself up, and headed into the arena.

A half hour later the queasiness returned when his team jumped out to a fourteen-point lead. He was giving up open shots and passing, but his teammates couldn't miss. His coach even yelled, "Way to be selfless, Jason."

During a time-out, he peered into the stands. Was one of Denton's associates at the game ready to inflict punishment? He pushed the thought from his mind.

The other team rallied, and by halftime they had closed the gap to ten points. His device was in the locker room, so he didn't see Denton's angry messages. The third quarter started the same; Jason's teammates were killing it. The lead jumped back to fourteen points. Jason grabbed a rebound and started down the court, only to botch a pass that led to an opponent's score.

The blowout bored the crowd, many of whom headed for the exits. His teammates stopped hitting shots, but the lead stood at twelve with just four minutes to play. His coach called a time-out. He walked over to Jason, and his stomach dropped. Was the coach onto him?

Instead, the coach put his hand on Jason's shoulder. "Well done. You showed a new side today. Mind if I swap you out and give Gary a little time?"

"Sure, Coach." He nodded and got up from his seat.

He buried his head in a towel. The clock ticked down. Gary was nervous and missed three straight shots. A scrub from the other team hit two quick three-pointers, then another at the buzzer to cut the gap to six. Jason looked up in disbelief.

As he walked to the locker room, the e-76ers scout complimented Jason on a well-rounded performance. Inside, he changed his shirt and picked up his device. There were thirteen messages from Denton, each angrier than the last, until the final one: *ur lucky AF.*

———

Sasha lowered the shades in her bedroom. A day free of obligations was a gift from heaven. And she knew how to honor such a gift. With a nap.

So when her device buzzed, she ignored it. The second time, too. The third time she muttered and checked. All were from Brianna.

Where are you?

You OK?

Who's William?

Sasha tried to make sense of her messages. She typed the best response she had. *Huh?*

William. Go on TMZ. Sasha's stomach seized.

The headline read, "Sasha Spends Anniversary of Mother's Tragic Death with Mystery Man." The images showed Sasha and William eating what appeared to be an intimate lunch for two. In one image, Sasha's left hand grasped William's wrist. Sasha recognized the restaurant—she and William and a large group of people from their last commission meeting had eaten there. She had grabbed William's wrist because she had just spilled her drink. TMZ had cropped out the others and waited until the anniversary of her mother's death to use it.

She sent messages back to Brianna.

I'm fine. You know William, I've mentioned him.

Oh, the cute professor?

Sasha ignored that last message.

She summoned the energy to get out of bed and examined herself in the mirror. Unshowered, unkempt. Yep, good enough for a coffee run. She navigated Mandana Boulevard, debating whether to tell William about the story. She decided against it. Too awkward. Making a left on Lakeshore, Sasha eased her car into a spot close to Starbucks.

Ten minutes later she walked out with a grande coconut milk latte, hold the foam, extra hot. And right into Freddy Tangier. He had tailed her from her house.

"This fling with your professor. How serious is it? Isn't that a little naughty?" he teased.

So much for goodwill. She avoided eye contact as she walked to her car, but as she slipped into the front seat, her coffee tipped and splattered onto the center console. Cursing, she struggled to wipe up the mess with her sleeve.

"Need help there? I might have a towel," offered Freddy.

She ignored him as she trudged back to Starbucks for napkins.

Freddy was waiting for her when she returned. "Sasha, do you remember Ginny Bolet? She just died of an overdose. Did you hear? Wasn't she your next-door neighbor?"

Sasha froze, napkins in hand. She and Ginny had been good friends back in middle school. But . . . Freddy had to be lying. Ginny wouldn't . . .

Freddy took her silence as a cue to move in for a conversation. He read wrong.

"Just fuck off, you asshole!" Sasha screamed.

"Bad day?" Freddy asked, all the while recording what was a rare feat: provoking Sasha to lose her cool.

Her seat cleaned, Sasha pushed the ignition button, and the Fiat Roadster came to life. Freddy put his face to the closed driver's side window. "Can't we be friends?"

Face burning, Sasha floored it. She could swear she heard Freddy laugh as she drove off.

She braced herself the next day as she left her town house. No Freddy. An accident on CA-24 East gave her plenty of time to think about what she would say to William. As she bounded up the stairs of Evans Hall, she noticed the disapproving looks. She shouldn't care whether people believed she'd had a fling with her professor. But still, it hurt.

Her device signaled an incoming call from Jason.

"The e-76ers want to meet with me."

For a moment she forgot her troubles. "Awesome! Are you still killing it?"

Jason talked about his last game but left out his point-shaving fiasco. If he told her about that, he would have to tell Sasha things he hoped to never share. "The e-76ers told me they'll decide by next month. And Denton's gone quiet."

"Denton's in jail."

"What? Where did you hear that?"

Sasha found a seat on a bench. "Brianna told me last night. A drug sting. Denton and another guy from high school she knows got arrested."

"Does it make me an awful person that I'm happy?"

"Not at all. He's a bad dude. I hope he rots in jail."

She put Denton out of her mind, even though she felt like a prisoner herself. She had enough to worry about: namely, the start of filming for her show.

Which was, to be clear, worse than she expected, as evidenced by her meeting with Summer Evers, the host who'd been hired for her show.

Summer Evers smiled sweetly, but her words were daggers. In their first official meeting together the next day, Summer harped on her own modest upbringing in a lower-class section of Baltimore, and Sasha lost count of how many times Summer claimed how "nice" it must have been for Sasha to grow up with so few worries.

The show's producer, Casey Madson, had a different approach. Her line of questioning barely touched on the Auction. Instead, she grilled Sasha on whether she had a boyfriend (no), if she went to clubs (rarely), when was her menstrual cycle (really?), and if she was into drugs (Sasha stared at her).

"C'mon, have fun with this!" Casey said playfully, mockingly. Then, narrowing her pointy face into something pouty, she added, "Why did you fight so hard to get this show?"

I didn't! Sasha almost screamed.

From there they moved on to wardrobe. A stylist proudly wheeled in racks of clothes she'd picked out for Sasha, but with every hanger—sequined shirts, minidresses, heels—it became more and more clear that no one on staff had even bothered to study Sasha—the person, not the idea—for a single second.

She fingered a cashmere sweater dress the stylist had held up, hope lighting up her face. Sasha forced a smile; she didn't want to get the poor girl fired. But the energy in the room was flat, and Sasha felt cut off, like she was watching it all from a distance.

Eventually they settled on some outfits Sasha could stomach, and even though they showed a bit more skin than she wanted, and were way more put together than she had ever managed to pull off, at least that item on the checklist could be crossed off.

"Coffee?" she asked hopefully when the clothes were gone. Casey snapped her fingers, and within minutes a carafe of black coffee was on the corner table of the conference room. Sasha felt her spirits rise.

"Let's talk about William," said Casey, glancing down at the open folder of show notes laid out in front of her.

Sasha, in the middle of a sip, choked, spilling hot coffee down her chin.

Casey didn't even notice, she was staring so hard at the papers. "William . . . what are we going to do with William . . . ?"

Tongue scalded, Sasha chugged some water and tried to catch her breath. Just as she was ready to speak, Casey beat her to it, scribbling in the margins.

"I know! We'll play up the professor angle, for sure. Make this a real Lolita-inspired plotline. He's handsome . . . and single." She glanced up for confirmation.

"No."

Casey applied her best fake smile. "We have time to sort that out."

Sasha eventually fled the PicaFlix offices and drove over to campus. She had to clean out her cubicle. She reached Evans Hall, and a middle-aged woman and teenage girl sitting on a bench rose to greet her. Sasha, not in the mood for fan attention, put her head down to walk past them.

"Ms. Cross, may we have a moment?"

Something in the woman's voice made Sasha stop. She didn't sound like the usual kind of fan—greedy, desperate. Instead there was something solemn to the pair. Something serious. "What is it?"

The sharp response unnerved the woman. "Is this a bad time?"

Sasha breathed. "Depends. What do you want?"

The older woman smiled gently. "I lead an organization that helps young women, mostly poor, who are victims of stalking and harassment. We heard the news about your incident."

Sasha headed toward the front door. "That's kind of you, but I don't need your help."

The woman shook her head. "You misunderstand. You don't need our help. But we'd like yours. Can we come in?"

Over the next twenty minutes, Tricia Carlisle outlined the mission of Safe-D, a group that worked with women seeking restraining orders and other legal protections against abusive ex-husbands, boyfriends, and stalkers.

The young woman, Christy, recounted how an ex-boyfriend hacked into her accounts, illegally filmed her in her home, and attempted to blackmail her with the video.

"Did you report him?"

"Yes, but it didn't do any good. He's a prominent lawyer and pals with the prosecutors. They took down my information, but nothing happened."

Tricia handed Sasha a printout. "If you're a Series D like Christy and you submit a report about someone in power, the police won't touch it."

Sasha shook her head. "When my mom had a stalker, an army of police arrived."

"If Christy was a Series A, police would have a patrol car parked outside her house," said Tricia.

It was true, and Sasha knew it. *Everyone* knew it. How was that fair? Sasha rubbed her temples, thinking. "How can I help? Would you like me to raise money?"

Tricia shook her head. "That's kind, but actually . . . I'm the founder of Safe-D. We need a new executive director. Someone who lives and breathes the mission, who understands what's at stake. Someone who, yes, can help raise money, but much more than that."

"I don't understand," Sasha said, looking back and forth between the two women. "Do you want me to, like, connect you to someone famous who fits the bill?"

"No, Ms. Cross," Tricia said. She raised her eyebrows hopefully. "We would like you to lead the organization. To become the executive director. To make a difference."

Inside her office, Sasha leaned back in her chair—hard, like she'd been hit by a truck. It was so silent she could hear her own breath, the birds talking in the trees outside the window. Beyond that, some shouts on the lawn below.

She almost laughed.

But Tricia's face. . . . She wasn't joking. She wanted Sasha to run Safe-D. She believed in her.

Sasha's fingers flew to her cheeks; she was flushing. Was she qualified? Her mind raced as she thought it through. Sasha's name would boost fundraising, garner media attention, educate people to the importance of the cause. She had a big network of old contacts who would probably be happy to throw money and time and attention their way.

Most of all, she herself had firsthand experience. And so did her mother.

It was the thought of Lacy that sealed the deal for Sasha. Doing this kind of work was exactly what her mother had longed to do—exactly what she'd want Sasha to do in her place.

Almost in a daze, Sasha nodded. She put out her hand. "I'll do it."

———

There was a lot to catch up on. But first, there was cake.

Sasha hadn't told anyone about her new job. She'd decided to save it for an in-person delivery. The opportunity arose two days later: Jason's birthday.

He seemed different, Sasha noticed right away. Settled. Peaceful. As he blew out the candles on the tres leches cake, his new boyfriend, Reji, livestreamed it on his device. The three of them, plus Ayana and Baker, sat at a table wedged into the corner of the small dining room separated from the kitchen by a sliding door.

Ayana passed slices of cake around the table. "Sasha, you don't remember this, but I was visiting when you came to Jason's fourteenth birthday party."

Sasha rolled her eyes. "Oh God, you were there?"

"Jason told us his girlfriend's name was Sasha Cross, and I remember thinking, not that child actress. She must be a stuck-up, hell-on-wheels prima donna. But this shy, tiny girl came into the house, and I thought, this can't be the same Sasha Cross."

Sasha laughed. "Then he dumped me the next week."

"You only had one Academy Award. I have standards," Jason teased. She flicked a piece of cake at him. "Where do you keep that thing, anyway?"

Sasha thought for a moment. "No idea. I haven't seen it since that night. My father must have it." She hated talking about her awards, so she turned her attention to Jason's boyfriend. Reji was smaller than the guys Jason usually dated—kinder, too. She grinned and wiggled her eyebrows. She, too, was feeling a new kind of peace inside, ever since she'd accepted Tricia's offer. "So how did you two meet?"

Reji and Jason cast sparkly, secret smiles at each other, the kind that made the single people in the room nearly faint with jealousy. "We sat next to each other on a flight from Los Angeles. We got to talking and realized we knew the same people in Philly. It went from there."

"Wait, the flight when you flew back after seeing us?" Sasha did the math. She whacked Jason's arm. "Why didn't you tell me?"

Jason gave her a look. "Just taking it slow. Anyway, I don't see Reji that often."

Reji put his hand on Jason's. "I'm on the road a lot. I handle the lighting for some musicians."

Baker finished his cake and patted his belly. "So now we have a ticket hookup."

"When's your next fight?" Sasha asked him.

Baker pointed at his knee. "I sprained it. I'm out of action for a month. And the way Ayana's feeding me I'll be too fat to fight when it heals."

Ayana handed him another piece of cake. "Nonsense."

Baker took one bite and set it down. "Sasha, are you excited for the show? When's the debut?"

"Six days. This is my last taste of normalcy. Filming starts when I get back. Unless you come out and force my father to cancel it?" she said pleadingly.

"My brother, Bobby, is still an LA cop. I could have him swing by," said Ayana. She bent over to fix Sasha's collar. "But why would you want to do that? You're Sasha Cross. You can do whatever you want."

She suppressed a groan. "What I want right now is another slice of that cake."

Later Sasha waited outside when Jason walked his boyfriend out to his car. As Reji's taillights faded into the distance, she stepped into the humidity of the Philadelphia summer night. He joined her on the porch swing.

"Why didn't you tell me about him?"

"I'm breaking up with him this week. He's a disaster. And I wasn't ready."

Sasha turned to him. "Then why are you still with him?"

"Who wants to break up around their birthday? I'll wait a few days."

She touched his shoulder. "You're a heartbreaker. First me, now Reji."

They sat in silence until Sasha broke it. "I have news."

He looked at her questioningly. She teased the words on her tongue; she knew once she spoke them out loud, there'd be no going back. "I found it, Jason. What I'm meant to do. After the show ends, I'm joining a nonprofit that helps women deal with stalkers."

Jason squeezed her hand. "Sounds perfect for you."

"Here's hoping. You're so close to your dreams, and I'm so far from mine."

"Speaking of dreams, the e-76ers asked me to come to their office next week."

She squealed. "Wow! It's happening!"

But Jason looked troubled. "I can't get my hopes too high. Every time I get close it slips away."

She squeezed his hand back and shook her head. "Not this time."

"It would bump up my Auction price, and Ayana needs that. She won't get any money for Baker, so I'm it."

The front door opened, and Ayana walked out. "Here are the pictures from Jason's fourteenth birthday party. Look how cute the two of you were!"

Sasha stared at the images of their younger selves. "I'd do anything to go back to that time."

"You miss your momma."

"I do."

Ayana put her arms around them. "And Jason misses his parents. It's a good thing you have each other."

"See this scar?" Mickey Callahan pointed to his belly. "That's where I got shivved my first week at Elkton."

Vincente examined the skin, faintly pink and mottled, but a bit too clean a line to look like an accident. "Really?"

Mickey pulled down his gown. "Nah. Gallbladder surgery. But I told newbies it was a shiv. That way no one messed with me. I got knifed in the stomach once, but with these flaps you can't see it." He inspected the loose skin that hung over his waistband. He had lost so much weight. Mickey had been a vain man once. He was well past that.

Vincente saw the pained look on Mickey's face and changed the subject. "Has the medicine made any difference?"

Mickey shook his head. "Not a bit."

Vincente watched as Mickey toyed with a metal object. "What's that?"

"My Saint Jerome medal."

He furrowed his brows. "Is that a Catholic thing?"

"You're straight off the boat from Mexico and you don't know your Catholicism?"

"Hate to break it to you, but Mexicans don't need a boat to get here," Vincente groaned. "And my mom left her religion in Guadalajara. What's so special about Saint Jerome?"

"The nuns gave me this on my eighth birthday. He's the patron saint of abandoned children." When Vincente raised his eyebrows, Mickey added, "I went into foster care six weeks after I was born. I've been lots of places, and the only thing that's been everywhere with me is this medal."

A coughing fit interrupted him. He put a handkerchief to his mouth. When he pulled it away, Vincente saw red spots.

"How long have you been coughing up blood?"

"Since I was in Elkton."

"I didn't see it on your chart."

"I told them when I got here."

Vincente punched in the code that pulled up Mickey's records. Only doctors were supposed to enter information, but all the nurses did it. He added notes to Mickey's file.

Mickey held up the medal. "In Terre Haute I had a real psycho bunkmate. He grabbed the medal one time and swallowed it."

"Shit! What did you do?"

"I beat him to a pulp, then waited next to the toilet every time he took a crap."

Vincente waved him off. "I didn't need to hear that."

The rest of the medical staff steered clear of room 226, but Vincente enjoyed Mickey's stories. He read the doctor's orders. "Tomorrow you'll get tests to check your kidney function."

"Why do they even bother?"

Vincente was used to the question. "It's standard for everyone." He tugged at Mickey's bed. "When did we last change your sheets?"

"I don't know. When was the last time you visited?"

"I was off yesterday, so Wednesday. Let's get you a fresh set."

Lyra walked by the room. "Hey, can you help me?" he asked.

A moment later she came in carrying sheets, and Vincente introduced her. "This is Lyra, the coolest person at Stewart."

Mickey eyed her. "Second to me."

"So this is the new best friend. I wondered who stole him from me," Lyra cooed as she pulled on the sheet after Vincente rolled Mickey to the side. Mickey grunted as he went from one side to the other.

"All done," Vincente said, then walked Lyra out of the room.

He came back smiling.

"You're sweet on her, huh?"

Vincente didn't answer right away. "She's the best thing here."

"Well, I've been in prison for nineteen years, so even seeing a woman is like a holiday. But take my word on this, be careful with that one."

FOURTEEN

"Shake their hands and look them in the eye," Ayana instructed.

"Yeah, you said that already." Jason tapped his fingers on the car window. A tractor trailer accident on I-76 East had traffic backed up, adding to his stress.

"Thirty years ago I took the same road to take Lennie to a job interview. He got that job and had it the rest of his life."

"You must miss him like crazy."

She nodded. "I do. But now I have you." Ayana patted his shoulder. "They wouldn't have called you in if it wasn't positive news."

"Maybe." He checked his device. The e-76ers had announced the signings of two players earlier in the week. If they wanted him, why didn't they do it at the same time?

The team's corporate offices were on the banks of the Delaware River in the Penn's Landing section of Philadelphia. Ayana pulled up to a gate where a security guard checked their names and waved them through. Ten minutes later they entered the e-76ers offices.

The receptionist area looked out over the river and the city of Camden. Framed pictures of e-76ers players hung on the walls. Even Jason had to admit that action shots of young men hunched over terminals didn't have the same excitement as a seven-footer soaring for a dunk.

"Jason?" A nondescript young man in a nice suit approached them. "Please follow me."

He took a last look back at Ayana, who offered a smile and a thumbs-up. When Jason entered the conference room, he nodded to the scout who attended many of his games. He shook hands with the e-76ers general manager, an older man named Scott Landry, and some other executives, the names of whom Jason forgot almost right away. His palms were sweaty; his mouth was dry.

"Thanks for coming in today, Jason," Landry said as he offered him a seat. "You've been on an impressive run, and what we like about it is that you did it knowing it was a key test. That tells us you can perform under pressure."

Jason waited, then realized Landry expected him to speak. "Thank you. Feel like I've hit my groove." He noticed he was fidgeting, so he shoved his hands into his pockets.

Landry nodded. "We want to talk to you today about joining the e-76ers."

Jason exhaled. He tried to keep his face neutral; he needed to keep his cool. "I'd like that."

Landry turned to the general counsel, who spelled out the terms of a standard e-NBA contract, and the head of communications, who explained what Jason would need to do to promote himself, the e-76ers, and the league.

Jason nodded through all of it. His palms had cooled; his stomach had settled. He couldn't wait to tell Ayana.

He was so excited he almost missed what Landry said next. "Before we can do this, however, we need to address a concern. Denton Long."

Jason would swear a boulder landed on his chest. He struggled to breathe.

"We get he was a high school friend." Landry peered at him, and Jason nodded. "But his history troubles us, as does your association with him."

The general counsel removed documents from a file on the table. "Los Angeles narcotics officers arrested Mr. Long weeks ago. Among the messages they recovered was one to you, with the word *six*. Did that message relate to drugs in any way?"

The room went blurry. Jason placed his hands on the table to steady himself. "No."

"What did it refer to?"

"I don't do drugs. I don't even drink. You can test me anytime," Jason stammered.

"Can we do it right now?"

Jason looked at the stone-faced general manager. He meant it. "Yes."

With that, the others stood, and Landry escorted Jason to a trainer's room in the facility. Jason rolled up his sleeve. The attendant rubbed alcohol on the crease of his left forearm, tapped it several times, then inserted a needle. Blood flowed into a vial.

Outside the trainer's room, Landry waited. He shook Jason's hand. "I hope this all works out, Jason. We'll be in touch."

The roller coaster Jason was on must've shown on his face, because as he entered Ayana's car, she grabbed his shoulders. "Tell me!"

He told her.

"Drugs?" Ayana fumed. "And it's all based on Denton?"

He nodded. He felt like he was underwater, swimming through a current to get some fresh air. He rolled down the window and gulped as she started the car and pulled out of the lot.

"So how did it end?"

He sighed. "They told me they'd be in touch."

Ayana signaled to make a right-hand turn onto the high-way. "So it will be OK. If you pass the test, they'll sign you."

"If?"

"Sorry, baby, I meant when. *When* you pass the test."

———

Vincente's moment of truth was at hand. He had arranged a movie night with Lyra. Tonight was it. In anticipation, he had ordered a fitted vintage black-and-white floral shirt that complemented his new blue weave dress pants.

He intended to tell her his feelings and hope for the best. But first, he had to finish his rounds. His last act was to swing by Mickey's room to deliver a slice of chocolate cake that he had smuggled out of the kitchen.

"There's my favorite Mexican," Mickey called out.

"You keep saying things like that out loud, everyone in the hospital wing will know you are a racist." He placed the cake on Mickey's tray.

"What? You are my favorite and you're Mexican. Why's that wrong?"

"Some words you shouldn't put together."

"Thanks for the cake. It's moist and creamy."

Vincente stifled a laugh. "Now you're just mocking me. You're in a good mood."

Mickey scraped the frosting off the plate. "That I am. I don't know if it's the drugs or I'm just losing my mind, but I feel better."

"That's why you can't give up hope."

"Are you going through with it?" Mickey asked.

Vincente took the plate and threw away the evidence. "Yes, sir. It's do or die tonight."

"I hope for your sake, it's do."

Mickey's assigned orderly entered the room, so Vincente got up to leave. "See ya, Mickey."

As Vincente left, he heard, "Good luck, my favorite Mexican!"

Captain Fisher, the head of nurses at Fort Stewart, intercepted him in the hallway. "Why were you in Mr. Callahan's room? You're not assigned to him today."

"I just swung by to say hello."

"And bring him cake?"

"I didn't think that would do any harm," he stammered. He could count the interactions he'd had with Captain Fisher, none of them good.

"Did you enter notes into Mr. Callahan's chart that he coughed up blood?"

"Yes, he did it in front of me, and I thought the doctor on duty would want to know."

"Then why didn't you inform the doctor, per protocol?" Captain Fisher asked.

"I just thought . . ."

Fisher interrupted him. "We need to run this floor efficiently. That means following protocol and not playing doctor. Making unnecessary stops in rooms of patients assigned to others isn't efficient. I'm concerned about your relationship with the prisoner."

"He seems harmless."

"Callahan is a felon convicted of a double murder."

Double murder? He'd never asked Mickey. He'd gotten only a few words out when Captain Fisher cut him off. "From this point forward, you only visit patients assigned to you. Clear?"

He replayed the conversation as he tidied up his apartment in anticipation of Lyra's arrival. Later, his device beeped as he stepped out of the shower. A message from Lyra read, *Hey, sorry, but can I get a rain check?*

He cursed under his breath. *Sure. Everything all right?*

I just have stuff to do.

Vincente paced, debated, and finally summoned the courage to act. *I actually really wanted to talk to you tonight . . . about us. Any chance I can stop by?*

Minutes went by without an answer. He resisted the urge to race the three blocks to Lyra's apartment. His resistance crumbled, and he headed toward the door. His device beeped.

I care a lot about you. Having a friend like you is the only way to stay sane here. But getting involved wouldn't be the right thing. Sorry. Friends?

Vincente didn't respond. He couldn't. His device lay in pieces on the floor across the room. He went over to examine the consequences of his fit of fury, then sat on the bed. He regretted lashing out because now he second-guessed the message. Did it mean she didn't like him in that way? Or was it too soon after her breakup? His stomach churned.

He worried all night about their interaction—about whether he'd been too pushy, or maybe not clear enough. But he never got a chance to find out. When he ran into Lyra the next day, she acted friendly but avoided being alone with him. His suggestion for a movie night was met with excuses of being too busy.

Weeks went by. He missed Mickey. Since Captain Fisher's reprimand, Vincente hadn't been assigned to him. He moped in his apartment. Without Lyra, he couldn't fathom his next eleven months at Fort Stewart. An envelope containing his mother's death certificate lay on the coffee table, propped against a bowl that once contained ice cream but now showed signs of mold. His white sheets had a gray tint. And he smelled. Disgusted with himself, he headed to the shower. Once clean, he stripped his bed and stuffed the sheets into a bag.

August was typically Fort Stewart's rainiest month, but the brown lawns reflected the drought the base weathered. The barren landscape also symbolized Vincente's life. Two months ago he would have spent the night teaching Lyra how to make homemade pizza. She'd flick flour at his face, and they would've had a full-fledged food fight. They would laugh until they cried cleaning up the mess, then devour their creation.

Why is it we never recognize the sweet moments in our life? he wondered.

Vincente, laundry basket in tow, cut across the quad that connected the three apartment complexes used for medical personnel. A nurse specialist approached.

She stopped. "Big night, huh?"

He held up the basket. "Oh, yeah. You?"

"Studying. I'm enrolling in nursing school in the fall."

"Wow. So you're getting out?"

"Heading home to New Jersey." She hesitated. "You always seemed like a decent guy. I wish I'd gotten to know you. I could tell you were sweet on Lyra. Sorry that didn't work out."

He blushed. "We'll see what happens."

"I guess," she replied. "But now that she's hanging out with Malik . . ."

He felt blood drain from his face. She took the silence as her signal to leave.

Vincente's mind raced as she walked away. Malik, the man he met the day of the amusement park? He felt anger, embarrassment, and resentment stirring at the same time. Vincente detoured toward Lyra's apartment complex.

He felt foolish when he reached the courtyard across from her building. What was the plan? Stand outside? As he contemplated his choices, fate intervened. The door opened, and Lyra stepped out. Malik held the door for her. Vincente stopped, then took a seat on a bench. The light from the building illuminated them. He watched as Lyra checked her device, then wrapped her arm into his as they walked away.

Vincente picked up his laundry basket and followed from a distance.

Malik stopped to tie his shoe. Lyra put her hand on his back while he did. Vincente trailed them until he reached the laundry facility. He waited outside until, arm in arm, the couple faded from his view.

He stuffed his laundry into two machines while considering whether to resume his pursuit. Instead, he pulled out his device and messaged her.

Hey, wanted to see if you'd like to hang out.

Minutes later he received a response. *I'm tired, so making it an early night.*

Pulverized, he resorted to petty revenge. He messaged her four times, on random and innocuous topics, hoping to distract her and annoy Malik. She never responded.

———

William popped his head into Sasha's cubicle. "I heard about Safe-D. That sounds like a perfect fit. Congratulations."

She brightened. "Thank you."

William's face turned serious. "But I need you to do me a favor."

"Sure, what?"

"Stop leaking stories to TMZ." He grinned and left.

"I hate you!" she yelled.

Sasha had expected a fight when she informed her father about Safe-D. But Judah took it well, especially after he ran it by PicaFlix, which thought Sasha helping poor, battered Series D women would make for compelling footage. Producers added plans for an episode all about her work there, and Sasha breathed a sigh of relief.

She counted on that relief to carry her through the next conversation she had to have. It wasn't going to be pretty. She met Brianna at a coffee shop just off the Berkeley campus. She made sure to buy Brianna's latte and croissant, figuring a little buttering up—literally, in this case—could only help her.

But when she broke the bad news to Brianna, the croissant sat in the middle of the table, untouched. "So . . . I'm really sorry, Bri, but PicaFlix is going in a different direction with the show's storyline. They just told me you aren't scheduled to have any scenes with me. Like . . . at all."

Across the table, hurt flashed over Brianna's face, followed by a stoniness Sasha had never seen before. "Did you at least fight for me?"

Sasha nodded. "I did. The producers want to spend more time with others who are going through the same process."

"I'm in the Auction, too!" Brianna shot back.

"I told them that." Exasperated, Sasha tucked her hair behind her ears and leaned forward. "I swear, Bri, I tried. I'm not in charge here. This whole thing sucks."

"Does your dad know about this?" Brianna demanded. She slammed her coffee cup on the table, and it splashed over the edges, leaving a big, dark ring that slowly creeped toward the croissant plate. Sasha stared at it, willing it to grow bigger, so big she could dive into it and drown. That's how much she didn't want to be having this conversation with her best friend.

"Yeah," she said softly.

"He's OK with you cutting me out? How is that reality?"

Brianna's voice had grown loud enough for others in the café to notice the argument. Sasha lowered her head. "Please, Bri."

"Oh, am I being too loud again? Too *me*?" Brianna snapped. "Tell me. What does your dad think about this?"

Sasha didn't want to tell her friend that her father had decreed it. He'd told her last night: producers intended to rely on other local Series As, fly Jason out to LA, and film a weekend with Sasha in Philadelphia. "Brianna's not compelling," someone at PicaFlix had said, and her father had latched on to that idea.

There was no way Sasha would tell Brianna that part, though.

"You act like I control this," Sasha said lowly. "Like I *want* this."

"Oh, that's right." Brianna threw her hands in the air. "The reluctant star. The poor little rich girl."

Tears welled in Sasha's eyes. "That's not fair, Bri."

"*This* isn't fair," Brianna hissed. She crossed her arms and glared at Sasha. "This is the story of our friendship, Sash. You get everything, and I have to beg you for scraps."

Horrified, Sasha leaped back in her seat, as if Brianna had slapped her. It almost felt like it, actually—her skin tingled. It took her a moment to find her voice again. "I never ask for a thing from you except to be my friend. These days, all you do is bitch at me about what you're not. Start treating me like a friend and not your meal ticket."

The two stared at each other, tears in both their eyes. It was a stalemate, and Sasha had had enough of those.

She grabbed her purse and the croissant, and walked out.

————

Armstrong ran his fingers along the plush velvet seat in his private box overlooking the stage. The Andberg Opera and Performing Arts Center was his favorite place to pretend to enjoy culture, and he never tired of the looks of envy he received when he arrived and was escorted to the best seats in the house.

It was a long tradition for the executives of the Big 7 to enjoy the opening night of each opera season together. Lisa Andberg from Chestfin dominated the arts and culture scene— she had donated $2 billion to turn the performing arts center into a magnificent hall that rivaled opera houses in Milan and

London, which in turn had lured the world's biggest stars to Olympia, Washington.

The audience in the majestic opera house burst into applause as *Madame Butterfly's* Cio-Cio-San appeared onstage. But Armstrong's mind was elsewhere.

His fingers thrummed as his brain worked through the latest news, fixated on the threat posed by the D Movement rabble-rousers. Of all the years, why had they insisted on this one? Their timing couldn't be worse—the year he was pushing the United Nations to get on board. With every new protest, every fatality, they got more and more spooked.

An hour after Cio-Cio-San slit her throat to force Pinkerton to take their baby, it was Armstrong who faced the knives. He and the other guests of the private box mingled after the show in a small room at the restaurant next door. Servers held trays of champagne and passed around shrimp and sliders. Armstrong surreptitiously chugged two glasses; he needed to brace himself for the onslaught he knew was coming.

As soon as they were seated for dinner, it started.

"Victor, you've botched this," Andberg scolded, her brow furrowed. She was seated across from Armstrong, and her booming voice captured the attention of the whole table. "Your ego and your big mouth created the D Movement. What do you have to say for yourself?"

The Global CEO bristled, unaccustomed to criticism. "You can't be that naive," he retorted. "You think all this happened because of an interview? They bombed my headquarters and hacked the Auction!"

The lines between her eyes deepened. Armstrong sipped the vintage whiskey a waiter had just placed in front of him. He had the spotlight now, and he needed to use it wisely.

He continued. "That takes planning and expertise. All of us are under attack—not just Global. They're waging a war against us!"

"What should we do about it, Victor?" Johnson countered, leaning in to join the conversation.

Armstrong sipped his whiskey, stalling to gather his thoughts. "Every good movement needs a countermovement. Right now, we stand for nothing in the public's eyes. So we need to create a movement of our own that speaks to the same issues the D Movement is raising. And then we need to strategically discredit them. And, ultimately, provoke them. Then the public will see their true colors."

For a moment the room went silent while the leaders absorbed what Armstrong was saying. Then Andberg went back on the attack, her voice incredulous. "You want to physically attack the D Movement?"

"Are you blind to what they are demanding?" Armstrong shot back. "They want the end of the Auction as we know it. Who here is ready to give them that?"

The table sat in silence. Eventually, Johnson stepped into the void. "Obviously, we all have a vested interest in maintaining the Auction."

"A very expensive vested interest," Andberg muttered. "If our investors start getting spooked . . ."

"Listen, if Victor is right, and this is a coordinated attack by protesters, we have to buy ourselves some time to map out a real plan." Johnson met each executive's eyes, taking her time around the table.

One by one, they all nodded. Except Armstrong. "That's it? We just wait until we're attacked again?" He searched the faces around the table. For the first time since the Big 7's creation, Armstrong didn't feel in control. He waved his hands. "You're making a mistake."

Armstrong fumed on his trip back home that night, looking over the city lights from the small windows of his private jet. Later, drink in hand—his private stash of whiskey was more impressive than what the restaurant had served him—he sat in the den of his compound in Los Altos Hills. He had built it to specification when he moved from Manhattan. It overlooked Portola Valley to the west and Palo Alto to the north. While he kept an apartment in San Francisco, he treasured his time in Los Altos Hills. The small town was an exclusive enclave. Three other billionaires lived on his winding street.

From his desk he had a view of the vineyard in his backyard. Each fall he held a grape-picking party. Afterward, guests drank the fruits of their previous year's labor.

He nursed his whiskey, thinking through his options. He had survived all these years by knowing when to cut his losses and when to act. And for years he believed it wasn't only Global but the Big 7 who had the will to do what it takes. The last few weeks he'd come to realize he couldn't rely on them. The Auction was in jeopardy, and his fellow CEOs were in retreat.

The realization was startling, and yet, Armstrong knew it deep down in his gut.

One of his household staff members interrupted him with a knock. "Mr. Armstrong, your guest has arrived."

He stood as Jessica entered the room. "Where do we stand with the bombing investigation?"

Jessica exhaled. That was one of the things he liked about her—she didn't need the niceties most other people demanded from him. She liked to get right down to business, like him. "So far a lot of dead ends. All the surveillance cameras caught was one man. A block away he got on a bicycle and rode to a parking garage on Spear. We found the bike. No prints. And checked the license plates of all the cars that came and went. Nothing."

Armstrong seethed. "I want you to dig up dirt on the D Movement leaders."

Jessica nodded. "To really do that, we would have to pull information out of the Digital DNA Archive in Oregon. It's illegal. Is that what you want?"

Armstrong hesitated only for a second. "Do it."

"Do we tell the other companies?"

Armstrong took a long swig, draining his glass. He watched the moonlight glisten on the vines outside. "Don't worry about them."

———

Ajani Odia placed his palm on the pad and stared into the retinal scanner. While collecting that data, the BioSignals system analyzed Ajani's unique scent. The system granted him access to the Digital DNA Archive—the very archive Congress forbid the Big 7 from using against citizens.

Ajani entered the facility intent on breaking the rules. He nodded at his colleagues as he made his way to the tiny room that housed the command center's main console. Ajani punched in a series of codes, verifying them with the officer on duty. Most were daily updates. Ajani added a code that searched the database for individuals who fit the profile of a Series D, lived near San Francisco, and were likely to engage in violence or protests.

The system signaled it had finished its query, and Ajani sent the file containing the complete digital history of more than nine thousand Americans to his device. He made a silent wish to the universe that the woman who had contacted him to do this job—the same woman who was paying him handsomely to break the law—wasn't some kind of secret informer, that this level of risk was worth the potential jail time. Completing his task, Ajani nodded at the duty officer and returned to his office.

———

Avery sat with Suni on the porch overlooking the tennis court at his parents' estate in Plymouth. Maybe the town wasn't the obvious choice for a wealthy, successful lawyer to reside, but it had family history. Avery's grandfather had built the estate eighty years ago, and Avery's parents split their time between the Plymouth house and a summer home thirty miles away in Grosse Pointe Shores on Lake Saint Clair.

Suni studied him. Abruptly, she said, "My mom is suspicious of you. Why were you snooping?"

He'd had time to create a lie. It wasn't very good, but it was the best he had. "I'm sorry. I saw this random letter and—I don't know, I had hoped it was from the Philharmonic about a permanent position for you. I picked it up and then realized it wasn't, and I was putting it back when your mother walked in."

Suni deliberated. "It's odd you would think that. I got offered a permanent spot."

He wrapped his arms around her. "That's so amazing. What does that mean?"

"It means I have a job, idiot."

"I know that. But does it pay well? Does it mean more travel?"

"It pays like crap, it's long hours, and no travel. But it's what I love, and it's the first step toward reaching my dream job."

"Which is?"

"I told you already. Since middle school my dream has been to play for the New York Philharmonic. But they're so selective, they only hire Series As."

"So, in baseball terms, what is the Michigan Philharmonic—like Double-A ball?"

She frowned. "I don't know what that means." Suni pulled a letter out of her pocket. "This is the letter you found on the mantel. It's from my father. He married two months ago and is moving back to Bangladesh." Suni handed it to him. "Read it."

When he finished the letter, he looked up to see tears streaming down Suni's face.

"That sucks."

"I don't know what I did, why he changed so much." She wiped her eyes. "When I was a kid, my friends loved coming over to the house. I was so lucky to have such a great dad. Then he just changed. And now I don't know if I'll ever see him again."

Avery put the letter back in the envelope. "You didn't do this. He did. You can't blame yourself because your dad's an asshole. If so, I'd be in nonstop therapy."

Suni put her hand on his chest. "At least I can tell my mom to trust you."

FIFTEEN

Sasha propped her feet up on her coffee table and stared at Jason's holographic image. "Do you remember Patty from school?"

"Patty Hatty? The one who always wore that ugly green hat?"

"The very one. Have you heard of cyber marriages? She's in one."

"Is that where they never meet?"

Sasha nodded. "Yep, he lives in Tokyo. They met online."

"How do they handle the sex stuff?"

"They each have a sex suit." Sasha giggled. "They put it on and it mimics their movements."

Jason shook his head. "The world's a weird place. Speaking of weird, how's Brianna been with you?"

Sasha bristled. "She's pissed she won't be on the show that much. Like I control that!"

Jason hesitated. "I shouldn't say this, but she called me last week talking shit about how you didn't want her on the show and how you're undermining her big shot."

Sasha's device beeped with an incoming video call from her father. She ignored it. "She's delusional. Even though she'll barely be on, she's staying in LA until we complete filming."

Jason shrugged. "That girl has always known what she wants."

Ayana entered the picture. "Hi, Sasha. Jason, it's time. We have to go."

Sasha waved. "Knock 'em dead!"

Two hours later, Jason sat in the same e-76ers conference room as before, surrounded by the same people. He couldn't stop tapping his feet. His body was humming with nerves.

Landry slid a folder in front of him. "As I'm sure you figured out already, you passed the drug test. We expected nothing else, but we need to do our due diligence."

Jason wanted to leap up and cheer. But he simply nodded. "Sure."

"This is a big commitment. We need to know you'll be a hundred percent devoted to the success of the e-76ers."

Jason leaned forward. A big, authentic grin lit up his face. "Mr. Landry, I'm all in."

Landry pointed to the file. "It's a standard contract. Have your lawyer review it. You'll also see a detailed schedule for practices and games, and a code of conduct."

"Should I open it up now?"

"No need. There's just one thing left we need to discuss. The contract is contingent upon you breaking off communications with Denton Long. If you associate with him, we can't associate with you."

It was an easy decision. When he told Ayana down in the parking lot after shaking hands with countless people inside the offices, she beamed and dove into him, nearly tackling him with her huge hug. "You did it!"

They were nearly home when Jason mentioned the stipulation that he cut all contact with Denton. She waved it off. "He's in jail. Baby, you don't have to worry about him."

Jason felt a surge of pride. It was happening.

He texted Sasha. She replied with a million emojis and *I told you it would work out!*

Baker even flew home to celebrate. At dinner Ayana showed the boys Jason's estimated Series A Auction bid. It had doubled with the news.

The hard work of Team Harris was paying off.

After dinner, Jason packed a bag for a trip to Los Angeles. Team executives were enthusiastic when he told them about *Auction Diaries.*

The e-76ers season didn't begin for weeks, so the team gave him time off to film. The Sasha Cross connection was a marketing boon and boosted their plans for their newest player.

———

Butterflies. Sasha tried to remember the last time she felt this way as she entered the conference room of Safe-D's offices in Oakland. The organization's board of directors sat around the table, thrilled to have recruited someone of Sasha's notoriety.

To say the Safe-D's office was modest would be an understatement. The dingy conference room hadn't been upgraded in twenty years. No pictures hung on the walls, and the view out of the windows was of a dumpster behind the building.

None of it mattered to Sasha. She smiled as she sat down.

"I'm excited to be here," she gushed as she introduced herself to the board. They walked her through the work they did.

"Series Ds are three times more likely to be stalked, attacked, or exploited than other women their age. And they are dying at twice the rate of other young people," Tricia explained. "The reason is they have subpar health care and authorities don't take their concerns seriously."

"But how do the police know their Auction status?" Sasha asked.

Tricia showed stats on a screen. "The first thing the police do when they get a report is to check the victim's profile. If she's a Series D, she's a low priority."

They discussed the timing for bringing Sasha on board. She wouldn't start as director until the PicaFlix series ended. But there was a lot she could do in the meantime, including diving into the group's strategic plan, reading their board reports, and getting to know its employees. Tricia had big plans for doubling the organization's budget in a year, and Sasha promised to do her best. It was invigorating, being needed like this for something other than her mother's legacy; it felt like someone actually saw what Sasha could bring to the table.

With her father's decree in her mind, Sasha hesitantly pitched her idea. She explained what was happening with *Auction Diaries* and presented a plan for involving Safe-D in the show, which would raise their profile and hopefully drive donations. They loved the idea, and Sasha left with an understanding of the organization (shoestring), her salary as its leader (peanuts), and an exhilaration that she had found her calling.

She also left with a massive, almost overwhelming, sense of relief. Maybe, if *Auction Diaries* showcased her new role with Safe-D, she wouldn't hate the idea of the reality show so much. Or of the Auction itself. Because she'd be doing something important. Something in honor of her mother.

Still, Sasha had another problem on her plate: Brianna.

They hadn't spoken since Sasha had stormed out of the coffee shop, but somehow, Jason had managed to get them on a joint message that had forced them to make an attempt at reconciliation.

It had started with a lie.

Hey, Sasha, Jason had messaged. *Did you tell Brianna what you told me about the show?*

Sasha, sick to her stomach—what on earth was he trying to do?!—had responded with a series of question marks.

His reply was quick. *Remember, you told me you put your foot down with the execs and demanded your best friend be a part of it?*

Sasha had nearly thrown her phone across the room. What was she supposed to say?

Before she could answer, though, Brianna had chimed in. *Sash . . . did you really?*

And Sasha could practically hear Brianna's soft, forgiving voice through her device. It would be so easy to lie, and the lie would start to heal some of their wounds.

So . . . Sasha lied. *I did,* she wrote. *I didn't want to tell you until I knew for sure. I'm still waiting to hear.*

Then she called up her father.

She'd done a lot for him—including agreeing to be on this show. It was time he did something for her.

———

That was how Sasha ended up in the PicaFlix studios flanked by both of her best friends. Jason, high off his first-class flight and luxury suite at the Beverly Hills Plaza, thanks to the e-76ers, was thrilled his little trick had worked. Brianna was beaming. And Sasha was just happy things had returned to some kind of stasis.

Of course, Sasha's dad sort of ruined the vibe when he entered the room. With barely a look at Sasha herself, he gestured to Jason and Brianna.

"You two are Sasha's connections to her adolescence. So during filming this weekend, talk about your childhood together. Don't be shy to ask Sasha about memories of her mom."

Sasha stared in disbelief. "I'm sitting right here."

"Would you rather I tell them privately and surprise you?" her father retorted.

Honestly, she didn't know. So she closed her mouth and let him continue.

"Tomorrow night all of you are attending Kelsie's play," Casey, the producer, informed them, pulling up a hologram of a busy, color-coded calendar.

"That will show how the arts are important to all of us and highlight Sasha's support of her sister's career," Judah explained.

Sasha's eyes glazed over as they went through the schedule minute by minute. Did viewers know how unreal reality shows were? She briefly considered filming an exposé into the whole thing.

But her anxiety really hit its stride when Casey pulled up the official series trailer. It featured a seven-year-old Sasha sobbing over the dead body of her mother. It didn't matter that it was from the movie they made. The only downer was the ridicule Sasha received. The next day, TMZ called her a "tool of the Auction." The publicity just boosted her Auction value, so her father loved it.

When Judah rushed out, Casey held the three of them back with a few more words of wisdom as they prepared for filming. "Let's have fun this weekend. Don't be shy about getting sassy and bitchy with each other."

Brianna snorted. "That shouldn't be difficult."

Jason's device beeped. "Be right back. It's my agent."

Without Jason as a buffer, Sasha turned to her friend. "How long will you be mad at me? I got you on the show. I should be the one still mad at you."

Brianna wouldn't look at her. "Doesn't matter. Jason and I are just props."

Casey gave them a thumbs-up. "This is all so, so great. But save it for the cameras!"

———

Sasha and her entourage rolled into the Studio City theater. A security detail attached to Sasha opened her door, checked the perimeter, and walked alongside her into the theater as cameras filmed her arrival. It was a little much, Sasha had to admit, but she still bristled in defense when Brianna made a crack about Sasha's notoriety. Jason sighed and shook his head at the shitshow.

It was hard to concentrate on the reason they were all in the theater, with Judah running around, checking on the cameras positioned on each side of the stage, and even stopping to fluff Sasha's hair. She pushed him away as Brianna howled. "Shut up," she hissed.

Luckily, the lights dimmed, and the show began. Kelsie played Elphaba in this production of *Wicked*, and Sasha had to admit, she wasn't half-bad. She lost herself in the costumes, the music. For a second, she wondered . . . *What if I missed my calling? What if I'm meant to be an actress, too?*

Judah arranged a special announcement at intermission thanking Sasha and the cast of the *Auction Diaries* for attending. By the time the young man playing Fiyero opened the trapdoor to release Kelsie's Elphaba in the final scene, Judah had what he needed.

After the show, Sasha stepped backstage toting a bouquet of flowers. But Kelsie was hunched over in her dressing room, tears streaming down her green face. The space was so tiny, the cameras could barely fit.

"What is it, Kels?" Sasha said, alarmed. She tried to squeeze her sister's shoulders, but Kelsie flung herself away, as if Sasha were poison.

"Tonight was my night, Sasha!" Kelsie said in between tears. She glared at her big sister, and Sasha noticed genuine hurt flash in her eyes. "But instead, everyone was talking about you. Applauding for you. It's always all about *you*, Sasha!"

Speechless, Sasha stared at the shivering green creature in front of her. Behind her, she heard a whisper. "Shit, the producers are gonna love this!"

It was Brianna, and Sasha hated that she was right.

Later that night, after the cameras had left, Jason and Sasha lay on the couch in Sasha's town house. Sasha crawled up next to Jason. "I'm afraid. I feel like I'm losing who I am."

He pulled her in close. "When I was sitting in that hospital five years ago, heartbroken over my parents and my body broken, I prayed that I'd die. I couldn't imagine living. And it took a long time, but today I'm glad I'm here. Have faith it will get better for you. Just remember who you are. You're Sasha Cross. You can do anything you set your sights on."

The crew filmed Sasha, Jason, and Brianna at brunch the next morning. Sasha felt like she had a hangover, even though she hadn't drunk anything the night before. Judah arranged for a famous hip-hop star to "just happen to walk by" and join them. Sasha had thought it would make Brianna's day, but instead, Brianna acted as cold as her mimosa, and Sasha struggled to understand what the point of all this was. Didn't Brianna see that the worse she acted, the less screen time she'd get? Sasha wanted to scream. Everyone expected her to play the game, but none of them wanted to play it themselves. It was infuriating.

Judah had one last surprise. While the trio sat in Sasha's living room, a courier delivered certified letters for Sasha and Jason inviting them to attend the Auction in Brooklyn. Their reaction? Jason shouted in glee, Sasha cringed, and Brianna stormed out of the room.

By Monday, Jason had headed back to Philadelphia, Brianna only spoke to Sasha when the cameras were on, and trailers for the show made Sasha look like a stuck-up brat.

Judah couldn't have been happier with the progress.

———

Thanks, bro, got the invite! Avery messaged his brother.

Garrett messaged back, *What invite?*

To the Auction, wrote Avery, looking at the golden ticket he held in his hand. He regretted not having trusted his brother to come through. But his childhood had taught him to be wary, and he had watched as Garrett screwed over Jeff to get ahead. Still, he should have had more faith. Garrett had promised if Avery gathered enough information on prospective candidates, he would be a Series A. And the intel he delivered about Suni's father remarrying and not leaving her a dime of his money was pure gold.

The annual Auction was a weeklong event, but day one was its Super Bowl. On that day the Big 7 would bid on the elite—the fifteen thousand Series A candidates. CNBC owned the broadcast rights. A select group of the Series As would be asked to conduct on-air interviews. Series As would meet with the Big 7 company that had chosen them to map out their future. Within a week their parents would receive from the winning Big 7 bidder the first of the annual payments to fund their retirement. It would be a glorious week for everyone.

Avery stared at the acceptance letter. If he had known Garrett's reaction, he'd have thought differently about him. His older brother messaged his boss. *We never removed Avery from the list. He got an invitation. What should we do?*

Let him go. He can still be useful.

Suni waited on her porch when Avery pulled up in his car. "Did you get yours?" he asked. Suni held up an envelope. "We're going to New York!"

They held each other in a long embrace. He smiled at her. "To the New York Philharmonic!"

She smiled back. "To whatever the hell it is that you want!"

———

Vincente watched the medevac helicopter carrying Captain Fisher depart the base.

The accident was gruesome. It usually is when a transport vehicle going full speed plows into a pedestrian. He went back to his rounds. A fresh batch of patients had arrived two days ago, and he needed to get to know them. Turnover was high. Travis never received a kidney and died of sepsis after his dialysis catheter got infected. Only Mickey remained from the old-timers.

A thought entered Vincente's head. He walked past the nurses' station and down the hall toward Mickey's room. Since Captain Fisher's edict, he hadn't been assigned to his friend. They only shared small talk if he ran into Mickey in the hallway on his way to a test.

He peered in the room to find Mickey adjusting his covers.

"Hey, stranger!" Mickey beamed at his guest. "How's my favorite Mexican?"

"I see you're still as racist as ever," said Vincente, coming up to the bed. "I never asked you about your family."

"Not much to tell. I have a daughter I haven't seen in fifteen years."

"That's it?"

Mickey shrugged. "That's it."

Vincente started to speak, stopped, started again. "Mickey, I don't know how to . . ."

The convict raised his hand. "Stop. Two counts of manslaughter."

"How did you know that's what I was asking?"

"Because everyone stutters when they ask that."

"I shouldn't have been nosy."

"It's the part of my story I can't run away from. I killed two teenagers crossing the street late one night. Heroin had me out of my mind. I can't do anything to change it."

Vincente struggled with a response. "Well, that just sucks."

"Sure does, kid. That's why my daughter never visits. But it doesn't explain why you don't come by anymore. What gives?"

"I got yelled at for spending too much time with you."

"Well, that's just silly."

"I know. How are you feeling?"

"I don't know if it's the treatments or a last gasp of life, but I feel better. I got my appetite back, and I've been badgering the doctors to let me go home."

"That's great, Mickey." He called up the medical chart. "No tests this week?"

"Enough tests. They checked my kidneys twice. I'm ready to go. Can you tell them?"

"I'll do what I can."

Mickey snapped his finger. "Hey, what's going on with that girl of yours?"

Vincente closed the chart. "Lyra. She's not my girl. She's somebody else's girl."

"Oh, damn. I shouldn't have mentioned it."

"Doesn't matter. I'll be able to see you more. What can I sneak you from the kitchen?"

Mickey shook his head. "Nothing. Just visit me once in a while."

Vincente opened the door, then heard Mickey say, "Maybe a chocolate milkshake!"

SIXTEEN

Showtime.

Sasha fidgeted under the glare of the lights. It was Tuesday, the first day of in-studio live interviews for the *Auction Diaries*. Offstage, her father gave her two thumbs-up. She cleared her throat and tugged at her clothes. She wore a forest green, long-sleeve Lulus bodycon dress, stylish pumps, and designer glasses. Instead of her usual ponytail, stylists had pulled her hair back into a tight bun. She rebelled by wiping off makeup in the bathroom, only to have it reapplied in the minutes before the show went live.

She felt wholly foreign to herself.

Next to Sasha, Summer Evers gazed into the camera. A former beauty queen with striking jet-black hair, high cheekbones, and natural good looks, Summer rose to prominence at Fox Business Network before PicaFlix enticed her away. She had the ideal background: barely thirty years old, it wasn't long ago that she herself awaited her own Auction.

"And we're live in five, four, three . . ."

Summer welcomed viewers. "When does someone come of age? With the Auction, it's at twenty-two years old." Images from Sasha's past splashed across the screen as Summer hyped the show. "In the coming months we'll watch, up close and personal, as a remarkable young woman comes to an important milestone. Every twenty-two-year-old faces Auction Day, but few with the scrutiny and expectations of Sasha Cross."

A never-before-seen home video of a four-year-old Sasha playing in the pool with her mother lit up the screen. She fought back a lump in her throat, and fought back the urge to rip out her bun, fling off her pumps, and run away.

"We'll get an unprecedented look at Sasha's private trials as she prepares for a defining moment. And we'll hear her remembrances of her mother, the unforgettable Lacy Cross."

In case the audience needed reminding, a video montage of Lacy played on the screen, followed by footage from the funeral. Close-up shots of Hollywood's biggest stars mourning Lacy appeared, followed by a slow-motion shot of a stone-faced Sasha at the grave site.

Sasha couldn't look anymore. She concentrated on her feet, on her pearly pink toes peeking out of the openings of her heels. *Just breathe,* she told herself, though she was finding that increasingly harder to do.

"She has always been a special girl," her father gushed on-screen, predicting that his daughter would return to the Cross family business. "It's in all of our blood." Sasha's dismissal of that prediction made for good television.

Thursday's live program featured Sasha answering Summer's questions about her hopes and dreams to balance a business and philanthropic career. Summer leaned into her guest. "Sasha, I remember seeing you at your mother's funeral. You were so poised for a young woman dealing with such a tragedy. What do you think your mom would think of you now?"

Sasha shifted in her seat, and to the audience she seemed to react to memories of her mother's death. Lacy Cross was the epitome of a star. Her first marriage to director Roberto Trevolini ended after a short and chaotic year. Judah Cross offered her a new direction in life. The marriage had troubles, but it lasted. Lacy died three days after their nineteenth anniversary.

The coroner deemed her death an accidental overdose. Sasha had always wondered, though, if there was more to the story. She knew that Lacy, despite her public image, was unhappy. She relied on painkillers to deal with a back injury suffered when Roberto flipped their SUV in St. Barts. And once she walked away from Hollywood, her marriage suffered. Judah didn't support her philanthropic work. Lacy isolated herself as she grappled with the choices she had made.

A college sophomore, Sasha had intended to use her winter break to spend more time with her mother, to really check in with her. She never got to. Her father and Kelsie were traveling in Asia, leaving Sasha to deal with the immediate details of her mother's death.

Now, just a few years later, it was fodder for entertainment.

Couldn't people see how grotesque this all was? Sasha wondered. She stared out into the live studio audience, their shadows and lights, and thought: *You're all responsible for her death.*

And then, even worse: *We're all responsible.*

"What would my mom think?" repeated Sasha. "She would ask why I'm doing this show, since I never expressed an interest in the entertainment industry."

Her eyes flared, a message to her father. Inside, something was growing. A tidal wave. She let it build. She couldn't stop it.

Summer nodded. "People are pointing to you as a symbol of what is wrong with your generation—a rich girl who has it all and an Auction that allows the privileged such as you to get more. Why is the Auction a positive thing?"

Sasha stared directly at the camera. "Who said I believe the Auction is positive?"

Summer faltered. Through their respective earbuds, the control room directed Summer to pivot. Immediately.

The next morning Sasha sat with her father in a satellite studio in Redwood as executives discussed the debut. Over a video conference call, Marcus Matthews, the PicaFlix head of programming, walked through the numbers. "We got the overnights, and we pulled a 4.2 for Tuesday and a 4.9 for Thursday," he reported. "That's good for eighth place this week."

PicaFlix executives were ecstatic, even if the reviews were harsh. "If Sasha Cross can convince viewers she's not an entitled princess who only cares about money and fame, she'll earn a Golden Globe this time for acting," a *Variety* columnist opined.

Marcus thanked the group, then turned to Sasha. "One final note. You can't diss the Auction. It's the only thing Global complained about."

Sasha fixed a stare at her father. "Global?"

Judah suddenly made himself very busy, shuffling papers and checking messages. He waved his hand at Sasha. "You know how it works. We shopped for financing to pay for the production costs, and Global made a generous offer."

"What does Global get out of it?"

"Standard stuff," he assured her. "A piece of the action, positive PR for the Auction, and you and I will do events and advertising. Don't worry, I won't ask you to do much."

She wished she had her contract in front of her. She'd signed it, but she hadn't really read it. Why had she needed to? Her father had assured her it was all normal stuff—no special clauses. "What do you mean, you and I?"

"Not this again, Sasha. What's good for the Auction is good for your show."

Sasha bit back a retort—it wasn't suitable for public viewing—and marched toward the door. On her way out, Casey held up her device. "What's this about?"

On the screen a headline blazed: "Reality Bites: Sasha Cross Pregnancy Scare!"

Sasha scrolled down to read about how seven months ago, according to a "close friend," she thought she was pregnant and would have to drop out of Berkeley. The story claimed the pregnancy led her to break up with her mystery boyfriend.

Sasha closed her eyes and inhaled slowly. The story was infuriating—because it was true. She had experienced a pregnancy scare but never reached a point where she had to consider ending it. By the time she visited her doctor, she wasn't pregnant. The doctor said she had an early miscarriage. And the so-called boyfriend? A dumb mistake with a classmate during finals week.

She handed the device back to Casey. "Don't ask." She stormed away.

Undeterred, Casey followed. "There's no shame in a pregnancy scare. We should address it on the show. It makes you relatable. Think of all the women you could help."

She pointed a finger at Casey. "I'll walk off if it comes up!"

Summer came to the rescue. "Casey, the girl's private life was violated. Give it a rest." She put an arm around Sasha. "I'm here if you need me."

"Thank you, Summer," she said, then headed to her dressing room.

Summer told Casey as they walked away, "We have a week to loosen her up."

———

In a small, nondescript room in the bowels of Global's San Francisco headquarters, Victor Armstrong stared at the large monitor on the wall as his security chief made last-minute adjustments. "Display results for Linda Patterson Cooper," she ordered.

As images appeared on the screen, Armstrong recognized the forty-something receptionist who worked in the main lobby of Global's office. "Her boyfriend bombed our building," said Jessica. Within seconds, a full profile of Joseph Randolph McKinley appeared. It displayed his digital footprint, known acquaintances, health information, and family history.

"Shit. Where is McKinley now?"

"Watch this. Give me the probable location of Joseph Randolph McKinley." The system analyzed McKinley's behavioral patterns and tendencies. Again, within seconds, the display showed an image of a vape shop near Oakland.

"Holy crap. How did you do that?"

"We applied our own artificial intelligence to the database. With this, we can predict what each of the targets in the database will do next." It was Global's crowning achievement.

Armstrong studied McKinley's profile. "You call this system the Global Ontogenetic Database?"

"Yes." Jessica turned to her boss. "Say hello to GOD."

The next day, Jessica focused on the drone hovering over the rundown vape shop in the Fitchburg section of Oakland. The light blue drone stood out against the dark, ominous clouds.

"Don't let it get too close," she warned.

"It's two hundred yards away, they can't see us," an underling responded as she subtly moved the joystick that controlled the drone. "You sure this is our guy?"

Jessica sat back. "The intel says he's the guy who left the cardboard box. But there's no way this dumbshit is the brains behind the operation."

"What do you want to do?"

Jessica picked up the handheld radio and barked orders. "It's a go."

She watched on a monitor as the team of three entered the shop. Each had a body camera so Jessica could watch the action. As they entered, a body camera showed cases of water stacked up against the wall. One of her operatives grabbed two bottles.

She watched as the team ignored the store clerk and veered right to the back of the store, trailed by a young, buff security guard. His buzz cut revealed a scar that traced from his left ear up to the top of his head.

Back outside, the sky opened up, and a heavy rain pelted the SUV, making it harder to hear the audio from inside the vape shop. Jessica turned up the volume.

The guard barked at the trio, "You can't go back here."

The team lead raised his hand. "Get out of the way."

The man puffed his chest and snarled, "Step back or there's gonna be trouble."

"You'll hit me if I go by you?"

"Damn straight, so step the fuck back!"

Her operative stared. "OK."

The response confused the guard. "OK, what?"

"Hit me."

"Boy, get the hell out of my face."

He repeated. "Do it."

Angry, the man struck a hard left jab that glanced off the operative's right cheek. Blood trickled from the cut.

"Again," he repeated. The guard frowned. He clocked him with a hard right. It sent Jessica's operative sprawling. But she watched as he recovered and stood closer.

"Again," he repeated.

He snarled, "This is fucked!" and turned. With a rapid flick of the wrist, another operative tased him. The guard dropped to the ground.

The operatives opened the door. A slight man behind a desk poured gunpowder into a PVC pipe. The man expected his bodyguard but discovered the strangers instead.

"You can't come in here!" That was as far as he got.

The team lead raised a water bottle and winged it at the man. *Crack!* Jessica heard the telltale sound of a nose breaking.

The operative opened up the second bottle of water. "Where's McKinley?"

"Go fuck yourself!"

It turned out Jessica's GOD was not omniscient. The Global bomber hadn't returned, prompting the operatives to resort to more direct methods. The lead used the heel of his right hand to jab the man's already broken nose. The man shrieked.

Another grabbed the PVC pipe and poured the gunpowder down the man's throat while the lead forced him to wash it down with water.

The man gurgled, "OK!" They stopped. The man caught his breath. "He's holed up in an apartment near the stadium."

The operative leaned in. "This is what will happen. Give me the name of every one of your customers. We're installing cameras in here. If you tip off anyone, I mean *anyone*, I'll pour the rest of this down your throat and light you up. Understand?" The wild-eyed man nodded.

"It's getting hard to control the drone with this wind," the operator warned.

Jessica ignored her and radioed the team. "Come get the equipment."

"Someone is approaching," the drone operator reported. She zeroed in on the subject. Through the rain, the screen revealed a murky face.

"That's McKinley." Jessica radioed the team, but it was too late. The lead operative and McKinley met at the door. McKinley clocked the operative in the head with a baton. As he tumbled to the ground, Jessica grabbed a knife and leaped out of the SUV.

McKinley watched her approach but the blinding rain hindered them both. Jessica caught him in the leg but couldn't evade his backswing that hit her flush on the mouth. As she crawled to the curb, McKinley came up behind her but the operative collided into him. McKinley stumbled on the curb and had no chance when a passing garbage truck clipped his side.

The operative helped Jessica to her feet.

They stood over McKinley's lifeless body. The garbage truck driver leaped out of his rig and gaped at the mangled body on the ground. Jessica radioed the team. "We need to leave."

Armstrong tapped his fingers on the desk after hearing Jessica's report.

"So, GOD worked?"

"For the most part, yes."

"The predictive part, you could do that with anyone we added to it?"

"Yes, but it only includes the Series Ds located around San Francisco."

The CEO stood and peered out the window at the Bay Bridge. "How hard would it be to add this year's Series A candidates?"

"All fifteen thousand?"

The CEO shrugged. "Think about the advantage that would give us."

"Each time we access the Digital DNA Archive we take a risk."

Armstrong smirked at her. "I know that. Do it."

Vincente sat on Mickey's hospital bed and pulled on the sheets. He couldn't believe he missed him. Fisher's replacement, Captain Starling, had made an offhand mention during the daily staff briefing that room 226 was vacant. Vincente rushed to the room.

The attendant at the nurses' station said he received a transfer to a facility closer to his home. At least he got his wish. As Vincente stripped the bed, he heard something fall to the floor. He leaned down and ran his hand along the cold ceramic tile. He grasped a piece of metal. He held Mickey's Saint Jerome medal in his hand. "Ah, no. He'll be pissed."

He walked to Captain Starling's office and knocked.

"Enter."

"Sir, sorry to bother you, but the patient in room 226, Mickey Callahan, left something behind that I know was important to him. Do we have an address? I can mail it."

"226? The convict. What is it?"

Vincente pulled it out of his pocket. "A Catholic medal. It has special significance to him."

The captain reached out his hand. "Give it to me. I'll make sure he gets it."

"Sir, I don't mind sending it."

"That's not procedure. If a patient leaves something behind, we need to catalogue it and then send it."

Vincente turned it over. "Can I get his address anyway? I'd like to check on him."

Starling shook his head. "You need to learn army procedure. Dismissed."

Leaving the captain, Vincente was so lost in his thoughts he tripped over the electrical equipment spread out in front of the entrance to the morgue. Workers had removed the facility's large metal swinging security doors. An electrician pulled out a circuit box and cut the wires.

"Sorry." He noticed the charred marks on the metal door. "What happened?"

"An electrical fire," the man replied without raising his head.

Vincente loitered, peering in hopes of a Malik sighting.

"Can I help you?" the electrician asked pointedly.

"No," Vincente said as he looked one last time, then left.

He'd walked barely twenty feet when Lyra approached. Vincente waited for her to look up at him, but she stared down at her device as they passed each other. He felt a burning in his chest. He stopped. Surely, she would peek back at him. But she didn't. Instead, she stepped over the electrical equipment and entered the morgue.

Vincente resisted the impulse. Nothing good would come from following her. And he didn't want to see Lyra and Malik together. He had things to do. He felt his chest rising. Anger. He retraced his steps back to the morgue. The electrician didn't look up when Vincente passed through the entrance. Once inside, he faced a dilemma. He didn't know which way Lyra had turned. He passed office doors marked Pathology and Surgical. He turned the corner and spotted a security guard. Pivoting, he hurried in the other direction.

Did he hear footsteps? He panicked and tried the door handle for the surgical office. It turned and he entered. Now what should he do? He took a moment to come up with an excuse for why he was in a restricted part of the base. Bright fluorescent lights cast a glow over the sterilized tools laid out on a tray in the center of the room. Plastic containers marked Kidney, Liver, Pancreas, and Lung were stacked against the wall.

Vincente heard footsteps pass in the corridor. Time to go. He waited a minute, then turned to leave. A corpse lay on the metal table in the center of the room.

He blinked.

It was . . . Mickey.

Confused, Vincente took tentative steps toward his friend. A plastic sheet covered most of his body. He grimaced. Mickey's eyes were missing.

Suddenly, he heard the door open. "What are you doing here?"

But Vincente couldn't tear his eyes away from Mickey's body. The guard's voice continued barking at him. "What are you doing in here? Let me see your ID."

Vincente stared at his friend. His head was spinning; his throat was blocked. He managed to choke out, "I got lost."

As the guard escorted him out of the room, Malik and Lyra came around the corner. Dazed, Vincente pointed at Lyra. "I was looking for her."

Fort Stewart security interrogated Vincente for two hours before releasing him.

As he left, he turned back to the security officer. "They told me Mickey got transferred, but his body is in the morgue."

"I have no information on that," said the officer.

When he returned to his apartment, Lyra was waiting outside his door, her eyes flashing, her arms crossed. "Malik received thirty days of barracks restriction. You happy now?"

Dazed, Vincente ignored her and tried to unlock his door. But Lyra wasn't finished.

"You're selfish, you know that? And you ruined my life!"

"What do you mean?"

"Malik wanted to show me where he worked. Nobody would have known if you didn't show up and then rat on me," she hissed.

He sighed. "Lyra, Mickey is in the morgue. He's dead."

Confusion blanketed her face. She shook her head. "No, he got transferred. Starling said so."

"I know what I saw." Vincente's key finally worked. He turned it and stepped inside. "They told us Mickey left. I gave

Starling the medal he left behind. He promised to ship it to him."

"It must have been someone else," Lyra insisted.

"No." He shook his head and looked mournfully at her—the girl he'd thought he loved, the girl he thought he'd have a future with. He barely recognized her now. "It was Mickey."

"Stop telling people it was Mickey. You sound crazy." She jabbed a finger in his chest. "And now I can't see Malik for thirty days. Thanks for nothing. Asshole."

His apartment was quiet once Lyra's sharp voice stopped echoing. Vincente lay down and closed his eyes. Somehow, this had to make sense. Mickey was in the morgue. He didn't have eyes. He said he was feeling better. The medal. He would never leave it behind. Something troubling stirred in his soul, and as it surfaced, it terrified him.

He reached for his device and messaged Jessica, *Something is wrong. Need to talk.*

In a far corner of Fort Stewart, a lone intelligence officer monitored a screen. When he read Vincente's text, he contacted his supervisor. "We have a text in queue. Recipient is a Jessica Garulli. Please advise."

The officer stared at a bank of monitors that displayed live footage from the apartments of Vincente, Malik, and Lyra. Having monitored Vincente for days, he'd grown bored with his pathetic life. Malik and Lyra had been added earlier that day. New meat.

If any left their apartments, a signal would alert him. A message came up on his screen.

Intercept message and delete.

———

Jason couldn't pick up Sasha's incoming video call. He stood at center court in McGuire Arena holding a basketball in one hand and a game controller in the other. The e-76ers season started in two weeks, and while it remained to be seen what contribution he would make on the virtual court, thanks to *Auction Diaries,* Jason was already a marketing success.

He experienced a style transformation, but unlike Sasha, it was his own doing. He sported a new, hipper hairstyle and designer shirts and jeans. His classic sneakers cost more than he'd ever paid in rent.

"Great work, Jason," the photographer said as he high-fived him. "We got what we need."

Jason put down the controller, then eyed the basketball hoop fifteen feet away. He straightened up, raised his arms, and launched the basketball. Air ball.

A voice behind him said, "Stick to gaming."

Jason turned around. "Baker! Cool, you made it."

"Any idea if you'll play?" his younger brother asked as a guard opened the gate to the arena employee parking lot. Jason clicked a button. The lights to a new BMW flashed, and its engine started. Baker walked around the car. "You bought this?"

Jason opened the driver-side door. "At a discount after I promised I'd drive Sasha around in it when she comes to Philly. Sweet, huh?"

Baker eased his way into the passenger seat. "I guess you got paid."

They parked in a strip mall and walked to a favorite spot for wings. After they were seated and placed an order, Jason's device beeped. "Give me a minute."

Sasha appeared on the screen. "Did you ever tell anyone about when I thought I was pregnant?"

"Slow down. No, why?"

"TMZ did a story. I can't figure out how it leaked."

"That sucks. Could it have been the doctor's office? With the show, the price for dirt on you is skyrocketing."

"I hadn't thought of that." Sasha paused to think. "How's it going with the team?"

"Couldn't be better. I just did a photoshoot. Look at us!"

"Yeah, look at us," Sasha responded, with none of the same enthusiasm.

Jason looked over at his brother feasting on a basket of wings. "Sasha, I want to talk. Just can't right now. Later?"

"Oh, sure. Sorry."

Jason sat back down at the table. "Did you know Ayana has a second mortgage?"

Baker bit into another wing. "She does?"

"I found a letter. She's behind on payments. When I mentioned it she got angry but admitted that Uncle Bobby has been paying bills. She agreed to meet with a financial adviser."

"What financial adviser?"

Jason pulled the skin off the wings, a habit that drove his brother crazy. "As a Series A, I get access to a money person. He said he would review Ayana's finances."

"You're getting all buttoned-up on me, bro."

"I'm just glad I have the money now to need an adviser. You'll see soon."

Baker grabbed the last of the wings. "Nope. I won't be a Series A. You're it."

The next night Ayana sat in her kitchen, looking like a scolded child. Jason was the one doing the scolding. He scattered her bank statements and bills across the dinner table. "How long has it been this way?"

She picked up her mortgage statement. "Five years."

"So when you took Baker and me in. You should have told us."

"Team Harris, remember?"

"I do. But now the team has a new finance director. I'm taking over the bills."

She reached for the papers. "You worked hard to get where you're at. You need to save your money. Spend it on someone, if you ever stop being so picky. This is my job."

He took her hand. "How many times have you come to my rescue? It's the least I can do. Ayana, it's my time now. You need to know Team Harris works for you, too."

From the other room, Baker bellowed. "Did she buy it? Can I come in now?"

"You're ganging up on me," Ayana grumbled.

Baker came into the room. "What time tomorrow?"

"The game's at eight."

"Are you nervous?"

Jason shrugged. "Don't know if I'll even play. Seems like they like me more for marketing than three-pointers."

Ayana gathered up her bills. "It's your first game. You have plenty of time for this later."

The next night Jason waited with his teammates in the bowels of McGuire Arena for his name to be called. His mind wandered back two months ago to the threat he had faced from Denton. Ayana was right; God has a plan.

Everything about the e-NBA was better: the crowds larger, the spread of food in the locker room gourmet, the gaming controls more sensitive to the touch. He heard his name called and raced out to the center of the arena, shook hands with teammates, and made his way to a monitor. His coach told him he would start. It took the first half for Jason to get over the jitters, but over time he settled down and scored eight points in a losing effort against the e-Celtics.

After the final horn sounded, he stood up and shook hands with the opposing team members and his teammates. In the locker room his coach launched into an angry tirade about how they played, but he didn't call out Jason specifically.

When Jason walked out of the clubhouse, Ayana and Baker were waiting. Ayana gave him a big hug. "Baby, you did it."

An ESPN producer interrupted the reunion. "Jason, can we grab you for five minutes for a quick interview?"

Jason looked over at the team's PR guy, who nodded approval.

Ayana and Baker stood by while Jason casually answered the producer's questions about how it felt to play in his first e-NBA game. He bounded over to his family. "How'd I do?"

Baker sized him up. "Fine, other than that booger hanging out of your nose."

"Oh, crap," Jason muttered as he wiped his face. "Really?"

Ayana smacked the back of Baker's head.

——

When Suni opened her front door, Avery stood on the welcome mat holding up a package. "Thai coconut chicken soup. I hope your mom likes it."

"Are you kidding? It's her favorite. Where did you find it?"

Avery handed her the bag. "A little place in Redford. I got there just before they closed."

Suni reached up to kiss him on the cheek. "Sit down. Let me check if my mom is awake. This flu is kicking her butt." She poked her head back in the room. "No opening envelopes!"

He walked over to the fireplace. Framed pictures of Suni covered the mantel. Her first day of school. Playing in a middle-school concert. High school graduation.

Suni came up behind him and put her hands around his waist. "My mom says thank you. Avery Langdon, you're a decent guy."

"No, I'm not." He felt an urge to confess. Instead, he picked up a picture. "Tell me about little Suni."

"She was daddy's little girl," she replied, taking the frame and putting it back on the mantel. "If you removed the frame, you'd see my dad is in the picture."

"Any word from him?"

"He left for Bangladesh last week. But in more positive news, the Philharmonic got excited I'm likely to be a Series A. They said I would be the first they ever had."

"That's cool."

They settled onto the couch. "How's the job search?"

"I have interviews, but I waited too long. The best jobs are taken. My brother says after the Auction he may get me something at Global."

"That's only two months away. It'll go quick. Global must pay well."

"It does. But it's a ruthless place. My brother screwed over his friend so he could get ahead. He says that's what it takes, but I don't know if I have the stomach for that."

"And Avery's heart grew three sizes that day," she said, draping her arm around him. "Do you remember when you said you wouldn't have sex with me?"

"Ha. Right after you said you wouldn't have sex with me."

She caressed his neck. "Are you firm on that position?"

"What would having sex mean?"

She touched his face. "It would mean we're having sex."

"Yeah. I got that. But, like, does that mean we're a thing?"

She bit his ear. "Do you want to be a thing?"

"I'd love to be a thing."

She kissed his cheek. "Good, let's be a thing."

Avery pointed to the stairs. "Your mom is up there."

Suni kissed him on the lips. "She's not going anywhere, and if she needs anything, she'll call me. If we're quiet . . ."

———

Jason's device beeped. He cursed. "Sasha, oh my God. So sorry I didn't get back to you. I had my first game last night."

"I know, I left you a message. I'm so excited for you."

"Thanks, it's been crazy. You OK?"

"Just a lot of crap, mostly because of the show. Have you been watching?"

"I'm sorry, they have me on a tight schedule. But I heard the ratings are strong."

No doubt about that. *Auction Diaries* was a hit. Stories about Sasha appeared on the websites for *Entertainment Weekly* and the *Wall Street Journal* in the same week.

EW asked if she was "The Face of Auction America?" Her story was the perfect recipe for American media: a mix of business news, entertainment, and celebrity. Matthew Marcus told Judah to add a Thanksgiving special. "This has legs!" he said. If only Sasha and William would hook up, he mused. During a production meeting. In front of Judah. Who stayed silent.

Business programs assessed the show's impact on her Auction value. "She had a bid target of twenty million before the show. That's likely doubled," said CNBC's Andrew Barby.

The producers had one dilemma: Sasha.

She wasn't playing along with Summer's questions. Asked what the best experience was about doing a show, she retorted, "Knowing it will all be over on November 15." Producers held daily conference calls on what to do about her.

Despite Sasha's open contempt for the show, or maybe because of it, the audience latched on to her. She was different from what they had expected of Lacy Cross's daughter.

Studio executives were already identifying a good-looking college senior, this time a young man, to build a new season in January. Sasha's show was about to become a series.

Sasha held her device close to her ear. "Jason, what's that noise, can you hear me? Where are you?"

"We're boarding our flight. I'll call you when I land." The line went dead.

She put down her device. "Sure you will."

SEVENTEEN

When Jessica didn't respond to his messages, Vincente showed up at Starling's office with a transfer request in his hand.

"Does this have to do with what happened in the morgue?" Starling asked. "Do you have a personal issue with Specialist Angelos? I want you to know if she makes a complaint against you, I'll put you up for a court-martial."

Vincente measured his words. "It's best for me to be elsewhere."

"I don't appreciate you requesting a transfer while you await disciplinary action, Specialist Arias. But given the circumstances, I'll consider it. Dismissed."

Two thousand miles away, Jessica shot down another Auction target proposed by her team. "Don't waste your time on Billy Edwards."

"Edwards is already worth more than hundreds of millions of dollars and has a new start-up. Why wouldn't we bid on him?" asked an analyst.

The cramped conference room was littered with scraps of paper and empty bottles.

"He's a bad bet. Move on."

An analyst eyed the rankings. "Why is Suni Yosar on the list?"

Another piped up. "She could inherit money from her father. But the finances are murky. He's shifted his accounts overseas. There's an escrow account that we can't access."

Global's weekly meetings sorted out which of the Series A candidates had the best chance for a big return. With the average bid of ten million for a Series A, a lot was at stake. Analysts poured through candidates' available financial records, school history, criminal records, and family history to glean clues, then reported their recommendations to Jessica.

Jessica's device chimed. She opened it up to find an ad for Chicago deep-dish pizza. She stood up. "Keep going," she ordered her team.

She took the elevator to the basement and nodded at security as they held open the door of the waiting SUV. The driver whisked the vehicle out of the garage, passed the demonstrators, and headed onto the Embarcadero, which separated San Francisco and its famous bay. She turned off her device.

As the SUV approached Pier 39, she instructed the driver to stop. She stepped out of the vehicle and walked briskly to a booth offering tickets to a ferry boat to Alcatraz. She tapped the shoulder of a middle-aged woman waiting in line.

"I'm sorry to bother you, but I'm supposed to meet my husband here and can't find him." She groaned as she held up her device. "And this broke at just the wrong time."

The woman eyed her. "Where are you from?"

"Chicago, you?"

"Omaha." She smiled at Jessica and handed her the device.

"Thank you," said Jessica, typing in a number.

Beech's Ursula Johnson answered. "Something is going down at Fort Stewart. Have you heard from Vincente lately?"

"Fort Stewart? And how do you know about my cousin?" she barked. The connection was dead. Jessica handed the device back to the woman and turned on her heels.

"You're welcome!" the woman yelled. So much for Chicago manners.

Back in the SUV, Jessica turned on her device and messaged Vincente: *Hey, checking in. How are you?*

No answer.

Two minutes later. *You OK?*

No answer.

As the SUV pulled up to the Global building, she punched another message into her device. *Whoever is getting these messages, put me through to Vincente or you're fucking dead.*

She nodded at security and barked, "Hold the elevator."

Garrett Langdon held the door for her. "Good to see you, Jessica."

By the fifth floor, she ruled out going to Armstrong.

"Jessica, not sure you know this initiative we have to get intel on Series As . . ."

She pushed the button to the seventh floor. The door opened.

She barked at Garrett, "Get out."

Without a word, the humiliated underling slunk out as the door closed.

Jessica took a moment. Breathing exercises slowed her heartbeat. She walked casually to her office. Fifteen minutes later, she summoned her assistant.

"Silas Parker is in trouble again, this time in LA. I have to deal with it."

"I'll tell the pilot."

"No need. I'll take commercial."

After a quick stop at her downtown apartment, her security pulled up to the departing passenger entrance at San Francisco

Airport. She navigated her way through the Monday morning travelers, passed through security, and found her gate.

Checking her device, she rolled her bag to the bathroom. She found an empty stall, removed her watch, took off her black sweater, unbuttoned her white blouse, and hung the clothes on a hook. Next off were her shoes and then her skirt. She waited in the stall in her bra and underwear. Five minutes later a woman entered the next stall.

"About time," Jessica whispered.

"Sorry." The woman, who shared Jessica's height, build, and hair color, slipped into the neighboring stall and, following Jessica's lead, removed her clothes.

"OK, let's do this." Jessica passed her clothes under the stall to the woman and took hers in return. Jessica pulled on a pair of ragged blue jeans, a T-shirt, and a blue Dallas Cowboys sweatshirt. Once done, she laced up her compatriot's Nikes and donned sunglasses.

The woman put on Jessica's clothes, then opened the door to the stall, when she heard, "Stop." She relocked the door.

"Your device," Jessica said. They swapped devices under the stalls.

The woman waited five minutes before leaving the bathroom. She rolled the carry-on to the gate where, as Jessica Garulli, she boarded United Flight 2114 to Los Angeles. When the woman landed two hours later, she used Jessica's device to message the Global team that she'd been called away and not to bother her for a few days.

The real Jessica boarded a United flight to Savannah. She pulled a gray, lead-lined sleeve out of her bag and slipped it on her left arm. The chip in Jessica's arm wouldn't transmit through the lead. Depending on the diligence of her team, it could be twenty-four hours before operatives who tracked the whereabouts of high-level Global executives noticed. She was counting on their delay.

When she landed in Savannah, she cut to the front of the line, and, ignoring the complaints, jumped in a taxi. "Fort Stewart," she told the operator.

———

The SFPD police sergeant leaned against the bulletproof glass in the lobby of the Market Street station. "If you fill out this form, we'll process it and visit your husband. We'll advise him that if he contacts you again, he'll get arrested," he instructed Rosa Cortez.

Sasha watched as the young woman stared blankly at the document. After a few moments, Sasha leaned in and, in perfect Spanish, explained to Rosa how to complete it. There were bruises on Rosa's wrist that Sasha surreptitiously eyed. Three weeks ago, her husband had kicked in the front door of Rosa's sister's house and dragged her by her hair to his car before peeling off. A week went by with no word from either of them. Fearing the worst, Rosa's sister contacted Safe-D, and together they tracked down Rosa and waited for her husband to leave late one night before breaking into the house. Inside, they found Rosa chained to a radiator.

She now stayed in a Safe-D community house until the group could find her an apartment. The *Auction Diaries* camera crew caught the shot of the grateful woman smiling up at Sasha and saying, "Gracias."

Tricia Carlisle stood off to the side. A producer sidled up to Sasha. "We need to finish up here. We're running behind." Sasha brushed him off.

Fifteen minutes later Sasha waved goodbye to Rosa. Once outside, an SUV pulled up to take her to the studio. "Wait! I forgot to give her my number," Sasha said. She hustled back into the station just as the sergeant escorted the woman out the door.

Sasha stopped in front of them. "What are you doing?"

The sergeant let go of Rosa's arm. "She got unruly and combative."

Sasha asked the woman in Spanish, "What happened?"

"I put down the wrong address," she said, wringing her hands. "I asked for another form. He told me they were out and I had to come back next week. When I asked why, he grabbed me."

Sasha glared at the sergeant. "She just asked for another form."

The sergeant pulled Sasha aside. "I don't have time to waste on this. We did your little filming. The cameras aren't on, so you don't have to act like you care. Now run along."

"Get your supervisor," Sasha snapped.

Tricia arrived. "Sasha, this won't help us. We'll find another way."

Sasha and Tricia escorted a distraught Rosa from the station.

"I can't believe that just happened."

"Having second thoughts?" Tricia asked.

Sasha shook her head and handed her card to Rosa. "Call me tomorrow, and I'll arrange for my lawyer to represent you. You won't have to worry about these people again."

Sasha couldn't get the morning out of her mind. And when the producers pressed for a solo interview with William, where they planned to play up the romance angle, Sasha fumed.

She'd barely spoken to William since filming had begun, but the studio had been acting like they were practically married. The whole situation was mortifying—more painful than a root canal. PicaFlix invited the speculation, linking to a fan survey asking whether William was too old for Sasha, and if they were in her shoes, would they "hit it" or "quit it."

While makeup artists prepared William for the live show, Casey, the producer in charge of prepping him, popped in to ask what he thought of Sasha.

William kept a neutral face. "She's a bright young lady, and whatever she does, she'll go far."

"No, what do you think of her as a woman? Is the age difference causing a problem?"

William blanched. Sasha stood in the doorway, watching the scene unfold, wishing the floor would open up and swallow her whole.

She couldn't take it anymore. "Casey, you are confusing us with your next show, *Whore Island*."

When filming ended and William fled, Judah cornered her. "We need to make some decisions."

"What decisions?"

"Endorsement offers. We need to decide which ones to accept. Clothing lines, shoe lines, flavored water. And at least three movie and music festivals want you to make an appearance."

"Oh no." Sasha began shaking her head even before he finished listing all her options. "That's not part of the deal."

"We don't have to make a decision now," her father tried to soothe her. "But it'd be silly to not do it. It's practically free money. And you didn't seem to mind it when you did that Rogue Deluxe deal."

"That was for Brianna!"

"Well, do this for me." He waited a beat. "And Kelsie."

She groaned. Kelsie hadn't spoken to her since her opening night, despite several attempts on Sasha's part. "Fine. But don't do anything without telling me."

Sasha's father had more on his mind than just endorsement deals. Minutes later, he said goodbye to his daughter and bolted to the garage, where he flagged down William as he was getting into his car. "I need you for a minute," he panted.

William's eyes were practically in his hairline. "Me? What now?"

"Listen, talk to our girl here," Judah pleaded. He needed to connect to William, man to man; it was crucial he get on board. "She's not helping herself, and she's not helping you."

"How's that?"

"Listen, Sasha's my daughter. I love her to the moon and back, and all that. But let's be real." He paused, and smiled in what he hoped was a genuine way. "She's dour. If she's not careful, she's gonna drag down the show. This is a big opportunity for you—lots of investors watching who could give you another chance." Judah let that hang there. "You have to explain that to Sasha, so she gets with the program."

"Why don't you do that?"

Judah laughed. "No one wants to hear from their dad! William, she likes you. I can see that, and you can make this work. If you can get her straightened out, PicaFlix will pay you."

He could see the war playing out on William's face; he could see there was a lot he probably wanted to say to him.

But Judah held all the power here, and William knew it.

"I'll see what I can do."

When Sasha's device rang that night, she froze at the sight of William's name.

But then she ran to answer it, nearly tripping over the leg of her couch and tumbling into the coffee table. "Hello? William?"

A pause, and then William's familiar voice. "Hi, Sasha."

From his tone, Sasha felt a flood of anxiety pool in her stomach. "Oh, God. What is it? What happened?"

William sighed deeply while Sasha ran through the possibilities. Maybe William was hurt? Or . . . maybe he was quitting the show? Or . . .

"It's your father," William said, and with that, Sasha jolted from her seat on the couch. "He cornered me today and told me . . ."

William's voice trailed off, but Sasha sunk her head into her hands. She already knew what he was going to reveal. Maybe not the specifics, but the general gist. She knew her father better than anybody.

As William relayed the conversation, Sasha chewed on her manicured nails. The glam squad for the show scolded her for ruining their work, but she couldn't help it.

When he finished, Sasha said darkly, "I hate this."

"Then . . ." William hesitated. "Sasha, why did you agree to do it?"

She paused, debating whether to tell him the whole truth.

Then she realized: If she didn't tell William, who could she tell? What did she have to lose? So, haltingly at first, she told him everything—the money, the risk, the lies. "And the worst thing is, not only am I now the latest spoiled Hollywood tart, but I'm supposed to cheerlead this thing. And somehow it's on me to save my family from bankruptcy." She paused, feeling tears pool in her eyes. "William, I'm barely an adult. But I feel like the weight of the world is on my shoulders."

When William spoke, he did so gently. "It's OK, Sasha. Let's just get through November."

———

The knock at the door startled Vincente. He wasn't doing much in his apartment—just pacing, really—so when he peered through the peephole and saw the eyes of Captain Starling staring back at him, he froze.

He opened the door. "Captain? Sir?"

Without any niceties, he dove right into the reason for his visit. "I'm here to let you know your transfer has been approved."

Vincente felt the relief zing from his head to his toes. "Thank you, sir."

"Know this." Captain Starling zeroed in on Vincente, his expression relentlessly serious. "If I had my way, you'd spend your last miserable hours on this base. What you did and said to justify your actions is plain horseshit. I can hardly look at you. I want you off this base immediately. I don't want you disrupting the medical personnel tending to our patients."

Vincente gulped. "Yes, sir."

"You're lucky your cousin is high-ranking enough to sort this out for you. Understood?"

Vincente nodded.

"She's coming here to meet with you. I hate the fact that because of your recklessness, she's visiting the base under these circumstances. She's arriving in two hours. Pack what you can. The rest of your belongings will be transferred to Madigan Army Medical Center at Joint Base Lewis-McChord. I don't want to hear you whine about going all the way across the country. It's only because of Ms. Garulli that you don't face a court-martial."

"Yes, sir. Thank you, sir."

Starling look at him with disgust. "Come to my office in an hour to process your paperwork."

A wave of relief swept over Vincente, followed by panic. He had to ship his belongings. His heart hurt when he realized he didn't have to contact his mother. He messaged Lyra, but received no response. Things had turned sour, but he wanted to say a proper goodbye. A few minutes later the doorbell rang. He opened it to find a large container of packing boxes, tape, and Bubble Wrap. Fort Stewart wasted no time.

Looking around at what to pack first, he zeroed in on his closet and began folding his blazers and dress pants and putting them into a large cardboard box. Next, he emptied his sock and underwear drawer. He waited to pack army dress uniforms last.

Forty-five minutes later he had packed the bulk of his belongings. It depressed him how little he had to show for his life. But he was only twenty-five years old and JBLM would be a fresh start. He brightened when he realized the base wouldn't have the same restrictions. That meant restaurants and bars, weekend passes, and the prospect of a social life. He thought of Lyra. She was beautiful and funny and smart . . . but she'd led him on. Hadn't she? Didn't he deserve better?

Still, his heart ached. He checked his watch; he had a few minutes to spare, so he left the complex in search of her. The search was short-lived. When he attempted to swipe himself into the patient facility, the system denied him access.

He tried again, then realized they had cut him off. The army was rarely so efficient.

"I surrender," he muttered to himself, changing paths to head in the direction of the captain's office, where he would sign his papers.

Captain Starling, an MP, and a nurse he didn't recognize awaited him.

The captain took charge. "Your papers are ready, Arias."

Vincente sat down at the desk and peered at the monitor. He did a cursory look at the forms, then digitally signed his name. Captain Starling checked the screen, then gestured to the nurse. "JBLM personnel are required to get a vaccine for Rocky Mountain spotted fever."

He gestured to the door. "She'll administer the vaccine while I submit the transfer."

The nurse escorted him to a conference room. Vincente rolled up his sleeve, and the nurse slipped on latex gloves. She wiped his arm with rubbing alcohol and inserted the needle.

He barely felt a thing.

"You're all set."

Vincente hopped off the table, but the room spun. He gripped the ledge to steady himself.

The nurse eyed him. "You OK?"

Vincente struggled to focus. The edges of his vision blurred, then darkened. He heard a man's voice—Starling, he thought—but it sounded very far away. Someone pressed him into a chair. Then . . . nothing.

———

The taxi driver looked at the crisp twenty-dollar bills in Jessica's hand in amusement. "That's old-school."

"Keep the change." When she reached the Fort Stewart security gate, she told the guard, "Tell Captain Starling that Jessica Garulli is here and it's urgent."

"Yes, Ms. Garulli." The guard looked at the monitor, then picked up his device. He handed it to her. "This person wants to speak with you."

Jessica put the device to her ear, then a cold fury swept over her body when she realized who was on the other end of the line.

"Jessica, come back to San Francisco," said Victor Armstrong.

"It doesn't have to be this way, Victor."

"You made up the rules. We need to follow them."

"He's my fucking cousin!"

"And you had him assigned to Fort Stewart. This is on you." The line went dead.

Jessica approached the guard and gestured to the gate. "Let me in."

"I'm sorry, Ms. Garulli, I can't."

Her face contorted in rage, and she flung the device at the glass enclosure. It shattered into pieces.

Moaning, Jessica fell to her knees. It was like every emotion she'd ever kept inside had realized it couldn't be contained anymore—fear and regret and anger poured out of her, leaving her limbs loose and shaky.

Just as quickly as it came, it left. Or rather, she forced it back.

Breathing heavily, the tears back inside where they belonged, Jessica stood back up and looked at the petrified guard.

"Send out an SUV to take me to the airport."

While Jessica waited, she took out the device her airport compatriot gave her and dialed a number. "I want to order a deep-dish pizza."

EIGHTEEN

As instructed, Sasha held her gaze until the floor manager said, "That's a wrap."

She stood up from the pastel couch used for her intimate one-on-ones with Summer without so much as a glance at the host. Other than the live interviews, the two were not on speaking terms. It was hard to say who was angrier—Sasha, for having to deal with Summer's inane questions, or Summer, who felt Sasha was sabotaging her quest for stardom.

Ever since she'd found out about her father's request to William, Sasha counted down the days until the show's end. Literally—she had a reminder alert her on her device each morning. It was the only way she could think of to survive it all.

Offstage, she checked her messages while she settled into the chair. As Deja removed Sasha's makeup, she said, "I like the Cosmos ad."

Sasha frowned. "What ad are you talking about?"

"The Cosmos perfume ad. My boyfriend ordered it for my birthday."

Sasha racked her brain, brow furrowed. Deja was super nice, but Sasha was sure she was wrong. She'd never filmed an ad for a perfume. "Can you show it to me?"

Deja put down the bottle of Bioderma and scrolled her device for a few moments. "Here!" she cried, showing Sasha the screen.

She leaned in. Her stomach fell.

"The Sasha Cross Collection" was painted across the top of the ad above a heavily airbrushed image of Sasha—she barely recognized herself at all, which felt fitting—as a series of brightly colored bottles tumbled down the page. Perfume, body wash, lotion, something called "texturing essence" that Sasha couldn't even begin to guess the meaning of.

Evidently she was now a beauty mogul, even though Sasha herself barely did more than shampoo her hair and slap on sunscreen.

Sasha shook her head at her father's latest broken promise. "Thanks, Deja. Hope it smells good."

"Silly." Deja laughed, tucked away her device, and wiped off the last remains of Sasha's makeup. "You know what it smells like! You created it!"

Face fresh, Sasha slung her handbag over her shoulder and headed for the door. A producer handed her an itinerary for the nighttime activities, which were primarily centered around a concert. Her bodyguard waited in the lobby and then escorted her to a waiting SUV.

In the car, she received a message with the latest news about Rosa Cortez: Rosa's restraining order was filed, and the police said they visited her husband to warn him to stay away.

Well, at least that's done, she thought.

Sasha was enjoying the silence of the car ride, but all too soon, the driver pulled up to one of the biggest concert venues in Los Angeles. The door opened; flashes popped and photographers yelled. She kept her head ducked and followed the security guards who had been assigned to celebrity duty. They led her right to a private suite backstage.

Unfortunately, the suite was anything but private.

"Sasha!" Her father called. He waved and pointed to the man next to him. "Come say hello to Jackson."

Whoa. Jackson Bridge. Memories flooded back. He had starred as her best friend in the movie she'd made with her mother. He'd appeared in over twenty films since, building a solid career that recently reached a new level. Sasha had seen previews for an upcoming film in which Jackson played the love interest of Hollywood's current favorite starlet.

"Jackson!" she sputtered. To her surprise, she felt a flush form in her cheeks. "I'm shocked to see you here!"

He came in for a hug. "Too long, Sasha. Do you realize it's been fifteen years since we worked together? That was my first movie, too."

"And my last," she giggled, a little too much. Why was she giddy?

Judah put a hand on his daughter's shoulder. "I need a drink. You two catch up."

Sasha studied Jackson's face. She could find remnants of the little boy she had played dolls with in between takes, but only if she looked closely at the rugged, bearded man standing before her. He was . . . handsome, she decided. Solidly, inarguably handsome. "Congratulations on the movie. When does it open?"

"Next month. Can't be soon enough. I feel like a trained monkey trotted out to promote the thing. Hopefully, it's a hit. Are you hungry?"

As they walked over to the servers, a light show signaled Zia's entrance. Jackson snapped up sushi rolls, and they were led from their suite to center-row seats. Sasha noticed Brianna sitting a few rows back, but they avoided each other's eyes.

The *Auction Diaries* cameras were positioned to capture the excitement when Zia hit the stage. The singer was the hottest entertainer in the world, finishing up a two-year tour that grossed $2 billion. Zia performed nonstop for two hours. An impressive troupe of dancers, magicians, and acrobats worked in sync with the music.

Sasha turned to see Jackson staring at her. She smiled back and danced.

The music slowed and Zia took a seat onstage. "We have a special group of people here tonight," he told the audience. A spotlight flooded the center-row seats. "When I was a nobody, my first break was singing backup vocals for the soundtrack for her movie. Sasha, I bet you didn't know that. This next one is for you."

As Zia sang a ballad about love, the spotlight remained on Sasha. She tensed. Jackson took her hand, and he whispered into her ear, "It will be OK." After the show, Jackson helped her put on her coat. "Let's talk about how we make this work. Dinner next week?"

He'd already decided they would go out? She felt that heat rising up her face again. She hadn't dated in . . . well, a long time. "I'm up for dinner," she said.

"Great! I'll get your contact info from the producers."

"No need. Take it now."

He leaned down to kiss her cheek. "Glad this worked out."

The camera crew followed her to the elevators. Brianna sidled up. Her friend only spoke with her when the cameras were around; it was so obvious. But Sasha played nice. "Hey, Brianna. Enjoy the show?"

"Amazing!" Brianna offered a radiant smile. "You and Jackson, huh?"

"He's an old friend."

Sasha could tell the sarcasm in Brianna's voice. "They're the best kind."

———

In an operating room that just moments before bustled with activity, Vincente's body looked as though it had been picked apart by vultures.

Given the patient's fate, the Fort Bliss surgical units hadn't bothered with precision. With gory holes where his eyes once were, and his mouth agape, Vincente seemed a character from a horror film. Entrails hung over the side of his bloody abdomen, and his chest cavity remained open. It was up to the orderly to pry off the rib spreader and prepare the body for cremation.

The army MPs that trailed behind the gurney were, in a way, a sign of respect to Jessica's capabilities. Even though she'd been turned away at the gate, the base commander ordered additional security to ensure that Vincente's procedure went off without a hitch.

Over the next few weeks, Fort Stewart transitioned out personnel who had worked with Vincente. Before Malik's barracks restriction ended, the army transferred him to a base in Minnesota. Lyra was sent to a medical facility in Oregon. The army sent a notice to Vincente's distant family in Mexico about his tragic death due to a toxic gas leak. The army's heartfelt condolences never reached them.

Jessica shipped what was left of the body to Lukeville so Vincente could be buried next to his mother. No service was held, and Jessica and the man who operated the backhoe that dug the grave were the only ones present at his burial.

A day later, Jessica sat in Armstrong's office being reminded how charming and persuasive the CEO could be. He placed a drink on the table and sat next to her.

"This is a horrible tragedy," he nearly whispered. "And I understand if you want to leave the company. But I know you can get through this. Your future is unlimited. You could have my job someday. Let's get through the Auction and then talk."

———

"What's my brother's car doing here?" Avery asked as he pulled up to his parents' house.

Suni opened the passenger door. "Does he know about us?"

"Yeah, kinda."

Avery opened the hatch, and the two of them slid the futon out of the cargo space. Garrett opened the door as they carried it to the house. "Let me take that," he said to Suni.

Once inside, the older brother turned to her. "Hi, I'm Garrett. What's your name?"

"I'm Suni."

Garrett turned to his brother. "Suni, huh?"

She tapped Avery on the chest. "Liar. You said you told him about us."

Garrett laughed. "Oh, he did."

Over lunch Avery's mother updated the boys on the home remodeling. "The master suite is complete, but they are still working on the bathroom. The new theater will be finished by Thanksgiving." She reached out for Garrett's hand.

"Suni, you're a cellist, right?"

"With the Michigan Philharmonic." She smiled at Avery. "You did tell him."

"Avery's gone on and on about you. Does it pay well?"

"No."

"That's too bad. You must have family money to fall back on."

Avery watched Suni tense. He said, "They manage, and anyway, who says everything has to be about money?"

Garrett laughed out loud. "Says the guy who only went out with the Rangers owner's daughter so he could get a job, then got wasted, and blew it. But glad to see you're evolving." He said it in a way meant to mock both Avery and Suni.

"Whatever you say, Garrett. Anyway, we need to go. Thanks for lunch, Mom. Garrett, take care."

They drove in silence until Avery spoke. "Sorry. I told you Garrett can be a jerk."

"I don't have an older brother, so I don't know what that's like. But after meeting him, I see why you were the way you were. He's your role model."

"I'm more like him than you know."

She rested her hand on his. "Maybe you were, but you're not anymore."

When Avery came back home later that night, his brother's BMW remained in the driveway. He opened the door and slipped into the house. A light gleamed from the family room. Garrett watched MMA highlights.

"Hey."

Garrett took a swig from his beer. "Dude, what are you still doing with her?"

"She's cool. I have a nice time with her."

"I thought I taught you better."

"Mind your own business. She's very talented. Someday she'll play for the New York Philharmonic."

Garrett turned to him. "You got what you wanted. She is, at best, a six. Move on. But hey, if that's your taste. But never mention her when you're around Global. If they knew you turned sweet on the girl you spied on, they'd never trust you or me again."

Avery crawled into bed. He messaged Suni: *A buddy of mine is in a band. They're playing in Dearborn tomorrow night. Want to go?*

Just you and me?

No, my brother, too. He wants to spend time with you.

Her response took a while. *Seriously?*

Hell, no. He's an asshole. Just you and me. And pizza.

Avery couldn't help smiling as he turned out the light. Suni had sent back a single emoji of a heart.

———

Freddy Tangier waited outside Sasha's house when she left the next morning. "Jackson Bridge? You could do better."

"Not today, Freddy," she shot back. He didn't have a camera in his hand.

"I'm not here for that. I wanted to pass on information. Your friend Brianna did you dirty."

She opened her car door. "What?"

"That TMZ story about your pregnancy scare. I know the guy she leaked it to."

She held the door and stared searchingly at him. Her own voice felt hollow when she said, "That's bullshit."

"He works at TMZ. Brianna's brother knows him. That's how she got connected."

Sasha bit back a scream. "Are you sure?"

Freddy smirked. "Just thought you'd like to know."

He began sauntering off, down Sasha's driveway, but a thought occurred to her. "Why are you telling me?"

Freddy turned around. "We all do what we have to do, but I don't screw over my real friends. I don't think you do, either."

Sasha couldn't get Freddy's words out of her mind all day. Sometime around ten in the evening, she made up her mind.

At nine sharp the following morning, Sasha donned a plain black T-shirt and jeans and her most neutral, professional expression as she waited in the PicaFlix conference room. Her father sat to her left, a lawyer for the network to her right. Camera crews occupied the back corners.

Hours before, a studio publicist had alerted Brianna that her services were no longer needed on *Auction Diaries*. As Sasha knew she would, Brianna had immediately messaged Sasha, asking to talk.

"You sure you want to do it this way?" Judah asked.

"Yes." There *was* no other way. Not now.

The door opened and Brianna stormed into the room, then came to a halt at the sight of the camera crews and the lawyer. For the first time, Sasha decided to take control of the meeting. And the show.

She had no choice. She was out of options, and definitely out of fucks to give.

"Brianna, please sit down."

The girl she'd known for so many years, the one she thought had understood her better than anyone—except maybe Jason—fixed Sasha with furious, flashing eyes. She held up the letter. Sasha didn't have to read it to know what it said. "Did you know about this?"

"I ordered it."

Brianna's nostrils flared. "I'm counting on this money to pay back my student loans!"

Another sheet of armor fell down inside of Sasha, sealing her off even further from her old best friend. "Then it's a good thing that you have that TMZ check."

Brianna's face froze. Sasha, in that second, knew it was true.

"Wait, what . . . wh-what are you talking about?" Brianna stuttered, looking at the cameras. "Do we need these other people in here for this?"

"You're the one who wanted the spotlight." Sasha shrugged. "Now you have it."

"Sasha, you've got to believe me," Brianna pleaded. "I didn't call TMZ!"

"C'mon, Brianna, don't embarrass yourself," she said coldly. "We know."

"Know what?"

Judah spoke. "We contacted TMZ and offered to match what the reporter paid you. He gave you up quick."

The lawyer slid an affidavit across the table to Brianna.

Sasha leaned back in her chair, crossing her arms and glancing out the window. She could see the rooftops of nearby buildings, could see inside other offices. She wished she were anywhere but here. "You're off the show."

"Please, Sasha," Brianna began to beg, tears spilling down her cheeks. "I'm sorry. I was angry after you told me I wouldn't be on the show."

Sasha shook her head. "You were always selfish, but I could handle that because you were never sneaky about it. I never had a reason to distrust you."

Brianna picked up the affidavit. "I regretted it immediately."

"So much so you never confessed."

The lawyer pushed another document across the table. "You violated your contract. We could sue you. But for now, this document stipulates that you'll not make broadcast appearances, conduct any interviews, or post on social media until the show ends."

The room was quiet as Brianna processed the deal. When Sasha had had enough, she waved her hand at Brianna. "That's it. We're done here."

Brianna wiped her eyes, stood, and walked toward the door. She lingered before blurting out, "One million."

Sasha turned. "What?"

She sniffled. "That's how much they paid me."

"Bye, Brianna."

After she left, Sasha instructed the camera crews to leave, then pointed at her father. "None of this footage gets on the air."

"C'mon! It's the juiciest thing we've filmed!" Judah cried. "Ratings gold!"

"None of it," Sasha ordered. "My contract says I have final say on anything that gets aired about my friends."

"But why protect her now? She's not your friend. She screwed you over."

Sasha stood. "We humiliated her. No need to do that in front of the entire nation."

———

Glenn Hammond waited outside Victor Armstrong's office. Labeled the "Bad Boy of Marketing," Global lavished him with an eight-figure salary and millions of dollars in stock options because his brand of crazy attracted advertising dollars. Sure, he sometimes got out of control, but the Global CEO had a bottom-line attitude. And Hammond got results.

Until now. It was a horrendous mistake to go on Gabberbate in his condition. But Hammond loved appearing on the number one podcast in the country. And he was in Vegas for a Global sales meeting. He was confident on the day of the podcast.

Speaking to Global's best salespeople, he announced the company would be the sole broadcaster of the Olympics— online and broadcast. The celebration started early, and he almost missed the interview. He rolled into Gabberbate's studio half wasted, then joined in the podcast's tradition of shots to kick off the show.

The conversation was wild as always, and the host got around to critics of the Auction. "A bunch of losers," Hammond slurred. "The money in my pocket is worth more than their lives, dude. That's the world, man. Mother Teresa would be a Series D today, dude. What did she ever do that made money?"

The small audience in the studio roared. "The algorithm is all that matters." Hammond pointed at the audience. "Each of you is just a dollar figure. Go fuck yourself with your charity BS. All that matters now is what dollar value you have to Global." Later he told his hosts that "the only Ds I care about are in bras."

Hammond woke up with a headache and a hundred messages. Global had been forced to issue an apology while he slept.

Three hours later he landed in San Francisco. As he walked into the office, he received congratulations: his interview was Gabberbate's most viewed podcast.

From the massive windows overlooking the city, he could see the construction on the new Giants stadium. Hammond had engineered the deal that led to its building. "Global Field" would be just the latest jewel in the company's Tiffany box.

Armstrong wasted no time when Hammond walked into his office. "Glenn, you're fired."

He laughed. Then realized he wasn't joking. "Really?"

"Look outside," Armstrong pointed at the demonstration. "It doubled in size today thanks to you. I received a call from LeCartrion at the UN, for chrissakes! You picked a bad time to make an ass out of yourself. There's too much at stake. You're out."

Glenn jumped in, "Victor, I've heard you say the same things in this room."

The CEO nodded. "I'm smart enough to only say it here."

When news of Hammond's dismissal reached the mob, they overturned a police cruiser in celebration. The demonstrators tasted blood. They liked it.

NINETEEN

When the doorbell rang, Sasha was nearly done cooking dinner. She led Jackson into her kitchen, and he inhaled appreciatively. "Smells delicious."

"Thanks." Sasha stirred vegan sausage and peppers in a pan. "I'm glad you're OK staying in. It's a hassle to go to restaurants." She dropped the pasta into the tomato sauce.

"It's easier for us to talk this way." He looked around her kitchen and peered into her living room. "Nice place. How's the show going?"

Sasha scooped the pasta into large bowls, then added the sausage and peppers. "It wasn't in my plans, but let's just say my dad can be persuasive."

"Is it a one-and-done thing? You don't seem to love the Hollywood scene."

Sasha tried to be blasé about it, but she suspected Jackson could see right through her. "I'm doing this for family reasons. Kelsie can carry on the Cross name in Hollywood."

"So what's your plan? I mean, you're Sasha Cross, which means you can do just about anything you want."

"So I hear. I'm working with a group helping poor women deal with domestic violence. It's early but I'm excited about it. How about you?"

Jackson carried a basket of Italian bread to the table. "I'll ride out the movie thing for as long as they'll have me."

Sasha poured prosecco into two glasses. "I hope you don't mind vegan sausage."

"All good."

"Cheers!" They raised their glasses.

Jackson soaked up sauce with a piece of bread. "Did you ever regret getting out of the business?"

"If my mom had stayed in the industry, when I got older maybe I would have liked to work with her again. But once she left I had no interest."

"She was a cool lady. One time on the set, I toppled over a lighting fixture. The gaffer, do you remember him? A really tall guy? He screamed at me. Your mother reminded him I was just a kid and brought me over to craft services to get a cookie."

Sasha sipped her sparkling wine and smiled. "She was very protective."

He refilled their glasses. "So let's get down to business. How do you want to do this?"

"Do what?" She took another bite. She was proud of herself—she didn't cook often, but apparently she'd been inspired by Jackson, wanting to impress him. She was beginning to like this version of herself.

"Arrange schedules." Jackson rubbed his hands together and then studied his device. "I don't know what you like."

She chuckled. "What are you talking about?"

"This." Jackson looked up at her. "You know. Us. This. Our relationship."

"What relationship? I haven't seen you in fifteen years!" She laughed out loud now. Maybe Jackson was kookier than she'd realized.

"That's what I mean. If the press is going to write about us we need to look like an actual couple." He began ticking off his fingers. "Dinner dates, beach trips, social media posts. Just tell me what you like. It's all here in the memo the PR team sent."

Sasha was suddenly having trouble swallowing. She glanced at her dish. It looked disgusting. "Can you excuse me a second?"

Jackson waved her off in between bites of food as Sasha fled to her bedroom, where she frantically dialed her father.

"Date over already?" he joked when he answered.

"This Jackson Bridge thing," she demanded, feeling a wave of nausea curdle her stomach. "It's a publicity stunt to bring attention to the show?"

"Yeah, and his movie, which I hear isn't very good."

"You didn't tell me that, Dad!" She tucked her hair behind her ears and paced the room. Shame rose up her throat, tasting like bile. Like regret.

"I thought it was obvious," Judah chuckled. "Sort it out. There'll be photographers at your place tonight."

"Oh my God," Sasha breathed to herself when her father hung up. She wrung her hands, checked her reflection in the mirror. She willed the pink in her cheeks to go away, and fixed a blank expression on her face.

Jackson could never know that she thought this was real.

Sasha returned to the dining room. "Jackson, would you mind if we cut the night short? I'm not feeling great. Also, could you send me that memo?"

"No worries," he said. "I'll send it to you now. It will be easier for our publicists to figure out schedules. I'm glad to see you again, Sasha. I have fond memories."

When he stepped out, a handful of photographers scrambled to get in place. Jackson loitered at the door to give them time. He leaned in to kiss her on the lips, but Sasha turned. The shooters followed Jackson down the street to his Tesla.

"No comment," he told them, smiling.

Only Freddy waited outside her house the next morning when she walked to her car. She opened the door to her Roadster, then stopped. "Freddy, put down the camera."

"Why would I do that?"

"Please."

He lowered it. "What's up?"

Sasha walked over. "Were you here last night?"

"When Jackson Bridge left? Yep."

"Did you file your story?"

"Yeah, why?"

She pulled a copy of the memo Jackson sent her. "Here. Have fun with this."

———

The headline was everything Sasha had dreamed of.

"Exposed! Sasha and Jackson's Romance Is Actually a Showmance," blared TMZ. Sasha sipped her coffee, her stomach burning from stress, and waited for the blowback.

It was immediate, and expected. On set, a miffed Judah informed the crew that Jackson would no longer be a part of the show. Anger emanated from him—so much so that no one met his eyes, and no one asked any questions. Judah dismissed them but glared at Sasha. She knew that look. She hung back as the others left the room.

Judah grabbed his daughter's wrist. "No more stunts."

"Dad." Sasha's voice quivered. The burning in her stomach had turned into a fire. "I can't handle this. I feel unsafe."

"We've got security in place."

"It's not the security. I'm suffocating." She swallowed hard. "Why is all this crap my problem to solve? Why can't I make twenty-two-year-old decisions?"

"These are twenty-two-year-old decisions to make." Her dad smiled, and Sasha realized he probably used it on dozens of actresses. "Go with me on this," he said, stroking her shoulder. "And give Casey more to work with. She's dying."

"You aren't hearing me," she pleaded. "I want out!"

Judah pulled his hand away. "Out? We have contracts. Millions of dollars are at stake. We've taken care of the security issues. There is no 'out.'"

"Please, Dad, I—"

"No, Sasha. Suck it up." He brushed away her attempts at an embrace. "Your mom would be ashamed if she heard you complaining."

Sasha snapped. "But she's not here because she couldn't stand you!"

Judah stood. "Stop acting like a baby. And be flirty. Casey needs sex appeal."

———

Armstrong gazed at the tent city encamped in the plaza across from the Global headquarters. Since the Hammond debacle, the size of the mob had swelled, but that's not what had his attention. A gaggle of about two hundred counterprotesters gathered a half mile away.

He messaged Jessica, *Are those our people down there?*

No, she replied.

The police set up barricades to keep the groups separate. But they underestimated the size of the demonstration. Armstrong watched a frantic attempt to stop traffic at the intersection of Embarcadero and Mission. The D Movement made the police's efforts difficult. They shackled themselves to idling automobiles mired in the standstill.

Jessica reported that incidents had escalated since the morning. An officer was injured when someone catapulted a cinder block into a police line. Sporadic gunfire filled the air. With hundreds of arrests in the past week, police were concerned the confinement centers would fill.

As a precaution, police closed downtown to all but pedestrian traffic. Chants of "Down with Global!" cascaded between the steel-and-glass buildings.

Armstrong watched as skirmishes broke out as police confronted the D Movement mob. Jessica reported the group of counterprotesters were moving toward the barriers. Soon, the groups were within ten yards of each other, separated only by Mission Street. For a brief moment, the two mobs halted in what looked to be an uneasy standoff. Competing chants bounced off the buildings, creating a wall of sound.

Armstrong flinched when a Camry shackled to a street sign exploded, sending metal pieces into the crowd. With that explosion, the counterprotesters surged forward, pushing aside the metal barriers. For all the preparation, the police were surprised by the suddenness of the action and struggled to hold the line that separated the groups.

When a D Movement leader stepped forward to signal his supporters to halt, a counterprotester lunged and tackled him from behind. Others joined in beating the man. The counterprotesters cracked the man's skull open. An officer tried to intervene, but got knocked to the ground. Armstrong saw a pool of blood expanding around the victim, who convulsed before his body stilled. In the aftermath, the D Movement, some of them teenagers, fled. But in the sea of people, dozens were trampled. The officer who tried to assist the man fell to the ground as if shot. Armstrong watched another approach the wounded officer, point a gun, and fire.

He texted Jessica, *What the hell is happening?*

CNBC reported that fourteen people died in the riots. Both the police and Global were blamed for not having enough personnel on hand to avert the violence.

When Jessica made it to his office, he demanded answers. "Who the hell were those people? Are you sure they weren't your recruits?"

"I know they are not."

"How can you be so sure?"

"Because I never built the army you wanted."

Armstrong went to speak, then stopped. CNBC played in the background. As footage of riots streamed on the screen, Britney Reynolds reported, "In a setback for the Big 7, Korea announced it is suspending its plans to implement an Auction system."

Turning to Jessica, he gestured at the monitor. "You need to get this under control."

———

Avery peered out of the lobby window at a hideous sight: the University of Michigan football stadium. He refused to call it the "Big House." The last time he'd been in Ann Arbor, he'd talked his way out of an arrest after getting in a fight with a food vendor. Now he wore a suit and tie and sat in a lobby shared by three companies. One was a two-person law firm and another was a real estate agency. Neither had any need for Avery. But the third, Michigan Premier Marketing, responded after he messaged them about a posting.

He needed a job. At a pre-Auction meeting with Beech a week earlier, the analyst scoured his record, then asked, "Is this a joke?"

"What do you mean?"

"Your college record is pathetic, you have no skills that I can tell, and you don't even have a job. You'll be lucky to be a Series C," the woman responded.

"I'm pretty sure Global will pick me."

"Good for them. We won't."

The moment he got home, he searched jobs listings. The only response came from Michigan Premier Marketing. He heard his name called and was escorted to a cubicle where an overly friendly HR person asked him basic questions.

Having passed that test, the HR rep ushered him to the office of Ross David, the company's director of field marketing. The compact room had a circular table and two chairs in it. Posters of mountains and eagles with inspirational quotes covered the walls.

"Avery! Thanks for coming in. You seem like a go-getter." Ross wore khakis, a black button-down, and an ugly black-and-neon-blue-striped tie. "Love this résumé, Avery. We've had a lot of luck with State graduates. Tell me why you want to work here."

"I enjoy marketing and . . ."

"Me too! It's where the action is," said Ross, tapping his pen on the desk. "You know what? I have a feeling about you. Let's go meet my boss. Let me see if he's available."

Avery put up his hand. "Do you mind if I ask a few questions first?"

"My boss founded this branch." Ross pushed a button, and the receptionist answered. "Is he available?" He listened, then stood and motioned Avery to do the same. "He's got a brief window. Let's walk over."

Avery passed a series of desks where other candidates filled out forms on monitors. They reached a large corner office, where the occupant waved him in. "I'm Nate. Glad the timing worked. So State? Me too, six years ago. That's the great thing about this place. If you show initiative, you move up quickly."

Avery shook his hand. "That sounds great. This process is moving fast. I'd love to hear about what the company does."

"You bet. Offices in nearly two dozen cities now, growing every day. That means lots of room for advancement for hustlers. I started this office six years ago."

"How many people work here?"

"Ninety. And we need more. The best thing is that it's not a boring desk job. You get out of the office, meet people, and visit retail shops. The more you sell, the more you make."

"How does the pay work? That didn't get explained."

"Simple. We pay you a guaranteed amount. Your sales exceed your quota, you get paid more. Better yet, you recruit others to join your network, then you get a piece of what they sell." As he spoke, his device beeped. Nate winked. "Every time you hear that, someone made a sale. That means money in my pocket."

"What would I sell?"

"We have a lot of products and services. It's not just about the selling. It's recruiting to your network. You look like a guy who has a lot of friends. That's important. If you're ready, we can sign you up today."

It took Avery twenty more minutes to escape the offices, and only after he agreed to come back tomorrow. He looked across at the stadium. Suni messaged: *How did it go?*

He took a breath. *Ugh, it's a Ponzi scheme. Getting the hell out of here.*

Suni responded quickly, *Can you come over to the house?*

Something about her words felt off to Avery. *Sure. Everything OK?*

Let's talk when you get here was all she said.

His mind raced during the short drive to Plymouth. Had she figured it out? His stomach tightened when he pulled into her driveway. She met him at the door with puffy eyes.

"What's wrong?"

"My mom's tests came back."

"You mean for the flu?"

Suni's voice cracked. "It's not the flu. She's got pancreatic cancer."

"Oh, no. I'm so sorry." He wrapped his arms around her. She was shaking, and he squeezed harder. "I can't believe it."

Suni buried her head in his shoulder. "When she didn't get better, she went to a specialist. She needs to get more tests, but they told her it's likely stage four."

Suni's legs wobbled as he led her back into the house. He set her down on the couch. "How can I help?"

Suni rubbed her eyes. "I don't know yet. She's staying overnight to complete her tests. I'll pick her up tomorrow. She's worried about me. Her financials are complicated."

"Why is that?"

"She told me this morning that my dad gave her money as part of a settlement."

"Why would that complicate things? Seems normal for a divorce situation."

"It's not a normal amount of money, Avery!" Suni wailed.

He paused, looking at his girlfriend—his crying, heartbroken girlfriend—and hated himself for thinking, *Garrett is gonna be so proud of me.*

"How much?" he asked quietly.

She gulped. "Ninety-five million dollars."

The number hung in the air. It was a lot to process. "Wow," he eventually breathed.

Suni nodded. Her sobs had quieted. "It turns out, a few years after the divorce my mom found papers that showed he hid money and lied to the court. He could have faced criminal charges. They settled it. That's why my dad cut us off." Suni leaned into his lap. "I need to tell my dad. Can you help me?"

He caressed her hair. "Anything you need."

"I don't know what I'd do without you."

———

Jessica lifted the police tape that cordoned off the area where the fourteen people died during the previous day's demonstration. She nodded at police investigators and then walked into the Starbucks across from Global headquarters.

As she made her way up to a barista, she ordered an iced coffee and searched her pockets for her device in a way that was highly visible to the people around her. "Not again! I'm supposed to call my boss and ask what she wants."

The barista hesitated, then offered her own device. "Here."

"That's so nice of you," Jessica said with the best smile she could muster. She scooted to the side of the line, punched in a number, and waited.

Ursula Johnson answered, "Go ahead."

Jessica turned away from the barista and whispered, "Rosa Cortez. Today."

———

Ayana pulled her Jeep into the area marked Private Aviation. Jason grabbed his suitcase. "Thanks, Ayana. See you Monday."

"Have a great game, baby."

His teammates and coaches were inside the terminal, waiting for the charter. His coach tapped on his device and held it up to Jason. "Look who's the fifth-ranked rookie in the league."

The team boarded the flight heading west for games in San Francisco and Seattle. Jason searched the rookie rankings. He checked around, but the charter flight offered large, private seats, so his teammates couldn't see. The season had not gone as planned for the team, but Jason was a bright spot. Between his play and the publicity connected to Sasha's show, the e-76ers were on pace for their most profitable year.

After the game against the e-Warriors, he would meet up with the *Auction Diaries* cast for filming and carve out time to catch up with Sasha. Satisfied, he leaned back in the seat and nodded off. He couldn't remember the last time he'd felt this at peace.

The next evening he stepped out of the locker room to message the show's producers. The late-arriving crowd reminded him of watching NBA Warriors games in the arena as a teen. After the team moved to Las Vegas, the e-NBA converted the old facility into a smaller arena. The NBA still drew crowds, but mostly middle-aged men filled the seats.

The e-NBA drew a younger, hipper crowd and would soon eclipse its parent as a moneymaker. Besides official games, the e-NBA staged tournaments that brought together rappers, musicians, actors, and YouTubers to play with and against e-NBA stars. Millions of viewers tuned in to listen to the spectacle, listen to the smack talk, and place bets on everything from the score to the total number of curse words uttered.

The e-NBA knew it made it when Lyle Sanders, a five-time NBA all-star, retired to focus on his e-gaming career. Jason was getting in at just the right time.

The only downer was his lousy team. The game's outcome was predictable. The e-76ers took an early lead but couldn't hold it and lost its fourth straight game. Jason scored thirteen points.

Spent, he toweled off after a shower and dressed. His car service was waiting outside the arena, so he zipped up his bag and darted out the door. The cool San Francisco night felt refreshing after the humidity of the arena. A gaggle of the homeless converged around a firepit across the street in the parking lot of the abandoned NFL stadium.

When he searched for his driver, he found someone else.

"My boy," Denton uttered, ambling out of the shadows and going in for a man hug.

Jason jumped. Panic threaded through his veins, but he tried to play it cool. "Denton, didn't expect to see you here."

"Can't keep a good man down." He grinned wickedly. "Back to work."

Jason pointed at his driver. His back felt slick with sweat, his tongue dry. "Cool. Uh, can we catch up sometime later? I'm late. There's my car."

Denton stepped toward the waiting sedan. "I'll come along. We have business to discuss."

"Naw, man, I—"

"Jason." Denton stared meaningfully at Jason and placed a hand on the door of the sedan. "I'm coming."

Silently, Jason slipped into the back seat. Denton slid in next to him. As the driver eased the vehicle onto 880 North and Jason kept his eyes focused on the scenery flying by, the silence was broken by Denton. "Next time I tell you to cover a spread, don't get cute. Guys get their legs broken playing cute like you did. But now's your chance to make it right. You're in the big time now."

Jason glanced at the driver and whispered, "We can't have this conversation now. We'll both get into trouble."

Denton laughed. "Is this a conversation about prison? You ever been there? Oh, that's right. You skated." He pushed Jason. "Maybe you need a stretch to harden you."

Jason hadn't thought this through. He looked into the rear-view mirror. The driver, paid for by the e-76ers, stared back at him. In a hushed voice Jason said, "We can work it out, but if you keep talking, the driver will report us and I won't be able to help you."

Denton changed the subject. "Have you seen Sasha's show? Wait! Of course you have. You get paid for that shit, right? I got sidelined for months, and you're rolling in it."

The driver pulled up to the restaurant. Jason got out of the car, then looked at Denton. "Aren't you getting out?"

Denton pointed at the driver. "He's on the clock. He can take me."

The driver nodded, and Jason watched the sedan pull away. He crouched down, put his hands on his knees, and heaved. He was glad his stomach was empty.

Still, he found he couldn't move. His limbs were stiff, and he didn't trust them to be able to carry his weight. So he stayed right there, hovering over himself, struggling to even his breathing, fielding incessant texts for the next hour: the *Auction Diaries* producer, wondering where he was; Sasha, peppering him with questions about his whereabouts, followed by concern that something might be wrong.

Jason ignored all the messages. He felt like his body had melted; he was all emotion: panic, fear, regret. Above him, the stars sparkled in the night, but he couldn't tell if they were real or if he was remembering the night of the car accident, when the moon had shone down on them—when he'd made a choice that would change everything.

When a cab appeared, the conscious, thinking part of him managed to flag it down. And when he arrived at his hotel room, he barely made it inside before he slumped to the floor of the bathroom. The night passed in a haze of memory and nightmares as he faded in and out of consciousness.

When he came to, a graveyard of miniature bottles of vodka from the minibar littered the floor.

Five years ago, his life had splintered off into a different path, and every day since then, he'd been waiting for it to end in an explosion.

It was a night like many others—Jason's parents arrived at the school gymnasium to watch Baker's basketball game. Jason and Denton showered after practice and made plans to go to a party. They stood at the locker room door watching Baker's team come out for the second half. As they waited, Denton opened a packet. "I've got something new."

"What is it?"

Denton rolled out what looked like a tiny pill. "It's a new type of MDMA. My man said it takes you places."

Jason eyed it curiously. "What does it do?"

"It makes everything brighter."

"Man, I gotta see my parents."

"The come-up takes a while. Take it now, they won't even know. We'll be gone by then."

Jason paused. "Really? Now?"

"We drop it now, and by the time the party gets going, we'll be peaking." Denton nodded. He extended his hand.

Hesitantly, Jason reached out. Denton was nodding, his eyes smiling. At the same time, they each put a tablet on their tongues.

Nothing was different as Baker's game ticked down to the final seconds. He felt fine—cool, even. He said a normal good-bye to his parents and to his brother, who was spending the night at a friend's house.

Jason's mom gave him a look. "Don't stay out late."

He had walked just a few blocks away when his device beeped with a message from his mother. *Come back. Our car won't start!*

He nudged Denton. "Shit. I gotta go back."

"I'll catch up with you at the party."

"C'mon, come back with me!"

The hood of his father's Acura was up when the boys got there. "It's the alternator. I'll get it towed tomorrow."

"I'm starving," Jason's mom moaned.

Jason chuckled. His mom's appetite was a family joke. Inside, he felt both hot and cold at the same time. He tried to ignore it, to stave it off until later. He just had to get through this moment, he told himself.

His dad fixed him with a stare. "Drive us home." It wasn't a question; it was an order. Before he could process it, Jason's parents walked with him to his Mustang convertible.

Jason got behind the wheel, his dad in the passenger seat. Denton and his mother wedged themselves into the back. He was sweating now, and lights were creeping into the sides of his vision—flashing and jumping. The drive home would take only fifteen minutes. He could do it. He *knew* it. He concentrated on staying in his lane, made harder by cars pulling up next to him on Sunset.

"Jason, the light turned." His father nudged him, then went back to making weekend plans with his wife. Jason heard Denton giggling in the back seat. They departed the quiet streets of Holmby Hills and sped past UCLA on their left. As they hit the flashing signs that signaled the highway, Jason panicked. He stepped on the gas pedal.

"Jason!" his father screamed as the Mustang blew through the red light and roared over the 405 overpass. He unbuckled his seat belt as he struggled to seize control of the wheel from his son. The car careened down Sunset before Jason lurched the car to the right down a service street that led to the Luxe Hotel. His father grabbed the wheel just as the car struck a concrete barrier at the entrance to the hotel parking garage. The force of the impact ejected both of them from the car. His mom and Denton lay unconscious in the back seat.

When he woke three days later, Ayana stood over him. His protector.

The beeping from his device pulled him back from his nightmare. In his hotel room, Jason raised his head and looked around in a daze. This wasn't right. This couldn't be right. What had he done?

His device beeped again.

Denton wrote, 5.

TWENTY

William put down his menu and smiled at the server. "A Mediterranean omelet, please."

"The same for me, thank you," said Sasha, looking down at her device for a message from Jason. He hadn't answered her texts.

William sipped his grapefruit juice. "My sister is watching the show."

"Send her my apologies."

A TV hung on the wall in the corner. The footage on CNN caught Sasha's attention. A rally of tens of thousands of people was crippling downtown Boston. "Police have lost control of the area downtown," the anchor reported. "An American financial center is paralyzed, and authorities lack answers."

Sasha took a bite of her rye toast. "It's getting worse out there."

When Sasha arrived at the studio later that day, Casey informed her of a special guest that night: Global CEO Victor Armstrong. Given the show's young audience, his PR team thought it would give him a chance to counter the bad publicity from the recent deaths outside the company headquarters and tout the Auction's benefits.

While Casey spoke, Sasha scooped up a handful of grapes on the snack table and dropped them one by one into her mouth. Deja pocketed a granola bar. "You coming?"

Sasha nodded. "Be right there." She pulled out her device and messaged Tricia: *Can you meet with our fundraiser tomorrow in the city?*

Casey intercepted Sasha as she walked to the makeup room. She handed Sasha a rough script of how the interview between Summer and Armstrong would play out. "Read this. Summer wants you to play off his answers during your segment."

"You look tired," said Deja as she wedged tissues into the front of Sasha's Jana Sequin Blazer.

"I am."

"Then close your eyes and relax." Deja applied concealer under her eyes. "By the time we're done, you'll look perfect."

Sasha's device beeped and she reached for it. Deja gently placed it back on the table.

"Hold still and keep your head up."

"Sorry."

"It's OK. You're just a little shiny. Hold on." Deja reached for a powder puff and dabbed Sasha's forehead. The device beeped again. The makeup artist leaned back to assess her work.

"Did you do Armstrong's makeup?" Sasha asked.

Deja shook her head. "He came in already done. Global has its own person. You're still shiny." When she turned to get a pad, Sasha used the moment to check her messages.

It was Tricia, responding to her earlier plea. *Sasha, I'm so sorry, but I have horrible news. Call me?*

Deja wiped off the excess foundation as Sasha frantically typed. *In the makeup chair, can't talk. Just tell me. What?*

Thirty seconds passed. *Rosa was killed this afternoon.*

Sasha put her hand to her mouth, gasping. "Oh my God."

Deja stopped. "What's wrong?"

Sasha stood, unable to answer Deja. *What happened?*

Tricia wrote, *Police said her husband did it.*

Deja touched her arm. "Hon, we're running behind."

Sasha shook her off. "I need a minute! This is an emergency. Please." Without waiting for a response, she dashed out of the small dressing room, dialing Tricia.

She picked up right away. "Sasha . . . I'm so sorry."

"I can't believe this." She felt sick to her stomach. "How did he find her?"

"She was visiting her mother. They think he waited outside. He's in custody."

Sasha pressed her hand to her chest and held back tears. "I don't know what to say. What's the point of a restraining order if this happens? Why didn't the police protect her like they said they would?"

"Sasha, I'm not even sure the cops followed up," Tricia said quietly. "We've seen this before. Sometimes . . ." She hesitated. "Sasha, sometimes they don't even tell the husbands or boyfriends that they're under a restraining order. It's how so many of these women slip through the cracks."

A moan slipped through Sasha's lips. "How did he do it?" She had to know. She didn't even know why, really; it just felt like she owed it to Rosa, to understand her last moments, to pay tribute to her life.

"She was on her way to work," Tricia explained softly. "He . . . he had a pipe, Sasha. Something he grabbed from the dumpster in the alley behind her."

"He's in custody?" she asked dully.

"Yes. But he denies everything."

Sasha ducked her head, and the tears flowed freely. "Thanks, Tricia."

"Take care of yourself, OK, Sasha?" Tricia pleaded. But Sasha hung up before responding. She didn't know what to say anymore.

As she searched for her lawyer's number, a production assistant approached her and whispered, "No devices allowed during filming."

"Fuck off," she hissed, and he slunk away.

Behind him she could see the open set where Summer and Armstrong were talking animatedly in front of the live cameras. In that moment, Sasha realized she *hated* them. Summer, because she was fake and smarmy and represented everything Sasha had always hated about Hollywood. Armstrong, because he was responsible for all of this. For the Auction, for this damn show. For Rosa.

Without even noticing she was doing it, as if her arm had a mind of its own, she flung her device against the wall. It shattered into pieces.

The sound was an explosion. It echoed through the studio, making heads swivel—even Summer and Armstrong, who both flinched.

No one moved. Sasha breathed heavily, daring them to approach her. But Summer and Armstrong, ever the professionals, returned to their live interview.

With the room quiet again, Sasha could hear them.

"We've got to stop the violence," Armstrong said. "I think people forget what it was like before the Auction. If you ask me . . ." He pretended to hesitate for a moment. Sasha could see right through him, and a firecracker of anger launched inside of her. "If you ask me, they're ungrateful. Thanks to the Auction, Americans have more money in their pockets. Health care for all. A vibrant economy. And Americans have never been safer."

Sasha couldn't hold it in.

She bolted down the corridor, pushing away the line of producers and assistants and camera operators blocking her way.

Breathless, red with rage, Sasha landed in between Armstrong and Summer, on live television.

"Safer?" she snarled. She barely recognized her voice. "Last night a woman named Rosa Cortez died, beaten with a pipe by her husband. She wouldn't matter to Global. She's just a housekeeper. She asked for help, but she's poor and of no value to people like you."

Behind her, Summer was nearly purple with frustration. She began to tug at Sasha's arm, waving at someone off-camera, hissing, "Sasha, this is not your turn."

"My turn?" asked Sasha, swiveling to face her. "My turn comes in six weeks when a company will bid on me because it thinks I can make it millions of dollars. Because I'm valuable, I'll get protected. But women like Rosa never get the protection they need. Or the chance they deserve."

Sasha pointed to Armstrong. "So don't sell us your bullshit, Mr. Armstrong. You have blood on your hands!"

Several producers had appeared onstage by then, all of them clawing at her. She held up her hands in surrender. "I'm going! I'm going."

The headlines were gleeful. "The Day the Auction Died?" said one, almost hopefully. It took the position that the last gasp of the Auction would be when rich people attacked it. "Sasha Cross is an unlikely face of a movement, but in today's America maybe the spoiled daughter of Hollywood royalty railing against a rigged system is what it takes to wake people up."

She skimmed them all and waited for the doorbell to ring.

Her father, ever predictable, pounded on her door as soon as the sun was up, right on time. She'd been holed up in her apartment since her on-air rant the night before, studiously ignoring her father's messages and calls. She knew he'd show up anyway; what was the point of responding?

"What brings you here?" said Sasha, feigning surprise as she opened the door.

"Do you know what you've done?" he demanded, pushing past her into her living room. His face was contorted with rage in a way Sasha had never before seen. "I hope you have your statement ready, because you're issuing it now."

"Why would I? You wanted me to parlay our family's fame into something bigger." She crossed her arms and stared at him, almost bored. "That's what I did last night."

"You violated your contract!"

She plopped down in an oversized chair and yawned. "That sounds like a you-problem."

As she hoped for, her nonchalance made her father's anger dial up ten more notches. "You don't have a clue what you've done! Global funded the show and its subsidiaries make up half of our advertisers. The president of the studio called me last night. The president! Demanding to know why I embarrassed the network!" He was tugging at his hair in frustration, making it stand on end so that he looked like a mad scientist.

Sasha smiled sweetly. "You told me to be controversial."

Her father stopped his frantic pacing. His expression changed to something earnest, pleading. He knelt down next to her.

"Sasha, baby, there are tens of millions of dollars at stake here. Your tantrum has implications. For the family, for me and Kelsie." He pointed at her device. "Start writing a goddamn apology statement. You were stressed, you're nervous about the Auction, you're sad about your friend Rosa, whatever. I don't care what it says, as long as it makes nice."

Sasha shook her head. "No."

"You aren't your mother at all." Judah turned away from her. "She knew how to get what she wanted and not break bones along the way. You're not only endangering your future, but Kelsie's and mine."

"You know what, Dad?" Sasha stood up and opened her front door. "You always talk about living with the consequences of our actions. Well, I think it's time we all grew up. Including you and Kelsie. I'm not your puppet anymore."

Awed, her father stared at her. She pointedly looked at the open door.

Her father knew a losing battle when he saw one. "We're not done!" he shouted on his way out.

She slammed the door behind him, and double-locked it for good measure.

When Sasha called her team at PicaFlix to tell them she wasn't going to issue a statement, that they'd have to deal with it on their own, they never picked up her call.

———

The e-76ers general manager glowered at Jason. "What the hell happened in San Francisco?"

The star rookie never showed for the game in Seattle. And for three days the team, and Ayana, didn't know if he was alive. He finally sent messages and flew back to Philadelphia.

When Jason didn't answer, the GM asked, "What's wrong with you?"

I killed my parents, lived with a lie for five years, and now the one person who knows about it is threatening to ruin my family's future unless I fix games you pay me to play. That's what Jason wished he could say. Instead, he muttered, "I slipped."

The GM sat next to him. "I know that. And we can deal with it. You just can't disappear on us. We have people who can help you. But you can't go AWOL."

He held his head in his hands. "I'm sorry."

"Listen, Jason, we have a lot invested in you. We want you to be part of this team. And we'll get you help. But if this happens again, we'll cut you."

He nodded.

It took everything he had not to scream, *I deserve to be cut!*

Ayana waited outside the team offices to take him home. Halfway there, she spoke. "You promised me a long time ago this wouldn't happen. You're so close."

"It's too hard, Ayana."

"Baby, what's too hard?"

Jason peered out the window at the charred remains of a row house. That was him, burned and hollowed out. "Nothing. It doesn't matter."

He holed up in his room. There were no Ayana pep talks or late-night deliveries of a bowl of cookies-n-cream ice cream. He thought back to the game he missed in Seattle. Instead of winning close, as Denton wanted, the team lost. Denton messaged, *Clever.*

———

Days later, Victor Armstrong still hadn't recovered from the on-air assault a rich, entitled Hollywood brat had screamed at him. And he was taking it out on everyone around him.

"This is all of your doing," he thundered at his team.

Jessica spoke up. "I warned against appearing on the show."

Armstrong turned red. "No, you told me I wasn't up to it. I handled it just fine."

Jessica crossed her arms. "Now when we cancel the show, she'll look like a hero."

"Then don't cancel. Sideline her and dig up dirt that we can leak first. Then we'll use that to pull the plug."

Armstrong's PR chief interjected, "If it ever came out that we were trashing her, the backlash would kill us."

"No, Victor is right," countered Jessica. "We have to soil her."

Armstrong nodded. Perhaps Jessica wasn't a lost cause after all. As the meeting broke up, he asked her to stay behind. "Run her through GOD."

The next day, Jessica showed up at Garrett's office. He jumped to attention.

"Your brother—we used him to spy on candidates, right?"

Garrett's heart raced. They'd learned Avery had fallen in love with Suni. "Yes."

"And how has he done?"

"Um, OK. He got intel on Suni Yosar. I guess a work in progress."

"He knows Sasha Cross?"

"They went to school together a long time ago."

Jessica contemplated. "Send for him, he might be useful."

She descended to the basement, walked down the narrow corridors where a solitary guard blocked access to a room marked Archives. When she scanned her retinas, she heard the whirring of the locks, and the door opened.

Three monitors on the wall came to life when she entered a long, complicated password she'd memorized. Once they were active, she said out loud, "Sasha Malleana Cross." The monitors lit up with data. The artificial intelligence scanned billions of records searching for data connecting Sasha, her family, and friends to arrest reports, postings, texts, and other digital records.

She took notes. After an hour, she had what she needed.

———

The street parking in William's neighborhood was always a problem. He circled around and around his block, growing more annoyed with each false hope. After the sixth trip around, police lights filled his rearview mirror. He signaled and came to a stop in the parking lot of a Chipotle on Shattuck Avenue.

It took an exceptionally long time for the officer to approach his window. "License and registration, sir."

Handing over the documents, he asked, "Can I ask what this is about?"

"You illegally crossed lanes," he responded, looking over William's license. Then he peered at William. "Have you been drinking tonight, sir?"

"No, of course not."

"Please exit your vehicle, sir."

William's mouth dropped open. He'd had the occasional speeding ticket, but he'd never been asked to leave his car before. "Um," he began, but when he noticed the officer tense up and place his hand on his weapon, he didn't bother continuing. Slowly, he opened the door.

Berkeley students leaving Chipotle gathered to watch. One raised his device to record.

"You sure you haven't been drinking? Your eyes look glassy," said the officer as he shined his flashlight in William's face.

"I'm positive," William said quietly.

"Do you consent to a breathalyzer, sir?"

William paused. "Yes."

He blew into the tube, confident in the results.

The officer peered at the device. "Sir, please turn around and put your hands behind your back. You have the right to remain silent . . ."

William panicked. "What the hell is happening?"

"You blew a .12, sir, that is legally intoxicated."

"That's impossible. I've had nothing to drink!"

"That's not what the test says, sir."

William spent an uncomfortable night in a holding cell with a half-dozen others. The video of William's arrest aired on YouTube, and the *Daily Californian* picked up the story. Within twenty-four hours, nearly twenty thousand people had viewed the clip. William was summoned to the dean's office, where he was suspended without pay until a formal review.

———

Avery stepped off a plane at San Francisco Airport, a conquering hero. He decided to wait to reveal the good news in person about Suni's worth. Suni's financial windfall justified her selection as a Series A because the Big 7 company that bid on her would get 25 percent of her inheritance. And, Avery rationalized, the information would keep Suni's dream alive of one day performing with the New York Philharmonic.

That Garrett had asked him to fly immediately to Global headquarters could only mean one thing: he'd shown his value, and they planned to select him as a Series A. Take that, Beech.

He recognized Makeda, one of Garrett's coworkers, when he got in the elevator. They made small talk as they rode to the eighteenth floor. Then she blurted out, "I just want to say I think what Garrett did to you was wrong."

Avery frowned. "I'm used to it. He never liked my girlfriends."

"No, I mean leading you on about getting selected as a Series A. That's a shitty thing to do to your own brother." She patted his arm awkwardly. "I hope things work out for you."

They stepped off the elevator. Makeda waited until a coworker passed before continuing. "I heard him telling his buddies about how you fell for the girl you were spying on and that you don't have what it takes to work here. I know he's your brother, but he's an asshole."

Avery walked in a daze toward Garrett. When he entered the office, he blurted out, "Am I going to be a Series A?"

Garrett dodged. "The Auction is in two weeks. Let's see."

"Am I on Global's list?"

"Where is this coming from?"

"Just answer," he demanded.

Garrett shrugged and avoided his eyes. "I don't make the list."

"You told me if I helped you, I'd be a Series A candidate. Makeda told me it's all a lie."

Garrett picked up his device to message her but thought better of it. "She's such a bitch."

"So, it's true."

"Nothing's decided. But dude, I have a new assignment for you. It comes from my boss's boss. If you do this, you'll be golden."

Avery took a step back. "Did you tell people about me and Suni?"

"You are missing the big picture here. I have your golden ticket. When you go to New York, I need you to work Sasha Cross. See what you can learn. We need to destroy her."

"Did you?"

"Yes, but seriously, if you do this it's a done deal you'll be a Series A."

"You're such an asshole." Avery reached for the glass-encased Tigers baseball. He winged it at his brother. It missed its target but shattered in pieces when it struck the wall.

The commotion caught the attention of Garrett's neighbors. Avery stepped into the hallway and began yelling, drawing a small crowd. "Want to know about the asshole you work with? Remember your old coworker Jeff? Garrett hired an escort to seduce him, then made sure his wife showed up to catch him. All to screw Jeff out of a promotion!"

Amid the gasps, Garrett yanked Avery into his office and slammed the door. He turned in a fury. "How do we have the same DNA?" Then he remembered why Avery was here. "Hold up, hold up. You've got to help me. This can be good for you. I need you to get in with Sasha."

"Screw you, I'm leaving."

Garrett's rage took over. "Now I know why Dad checked to see if you were really his."

Avery turned in shock. "How do you know about that?"

"Dad told me when I turned twenty-one. He said don't let the fact I have a loser for a brother hold me back."

Avery's eyes filled with tears as he stepped past his brother. Garrett said, "I know you feel humiliated, but don't worry. I won't tell anyone."

TWENTY-ONE

The *Auction Diaries* lifted Sasha's suspension after a week. The show would go on, although now without the disgraced William, who hadn't returned any of Sasha's messages. PicaFlix couldn't wait to get Sasha back on the air. The confrontation with Armstrong boosted ratings, and in an instant she went from Hollywood royalty to "bad girl," and PicaFlix doubled its budget to promote the remaining shows. They even offered Judah a hefty bonus if he could get Sasha to extend the show for another year.

Blissfully, Sasha knew nothing of the negotiations. She kept herself busy reading and responding to the thousands of messages from Series D people thanking her for standing up for them. The task reminded her how she was stuck between two worlds, a visitor to both. She wasn't with the D Movement, yet she detested the Big 7 manipulations. She rejected Hollywood, yet was the star of a reality show. She revered her mother, but didn't want to go down the same path she had. Who was she?

Jason made clear what side she should choose.

"You flake on me in San Francisco and now you tell me to shut up?" Sasha shook her head at him.

"I'm not telling you to shut up, Sasha." Jason searched for the right words. His hologram revealed how skinny he'd become since the last time Sasha had seen him. She was beginning to worry. "Just understand that I'm under pressure because of what you did. There's a lot at stake."

She studied him—the ghosts of worry lines on his face, the urgency in his eyes. "Jay . . . what's with you?"

"No, what's with you?" he shot back. "Where's the person who didn't want any part of publicity? I don't recognize this version of you."

"You know there are bigger things at stake than just me."

Jason was quiet for a moment. "Just don't make me your collateral damage."

"I would never do that," she promised.

His voice softened. "I know, it's just been . . . weird. Tough."

She didn't want to let on that she had noticed. "Talk to me."

"I missed a game. I . . ." He paused, and Sasha could see him debating. *Tell me*, she urged to the universe. "I had a drink, Sasha. Or . . . more than a drink, a lot of drinks. And the team knows what happened, and now I'm on thin ice."

She bit her lip. "Oh, Jason. I'm so sorry. Are you getting help?"

"Yeah."

She wiped away the tears that had pooled in her eyes. What kind of friend was she, who hadn't even known he'd fallen off the wagon? Hadn't even seen how bad things were getting for him? "I didn't realize you were under so much stress. I wish you would've called me."

He wiped his eyes, too. "It's not just that. Denton showed up after my game. Threw me into a tailspin."

"Shit!" Sasha yelled. No wonder Jason was a mess—she'd been telling him for so many years Denton was trouble. "You need to call the cops!"

"No cops. If the Denton thing made it into the news, I'd get cut."

Sasha pleaded with him, begged him, to get more help. Someone who could really set Denton straight—who could protect Jason. But he refused.

"Jason . . . this is your whole life we're talking about," Sasha said, trying one last time. "Do it for Ayana, if no one else."

Jason narrowed his eyes. "Drop it, Sasha."

"But—"

"I have to go," he said quickly. Almost immediately, he vanished, and her line went dead.

———

Jason rolled off his bed and then pulled it away from the wall, reaching for a hidden plastic container. He lifted the lid and looked at the Glock 9 mm pistol that once belonged to his father. He touched the trigger. The craving returned.

He put the gun back behind his bed, gathered his keys, and headed out.

As soon as Jason unlocked the front door, a light in the living room clicked on. Jason jumped, his heart thumping. "Where are you going?" Ayana sat in the dark in an oversized love seat.

"Out."

She stood and relocked the door. "No."

"I'll be back soon."

She blocked the exit. "No."

"I can't take it anymore."

"What can't you take?"

Jason slumped into a chair. "The guilt."

"We all have guilt, Jason. You can't let it eat you up."

He struggled to breathe. "I did it."

She embraced him. "Did what, baby?"

"I did it!" he yelled. "Don't you get it? It was me behind the wheel." He stifled sobs.

Ayana kissed his cheek and caressed his head. "I know, baby."

Ayana's words took a moment to hit Jason, who continued to sob. But eventually they did, and he stuttered, "Wh-how?"

"That night, I talked with your mom while your dad tried to get the car running. She told me you were driving them home." She kissed his cheek, still holding him tight. "But it wasn't your fault. It was just a horrible tragedy."

"They would be alive if not for me."

"You can't know that for sure," Ayana protested. "No one can know that. So we have to move past it."

"Denton is hanging it over me."

Ayana gripped him tighter, not in sympathy but in anger. "I can't believe he posted bail."

Jason straightened up. "How do you know about that?"

"I asked Bobby to keep an eye on him. He pulled him over and found enough heroin to charge him with intent to distribute. Bobby said he'd be stuck in prison until his trial."

Jason wiped his eyes. "I should have confessed to that police officer in the hospital."

Ayana scoffed. "Why? So you'd be another Denton? You made a mistake, but it doesn't have to define you. You've done wonderful things since that night. And you're making something of yourself. You're giving this family a future."

———

The online site *StAuctor* ran a short story next to images of the twenty-two-year-old daughter of a celebrity as she sunbathed nude. The story next to it displayed a photo of Suni with the headline "Sad Song: Cellist Booted from A-List." The story revealed the Michigan musician had been dropped as a Series A candidate because she wouldn't inherit her father's wealth.

Suni held proof in her hand: a letter from the Auction Combine informing her she no longer needed to travel to Brooklyn. She let the letter drop from her fingers; it danced to the floor. She sniffled.

"The New York Philharmonic orchestra was a pipe dream, anyway."

"Garrett," Avery muttered to himself.

"What?"

Avery's jaw was a block of steel. "I think my brother did this."

"What? Why would he go out of his way to screw me over? He hardly knows me." Suni sunk into her chair. "I should cancel my flight."

"Don't." Avery stood. "Give me a day. Do you have rehearsal?"

She rubbed her eyes. "We have off until Friday."

Avery searched on his device. "Keep our reservations. We're driving to Chicago."

"What's in Chicago?"

"Beech. I need you to bring the paperwork about your dad's money. When we're done with this, you'll never want to see me again. But for now, please trust me."

Suni was waiting outside her house when Avery pulled up early the next morning. It took Avery almost the entire drive to explain the reason he first reached out to her, what Garrett had promised him in return, and how his feelings had changed along the way.

Near Kalamazoo, he had to pull the car over and then coax Suni to get back in. She called him hurtful names, all of which he deserved.

But by the time the Chicago skyline came into sight, she agreed to his plan.

They sat in the lobby of the Beech headquarters. A receptionist called their names, and a security guard escorted them to a conference room.

A few minutes later a frazzled junior associate walked into the room. Avery pointed at his friend. "This is Suni Yosar, and if you pick her in the Auction, you can double your money in twelve months."

An hour—and one long, intense conversation—later, Avery and Suni shook hands with the Beech vice president who'd spoken with them in a hidden conference room. When they were finally alone again, waiting for the elevator, Avery handed Suni a plane ticket.

"Thanks . . . I guess."

"I hope you get everything you want. You deserve it, Suni."

She pushed the elevator button, then turned to him. "Remember when I told you how much it hurt when Derrick died?"

"Yes."

"This is worse." The elevator door opened, and she stepped inside.

Avery waited until the doors closed, then returned to the conference room. The vice president was still in there, and he looked up eagerly when Avery reappeared.

He stepped inside, pulling papers from his pocket. "I have something else to offer."

———

Jessica sat in Armstrong's office overlooking San Francisco Bay.

"Tomorrow the *Wall Street Journal* will publish a story that Judah Cross is under federal investigation for misuse of funds from his late wife's charitable organization."

"Was his daughter involved?"

She shook her head. "No, but it dirties the family. Isn't that what you wanted?"

"I guess."

"What do we do about Fort Stewart?" she asked. Since Vincente's death, Global had hit pause on the project while the company swapped out any personnel deemed a risk.

"If we restart, how many can we do a month?"

"If we expand Fort Stewart and add other facilities, we could do fifty thousand a year if we just focus on prisons and military hospitals."

"And that gets us . . . ?"

"We'd have organs for any Series As and Bs that need a transplant. That's billions of dollars in our pockets each year by keeping those Series As alive and working. And now that we've perfected the cryogenic process, any unused organ can be sold overseas."

Armstrong nodded, thinking. Jessica rushed to further explain the benefits.

"If you add in the cost savings, it's tens of billions of dollars more. That's fifty thousand people we don't have to provide with health care or pay for them to sit in the prison."

"When can we restart?"

"Well, there's still the problem of how we launder the bodies," Jessica explained. "If we eliminate that many people, we'll need to adjust the population numbers."

Armstrong glanced at his calendar. "I'm in Washington in two weeks. I'll tell President Sanford it's important that we win the bid to operate the census."

———

Jason walked stone-faced to the locker room. He knew what it meant now, to rise early and fall hard. In the three games since his return, he had played so lousy that tonight the coach pulled him in the second quarter. Ashamed, he couldn't even bear to search the McGuire Arena stands for Ayana the way he normally did when he knew she was in attendance. She had been a constant presence, bucking him up, reminding him what he was reaching for. She was no fool, though; she searched his room for booze and drugs daily.

He tuned out his coach's postgame rant. He wondered about the impact his slide would have on his Auction. A lower bid meant less money for his aunt. After all the grief, he prayed his Auction would bring her millions of dollars. He was her last shot.

The team meeting broke up, and he sat down in front of his locker.

"Jason?" The coach stood in front of him. "It might be better for you to sit out a few games, just practice on the simulators."

"I just need to regain my rhythm."

"I think you need a break."

He felt his stomach tighten. "Coach, I need to play. I need it."

The coach pursed his lips. "OK, let's give it another game. Then you'll miss one anyway when you're in New York. That break will help."

"Thank you, Coach."

He had one more shot before the Auction. He would refocus. Practice. Jason had been down before. He thought about that miracle shot he made months ago, and the games that followed when he was on fire. He could do it again.

His heart fell when he saw a message come in from Denton: *Coming to NY. Got business. You and I need to chop it up.*

In the car, Ayana tried to soothe him. "Tough game."

"Yeah."

"What did your coach say?"

Jason sighed, looking out the window. "He wants to bench me. I convinced him to give me another game."

"When do we leave for New York?"

"Friday."

"Remember. Team Harris."

TWENTY-TWO

Six months.

That's how long it had been since Avery had walked the concourses of the Brooklyn Dome. Back then, he'd had a hot girlfriend, big dreams, and not a goddamn care in the world. Now, everything hung on what Beech thought of him.

Inside he wandered, searching for Suni. He couldn't be sure she had even come. It didn't matter, as long as Beech stuck to the deal. Getting into the facility had been a challenge. Avery didn't appear on the list of candidates. It took an intervention by Beech to get him credentials.

That explained Garrett's surprise when he came upon him. "What the hell are you doing here? We're not selecting the Series Cs until later in the week."

"Get lost, Garrett."

His brother put his arm around him. "Please don't think that stunt you pulled about Jeff had any impact. Global only cares about one thing: making money."

Avery pushed him away. "I know."

"I ran into your girlfriend. I'm not sure what she's doing here. I played nice, but she slapped me. I can't believe you told her. Everything you touch turns to absolute shit."

Avery's heart raced. It always did when he fought with his older brother. Garrett had always been smarter, more ambitious, better. "You win, Garrett. You always do." Avery left in search of suite 338. The Beech executive he met in Chicago was waiting for him at the entrance.

"Are you sure you want to do this?" the executive asked.

Avery handed him a piece of paper and walked away. No turning back now.

———

Even though his own was just a memory, Garrett loved the adrenaline rush of the Auction. The Big 7 would risk hundreds of billions of dollars, and it all came down to which company had the best information.

The intelligence being discussed had taken months for Global to compile. Dark drapes covered the windows. Security swept for listening devices on the hour. Jessica sat at the head of the table while company executives made final arguments for who they thought were the best Auction candidates. Garrett sat in what analysts called the "speak-when-spoken-to row." They were there to provide color on a candidate, add a data point, or verify what showed up in a file.

He considered it a huge vote of confidence that he was in the room at all. The only stain on a perfect trip was Avery. He had to explain to Jessica why his brother couldn't spy on Sasha.

Candidate banter continued. He resisted the urge to speak when he had information on a candidate under discussion. Sasha Cross's name came up. She got labeled an "evergreen," meaning even if she didn't make money for the company right away, her level of celebrity meant someday she would pay out handsomely.

The conferees around the table discussed an inventor from Kansas. They made a bid based on information Garrett gathered. His boss, in the second row, glanced back and nodded. Garrett schemed on what it would take to be in the second row at next year's Auction.

He reached for his device, then remembered Global forbade them in the room. Like a casino, it had no clocks and fresh air was pumped in through the vents. In each corner a small speaker played chamber music to hinder efforts to eavesdrop on the deliberations.

Garrett's mind drifted to his second-row plan. The door opened, and a member of the Global security team entered and placed a note in front of Jessica.

"We need to take a break. Please leave the room," she ordered.

Garrett shuffled toward the exit. Jessica stopped him. "Take a seat." Security entered and guarded the door.

"Anything you need to tell us?" she asked him.

Baffled, he tried to chuckle, but found his throat was stuck. "No, I don't think so."

"Before the meeting, someone used your username and password to hack into our system and steal Auction files," she informed him.

"I don't have any idea what you're talking about," Garrett sputtered as his heart raced.

She nodded to security. "Go with them. We need to sort this out."

Garrett looked over at the poker-faced guards, then back at Jessica. "I had nothing to do with this!"

She eyed him. "You better hope not."

———

Sasha read the *Journal* story about her father—again—and tried to figure out what it meant that he still hadn't returned her calls.

The truth was, Sasha believed every accusation it listed. So maybe it was better they didn't speak for a while; she didn't know what she'd say.

The SUV came to a stop. "This is as close as we can get," her driver announced. A massive mob had gathered outside the Brooklyn Dome. Police had set up a perimeter, but that created a gauntlet that Series A candidates had to walk through.

Global had nixed filming of Sasha's arrival because they did not want to publicize the mayhem. The two security guards assigned to her escorted her through the barricades that held back the demonstrators. She walked through it; a mix of insults and cheers flooded her head as she pushed her way to the entrance. She shrugged off her handlers' efforts to keep her moving and looked back at the rally. Brilliant sunshine gave the crowd an eerie glow. A young woman pressed up against a barrier held a sign that read, Hear us. See us.

A hand cupped her elbow and pushed her into the arena. Spooked by the violence, many candidates had refused to travel to New York. Sasha counted her blessings that at least this time she didn't enter the stadium covered in a strawberry smoothie.

Jason had told her he was in the back row, and she found him easily. Even by Jason's standards, the hug lasted long. But Sasha sniffed, recognizing the scent of booze.

"Jason, not again."

"I'm fine." When he let go, Sasha noticed a stain on his shirt. She wrinkled her nose. It looked and smelled like vomit.

The same woman who introduced them to the Auction six months ago strode to the podium. "Welcome back, and congratulations on your upcoming Series A selection. Today's session will go over what you should expect in the next three days."

Jason's eyes closed. Sasha nudged him.

The speaker continued. "Today you'll get your last pre-Auction physical examination. Tomorrow you'll sit for taped interviews. On Monday afternoon we'll start the big show."

Sasha stared at her friend's bloodshot eyes.

The briefing broke up, and Sasha left arm in arm with Jason. Casey loved it, not understanding that Sasha was keeping her friend upright. "Let's get you a cup of coffee."

They sat at a small eatery. "Jason, we need to clean you up before your physical."

"Denton's out of jail. He's coming here."

"For fuck's sake, Jason, call the police. He's torturing you."

"No police." He sipped the coffee.

"Why not? Why are you so afraid of him?"

He mumbled, "My parents. No police."

She snatched the piece of paper from his hand. "Your physical isn't for two hours. Drink your coffee, then we need to clean you up. We need clothes. Where's Ayana?"

"At the hotel."

Sasha shook her head. "They'll never let her inside." She surveyed her choices, then pointed at the cameraman. "Come over here."

The man looked at Casey, who shrugged. Sasha touched his shirt. "What size are you?"

He frowned. "Large."

"Go to the bathroom. You and Jason are swapping shirts."

He lowered the camera. "I'm not giving him my shirt."

She glared at him. "Should I call my father?"

A voice from behind Sasha said, "He can take mine."

Sasha turned to discover Avery pulling his MSU sweatshirt over his head. He handed it to her. "It'll fit better than his, anyway."

She hesitated a second, then took it. "Thanks."

As Jason wobbled to the bathroom to wash up and change, Avery pulled Sasha aside.

"Is he going to be OK?" he asked.

"Don't worry about it."

The two stood in silence until Avery broke it. "Listen, I need to tell you something. My brother works at Global. You really spooked them. They are searching for dirt to discredit you. So be wary of someone like me suddenly acting friendly while you're here."

"I don't let anyone I don't know get close. And who would be that big an asshole?"

Avery ran his hand through his hair. "This asshole," he said, pointing at himself. "The only reason I was invited to the Combine was to collect intel for my brother."

The disgust on Sasha's face turned to curiosity. "Why are you telling me this?"

"I hurt someone doing it. And I don't want it to happen to anyone else. And I always felt bad for that cruel trick I played on you. The fake date. I don't know if you even remember it."

"Remember?" She threw back her head and laughed. "You really are an asshole. It scarred me. I still hate you for what you did."

Avery nodded. "That's fair."

Sasha touched his arm. "But I appreciate everything you did just now. Take care of yourself, Avery."

Jason returned a few minutes later, still glassy-eyed but more presentable. Sasha combed his hair and cleaned his face. In the corridor she handed him water and a blueberry muffin. "Drink. Eat. I need to get to my physical. Will you be OK?"

Jason nodded. He lingered on the bench. Everything he worked to achieve was now at risk. Because of Denton. He couldn't give Ayana the future she deserved. Because of Denton. He picked up his device and typed a message. *You are a fucking low-life.*

Seconds later he got a response. *Mommy killer.*

Jason thought for a second, then typed, *Fuck you.*

Say it to my face.

Jason tapped furiously. *Come to the stadium.*

Main entrance. Twenty minutes.

———

CNBC showed a split-angle screen of protests in New York and San Francisco.

Armstrong didn't need to look at the monitor to see the action. The demonstrators were thirty floors below him outside Global headquarters. The company's security team struggled to contain the protests that immobilized traffic. A tent city at the nearby plaza became Protest Central.

Across the country, tens of thousands of demonstrators wearing black D Movement shirts gathered outside the Brooklyn Dome. CNBC showed looters overrunning shops at the intersection of Flatbush and Seventh Avenue. As nightfall came, images of city buses on fire and store owners guarding their property with shotguns flashed across the screen.

His assistant alerted him for the call he'd been waiting for. "No, Mr. President. Don't listen to the secretary of treasury. If we postpone the Auction, there's no certainty we can get it going again." Armstrong listened before interrupting, "Mr. President, yes, I've seen the story and there is absolutely no truth to it. Goodbye, Mr. President."

Armstrong turned to the monitor on his desk. A headline blared: "Congress to Investigate Secret Global Holdings Operation to Spy on Americans."

He yelled out to his assistant, "Where the hell is Jessica?"

"She's not responding, sir."

Armstrong had difficulty concentrating due to the chants of the mob below. After the story broke, Beech's Johnson called a meeting of the Big 7 CEOs.

He needed information.

He needed Jessica. "Message her again!"

Armstrong looked out at the thirty-foot letters on company buildings that spelled out GLOBAL. Altogether, a hundred thousand employees worked in the massive complex. There were walkways and skyways that connected the ten-block campus.

The mob in the plaza across the street blighted the view. With each chant, his dream of expanding the Auction overseas grew more distant. He shrugged that off. That could wait.

The immediate threat was GOD. He needed to shut it down. Erase any record. He needed that done before he faced his fellow CEOs. Without Jessica, he'd be flying blind heading into that meeting. An icy shiver ran through his body.

"No," he said, loud enough for his assistant to hear.

"No, what?" she asked.

"Nothing. Call her again."

Armstrong stared at the vanity wall filled with pictures of him standing next to world leaders, scientists, entrepreneurs, and artists. In the center was a framed *Time* magazine cover proclaiming him Person of the Year.

He heard a sound at the door and turned, hoping to see his security chief. Instead, his assistant held a small box. "This came for you, sir."

Armstrong placed the box on the desk, then lifted the top. Inside was an ornate chess piece. A bishop. In chess, the bishop could move any distance, as long as it was diagonal. Its value was its ability to attack without notice. When he picked up the chess piece, he noticed a note underneath.

It contained just two words: *Small Details.*

Jason spit blood from his mouth. He crawled on the dirt path used by construction to enter the half-completed railroad terminal two blocks from the stadium.

After his messages with Denton, he had rushed out past the demonstrators. While he waited, the fear set in. But it was too late. Denton came upon him fast. "Let's go," he said, sticking a gun in Jason's ribs and grabbing his arm.

They walked a block to the Atlantic Terminal, past the commuters to the construction site. "Denton, I'm sorry . . ." He didn't get to finish. Denton pistol-whipped him.

"C'mon, tough guy. Say it again."

"Denton . . ." He crumpled after his ex-friend delivered a kick to the stomach.

"Say I'm a low-life. Say it."

Jason righted himself and leaned against a bulldozer. "What do you want from me?"

"Everything I got coming. You owe me for five years of silence." Denton leaned in close. "They cut me out of the car. Your momma was still alive. She kept asking what happened, asking for your daddy. But he was in pieces in the parking lot."

Jason looked away. "Don't."

"Your momma lived for ten minutes and never asked for you."

"Tell me what you want."

"You and I are gonna be partners for as long as I can ride your sorry ass. Now get up."

They walked down Atlantic Avenue toward the stadium. Denton shoved him. "You trifled with me, my man. And it's my fault. I treated you too nice."

"Denton, let's figure out another way. I can make you money, just another way." Jason's device beeped. He missed his physical. Sasha messaged him asking where he was.

Denton slapped it away. "I'm talking!" Jason scurried to retrieve it before commuters hustling to the railroad terminal trampled it.

They reached the wide set of concrete steps that led down to a sculpture garden across from the stadium. Denton took a step down, so he was in Jason's face.

"You're now my top earner," he said, leaning in. "Or it's not just you I'll hurt."

Five years of rage surged in Jason, and he rushed forward, hitting Denton in the chest with all his might, sending both of them flailing down the steps. Jason's leg caught a metal railing, and he screamed out in pain as he came to a stop.

Nothing impeded Denton. He reached for a handrail but missed as he hurtled down the long stairway until he came to the bottom. His head bounced, followed by his body.

Jason didn't stick around to see what happened next. He crawled up to the concourse. A small gaggle of people hovered over Denton's lifeless body. By the time they looked to the top of the stairs, Jason had vanished.

———

"C'mon, Jason, pick up," Sasha muttered, staring at her device. She thought the worst: he was sitting in a local bar getting drunk. Out of options, she messaged Ayana. *I'm worried about Jason.*

Sasha waited. Minutes dragged by. Finally, Ayana reported back: *No response. I'm coming.*

Sasha sat outside the Brooklyn Dome in the same spot Jason had waited for Denton. Ten yards away police struggled to contain the demonstrators. Some had handcuffed themselves to the metal barricades. She started to film the confrontation.

A stadium security guard approached her. "Filming is not allowed."

"I filmed at a concert here a few months ago."

"It's an Auction rule."

She pointed at her camera crew.

"They have special permission. And they aren't filming the demonstration."

"That's bullshit," Sasha said, but pocketed her device.

Ayana's face emerged from the crowd. Frantic, she rushed up to Sasha. "Any word?"

"No. Let me try again."

"When did you last see him?" asked Ayana.

"About three hours ago. He'd been drinking."

"Oh, lord. And you let him go?"

"We had physicals," Sasha protested. "We agreed to meet afterward."

Rachel, one of the security guards assigned to Sasha, interrupted the conversation. "Ms. Cross, maybe this will help. There's a tracker on Jason's device. After he didn't show in San Francisco, your father ordered it."

For once, Sasha's father's malice was paying off. "So, do it!"

"Your father has to approve."

She rolled her eyes and called her father. When he didn't pick up, she messaged him. *Dad, listen, you need to order the crew to activate Jason's tracking system. Right away. Find out where Jason is! 911!*

Five minutes later Rachel gave a thumbs-up. They rushed to the Atlantic Terminal.

"How accurate is the tracker?" Sasha wondered, peering through crowds.

"Within five yards."

At the steps of the sculpture garden, they spotted emergency vehicles. "Oh God," Ayana screamed as she rushed past the yellow security tape. Sasha followed behind.

An officer stopped them.

"Who's down there?" asked Ayana.

"I'm not at liberty to tell you."

"It may be my boy!"

"What's his name?"

"Jason Harris."

The officer shook his head. "No, that's not him."

Sasha burst into tears. Ayana squeezed her in relief. As they walked away, the officer yelled, "Hold up!"

They doubled back. Sasha felt herself holding her breath.

"Did you say Jason Harris?"

Ayana nodded. Fear lined her face.

"Do you know his whereabouts?"

Sasha looked at Ayana. "No, we're looking for him. Why?"

"He's a person of interest in this homicide."

"Homicide?!" Ayana clamped her hand over her mouth.

"Who's down there?" Sasha choked.

She knew the answer before the officer said it. "A man named Denton Long."

Sasha opened her mouth, but couldn't find any words. Rachel approached holding a cracked device. "We found it in the shrubs."

"He's not here," Sasha said dully. On their walk back toward the stadium, Ayana fumbled through her contacts. "I need to call my brother. I should have stayed with Jason."

When they returned to the Brooklyn Dome, police were struggling to dislodge the protesters who had chained themselves to the barricades. Giving up, they dragged the people and the barricades to a holding area off Sixth Avenue while they waited on the delivery of an electric saw. It took too long to arrive. Shots rang out, sending protesters across Sixth Avenue, over and on top of the defenseless handcuffed men and women.

As Sasha scanned the crowds, looking for Jason, a young woman caught her eye. It was the same person Sasha had seen holding the sign earlier in the day. She watched as the surge knocked the woman to the ground, and her repeated efforts to regain her footing were thwarted by panicked protesters climbing over the barricades to escape the police.

The woman lifted herself up, only to get shoved down by the next person scrambling over the barrier. "Stop!" Sasha called weakly as a heavyset man stepped on the woman's chest as he stumbled to flee. Sasha tried to make her way to the woman on the ground, but the crowd was too thick, and her security team had her surrounded. She watched, helpless, as a young man jumped in the air and landed on the woman's neck. She made one last push to get up, but protesters toppled over the barriers onto her. Sasha lost sight of her in the mix of bodies.

"Help them!" she screamed.

She turned toward the camera crew. "Stop pointing the camera at me! Film this!" But the crew had their orders: the cameras remained trained on the reality star.

Panicked, Sasha turned to Ayana for help, but she was gone.

———

Inside the little rundown dive bar a block from the stadium, Jason couldn't hear the chaos outside. He was focused on the bottom of his glass, watching, mesmerized, as it appeared to fill and drain all by itself.

Eventually, he summoned a car service to take him back to Philadelphia. The driver filled the two-hour trek with small talk after learning his passenger was an e-NBA player. He was not a fan of gaming, but his teen sons loved it. Jason signed autographs for each of them.

"When is your next game? I'll make sure they watch."

"The season's done."

"Already?"

"For me it is." The stabbing pain in his ankle, numbed by the alcohol, returned. He stretched out on the back seat and

fell asleep. He only woke when the sedan came to a stop. Jason
unfolded bills and handed them to the driver.

He protested. "This is way too much!"

"I want you to have it."

"You're one of the good guys. My sons and I will root for
you."

Jason watched as the taillights faded from view. He limped
up the steps. Ayana was in Brooklyn. Baker had left for a fight
in New Orleans yesterday.

The quiet calmed him. He passed the pictures that traced
his family history in reverse. Ayana and him at a wedding. A
photo of Baker. Ayana with her daughters. A family reunion. A
photo from Jason's sixth birthday. He had insisted Baker have
the first pony ride with him. In the picture Jason is smiling,
and Baker is looking up at his older brother.

He grabbed the railing as he gingerly made his way upstairs
to his bedroom. The door to his closet was open. Jason pulled
out his best suit. He undressed, taking care to fold his clothes
and place them on the bed. He pulled the designer pants from
the hanger and put them on. He looped his belt and fastened it.
Jason slipped on the jacket, then found his favorite pair of black
dress shoes. He smiled when he looked in the mirror. Baker
loved his single-breasted, wool-blend suit jacket. Jason picked
out a matching pair of pants and hung them in his brother's
closet.

The siren of a passing ambulance unnerved him, and he
fumbled as he brushed his teeth and did a quick shave. But
looking in the mirror, his eyes were clear and confident, and
he regained his calm. Back in his bedroom, discarded clothes
littered the floor. He scooped them up and dumped them in
his hamper; he straightened the pillows on his bed. The whole
time, he breathed evenly. Everything was as it should be. He
moved like a man on an inevitable mission.

In his desk drawer he found a copy of his e-76ers contract. He took it downstairs and placed it on Ayana's desk. His aunt had printouts of media coverage all about him, tons of photos, and box scores from his games. One article included a picture of him the day he signed his contract. The headline read, "Local Boy Makes Good."

He stared at it for a moment, remembering. Then he folded it and put it in his suit pocket.

Jason turned out the light in the kitchen and opened the door to the garage. Ayana complained the boys crammed so much junk in there that she couldn't park her car.

He pulled at a large box marked Jason's Stuff perched on a shelf. He dug through it until he pulled out a long, thick rope. He'd made the noose at his lowest point after the accident.

He felt relief he hadn't discarded it.

Jason was clearheaded. His e-NBA career was over. So was Denton's life, which meant he'd most likely end up in jail. Ayana would get nothing for him in the Auction. And he would kill the family's last chance at financial security. Team Harris needed him gone. And Jason was a team player. He just hoped the police would arrive before his aunt. He didn't want her to find him this way.

He looked at the heavy bag that Baker used for training. Jason thought back to how many hours the two of them spent in the garage, fighting and hiding out from Ayana. He followed the heavy bag up to the ceiling. The mount installed to hold it in place was perfect.

He set the noose down on a table, then grunted as he pushed the heavy bag up to unhook it. The dull throb in his ankle turned sharp as he placed the bag on the ground. Jason noticed the effort wrinkled his suit. He considered changing, but time mattered. He stepped onto a three-legged stool. He found it difficult to steady himself. He took a breath and slipped the rope over the mount, then tied a double knot to secure it.

Jason placed the noose over his head, bristling at how the rope irritated his neck. When he was in position, he took one last look around.

A car pulled into his driveway. He turned toward the noise, forcing himself to place weight on his throbbing ankle. His movement tilted the stool forward on just two of its legs. Jason balanced precariously as the stool wobbled. He clutched the noose with both hands but felt the stool slide, causing him to drop an inch. The noose tightened.

He hung on, his life on the edge of the tiny stool. Like a python, the rope tightened around his neck. Above the ringing in his ears he heard shouting. He choked out a scream, but only a low gurgle left his throat.

He heard movement. Then: "No!" Ayana, screaming.

Unable to speak, Jason pleaded for help with his eyes as the stool teetered. Ayana ran toward him. She reached the stool and steadied it. Jason struggled to loosen the rope. Tears filled her eyes. She sobbed and held Jason's hand.

She paused a moment.

"Baby, you don't have to worry anymore," she said, kicking the stool out from under him. Ayana watched as he struggled, but it didn't take long, and soon Jason was free of pain, doubt, and fear. She kissed his hand, then kneeled on the cold concrete and whispered a prayer for the soul of her beloved Jason, and another for the health and prosperity of Baker.

She rose and kissed his hand one last time. Then left to call 911.

———

Judah gripped his daughter's shoulder. "Everyone will understand. We can pack up the crew and be in Philadelphia in just a few hours."

Sasha watched the sun rise over Brooklyn. She barely heard her father. Instead she was empty, hollow.

It was silly, she tried to tell herself. People die all the time. The world moves forward. And what was the death of an alcoholic e-gamer with a limp who had killed his parents and lied about it for years, anyway? She chewed her lip as the reminder of that last salacious detail thundered into her. Denton had recorded his conversations with Jason—dozens of them, going back to their meeting at the Auction Combine. The media had reported on them in gleeful detail.

Poor Jason, having to carry so much guilt when he was so alone.

And still, the wheels of progress churned forward.

Overnight, the e-NBA put out a statement promising to investigate point-shaving allegations involving Jason Harris. The statement pointed out that he had only been in the league two months. By morning, the e-76ers had removed him from their website.

An Auction handicapping site had already added Baker to the list of the class two years from now. As a rising MMA fighter, he was placed in the "Series A Wait and See" category. The site noted that Jason had chosen an opportune time to kill himself. If he had waited another two days, Baker wouldn't be eligible. But Jason died before the Auction, so Baker was now eligible, and his guardian Ayana Harris stood to reap millions if he got a golden ticket.

Even with an active investigation of the deaths of a dozen protesters at its entrance, workers prepped the Brooklyn Dome for what would be a big day of interviews for the Series A candidates. No one could accuse the Big 7 of bad taste: They planned a moment of silence before the day's events. Thoughts and prayers.

"Honey, do you want to go to Philadelphia today?" Judah asked again.

Sasha looked up, surprised to see him there. "I'm staying here. There's a vigil for the demonstrators trampled yesterday. I saw it happen. I should be there."

She fixed her eyes on her father, remembering that she'd been trying to hear from him for days. "Are we going to talk about Mom's foundation, or not?"

He fidgeted. "It's all a misunderstanding. Don't worry about it."

Saved by the bell—his device beeped with a request from PicaFlix. "They want to film a special show about Jason. Stay sad; they want to see your grief." At her shocked look, he clarified, "It'll help the rest of the viewers. Remember, they're grieving, too."

———

Knock! Knock! Knock!

Avery woke up with a start. "No, thank you," he mumbled, pulling a pillow over his head.

Knock! Knock! Knock!

Irritated, he pushed away his covers and stumbled to the door. When he opened it, a force propelled him backward. He toppled over the corner of the bed and landed on the floor with a thud. He recovered in just enough time to see Garrett cock his fist. It glanced off the left side of Avery's head, giving him time to push his brother off him.

"What the hell is wrong with you?" Avery screamed, rubbing his temple as he positioned himself behind the desk chair for protection.

"Why did you do it?" Garrett screamed louder. Wide-eyed, he punched the wall. He clutched his hand as he fell to his knees. Garrett's eyes were puffy. Avery couldn't recall the last time he'd seen his brother cry.

"Why?" Garrett shouted again.

Avery didn't feel like lying anymore. Instead, he stayed silent.

Garrett stood. "I'm out! Global fired me this morning. I had a choice: Confess that I shared my log-in information with you or get accused of selling the information. Why would you do this to me?"

Avery walked over to his older brother. "Tomorrow Beech will select me as a Series A, or they must pay me fifteen million." He stared hard at his onetime hero, the man he always wanted to become. "One more thing, brother. Suni's getting $95 million from her father. That's what I came to tell you in San Francisco. She'll be worth more money than you'll see in your lifetime."

Garrett lowered his eyes. "I'm ruined."

Avery leaned in. "I know you feel humiliated, but don't worry. I won't tell anyone."

———

At noon, the bells of the local Brooklyn churches rang in unison, signifying not only the time but the number of lives lost during the tragedy from the day before. Ten thousand mourners came out, in a steady drizzle, to pay their respects. Sasha stood among them. Many of her fellow candidates defied the Big 7 to attend. Media labeled it the "Sasha effect."

After a prayer, the organizer nodded, and Sasha stepped forward. She pulled off a plain sweater to reveal a black D Movement T-shirt. A hush ran through the audience.

The light rain dampened her note cards. Sasha took a long breath. "It may seem strange that I'm speaking to you today. It's strange to me."

She gazed at the crowd. Her eyes fixed on a familiar face in the front row. She had freckles and a red ponytail. She nodded at her before continuing.

"What could a privileged reality star have in common with you? What about the daughter of a Hollywood icon who's only in town because a bunch of unethical companies want to pay millions of dollars to buy her future?" Sasha shook her head and choked out a scoff. "I'll tell you. The Auction distorts each of us. Distorts what we value. It made a shy young woman who wanted nothing to do with celebrity prostitute herself for her family."

Sasha held up a picture of Jason. "It made a sweet young man keep secrets because it meant he'd be worth something and be able to take care of his family." She pointed at the pictures lined up behind her of the fallen demonstrators. "And it makes a system destroy those who call out against injustice. We're all victims of the Auction."

Her voice wobbled. "This is difficult for me. Despite my famous mom, the spotlight is something I've never sought. But some things are more important than our own fears. Somewhere we have to make a stand. It may not mean much, but today is mine."

She pointed at the stadium. "I'm not walking back in there, and if you are here for the Auction, I hope you won't, either. Times are changing, and we all need to choose a side."

———

It didn't take long for Sasha to pack her bags. She was going home—alone. On the way back to the hotel from the memorial service, the camera crew had abandoned her. PicaFlix had canceled the show before her speech was even over.

Rachel met her in the lobby. "Ms. Cross, it would be a privilege if we could escort you."

"You know I'm damaged goods?" But she smiled. Rachel had always treated her well. "I'm going to Philadelphia. You sure?"

Jack joined them. "Our job is to deliver you to your destination."

"OK, but only if I get to sit up front."

Rachel shook her head. "No."

Sasha shrugged. "I tried."

As she sat in the SUV, she turned off her device and closed her eyes, but all she saw was Jason's face. The vision lasted until they pulled up in front of Ayana's house.

Rachel and Jack stepped out of the car. Sasha lingered on the sidewalk, pacing. "I need to go in there and tell Ayana that everything will get better, but I don't know if I believe it."

"Jack and I served in the Special Forces. We said goodbye to a lot of people. You can't say it will get better, just that you'll be there no matter what."

Sasha walked up the steps. Ayana answered the door and wrapped her in a big hug.

It was awkward at first, but soon, Ayana fed Sasha and Baker cake as they scrolled through pictures to use for Jason's memorial. All the emotions Sasha had held inside—not just grief, but anger and regret and fear and worry—flowed out once she was in the company of Jason's family. "I wish he had told me," she said, wiping away tears.

Ayana brought coffee. "Once you bury a secret, it's hard to let it surface. He had his reasons for the things he did. Whatever mistakes he made, he did it for his family."

"I found this in his room." Sasha held up a piece of paper. "It's a Russian poem."

She handed it to Ayana, who wept as she read:

> Wait for me and I'll return, but wait
> patiently.
> Wait even when you are told that you
> should forget . . .
> And when friends sit around the fire

drinking to my memory
Wait and do not hurry to drink to my
memory too.

Ayana put down the poem. "How long can you stay, dear?"

Sasha shrugged. "No rush. I'm unemployed."

"I thought you were joining a nonprofit helping battered women," Baker said.

Sasha smiled ruefully. "I did, too, but they cut ties with me today. They get a lot of funding from the Big 7."

"That sucks. Do you have a plan B?"

Sasha considered the question. "I think so." Her device beeped.

She stood. "Give me a minute."

Sasha slipped on a jacket and stepped outside. The morning rain had cleared, but the fall breeze blew leaves across the lawn. Patches of the grass were turning yellow, a telltale sign of winter coming.

She walked down to her father's sedan. Somehow he'd known where she would be.

Judah put away his device and removed his sunglasses. "Why didn't you tell me what you planned to say yesterday?"

"Because you would have tried to talk me out of it."

A TV news van pulled up. Soon the suicide of an e-gamer would be fodder for tonight's entertainment.

Judah turned back to his daughter. "For your own good, yes. There's a lot at stake here. My career, for one. I'm hanging on by a thread at PicaFlix. We need to walk it back. The show is a lost cause, but there's still a place for the Cross family in film."

"I agree."

"You do?"

Sasha folded her arms against the wind. "Whenever you talk about Mom, you only mention what she did in Hollywood.

But she had a second career. You might not have liked her philanthropy work, but it was important to her."

"What does this have to do with you?"

"I'll follow in Mom's footsteps. But I'm not taking anything back. I will not be quiet for you or anyone. I'll say what I want, about whom I want, when I want."

"Sasha, that just tells me you don't get it. To fund these projects, we need the Big 7. We need Hollywood. You can't expect them to finance projects if you criticize them."

"I don't. A while back you said I belong in the industry. I disagreed, but you were right."

Judah smiled and put his hands on her shoulders. "When this is over, let's chart a future."

Sasha took a step back. "No need. I'm going to make documentaries. About the issues I care about, and think other people care about, too. Like how we treat the Series Ds. And the power the Big 7 wield. About the unfairness, corruption, and distortion the Auction creates."

Judah's smile vanished. "No, Sasha. You'd turn against everything we've worked for all these years. You'd ruin me, us. I mean it. You can't do that."

She turned to go inside, then looked at her father.

"Don't you remember? I'm Sasha Cross. I can do whatever I want."

EPILOGUE

At Ursula Johnson's urging, the Big 7 held an emergency meeting. Victor Armstrong wasn't invited.

Johnson revealed that Global had not only built a database that they used to spy on Americans, including celebrities such as Sasha Cross, but intended to steal organs from prisoners and veterans under its care. If that information leaked, she told the others, it could destroy the Auction and the Big 7. Left unsaid was that the database gave Global a leg up against the other companies.

The Beech CEO informed the group that she learned about the scheme from Jessica Garulli, who came to her with concerns once she realized the danger of one company having so much power. She recommended, and the other companies agreed, that Jessica should oversee the dismantling of the system so arrogantly named GOD.

Global's stock price plummeted, along with Armstrong's reputation.

More ominous rumors about Global circulated. Johnson told her fellow CEOs that she'd had discussions with the White House about what to do with Global. But given its size and importance to the economy, the White House didn't see how it could punish the company. The CEOs agreed it was a problem only they could fix. They needed to formulate a plan.

Johnson ended the meeting. "Let's make sure each of us is ready."

———

The day after the Auction ended, CNBC's Andrew Barby presented his annual recap. He picked his winners and losers, then noted that the two biggest surprises among Series As both hailed from Michigan State University.

"One, Avery Langdon, never appeared on anyone's radar, and the other, Suni Yosar, had been dropped as a Series A candidate," he said. "They both seem like risky bets. I doubt Beech, which took both of them, will ever see a return on those investments."

Much to the delight of their parents, the Big 7 spent a record amount on bids for the Series A candidates. Still, CNBC fretted. Ratings for the Auction dropped. Viewers were turned off by the violence and demonstrations. For the first time, experts began to voice out loud the idea that the Auction might not last forever.

———

Judah Cross sipped a vodka martini at the Aruba Marriott Resort & Stellaris Casino. He had fled Los Angeles after his ouster from PicaFlix.

Plus, he wanted to be far away from LA when he told Kelsie that she would have to leave Crossroads.

After his fourth vodka, he couldn't stop his mind from wandering. The night he met Lacy. Producing *My Last Year*. The fight with the director, Elliot Fasteni. Storming out.

Certain that his fellow investors would choose him over Fasteni. Shocked when they didn't. Watching from the audience when his former partners accepted the Academy Award for Best Picture. *My Last Year* set box office records. Judah had never recovered.

That was why he chased project after project: to prove them wrong. Life is the sum of the decisions we make. He made a good living and was still the husband of Lacy Cross. But she never looked at him the same. Now he was the ex-producer of TV reality shows.

Judah motioned for the bartender to pour another vodka and peered out at the ocean. He felt the urge to venture out into the waves and disappear. But he didn't want to ruin his Rolex.

———

After Jason's memorial, Sasha flew to California. It felt like a lifetime since she'd been home. She began talks to create her own production company. The first project would be a series of documentaries spotlighting the candidates for next year's election. Sasha intended to start with Sen. Nancy Taylor, the only candidate to call for the Auction's abolition.

That weekend she visited her mother's grave site.

Dead flowers from fans who missed Lacy Cross, and one who stalked her, cluttered the grave. Sasha tossed them in a trash can and pulled away the grass that overran the marble. She took out a picture of her mom and her on the set of their movie. Shot between takes, it showed Lacy fixing her daughter's hair. Sasha looked up at her.

Sasha touched her mother's gravestone. She laid the picture next to the inscription that her mother used to close out her speeches: "The noblest cause is to serve others."

ACKNOWLEDGMENTS

For me, writing *The Auction* was like taking a masterclass in novel creation, and I had so many instructors. Toby Ball, Amy Stern, and Morgan Baden took the first and last versions of the book, respectively, and made it better. My five children—Gaby, Tom, Kevin, Lucy, and Hannah—were invaluable sounding boards and came up with important plot angles. My sisters Teri, Beth, and Kathy read drafts so many times they probably have it memorized. My sister Judy and brothers Andy and Bob offered insight and support. My wife, Jennifer, encouraged me to complete it when life inevitably got in the way. Finally, I owe a huge debt to a person I've not yet had the pleasure of meeting in person: Lisa Zupan. Academy Award–winning producer and friend Wendy Finerman was gracious enough to take an interest, and pass it along to her colleague Lisa, who became my guide and champion. She took a mess of a first draft and pointed me in the direction of something that resembled a real novel. The Auction would not exist today without her support and wisdom. To all who played a part, thank you.

ABOUT THE AUTHOR

Tom Galvin spent over a decade working as a Washington political reporter, breaking stories about Capitol Hill and the White House. He then moved to Silicon Valley as a technology executive, gaining a front-row seat to the internet era. His experience in the political and technological arenas has given him a unique perspective on the intrigues and dangers when power, technology, and greed are mixed together. Though his careers have changed, Galvin's love of writing has remained. He and his wife, Jennifer, split their time between the Gulf Coast of Florida and the Jersey Shore. *The Auction* is his debut novel.